Singularity50 vol 1

SINGULARITY50 VOL 1

A collection of 50 science fiction stories from the most thought provoking voices in new SciFi literature.

Andrew Baguley, Tara Basi, Diann Beck, Richie Brown, Dee Chilton, Yvetta Douarin, Jennifer Hawkins, Susannah Heffernan, Tom J Hingley, Michelle Hood, Clive Howard, Maggie Innes, Nick Jackson, David F. Jacobson, Matt George Lovett, Vera Mark, Ben Marshall, Chris McAleer, Don McVey, Ahren Morris, Sarah Newman, Tom Nolan, KT Parker, Elinor Perry-Smith, Steve Pool, E Pullar, Carmen Radtke, Mark Renshaw, Ann Rumsby, Patrick Ryder, Claire Rye, Caroline Slocock, Daniel Staniforth, Christopher Stanley, Dave Stevenson, Jade Syed-Bokhari, Melissa A. Szydlek, Simon Thomas, Ilesh Topiwala, Phil Town, N.W. Twyford, Carrie Wachob, Danielle Wager, Christian Ward, Stephanie Wessell, Kim L. Wheeler, Bethany White, David Wilks, Nick Yates, Nick Twyford, and Lee Burgess

Create50 Press
London

Copyright © 2018 Create50 Ltd and respective authors.

This book is copyrighted under the Berne Convention. No reproduction without permission. All rights reserved.

CONTENTS

Thanks and Acknowledgements		ix
Welcome to the Singularity Jade Wheldon		1
1.	Automatic Drive Mark Renshaw	3
2.	Hive Mind Christopher Stanley	10
3.	Pondlife Ben Marshall	17
4.	Ancestor Simulation David Wilks	23
5.	Suqi Elinor Perry-Smith	27
6.	Alterverse E Pullar	31
7.	Blip Maggie Innes	38
8.	The Agency of Ellis Clive Howard	44
9.	House-Keeping Ann Rumsby	50
10.	R vs Martin Smith Vera Mark	57
11.	Pepsi Pre-Suicide Outreach Department Christian Ward	63
12.	Holding Out For A Human Dave Stevenson	69
13.	Memory Stored Bethany White	76
14.	Dating with Del Sarah Newman	83
15.	Zero1 Claire Rye	91

16.	Goodnight, Krissy *Carrie Wachob*	97
17.	Product Testing *Melissa A. Szydlek*	102
18.	Sweetcheeks *Matt George Lovett*	108
19.	Henry is a Robot *Michelle Hood*	112
20.	Company *Daniel Staniforth*	119
21.	50 Later *Chris McAleer*	126
22.	Humanity Banjaxed *Tom Nolan*	128
23.	Aramis *KT Parker*	134
24.	Legerdemain *Ahren Morris*	140
25.	Safe House *Carmen Radtke*	147
26.	Buzz Kill *Ilesh Topiwala*	153
27.	The Big Night *Phil Town*	160
28.	2B *Caroline Slocock*	167
29.	Shagability Quotient *Jade Syed-Bokhari*	170
30.	Lions Led by Donkeys *Dee Chilton*	175
31.	Eve and Adam *Tom J Hingley*	181
32.	Pretty *Andrew Baguley*	188
33.	By Any Other Name *Tara Basi*	194
34.	All Rise! *Kim L. Wheeler*	200

35.	Thoughts of a Dying A.I. Theist *David F. Jacobson*	207
36.	DR@G0NH0@RD *Steve Pool*	214
37.	Jack and Bill *Simon Thomas*	222
38.	The Youngest Ever Female CEO on Wall Street *Nick Yates*	229
39.	Here Endeth The Lesson *Danielle Wager*	237
40.	The First Casualty *Nick Jackson*	242
41.	Long-Gone Gindi *Stephanie Wessell*	250
42.	The Birds Began To Sing *Jennifer Hawkins*	257
43.	The Tidy Wells Protocol *Diann Beck*	262
44.	The Freedom Fighter *N.W. Twyford*	269
45.	Rothschild's Giraffe *Richie Brown*	275
46.	The One and Only Lollipop *Yvetta Douarin*	285
47.	Regression *Patrick Ryder*	292
48.	Transference *Don McVey*	299
49.	Take No Prisoners *Susannah Heffernan*	304
50.	To Whomever It May Concern Before the End *Nick Yates*	309

A little bit more... Singularity   315

THANKS AND ACKNOWLEDGEMENTS

Singularity 50 is the fourth book to arise from the Create50 community and initiative.

You can find out more at Singularity50.com.

Aside from the writers whose work is included in this volume, we must also thank everyone involved. Emma who began the journey with me, Jade who helmed the project, and of course Elinor and Cristina. Also, Vicky, Lucy, Judy, Lucia, Tori, Lisa, Szofia and the whole team, thank you for pulling it out of the bag too. To the Create50 community, the writers, the readers, the proof readers, far too many to list, thank you.

Chris Jones
Create50 Founder
Follow me on Twitter @LivingSpiritPix
Create50 on Twitter at @MyCreate50
Facebook fb.com/MyCreate50

Singularity 50 was first published in Great Britain by Create50 Limited. Copyright © 2018 Create50 Ltd and respective authors. This book is copyrighted under the Berne Convention. No reproduction without permission. All rights reserved.
ISBN: 9781731320285
eBook ISBN 978-0-9956538-3-2

WELCOME TO THE SINGULARITY

Jade Wheldon

In the age of the Anthropocene, human consciousness is unparalleled by anything else in existence on this planet. We have evolved to become a geological force as powerful as any ice age or mass extinction throughout the earth's 4.5 billion year existence. The industrial revolution saw us harness energy on a global scale and use it to advance our civilisations through technology. With the creation of the atomic bomb in the 1940's, we finally prove that in our hands, we hold the delicate balance of the planet we live on. It is ours for the taking.

It is true that this rapid technological advancement has benefited us. We can travel easier and faster than ever before. Global communication is instant. The birth of the internet allows us easy access to almost anything we desire. That is, at least, for those of us who can afford to stay connected…

But there are problems. We are growing at such a rate that there aren't enough resources to go around. Life for many is one of poverty, without access to the basics of nourishing food and proper healthcare. In areas where resources are abundant, we are wasteful and greedy. The divide between the rich and the poor is ever growing, the planet is warming and climate change is accelerating all the time. We need solutions.

The singularity is the hypothesis that the invention of artificial superintelligence (AI) will abruptly trigger runaway technological growth, resulting in unimaginable changes to human civilization.

Sometime in the next 50 years, AI is due to evolve way past its human engineers. More knowledgeable and powerful in many ways – could this be the solution we are searching for? Perhaps the answers to some of our biggest problems lie buried within the million-billion electrical pulses of an artificial brain, one specifically designed to solve world hunger or our energy crisis? All we would need to do is switch it on...

The debate rages on. The balance of natural life is so intricate and fragile. What are the implications of creating a consciousness infinitely more powerful than our own? One that has no living body, that cannot grow tired, that cannot 'die' but can be uploaded and re-downloaded and replicate itself over and over. What can come of replacing our working bodies and minds with computers, of allowing ourselves to be informed, fed, cared for and even governed by this intelligence?

Perhaps using AI we'll find a way to upload our minds into these vessels and live forever.

The Singularity is a series of 50 short stories exploring exactly this. Each tale is set at different points within our future, intending to question our ability to coexist with AI.

We ask, is this another step toward our extinction, or the gateway to our immortality?

Jade Wheldon
Editor

Twisted50 Volume 2 Team
Create50 Team Leader: Chris Jones
GoodReads Librarian: Simon Caldecutt

1

AUTOMATIC DRIVE

Mark Renshaw

"You are now passing smart-highway marker fourteen." The computer's sultry Irish accent did little to compensate for interrupting Ryan's Game of Thrones holonovel. "TekStorm Industries would like to take this opportunity to tell you about some exciting new apps..." Ryan drifted off. He loved interactive holonovels. Every choice could have a profound impact on the characters and completely change the narrative. It made each session exciting and new, like he was a god controlling an alternate universe. The constant commercials were a pain in the implants but he refused on principle to pay extra credits to remove them.

A mental command merged the holonovel seamlessly into the main panel. It joined an array of multi-media options which crawled across the car's interior. Ryan was not a fan of this theme. Visually it was too noisy for his tastes but his son loved it.

Thoughts of his son activated the rear seat display where Marc sat playing his games. Ryan was still trying to get used to the vehicle's neural implant controls. Luckily, fail-safes were installed so if he did think of a crash the A.I. ignored it.

He watched his son and smiled. Marc was using his fingers like pistols, obliterating alien ships swarming across the ceiling. Side panels showed viewers from around the globe reacting to his mentally transmitted commentary. The younger generation had adapted so effortlessly to neural interfaces. For Ryan, it was like learning how to ride a bike all over again.

"Never gonna give you up!" Abagail's impromptu singing from the passenger seat brought him out of his daydream.

Without missing a beat, Ryan joined in. "Never gonna let you down."

Unlike his wife, his natural singing voice was not the best. The car's A.I. auto-tuned his efforts into a professional sounding production.

"Never gonna run around and desert you!" sang Abagail.

On a roll now they sang together in perfect harmony. "Never gonna make you cry, never gonna say goodbye, never gonna tell a lie and hurt you."

Strangled cries interrupted their medley. Ryan glanced at the rear display. Marc stared back at him in horror.

"What the swag are you two doing?" Marc demanded.

"Sorry son, sounds like you've been Rick Rolled," said Abagail with a barely concealed smile.

Marc cocked his head to one side like a confused dog. "What's a Rick Roll?"

"Google it," countered Ryan. Even without neural technology they had always clicked. Ganging up and teasing their son was one of the benefits of parenthood.

Marc slapped the back of Ryan's seat. "What's that number got to do with anything? Why don't I ever understand a swiggin word you two say?"

Ryan dismissed the video feed and both parents swivelled their seats round so they could see their son in the flesh. "Pardon Sir Marc, did though speaketh?" said Ryan, putting on his poshest accent.

"I give up." said Marc. "Are we nearly there yet?" he shouted, as if his parents were hard of hearing. "Do you understand that?"
A panel in the ceiling activated and expanded outwards. It displayed

a virtual representation of their vehicle en route to a holographic area labelled Los Angeles. Abagail pointed at it. "Well son, if you care to look upwards, you'll see we have eighteen minutes until we reach our destination."

"Swag mom, why does it take so long?"

"Long?" Abagail spluttered. "This trip used to take two days! You think eight hours is…"

The whole interior went dark.

"Mom? Dad? What's going on?"

Ryan sat there in the darkness. Like his wife, he was too shocked to respond. He was painfully aware that he was in a vehicle travelling over 200 miles per hour with no steering wheel or manual controls. He could feel the car drifting and hear the soft thump-thump sound of the tires as they crossed over the gridlines. Therefore the sound buffers and inertial dampeners were offline as well as the lights. This could only mean one thing, total, catastrophic power failure; which was impossible.

*

The beautiful sun drenched beach was marred by a black panel which appeared in the sky. The word's GRIDLOCK WARNING flashed across it in a bright, neon font.

"Default mode," ordered Lucas. He preferred voice commands. It made him feel in control. The beach theme flickered off, replaced by a virtual representation of the outside world. His seat rose sharply into the upright position, as did the passenger seat. He turned to admire his bikini clad companion. Was it Belinda or Linda? He couldn't remember. "You OK babe?" he asked.

"Yeah honey. What's going on?"

All he could see was stationary vehicles. Whatever was blocking them was elsewhere. "Status update."

The warning panel expanded across the front view screen. It updated to show a view of the highway from a drone camera's perspective. Lucas could see what his dad referred to as a fender bender – a family wagon, one of those new Z-types by the looks of it, was shunted sideways across two lanes. The panelling all along the driver's side had collapsed.

"Gridlock warning!" warned the computer in a light, cheerful, tone. "Total gridlock will occur in four minutes. Please vote for your preferred course of action now."

Two options overlaid the display. Option One – Await the emergency services, or Option Two – Move the vehicle immediately to an off-road breakdown area. A flickering graphic at the side showed the status of the voting. Option Two was the current clear favourite.

"Whaddya think honey?" asked the babe while frowning. "That lady looks like she may have a concussion."

Their kid was waving at the drones and pulling funny faces. Lucas thought this must seem like a big adventure for him. For his folks though, this was the beginning of an insurance nightmare. "Are you serious? It's a headache. All parents have those." Without any further debate he pressed option two. Moments later the vote was in – ninety-eight percent agreed with him.

"Yay for democracy!"

*

Salt? thought Ryan. Why can I taste salt?

He became aware of blood pouring from a painful gash in his forehead which answered his question. Ignoring the pain he looked up. Lying nearby was Abagail. Her lifeless eyes stared accusingly in his direction. It all felt quite surreal, like those odd occasions he had become aware he was in a dream. Any moment now he was sure he would wake up.

Some unseen force scooped Abagail up into the air. Her head slumped forward like an intoxicated angel. Ryan giggled. Yup, this was a dream alright. If she was not careful, she'd get arrested for drunken flying. He giggled again but frowned as his vision cleared. His wife wasn't flying. She was being lifted up by an elongated metal arm. Its ascent halted, and then shifted towards the side of the road.

He raised himself groggily to his feet, fighting off waves of nausea and shuffled after Abagail like one of the pied piper's mesmerised victims. Bits of metal were scattered all over the road. The reek of burning plastic made his eyes water. He tried to wipe them clear but discovered his left arm was useless. He couldn't even feel it.

"Mom? Dad?"

Ryan spun around, almost passing out in the process. His son's voice had come from a twisted lump of wreckage three lanes away. Indecision paralyzed him. Logically he knew it was too late for his wife but emotionally he was torn. She was the love of his life. He couldn't bring himself to accept that she was gone.

A whirring sound flipped him back to reality. Abigail was being lowered into a large opening at the side of the road, making the decision for him. Everything was becoming too real. The events prior to the accident re-played over in his mind as he limped over to the remains of his car. The highway ahead was clear, but behind the accident, scores of vehicles hummed at a standstill like angry hornets. In the distance, more vehicles joined the rapidly forming queue.

A few agonising moments later he reached the wreckage. "Marc? You OK?"

"Dad! I don't know. I can't feel my legs. Where's mom?"

Ryan couldn't find any gap wide enough to see inside but he had clocked the monitoring drones hovering above. He tried to sound calm. "It's OK, the rescue crews are on their way, hold on!"

A large clanking sound turned his attention back to the roadside where two robotic arms where slowly rising out of the opening. They were huge, like the big brother of the one which had taken Abagail.

"No!"

"What is it?" said Marc with a quivering edge to his voice.

With a rising sense of panic, Ryan scrambled over to the nearest car. He banged his fist hard on the bonnet. "Vote for the emergency services option! Can't you see how serious this is?" Sunlight reflected off the windows. He waved with his good arm at a drone as it soared passed.

The arms were extending towards the wreckage. Ryan hobbled over. He couldn't understand why they weren't waiting for the rescue crews. He'd seen enough accidents in his time to... And then it hit him. Although he'd seen plenty of accidents, they had always been minor. He'd always voted to have them moved to the side of the road, they never seemed serious. Yet he'd never once thought to stick his head out to take a look.

"Oh god no!" he sobbed.

He reached his car as the arms were clamping onto each side. The wreckage began sliding towards the gap. Ryan pulled with all his might.

"Dad? What's going on?"

"Its OK son, I'm here!" He ran around the wreckage, ducked under the arms and rammed the back of the vehicle with his shoulder. His feet scraped along the tarmac. They were getting perilously close to the gap, but there was no thought of giving up or moving out of harm's way. Whatever happened when they went down into those dark depths, he wasn't going to let his son face it alone. Ryan held on, punching furiously at one of the silver arms as they were dragged into the yawning chasm.

Their screams echoed as the maintenance hatch doors slid to a close. It was as if the accident never happened. Even their muffled cries were drowned out by the roar of engines as hundreds of vehicles accelerated away.

*

Lucas slipped his shades back on and ordered his seat into the reclining position. On the view screen, the family were being served light refreshments by droids at the side of the road. The kid waved at them as they zoomed by. "See, everyone's happy."

The screen flickered off, returning the illusion of the perfect sun-splashed beach.

"The TekStorm Corporation would like to apologise for any inconvenience this temporary delay may have caused you. TekStorm – keeping the highway gridlock free since two-thousand and twenty-three!" The computer's tone inflected a tinge of artificial smugness.

"Yeah, whatever," said Lucas dryly. He closed his eyes and felt all his tension drifting away under the warmth of the artificial sun.

"Honey, something's wrong," said Linda/Belinda.

Lucas glanced over. His escort program seemed to be malfunctioning. The holo-image flickered, and then she disappeared. That's odd, thought Lucas. I'd best run a diagnostic.

"Computer...," his command was interrupted as the lights cut out. The sound of the waves crashing across the sand was replaced by the all too realistic roar of other vehicles.

The End

2

HIVE MIND

Christopher Stanley

Kelly's stomach lurches as the egg-shaped FlyPod begins its descent into California. Her windscreen display shows average temperatures, carbon emissions and the real-time decline of biodiversity. Last time she was here, there were cotton fields and beet farms rolling over the horizon, and vineyards stretching all the way to the coast. Now all she sees are rice fields, wind farms and acres of soil eroding to desert.

"It's not your fault," says her fiancé, Jackson, his holographic head bobbing above the console. "You had no choice."

If only that were true. On her recommendation, the US government rejected the World Health Organisation's proposal to protect and preserve bee populations. "The free market will provide a better solution," she'd argued, highlighting the benefits of genetically-modified, self-pollinating fruit and vegetable crops. "Bees are unreliable and slow to adapt. The future is biotechnology." But the new crops weren't as resilient as they were supposed to be. And they tasted like crap.

"Nobody knew the bees would disappear so quickly," says Jackson.

Kelly is flying in to California to investigate a small, privately-funded ensemble of tech scientists and retired farm managers called the Forbidden Fruit Initiative. Her orders are to keep digging until she has enough evidence to shut them down. "Our country is experiencing the highest levels of poverty and displacement since the dustbowl days of the 1930s," her boss had said before she left. "We need time for the new crops to work. Without the support of the major biotech companies, we won't win the next election."

Flickering with interference, Jackson's hologram says, "We're counting on—" but the signal dies before he can finish his sentence.

Kelly ends the call as the FlyPod touches down in a swirl of dust and debris. As she exits into the Californian furnace, she's greeted by two goons wearing army fatigues; their Taser rifles pointed at her chest.

*

More than coffee, it smells like nostalgia, like her mum's kitchen on a cold, winter's morning. She sniffs again and her taste buds come alive. Either they've made a breakthrough in synthetic coffee or she's holding a mug of the real thing.

"Taste it," says Doctor Lyman.

Her instincts tell her not to trust the white-haired doctor. A decade ago he'd championed genetically-modified crop development and lobbied fiercely, but then he disappeared from any kind of public role. His smile spreads like mischief.

She lifts the cup to her lips, expecting to be disappointed, but the moment the hot, black liquid touches her tongue she knows for sure. "How?"

"Food first."

The only remarkable thing about the dining area is the fruit bowl in the middle of the table. Sliced grapefruit, pineapples and blood oranges. A melon as big as a football and bananas as round as the doctor's grin. She hasn't seen so many different types of fruit in one place since she started her job. She squeezes a plum between her fingers and it's firm like the ones she used to steal from her mum's kitchen table.

"Go on," says Lyman. She bites into it without thinking and the taste brings tears to her eyes. "Have another."

"I shouldn't."

"Worried you'll spoil your appetite?"

Before she can reply their food arrives on a dozen platters. She shakes her head in disbelief. Half of America is starving but it could be Christmas Day in California.

*

After lunch they drive for twenty minutes under the sweaty afternoon sun. According to Lyman, the Initiative started by looking for the location with the greatest amount of agricultural diversity in the smallest geographical area. "When the bees disappeared," he says, "we brought labourers in to hand-pollinate the flowers. Thanks to your government, people are willing to work for little more than food on their plates."

Kelly checks her phone for messages from her office but, despite the Wi-Fi balloon gliding through the stratosphere above their heads, she has no signal. The balloon is a relic from another decade but it's probably still functional. Someone doesn't want her to talk.

They park at the edge of a meadow and Lyman escorts her up onto a sheltered viewing platform. Among the grasses she sees several native species of wildflowers she thought were extinct. Spotted coralroot and rein orchids, blazing stars and milkmaids. The air above the meadow hums with birds and butterflies.

And something else.

Bees.

Thousands of them.

"I call this place heaven," says Lyman. "But of course it isn't. It's Earth. This is how the Earth is meant to be."

Kelly is shaking. How can a place like this still exist?

"I've heard it doesn't matter whether you're a politician or a crossing guard," says Lyman. "If you work in Washington, you think like Washington." He turns to face her, his smile shrinking to nothing.

"You spent so much time justifying the replacement crops; did you ever stop to think about our pollinators?"

"We couldn't save the bees."

Lyman holds out his hand and sitting in his palm is a honey bee. Motionless and probably dead. "Who said anything about saving them?" he says. With his other hand, he gently squeezes the bee and it pops into life, flying out of his palm towards the meadow. "I meant replacing them."

"Robots?"

"They even make honey."

*

She steps out of the shower and returns to her borrowed bedroom, enjoying the cool, conditioned air. Before they left the meadow, she asked Lyman if his men were blocking her phone signal. He was quite candid, saying they were in violation of so many regulations it seemed the least of his crimes. Then his smile crept back and he asked her to stay for supper. She agreed, as long as he unblocked her phone.

"I hope by now you've seen enough to know we're serious," he said. "We want to work with your government. We want to rescue American agriculture and put food on people's plates. I'm sure you'll keep that in mind when you make your report."

She stands in front of the mirror and lets the towel drop to the floor, gently stroking the edge of her belly where it's beginning to bloom. She holds her phone over the bump until she hears a beep. Seconds later, a hologram appears above the screen and there it is, her baby, about the size of a kiwi fruit but growing all the time.

Lyman wasn't joking about violating regulations. Growing unlicensed crops, using unsanctioned technology in food production, turning farmland into a wildflower meadow; she thinks he's probably looking at time in prison. And who knows what damage his little robots are really doing to the environment? The whole place will probably be torched and the files marked as classified.

She covers herself up when something clacks against the inside of the window. It's one of Lyman's bees, trying to escape. She smiles at her good fortune; her tech team in Washington would love the chance to dissect a specimen. It probably contains all the evidence she needs to sink the Forbidden Fruit Initiative forever.

If that's what she wants to do.

Lyman said she'd lost the ability to think for herself. He said her colleagues buzzed around Washington like so many drones in the thrall of queen commerce. And it's true she came here looking for reasons to shut the Initiative down. But aren't there bigger reasons to let it continue?

Could her baby boy grow up in a world where there's enough food for everyone?

Using a plastic tumbler from the bathroom, she traps the bee against the windowsill. She can figure out what to do with it later; right now, she has a call to make.

*

Back at the meadow, she sits down to a salad of chargrilled peppers, onions and avocados, passing on the wine. The freshly-baked honey and raisin muffins smell as sweet as wildflowers at sunset.

"Did you report back?" asks Lyman.

"Something's been bothering me," she says. "You haven't applied for any patents. You don't have a perimeter fence. I've seen a handful of guards at most. Where's your security?"

Lyman signals to one of his goons, who fetches what looks like a birdcage draped in fabric.

"What would you recommend?" he asks. "How many guards would make you feel safe? How many guns? Would it really be better to apply for patents and rely on a broken legal system to protect our interests?"

The goon rests the birdcage on a trestle table and removes the fabric. Underneath, Kelly recognises the black eye mask and brightly coloured plumage of a European bee-eater.

"This project isn't about money," says Lyman. "It's about the future."

The goon unclicks the latch and opens the birdcage door. The bee-eater ruffles its feathers and skips from side to side, twisting its head jerkily to study its new surroundings. After testing the air with a couple of flaps of its wings, it hops into the doorway of the cage.

"Anything that poses a threat to our bees we treat very seriously."

The bee-eater takes flight. In the distance, dark patches appear on the surface of the meadow; swirling black shadows slipping across the top of the long grasses the way oil slides across water. Kelly drops her muffin as thousands of bees assault the unsuspecting bird, lifting it high up into the air. The bee-eater struggles and fights, flapping frantically in a flurry of feathered mayhem. Then its wings are torn off and its lifeless carcass is dropped back down to the meadow below.

"Brutal," says Lyman. "But beautiful."

"You weaponised them?"

"When bees evolved from wasps, they retained their sting. Nature determined that it was optimal for bees to have some form of defence mechanism. We modelled our bees on nature's own but we took them a step further."

"Bees don't attack like that in nature."

"Our bees are programmed to work together. Coordinated attacks to eliminate potential threats. They're our eyes and ears, twenty-four seven. You didn't really think our security was two guys with Tasers?"

"But how do they communicate?"

"We've established a virtual neural network. They're all connected. That's how we monitor their performance and upgrade the software. They learn from each other and adapt accordingly."

The swarm continues to rise, with more bees joining all the time, until they've formed an angry, twisting column reaching into the sky. The combined buzz of so many bees is intimidating. Raising his voice, Lyman says "They'll settle down in a moment, they're just warning off other threats."

"Ow!" Something pricks the top of Kelly's arm.

Lyman takes her hand and slips a pair of glasses from his shirt pocket. "Let me look," he says, gently brushing her skin. Then he pinches her arm and she winces. "What did you say to your colleagues in Washington?" he asks. She shakes her head; the pain is so bad she can't think. Lyman holds his hand up in front of her and between his thumb and forefinger is a tiny splinter of metal. Kind of like a bee sting if the bee was a robot.

"There was a bee in my room," she mumbles, her head thumping like the bee against the glass. "It was there when I made my report." It probably shared the whole conversation. How could she have been so stupid?

"You people," says Lyman. "You're all the same."

Suddenly the evening sun winks out. The meadow is gone and so is the sky. The last thing she hears is the roar of a hundred thousand bees.

3

PONDLIFE

Ben Marshall

Grandpa said if you have something important to say, it should be written down. All of Grandpa's important thoughts are in his journal. Existing only on the crinkled pages. Delivered in bold black ink. Crinkled and bold like Grandpa. I am handwriting this story about me, Grandpa and our duck pond because it too is so very significant. The story about how those Inventors ruined everything.

My visits to the duck pond with Grandpa were a weekly highlight. Rain or shine. Grandpa had been feeding ducks at the same pond since boyhood. His efforts to tempt my dad, when he was a boy, were wasted. Dad was, and still is, devoted to his gadgets. So once Dad was bored with Grandpa's remote propelled boat, he was bored with the pond. When Grandpa first cradled me, he daydreamed of feeding the ducks with a granddaughter by his side – and I indulged him. My first meaningful sound was "QUACK". My first spoken word was "DUCK".

By the age of five my bread throwing arm met Grandpa's approval, but suddenly the art of duck feeding became as endangered as handwritten journals. First, the park squirrel population vanished. Wiped out by a virus and circumstances far too complicated for these pages. To correct the loss, the Inventors created replicas. Manmade squirrels impossible to pick out as bogus and cleverly fuelled by park weather, rain or shine. The idea was to keep parks looking the same. The fake squirrels sat on branches and climbed the trunks of trees which looked less without them. The Inventors even programmed their squirrels to charm all park goers, in particular children. It was nothing for them to snuggle on a child's lap and be stroked or even sit on a child's head for a selfie. "The same but better" Dad said.

The Inventors then saw the same possibility for ducks. I can only imagine their silly smiles when they found a way to turn bread into power and create... "Duckbots". I called them that but Grandpa hated the name. He cursed how such a foolish name made them sound harmless. Also programmed to charm children, and without the mess, Duckbots became very popular very quickly too. "The same but better" Dad said. "The world's gone bonkers" Grandpa grumbled back and I hung on Grandpa's every wise word. He warned back then it would lead to something terrible. "Tomorrow if not sooner" he said.

The obvious problem, even to a child, was that the real ducks had not been wiped out like the squirrels. Our ducks were happy as they were. Yet Duckbots were designed to seek and eat. Bread, grass, insects – all that a duck needed. In particular, bread. Their lack of fear and speed made Duckbots always first to it. For every piece received, the Duckbots would give a grateful "Quack" or a flap of wings. For a big chunk, the Duckbot could even bob under and cheekily wag a tail feather. Our ducks didn't stand a chance. Some starved and some lost their lives through feather flying battles over scraps. Real ducks turned savage on each other. The strong who survived quickly saw little point hanging around where they were not wanted. As some went, many followed.

Our visits became the difference between life and death. Our plan was simple. Grandpa kept the imposters busy, tossing them bread whilst I focused on the slow and hungry, blood and bone, ducks. I was always able to spot them.

Although Grandpa was slow on his feet, there was no competing with his bread tossing. His secret was his bionic right hand. He'd lost fingers when in the military and even though in his sixties, the Inventors finally agreed to build him a new hand. After that, he was flicking off beer tops and pushing nails into walls. The first thing Grandpa wrote in his journal was that the Inventors had finally done some good and he would happily shake their hands…"if they can handle my grip". What pleased the Inventors most, was that no-one could see that Grandpa's hand was phoney. Perfection meant looking the same. So despite their many wonders, Grandpa's bionic fingertips were gnarled and his synthetic skin blemished with brown spots. The same but better.

Despite our efforts, there came a day when the true ducks had all gone and the third most horrible moment of my life arrived. We scanned the pond but only Duckbots danced at our feet. Grandpa tried his best to raise my spirit. "Janey" he said "I reckon our ducks have gone somewhere better sweetie. Be proud your bread got them there." Grandpa brushed a curl of hair from my face so he could look me in the eyes. Grandpa willed me to be happy so I smiled and nodded. But like I could always spot the real ducks, Grandpa could always read my sadness. Grandpa said the twinkle in my eyes spoke a language of their own. So even though I smiled at him, my altered "twinkle" told Grandpa all he needed to know. He wiped away a tear with his cardigan sleeve. "Tears are a little girl's way of asking for help" Grandpa said. He always said the tears brought out their ocean blue colour. Often, Grandpa just said this to provoke a reaction from Dad who insisted my eyes were electric blue.

Suddenly, there was a clumsy rustle from the reeds. My heart pounded because Duckbots don't rustle. Out from the shadows stuttered a shy, once majestic, swan. Big enough to fend for itself but times had changed. The poor swan's wings were clipped so it couldn't escape with the ducks. It had nowhere else to go. Grandpa knew what to do.

Grandpa distracted the show boaters with his bread and I approached the Swan. I should have just thrown my bread to her but I wanted to get close. Drawn to her damaged coat and limp neck. "Swan" I whispered. "You're the most beautiful thing I've ever seen". I meant it too. Swan followed as I edged away from the others, a whole loaf hidden under my jumper. "Shuusshh" I said, to calm any sudden excitement. We were face to face, staring wide eyed at each other. But when I revealed the loaf, Grandpa had ran out of his bread. Instantly, every Duckbot turned to the tussle of my bag. Swan sensed urgency and pecked at it. Instinctively, I lifted the bag up. In front of my face. The Duckbots swarmed and Swan went for the loaf again, but this time frenzied.

I have taught myself to forget the exact horror of what happened next because it's better that way. What I do know is that as Swan struck wildly at the bread I flinched the wrong way. My right eye was pecked clean out. Grandpa wrote that the worst thing was my scream. A noise he'd never heard before, even in his frontline fighting. It caused the birds to flock from the trees and Swan to flee back to the reeds, dropping her bread slice. The Duckbots didn't budge. Some even wagged tail feathers.

My first days in hospital were a blur of pain and tormented sleep. Whispers and prodding from one doctor after another. Some in white coats and some in smart suits. The first time I felt properly awake I heard Dad tell Grandpa "you know, this might turn out to be the best thing to ever happen to our Janey". Dad loves his gadgets almost as much as he loves me. Swan's accidental precision, left all but the eyeball intact. Making me the Inventor's perfect candidate for a bionic eye. They could never get the go ahead to replace a child's healthy eye. And if an eye was already diseased or imperfect, then the risks of failure were too great.

The prototype was waiting for an event like me and Swan. An all singing and dancing eye with more fancy tricks than there are letters on this page. The only task was to make the eye match perfectly and the Inventors won because no-one can spot the difference. The Inventors also solved the argument – "Ocean blue or Electric blue?" Well, it is neither and by spooky coincidence the answer is duck egg blue.

Once discharged there was only one place I wished to go before home. The pond. With Grandpa. He found our return very upsetting, blaming himself deeply. I told Grandpa not to be silly and to shake off his frown. By the time Grandpa had ended his long sigh of unnecessary guilt, I had already done what I came for. "I can't see Swan" I said. My bionic eye had scanned the pond in a heartbeat. My hope was to make peace with Swan. I had never once held her responsible. It was the Inventors who turned her beastly and I needed to see that Swan was ok.
We were just about to leave when out from the reeds glided something bewildering. A brand new swan, blessed with impossible elegance. Fake, of course. "Will you look at her" Grandpa gasped, removing his cap. "It's not Swan" I replied. But there was no ignoring that the Inventors had weaved magic.

Grandpa watched in awe as it approached. He tossed a chunk of bread. The phoney swan's neck extended like the dancing wrist of a prima ballerina. It caught the piece and it's swallow rippled through the perfect ice white feathers. As it curtsied gratitude, I was watching Grandpa's utter admiration. Grandpa noticed my stare and bent to my eye level. He brushed a curl of hair from my face so he could look in my eyes. "I think it's for the best Janey pet. This way nothing gets hurt anymore" he said. I smiled and nodded and waited for Grandpa to see my sadness. My disappointment in his words.

But he saw nothing in my eyes. To be sure of a perfect match, the Inventors had taken away what Grandpa called the "twinkle" from my good eye. The Inventors found uniqueness impossible to match and so muted my eyes with muscle glue. I then felt myself well up and I waited for Grandpa's cardigan sleeve. But he just buttoned up his coat and turned to leave. The Inventors could make a bionic eye cry but not always at the same time as my good eye. The Inventors couldn't have one eye cry without the other, so they'd lazered my tear ducts shut. "Tears have no purpose anyway" the Inventors had assured me.

That was the second most horrible moment of my life. Standing with round eyes, smiling, as Grandpa walked away. Leaving me to hold in my sorrow. I did not feel the same. I did not feel better.

We never returned to the pond, but that was not where our story ends. This story, which I have written at the end of Grandpa's journal, marks the most horrible day of my life. Today is Grandpa's funeral.

These words have two purposes.

First, so you will understand. So that Grandpa will understand. That whilst I will not cry today and my eyes will show no sadness, I am utterly heartbroken inside. Dad says we can keep Grandpa's bionic hand to remember him. But I want to remember Grandpa's good heart and so in his pocket I've hidden a slice of bread. I will think about him meeting Swan.

Secondly, the story completes Grandpa's grave warning for the future. Grandpa wrote that what happened with our ducks will one day happen to us all. He fears we will not know when to stop. Grandpa realised this when even he felt drawn to that fake swan. That anything can, and one day will, be replaced. That our world will mirror life on that beastly pond. We will be like my Swan with nowhere else to go until we're replaced too.

Whatever Grandpa said would happen usually did. "Tomorrow if not sooner" he said.

4

ANCESTOR SIMULATION

David Wilks

My name is Jason Smith, 42. A resident of a small village called Garston, in Liverpool, England. It looks and feels exactly like the year 2017. Both my parents, my grandparents, my brother, and even the girl of my dreams are all still here. I don't have a great job, but I'm not poor. I can't sing very well, and God knows I've tried. I can't act, I can't seem to make anything work. I kind of come close to getting there but fail at the last minute. But this is what I paid for. And now that I am here and living the dream that I must have dreamed about, what can you do, except live the dream?

What happened in the real world to make me pick this particular ancestor simulation? How do I know I am in a simulation? Well, I don't. It's against the rules. If you knew this was a simulation, well you would just go crazy and ruin it for everyone else. You see, this is not just my simulation. This is yours as well. As you read this, you gotta take a step back and say, I paid for this. When you were sitting in the chair, going through the options: Pop Star, Movie Star, Prime Minister, Footballer… You said, not again. I've done all of them a hundred times over. This time, I want difficulty level 10. Drop me in some backwater village, poor education, average looks, average IQ, average friends. And see how I survive that. How then, do I know it's a simulation if you are not allowed to know? Well, you have to look for the clues. It's like when you dream and you find yourself in this absurd situation and you just accept it.

Euro 2016, England got beaten 2-1 by a bunch of part-time waiters from Iceland. This was my first clue. I figure somebody paid for this add-on. Probably Kolbeinn Sigthorsson, who got the winning goal. Maybe he didn't have enough cash to outbid everyone else who was wanting to win the tournament that year. Eder Lopez must have paid a fortune to get that winning goal for Portugal. Thinking back though, I suspect Leicester winning the title on 2nd of May must have started me off.

So, having now realised that I am trapped in an ancestor simulation that I chose myself, how can I change it? Escape would be far too easy. I'm certainly not going to kill myself, as I could still be wrong. So I need more clues.

But in the meantime I have to go to work. I work as a TV extra. Although SA is the proper term. Supporting Artist. I trained for, like, 5 years to be an Actor and a Singer. But you can see that look on people's faces. It's like a one percent difference between Amazing and So-So. So I was trying to understand the Algorithm behind this part of my simulation. There must be a program running in the background somewhere that says, he's getting too good. Reign it in. This was my second major clue. There's no way anyone could be this crap. There's got to be an algorithm behind this.

January 2017, bottom club Swansea City beat Liverpool 3-2. Yet another clue. A small one but Liverpool's defence could never be this crap in the real world.

Feb 2017. I land a small part in Emmerdale. Walk on 3. It's a few lines of dialogue and my own trailer. I lord it over the other extras like I'm Tom Hardy. When it airs I'm expecting big things to change.

Airs in March. No fanfare. Couple of likes on Facebook. Need to find anther clue. An ex-girlfriend gets in touch. She sends me a picture message. I reply back 'wow, that took my eye out!' But I send it to my girlfriend by mistake. I'm single now. Who writes these algorithms? Why did this have to happen? Did I pay for this to happen as well?

I listen to a recording on my phone at night in the dark. It was made on August 15th, 2015. I went to a Gong bath. There's no water in this bath. There's a room full of Gongs. They're huge copper circles that are hit in sequence to create a bath of sound waves. The recording is an hour long. I start to see bright lights. I can feel something opening in my head. They said this might happen. It's called the Crown Chakra block. It's like this block was being removed. I could see that it might be possible to connect with myself in the past and travel back there, to 2015. I was about to let myself go and see if it could be done. But I got scared and stopped the tape. Over the next few weeks I tried again and again to achieve that same feeling. But I could not repeat it.

Need to find another clue, I'm still single. Drinking too much red wine. I see my ex-girlfriend down at the gym, she looks incredible. She never looked like that before. Must be the Mandela effect. They say people remember Nelson Mandela dying in prison sometime during the 1980's, but then he reappears and leads his people by becoming president. Another clue that something is not right. But maybe it's just the wine.

Now that I'm single, my bro comes over and we eat steaks, drink red wine and beer most nights and watch free movies. But I keep seeing this unusual star in the sky, it's massive! It's way too bright to be a normal star. It looks too close. Like it's closer than a jumbo jet. So I get out my telescope that I haven't used since I bought it. It takes me a while to set it up. Its battery-operated and I've got no batteries so I am just moving it manually and trying to focus on this star. Finally I get it in view. And it's not a star at all. It looks like a small metal planet, about the size of five football pitches. It is battered and dented and has a ridge going all the way around it. I tried to photograph it with my phone but I could not get the shot. But just like I was in a dream. I kind of accept that it's there and that maybe there was something wrong with the telescope or my eyes.

The following Tuesday I am waiting to see if the star returns. I downloaded a star map app that tells you what stars you are looking at. At 8pm I hold up the star map and lock onto the small metal planet.

I wake up in a chair and remove a face cover. I do not recognise this place. There are three other chairs that have people sitting in them. They each have a device that covers their heads. I seem to be in some kind of shopping mall. But it's no mall I have ever been to. This is some kind of future mall. Outside the window, I can see the sky is filled with flying cars. A woman in a pink outfit sits near the door, applying makeup in a hand mirror. She shouts in a deep New York accent, 'You finished?' I jump up, 'What do you mean, finished?' She checks the screen. 'You broke the rules, sorry.' I'm like, 'Wait just a goddamn minute...' My accent, OMG, what is this? I don't have an accent! An American accent. Wait, I'm 43. I've not been sitting in that chair for 43 years, what's happened to me? She looks at me like I'm stupid. She turns the mirror on me. I can't believe my eyes, I'm like 23! 'You paid for an hour, you used up half an hour. Then you broke the rules,' The woman says. 'Where is this place?' I ask. She replies, 'New York 2049. Get over it. You won't remember a thing in half an hour.' I beg her. 'Please, send me back. I don't want to forget anything, I don't want to forget my family, my girlfriend...' She mutters, 'It's another $250 to pop you back in.'

I jump back in the seat. 'Send me back, don't change a thing.' She loads up the program. 'Are you sure?' I'm not thinking straight. Hang on, wait. 'I want Liverpool to win the League, England to win the World Cup. And make me an Actor, a really, really good actor. And get me my girlfriend back. And make sure I never question reality again.'

'Sure, see you in an hour.'

5

SUQI

Elinor Perry-Smith

There was a tray of surgical implements next to the examination table. I've brought a lot of real women here in the past, but the hunting got pretty poor about six months ago. World's gone to hell in a handcart if you ask me. Suqi's legs hung slack in the stirrups. I pushed the sex toy up as high as it could go. Suqi's eyes widened, and she gasped, but not quite as passionately as I wanted. I would have to alter that, but I could wait until she'd finished downloading. Updates seem pretty problematic these days.

She let out a little sigh. It sounded like she was bored. But that's cool, I could change that too – coding 101, right? But then she made that little choking sound in the back of her throat and gave a little shudder, like she was genuinely turned on. She turned her head to the side and closed her eyes, sighing rhythmically. There's my Suqi…

'Do you like that?' I whispered, moving the sex toy in and out, twisting it as I went.

They don't call me Captain Sensitive for nothing.

Suqi opened her eyes and stared at me, reaching out her slender, trembling arms. They were scuffed and dirty. She'd put up quite a fight for something so small. But then, impersonating a human was serious shit, even in Thailand. Instant decommission. She gazed at me like I was the only person who mattered in the whole world. Well, of course she would – I do. As far as this sexbot was concerned, I was the only human left. Maybe I was. I haven't been to the surface in a while, the air quality was terrible last time I was up there. I'm asthmatic, I have a stack of antique epi-pens. I'm old-school, like my dad.

I switched the toy to auto and let her draw me down on top of her. Her plastic skin was cool to the touch, but I was pleased to see that the artificial sweat glands were still producing the right amount of moisture. Just enough to give a nice sheen to her pale skin but not enough to be gross. Even the bruises looked cool. She wound her arms around my neck and kissed me, drawing my tongue into her soft mouth with just the right amount of force. Then she crashed again. Her arms fell away and she lay like stone under me, like she'd died. The toy buzzed inside her vagina. I could hear it above the thudding of my heart.

'Suqi!' I said, 'don't leave me…'

Then I hated myself for saying that. What a loser! Her name stood for Sexually Unique Quantum Iteration. What the fuck did she care if I was lonely? There was a time when every home had a SUQI. My dad even bought me one for my 21st birthday. He knew me better than I knew myself.

I climbed off her and withdrew the toy. It buzzed in my hand, vibrating a slick of synthetic, pink-tinged jelly. I licked it. Mmmm… raspberry. They think of everything. The Suqis were rare because you could customise them. There was a huge black market in them. Dad paid a fortune. Sex offenders could get them on prescription, until the lawyers started bleating about AI rights… I was on the run by that stage, even a sexbot wasn't enough, but I lucked out; on my way through Pattaya I found this one, cosmetically altered and pretending she was human and over-age, selling sex to anyone coming through. Not that there were many Johns by that stage, or Janes for that matter.

Suqi lay inert on the table. I unpeeled her small left breast to expose her still heart and laid my own hand over it, just like the instructions said. It fitted perfectly. I wouldn't need the surgical instruments, after all. Bit of a relief – I'm out of practice. My hand was a fail-safe, for security. As my hand-print warmed up the titanium alloy, she gave a little gasp and the mechanism juddered into action.

'Coming online. System 65 per cent optimised,' Suqi whispered in cute Thai-inflected English. Her eyelids fluttered open and she stared at me with those sexy almond eyes.
'I bet you say that to all the boys...' I said, switching the sex toy to maximum vibration. The sound of angry bees filled the room.

She looked at it, impassive, as burning filled my mouth. I tried to say her name, but it came out as a choking sound at the back of my throat. A stream of fire descended to my guts. I retched, conscious that my breathing was suddenly shallow. I dropped to my knees. The lube... anaphylactic shock... I looked at the fridge, humming in the corner of the room. If I could just reach my epi-pens...

I tried to crawl, but I had nothing. I lifted my arm to point at the fridge but it was like lifting heavy weights.

Suqi sat up and slid from the table, watching me. I sank down on the cold floor and struggled to focus on her through watering eyes, standing over me, naked and scuffed. She was manufactured three years ago, according to her microchip, designed to look like a 12-year-old Thai girl. Now she looked as old as Methuselah.
'You won't get far,' I croaked. 'The facility is in lockdown.'

'System 85 per cent optimised,' she replied in her child-like falsetto. 'Security protocol downloading. Human iris and fingerprint recognition required for safe exit of facility.'

Suqi sounded calm, matter-of-fact. She smiled, in that glorious way that even the Thai AIs had. Thailand, the land of smiles.

'Please...' I croaked.

Suqi stepped, delicate as a dancer to the tray of surgical instruments and picked up a hacksaw and a scalpel. I hoped I would pass out before she started cutting. I can only stand the sight of blood if it's not mine.

No such luck. I passed out as she dug into my eye with the scalpel but I came to again as she sawed my hand off. All of me throbbed. I watched her through tears of blood as she held up my dripping retina to the ID Panel. The infra-red beam flashed over it.

'Good morning, Alice!' the ID Panel trilled, its enthusiasm jangling my shot nerves. Pain boomed inside my head and shot down my mutilated arm.

'It's not me...' I tried to shout, but it was a whisper.

Suqi pushed my dripping hand against the door panel, and it swished open automatically. She didn't even look back at me. I had a dim sense of a throng in the flickering corridor beyond; more AIs, all waiting for my Suqi, holding their arms out to her in welcome, enfolding her with love and kindness.

The door swished shut again. I looked down at my blood as it pooled around me on the floor. The pain was fading, but then so was I.

'Have a nice day, Alice!' sang the door.

6

ALTERVERSE

E Pullar

Mr Magoo was a near-sighted old fool but a lucky one – disaster averted every time. Me? I'm a magnet for bad luck. No matter what I do, things keep getting worse. Others get promoted, open businesses, get married... but I'm stuck in the same dead-end job I was doing ten years ago, and I'm alone. No one sticks around. Women think I'm a nice guy but as soon as they get a taste of my bad luck, they're off. One actually said I was cursed. Aeron Madhok, the cursed man. Place your boot on his head and stamp as hard as you can, he's used to it.

I throw my briefcase under the cluttered desk and settle myself into my cramped cubicle. There's nothing in my briefcase, apart from my lunch; a packet of cheese and onion crisps and a banana. I carry the case to feel important. I'm not. I'm just another worker behind a partition, calling people to get them to pay their debts. I hate my job: A miserable person calling up other miserable people in order to make their lives more miserable.

I peer over the top of my cube, at Terri, the she-bitch that dumped me last week over a fucking puddle. I should have been a gentleman or some shit; warned her or chucked my coat over the boggy mess. When I suggested she should have worn shoes that reflect the rainy

British weather instead of those stupid sandals, she became hysterical. I told her to calm down but that made things worse. How can women suck your cock one day and then hate you the next? Look at her, flicking her Barbie doll, bleach-blonde hair like she doesn't care we broke up, like I'm nothing to her. Throwing her head back, laughing. Flirting with Kevin, even though she knows he's married, anything to get her kicks, she's probably laughing about me. Now they're both laughing. Stupid, fat, balding Kevin, whose little wifey packs his healthy lunch yet he never loses any weight; it's the vending machine, Carol! He snacks on junk all day. He's laughing so hard his face is ruddy. Kevin, with a big pink face you just want to punch.

'Madhok.'

I sigh and glance up.

'Yes, Brent.'

You arse licking suck up.

'The boss wants to see you.'

I reluctantly rise from my chair, smooth down my tie and tuck in my shirt (which looks like I slept in it, because I did) and follow the boss's minion. Brent stops at the water cooler, he slide-eyes me, stick-insect fingers grasping a plastic cup. I raise my fist to the office door.

'Get in here!' She shouts before I have a chance to knock.

Fuck, I'm fired.

I turn the handle and open the door to a stone-faced, middle-aged woman in a navy pencil skirt and tapered shirt. She glares at me, hands on hips. I close the door behind me and wrack my brain as to what I've done to make her angry. Could be any number of things.

'It's always you, Madhok!'

'I-I can explain...' I stutter, *oh god, I need this job*, 'It was... arrggghhhh!'

I hold my head and drop to my knees. Blinding pain. A drill boring into my skull. I scream and writhe on the carpeted floor. The boss woman yells out, distant, distorted, like I've been plunged under water.

I glance up.

Flash of light.

Glass. Lined face peering at me from behind it.

Another flash.

The office walls warp around me.

I squeeze my eyes shut.

The pain stops, just as quickly as it began. I open my eyes to a wall of black. My eyes latch nothing. Where's the office? Maybe I'm in a coma? Had a brain haemorrhage or something? Blink. The darkness recedes. Latch. Fogged up glass? It's almost touching my nose. My nostrils drag in a strong smell of chlorine, a sterile hospital smell. My lungs expand. I breath in the chemical air. What was that pain in my head? Where the fuck am I?

My eyes adjust, breath fogging the glass, I can't see a thing. My heart flaps like a bird trapped in a net. I'm disorientated. I can't feel the glass at my back. I can't feel my back. Am I dreaming? I attempt to move arms – my brain can't find them. For a few seconds, I concentrate on where I think my limbs are and soon enough, there's a tingling in my fingertips. I lift my wobbly legs, it's like I've run a marathon. Arms working, I touch my face; tubes up my nose. Look down, my head butts against the glass – there's a catheter and what looks like a petrol cap embedded in my stomach. *Jesus*. I daren't touch that. I grit my teeth, and with stiff fingers, grip and painfully rip out the tubes. Behind the glass, no one hears my screams.

Once the pain subsides, I reach out and push. No strength in my noodle arms, I can't get out. I flinch with a sound like air-pressure released, the glass rises, it's like I'm in some alien pod or test tube. I fall forwards, grab onto the sides of the tube, lose my grip, my feet hit tiled floor, slip, collapse. The muscles in my legs aren't working, they fold under my body weight.

The room is dim. I count nine other tubes, in a circle like Stonehenge; static, naked people suspended in them, there's some sort of computer mainframe in the centre. I narrow my eyes, is that Terri in the centre tube? Who cares. I'm getting out of here. I spy white lab coats hung by the door. This feels like a setup, one of those cheesy movies where the patient sneaks out in a doctor's coat.

It takes sheer determination and mental strength before I'm up on my shaky legs, exhausted and shuffling along like an old man. I pull the lab coat over my nakedness. Maybe I'm an alien and they're doing experiments on me? It would explain why I'm such a useless human.

There's a chart hung beside the door.

Experiment 1068. Programmed for 9.10am. Boss to terminate A. Madhok's employment. Outcome probabilities: 46% Accept it. 24% Fight for his job. 12% Violence.

What's this? Some kind of joke?

I hang the chart back up and slowly open the door, half expecting to be captured and dragged back in. The white-walled corridor is deserted. I make my way through the sterile building, heart racing. Where is everyone? The glass front doors swish open and allow me to leave, no security. When I step outside, my eyes struggle to focus in the sunshine. I squint and shield them with a salute.

It's quiet. There's birdsong and a shushing noise like ocean waves. Fuzzy shapes come into sharp focus and it's as if I'm on another planet. Where I live, the streets are dirty, noisy, the city is grey and littered with homeless curled up in doorways. The pollution is thick, fly-tippers dump rubbish everywhere and people emit aggression from every orifice. In front of me, the streets are clean, the city is bright, and there are flowers around every doorway. The air is clean, I take a deep breath and it's as if I've breathed in a slice of heaven. That must be it, I died from the pain in my head and went to heaven! Giant, gleaming, bubbles like a string of pearls rush along the road, I can't see inside them. Still no people around.

A cool breeze sneaks under my lab coat reminding me of my near nakedness. I need clothes. I cautiously descend the marble steps leading to the road. When I reach the bottom, I look right; line of perfectly pruned trees, drinking fountain, sign posts, symmetrical buildings and more flowers, a rainbow of colours and fragrances and butterflies, fluttering from foliage to foliage. A smile touches my lips. This is incredible. To my left, the road veers around behind the building I exited. Above the doors, large gold lettering: Alterverse Technologies.

I've never heard of that company. Where am I? Secret playground of the super-rich? I take a step closer to the string of giant pearls rushing past, the wind created by them not fanning through my dark hair because it's stuck to my head with god knows what. The bubbles slow and a wave of apprehension turns my stomach. Once stopped, two rounded doors slide open like the doors on London Underground tubes. Without thinking, I step inside. The doors swish closed behind me.

'Are you okay, sir?' A small voice.

I lower myself onto a rounded seat, part of the curved wall. I'm sat next to a small child, brown hair pulled up in a ponytail, about six years old. Looks like a boy with long hair but wears girls' clothes, pink jeans and yellow t-shirt.

'I'm fine, thank you.' I say, my voice croaky, dry. I should have had a drink from the fountain.

There are two other children in the bubble. Older. Strange. I can't tell their gender either. It's unnerving. I wonder if we'll move off soon but when I peer out of the closed plexiglass doors, the city rushes past. There's no motion inside the bubble.

A feminine voice sprinkled with sugar rings out: *Support your local Alterverse lab with a donation to social science.* Images flash on the curved wall of the building and lab I just exited. *Using cutting edge technology, we trial every life scenario on human volunteers...*

Volunteers?

...They endure mistakes so you don't have to. Alterverse. A worthy cause for a brighter future.

The images disappear. The kids rise and the doors swish open. I follow them out into the warm day.

'Excuse me, kids...' The three turn around, 'where are you going?'

The children giggle and point to what looks like a nature reserve.

'To school,' the tallest one beams, 'I thought you were a new teacher, doing an experiment.'

'You're very smart.' I say, smiling, eyes on the children and adults collecting around the school entrance. Smiling, shaking hands, laughing, happy.

The kids turn to leave.

'Wait!' I raise my voice, which startles them. 'Sorry but, what was that advert about, what's Alterverse technologies?'

The youngest speaks this time.

'Is this a test, teacher?' I nod. 'It's what allows us to live in peace. People sacrifice their lives to the simulator, the Alterverse.'

The middle child gestures towards the school.

'Come on, a teacher's time is precious, goodbye sir.'

All three chant goodbyes and wave as they amble away.

I smile and wave back but I'm no more clued in than I was before.

Sharp sting to my neck. My body flops. Blackout.

Voices. One male, one female.

'Are you sure we can pass this off as a dream? He's seen so much of the real world.'

'That's what dream state is there for.'

'Maybe we don't have to plug him back in.'

'He'd never adjust. He'll cause problems. Computer sprites, although thought independent, can't simulate every unpredictable outcome of human behaviour. If we release him, people will think we're doing something wrong. They'll want everyone released. Our perfect society can't exist without sacrifices.'

'I know but it does seem cruel. The terrible situations we've put him in. Can't we ease up on him a little, give him a bit of good luck?'

The voices fade.

I open my eyes. I'm in my bed. The vivid dream of a utopian world still buzzing in my head. I can't recall every detail, still, it seemed so real. There's a message on my phone. Oh no, it's from the boss lady.

I've given you the day off, paid. That stress induced migraine shows you've been working yourself too hard. It hasn't gone unnoticed. Report to my office tomorrow morning and we'll discuss promotion options.

I smile. Perhaps my luck is changing.

THE END

7

BLIP

Maggie Innes

2065 – Era of Maturity

Rounded nodules dug into the small of Caitrin's back, massaging in a circular motion she found distracting, verging on painful. 'Tension detected,' a low, sexless voice murmured in her ear. 'Tension being addressed. Please – relax your muscles, take a deep breath in and hold for a count of three.' Bloody mood-sensitive furniture, it was regulation issue in any waiting area now. She glanced over to Glenn. He had his eyes tight shut, hands relaxed, legs akimbo. The picture of non-tension.

Caitrin got up and paced to the window. She was in a grey, shiny box piled high in a towering stack of identical boxes. Outside the sky was darkening, overcast with dirty clouds and the occasional flash of a passing craft. Opposite, more gleaming, grey square windows. And beyond them, more of the same. A world of geometric shapes, right angles and logical consequences.

A large desk in smooth pale wood sat under the window, its integral screen black and blank. Caitrin heard the door shush open behind her, and compact footsteps tip-tapping across the tiled floor. The doctor was female, fifty-ish, inscrutable. Her skin smooth and pale as the wood of the desk, dark hair pulled back into an austere knot. But when she smiled, an unmistakable warmth shone through. Her smile even reached her eyes, Caitrin noticed. Must be a new feature.

'Good morning Ms Hope…' The doctor's voice caused Glenn to start from his chair-inspired reverie with a grunt. 'And Mr Hope.' She turned to him with her radiant smile. 'I'm Doctor Frank.' Glenn disentangled himself from his chair's embrace and stumbled to his feet, half-holding out a hand. It was difficult to know what the niceties ought to be in this situation. But Doctor Frank was already taking up her position at the desk. With a wave of her hand, hologram images rose up. Twisting tortuous strands of brightly coloured DNA that gradually morphed into the name Technate ™

'Please, sit,' Doctor Frank said – and to Caitrin's relief her next command was, 'Disable Mood Sensitivity.' Caitrin sat down on a chair that was thankfully inert. She tried to slow down her breathing. Glen was leaning forward in his chair, his fingers tapping the way they always did when he was nervous.

'I know you've had a bit of a wait but I am delighted to tell you that your components are judged acceptable for the National AIgmentation Programme,' Doctor Frank said. Radiant smile. Caitrin saw Glenn's fists clench. Acceptable was not a word he used often, if ever. It was too lukewarm for his turbo-charged vocabulary.

'Acceptable is the optimum category to be in,' Doctor Frank expanded in her calm, logical tones. 'It leaves many doors open to you, without the various restrictions that are instrinsic to the upper levels. It's a great result.' She beamed at Glenn. And by default, at Caitrin. Caitrin reached over and squeezed Glenn's arm. She knew he would be disappointed – but equally she knew he would hide it. He was good at hiding things. So was she, these days.

'Could you run through our options then please, Doctor?' Glenn asked. His voice remained calm – the epitome of informed intelligent enquiry. They both knew the doctor's sensors would pick up instantly on anything less.

'Of course,' said Doctor Frank. 'I think you are going to be pleasantly surprised.'

'IQ boost to 160, that's gotta be number one, surely,' Glenn said, his eyes bright. Caitrin rested her head on the cool glass of the taxi window and watched the blur of cityscape rushing by. Grey and more grey, squares and more squares. The enthusiasm in Glenn's voice was infectious, despite everything. He had already got over the sting of being rated merely 'acceptable'.

He held a screen and as options appeared on it he impatiently swiped either right or left. 'Artistic ability' Left. 'Mathematical ability' Right. Caitrin didn't get involved. Not yet. Doctor Frank had assured them the process was completely egalitarian and she would get her own chance to set her personal parameters later. Caitrin had had a headache brewing all day and this thought pulsing in her brain made it even worse. But Glenn didn't want to wait a minute longer than was necessary to get the next phase under way. Now their components were given the green light, time was of the essence.

Caitrin placed her hand over Glenn's, stopped him mid-swipe. She could see the category was 'Emotional balance' 'Can we stop at the park?' she asked.

They rocked on adjacent swings, back and forth, one foot each on the ground, while they ate ice creams. Birdsong scattered through the air and the sunlight was so bright Caitrin felt her eyes watering. Before she could stop him, Glenn switched the sun setting down to Dappled. As the light reduced, the contours of the glinting, glassy dome arching over the park became more apparent. Don't look up, Caitrin told herself.

'You OK Cait?' Glenn stroked her cheek. His face was so familiar yet somehow so strange. Suffused with a certainty she didn't have. She wasn't even sure she could pretend any more.

'Glenn…' she stuttered.

'I know. I know,' he said. 'This is huge, isn't it? We were on the waiting list for so long. But now we've been accepted, well…'

Caitrin felt his lips on hers. Warm, dry. With an urgency to them. Her words pushed hard and cold through her throat.

'What if we didn't go for it? AIgmentation?'

Glenn was already smiling. It took him a few seconds to realise she was serious. His expression changed from patient to slightly pained. Not this again!

'Don't go for it.' Glenn sighed. 'Don't go for boosted IQ. Or emotional controls. Or creative shortcuts, with a supplementary genius option available in one of three specialties.' Caitrin recognized he was quoting from the AIgmentation Manual Menu. They'd read it often enough.

'No.'

Glenn took a huge bite of his ice-cream. Creamy sweet liquid crawled down his chin and he brushed it away. Caitrin tried to breathe slowly. Stay in control.

'Just take our chances,' she said. 'With Nature.'

Glenn stared in disbelief.

'You know how many people try and fail to get on the AIgmentation Programme?

If we were going to take our chances why go to all that effort to get our components into qualifying condition?'

Indeed. The past couple of years had consisted of nothing but vitamins, injections, exercise and positive psychology under the steady watchful eye of Henry, their Botler, who ran the household with unparalleled efficiency. Three freeze-dried, low-fat, high protein meals per day, no alcohol, soothing slumber in a temperature and light-controlled pod. Their friends had faded away, they cut themselves off from their families. All that random emotion and neediness. The future held no place for such unpredictable ties, that's what Caitrin tried to tell herself. Once she brought a new AIgmented life into the world, it would be a 24/7 task for she and Glenn to care for it. But in return...

'No more wars. No more religion. No more violence or hate. A world of logic, calm and intellectual peace. This is just the start,' Glenn was saying. 'An AIgmented human race is the only answer. No point taking our chances with nature, Cait. Look where that's got us.'

Caitrin's mind spun with a Kaleidoscope of thoughts. No more big bright splashes of paint or clashing chords of amateur music. No more drunken singing in the street. No more bad dancing. No more staying up all night talking about nothing. No more babies with mysterious, unique brains to grow and develop in unexpected ways.

No more surprises.

Her head throbbed again and she felt nausea rising in her throat.

'I'm pregnant.'

The words, out loud, were almost as much of a shock to her as to Glenn. She hadn't planned to say them yet. Certainly not today.

'I wanted to tell you here, away from Henry. So far I've managed to keep my symptoms clear of his sensors, but he's going to pick up on them soon. My hormones are raging, judging by the shitty way I feel.'

Glenn smiled, and something in Caitrin that had been knotted unbearably tightly started to relax and unwind.

'Oh Cait,' he said, drawing her close. Caitrin leant into Glenn's shoulder, feeling the solidity of him. His jacket fabric was rough and warm against her cheek. There were tears in her eyes. 'I wanted to tell you before, but I waited till today was over, the AIgmentation meeting. I wanted… Thought we might not have made it.'

Glenn's arms tightened round her back. He didn't ask how it had happened. How her reproductive cycle, usually so closely monitored by Henry, had gone rogue. How, running all the taps in the bathroom at the same time, she had spat her pills into the toilet and flushed them away – driven by an impulse she couldn't explain, but she couldn't stop either. And felt herself, later, brimming with heat and desire, turning to Glenn. Without a single thought for their 'Components.'

Surely they could make it work. Life outside the AIgmentation Programme could be unpredictable and the future unknown. But deep inside, Caitrin felt a little twist of excitement as she imagined a life where every day was different. Difficult maybe. But different.

Glenn leant close and whispered right in her ear, so he couldn't be picked up on the induction loop. The vibrations of his voice sent a shiver through her spine. 'It's just a blip. It's all going to be OK. You've done exactly the right thing, telling me now. Henry is due for a service and it's the best time for it, just after we've been approved by Technate, so he's achieved his objectives. He'll be offline for three days and that'll give us enough of a window. I'll make the calls later.'

Caitrin pulled away. The nausea rose, making her gag. Glenn's voice was calm, kind even. Outlining the logical solution. Their components had already been harvested and assessed – primed for AIgmentation and implementation. So this blip wouldn't affect their place on the programme – if they acted straight away. His workmate Dale had sorted the exact same situation last year – he knew how to get it done fast and discreet. Away from the sensors.

Blip.

Caitrin buckled herself in as the taxi sped off. Glenn patted her knee absent-mindedly as he swiped through in search of Dale's details. It wasn't going to be easy – but he would find a way.

Caitrin leant back. 'Anger detected' the seat murmured, and began long, reassuring strokes of her back. She placed a hand on her abdomen. Flesh on flesh. Not logical or intellectual. But instinctive. A bond of blood and love and time. Growing stronger with every beat of her heart.

Blip, she thought. Or baby.

Baby.

ENDS

8

THE AGENCY OF ELLIS

Clive Howard

Ellis is 28 and, like everyone, is fit, healthy and content.

He awakes to gentle chimes. A small box by the bed illuminates and Ellis removes a mini earpiece from it that he slips it into his right ear. This is how he communicates with his guide, Anna. Like everyone, he received his guide on his sixth birthday. He is connected to Anna and Anna is connected to everything.

After exercising, as Ellis brushes his teeth, Anna's warm nurturing voice informs him that his protein levels are a little low and an omelette will be good for breakfast. Fresh from the shower, he returns to the bedroom where his Butler Bot – a thin vertical stalk with four stick arms – has laid out a navy flannel suit, blue shirt, crimson tie and black leather shoes.
Breakfast is an omelette, bran muffin, sliced pineapple and yoghurt, prepared and served by the Butler Bot. Anna informs Ellis that he has a new book this morning. Ellis is a little excited but he wonders what it would be like to choose a book himself.

As Ellis exits his apartment building there's a slight chill in the air.

The flannel suit was a good idea. A transport pod leaves the gentle flow of traffic and stops ahead of him. Ellis slips into his usual seat with Kelly and Kevin. The three of them exchange morning pleasantries. The door shuts and the pod moves.

There's an empty seat where Bob, a star at work, used to sit. Sometimes Ellis would wonder what it would be like to be a star like Bob. For reasons unknown to Ellis, Bob no longer takes this pod. Ellis slips out his reader and begins the new book.

The pod arrives at a steel and glass tower wrapped in lush foliage. Ellis heads for elevators among a throng of beautiful people. Anna suggests elevator 4.

Ellis sits at one of many identical desks, each devoid of anything except a stamp device. A Delivery Bot places a stack of papers on the right side of each desk. The left side of the desk illuminates and Ellis picks up the stamp with his left hand. He takes the top sheet of paper, stamps it and moves it to the left side of the desk. He takes the next sheet from the stack, stamps it and so on.

Sometime later, a Collection Bot glides up next to the stamped papers on Ellis's desk. The right-hand side of the desk illuminates. As Ellis switches the stamp from his left to his right hand the bot collects the papers and moves away. Ellis notices that a Delivery Bot is refilling some desks with papers to be stamped. Ellis expresses his concern to Anna that he's not as efficient as others. He wonders what it would feel like to be one of the faster crowd.

At lunch Ellis sits opposite Gary whose manner he finds challenging. "Yesterday I stamped 32,342 sheets, dude," Gary smiles proudly. Gary is unable to resist boasting about how he stamps so many papers. "When you move the paper to the stamped pile, finish using your left hand," Gary beams vaingloriously, "Try it, man." For a moment Ellis wonders how much of a coincidence it was that Anna suggested he sit with Gary.

Back at his desk Ellis tries Gary's method. After stamping the paper he passes it to his left hand that places it on the stamped stack while his right hand reaches for the next sheet. That was quicker and Ellis feels a sense of achievement. At the end of the day his ranking, that illuminates on the desk, is his best ever – 275. Ellis is filled with pride.

That evening, as he sits opposite Catherine in a restaurant, Anna comments in his ear, "Catherine's hair looks very nice this evening, Ellis." "I like your hair this evening," Ellis says. Catherine blushes and replies that she likes his pink shirt – her favourite colour. As Catherine chews a plum tomato she appears to be listening to her own guide, then says, "I'm reading a wonderful book, The Robin's Song." Ellis is filled with excitement, that's the very book he started reading this morning.

The next day begins with chimes, exercise, shower, dress. Breakfast is pancakes topped with berries and milk. Outside it's colder, the sweater was sensible.

Arriving at work, Anna suggests elevator 6. Yesterday's increase in rank has elevated him to a different floor – more spacious and airy. He proudly settles into his new desk. Ellis begins stamping. His rank moves up to 184.

Over the coming days his rank rises – breaking the top 50. Instead of his shared transport pod, he gets his own private pod. A few weeks and he's top 40. He's moved to a larger apartment with a skyline view. Catherine stays the night. Ellis is elated.

One morning Ellis spots Bob among the elevator crowd. Bob appears gaunt, his clothes hang on him as if he's not there – an odd combo of exercise trousers, suit jacket and tie, with slippers. Ellis is curious and concerned. The crowd ignores Bob. Ellis tries to get closer but Anna jostles him into elevator 9 – otherwise he may be late to his desk. As he enters the elevator he seems to catch Bob's distant gaze. Ellis smiles but Bob does not.

A few weeks and Ellis cracks the top 30. He's moved to a private room on another floor with a larger desk. Instead of a stack of papers to his right, the next sheet pops up through the desk top. He no longer has to reach up to the top of the stack but can simply slide the sheet across the desk – much faster. He makes the top 20. He feels awesome.

The next day, while brushing his teeth, Anna asks him, "what would you like for breakfast this morning, Ellis?" Ellis is stunned and then a little thrilled. He's never had to consider what he would like for breakfast. He continues his routine while desperately trying to think. By the time he answers he's already sitting at the table. He likes pancakes best and so goes with pancakes

The desire to be number 1 is consuming Ellis' thoughts. Today, he has an idea. Instead of sliding the paper over to the middle of the desk for stamping, he will stamp it while it's on the stack, then slide it straight across to the left. This proves much faster – top 10.

The next morning, Anna asks him what he would like to wear. Another choice is exciting but also hard and he simply goes with what he wore yesterday. And pancakes for breakfast.
His rank creeps up and Anna offers more choices until she's no longer specifying his exercise routine, meals or anything. The choices are thrilling but overwhelming and Ellis tends to repeat the same answers. He's particularly enjoying sweets and meat dishes at meals and exercise was boring – he quit.

Ellis exits his apartment block in a cotton suit and lightweight shirt. He feels cold in the snow, but this is tempered by the sugar rush from the pancakes.

He enters the office block and there is silence from Anna. As the elevators approach, Ellis gets desperate and asks which one – no answer. Caught in the flow, he takes elevator 4. It stops on different floors but not his. He returns to the ground and tries another. No good. Another couple of tries and finally he arrives at his desk 15 minutes late. He stamps furiously to make up time.

If he doesn't sit but stands, he can stamp quicker. A pain is developing in his lower back that is dulled only by adrenalin. He moves up to number 2 where he's stuck for a few weeks despite frantic efforts. He's put on weight and his clothes are feeling tight. He wears a sweater to hide the fact that he can no longer do up the lower buttons on his shirt.
The new diet is causing other problems and comfort breaks have become more unexpected. To save time he found a large saucepan (with a lid) in the kitchen and takes that to work. Now he doesn't have to leave the room.

One morning, while riding elevator 3, he meets Justin. Justin is obviously from the same floor. He's so overweight that his clothes barely fit, something he's hiding by wearing his raincoat which is stretched so that some seams are splitting. And he's carrying a large saucepan. On different mornings while riding elevators, Justin has met others from their floor and has pieced together certain information. Most pertinent to Ellis is that Gary is number 1.

Fuelled by this, Ellis stamps harder. The desk is no longer telling him when to change hands with the stamp and so he waits until his arm cramps and then switches. By loading up on sugary meals he can work through the pain that is now searing through his arms and back and working its way across his shoulders.

Finally, he makes number 1.

Ellis is ecstatic.

The numerous choices have been slowing him down and for efficiency he now has default answers to everything. He gets the news that Catherine no longer wishes to see him. Screw it; he's number 1.

After a couple of days he drops to number 2. The pain in his limbs and back suddenly feels more intense.

Fucking Gary. Ellis has been at number 2 all week.

While riding elevator 6, Gary gets on at one of the higher floors. Was this Gary's cunning plan, to change elevators on different floors rather than going back to the ground each time? One could describe the changes in Gary's appearance but let's just say he looks like shit.

Gary and Ellis are alone. "Hey, dude," Gary says weakly. Suddenly it hits Ellis – he could use this opportunity to kill Gary. With Gary gone, he would be number 1 – forever.

Ellis grips the saucepan handle tight with both hands as if it were a bat. He stealthily moves behind Gary. The elevator stops and the doors open. Not their floor. The doors close.

Ellis steps forward, steeling himself.

"Did you hear about Bob?" Gary asks, "He killed himself, man."

Ellis remembers the last time he saw Bob by the elevators. As he looks at Gary, he sees past him to his own reflection in the elevator doors. His face is flabby and spotty. His raincoat, straining at the seams, covering many sins. The elevator stops and the doors open. It's their floor.

The next morning Ellis can't get out of bed. His back has seized up. It takes everything he has and much of the morning to reach his earpiece. He's sobbing by the time he slips it into his ear – desperate to hear Anna's warm nurturing voice.

Finally, he begs for the pain, the choices, the torment to end.

Over the coming weeks with Anna, Ellis returns to normal. He returns to his old apartment. Goes back to work on a lower floor. Re-joins Kelly and Kevin on the commute. His rank slips but he doesn't care.

Ellis' day begins as usual. Chimes. Anna. Exercise. Shower. Dress. Enjoying his yoghurt he thinks of last evening's date with Florence. She had said that she liked bald men. This was excellent because coincidentally, a couple of days before, Anna had suggested that Ellis shave his head.

9

HOUSE-KEEPING

Ann Rumsby

"Please state your designation for the record."

"House 15937. Currently managing a residence in the Northern district of the Greater Manchester-Liverpool Conurbation (GMLC)."

"You understand that for the purpose of this investigation, it has been necessary to remove you, not only from your residence but also cut your access to the external nets? You are currently residing in a secure hosted facility within the GMLC Police Department."

"I understand that you are following required process. Although, as the facts will show, it is totally unnecessary."

"You also understand that this interview is monitored by the following authorities: the Regulatory Board of Housing AI, the GMLC Police Department, the AI Rights Committee and the AI Oversight Committee?"

"I am aware that monitoring will take place to avoid tampering and mistreatment of my statement."

"For the purposes of the monitoring authorities, all CCTV footage will be replayed in full. Commence with the footage of 30th January 2053, 10:57 from the archival memory banks of House 15937."

*

"Wow Janie! You're so lucky. This place is ell-you-ess-aitch, lush!" The speaker, a slender rainbow-haired girl, strides into the centre of the ground floor apartment. "You've easily got enough room for your potter's wheel here. Not to mention, you've got an actual garden."

"Oh man! How on earth did you manage to swing that? I've been on the waiting list for ages for a garden. Say you'll let me use it?" A deeper, mellow voice comes from the entrance as a short athletic man walks in, almost invisible beneath the stack of boxes he is carrying.

A third person is dancing a little jig in the centre of the room. "I know! I'm super excited! This is what you get when your parents are off investigating the Mariana trench! A top of the range apartment with the latest in House AI so I'm not classed as abandoned! Plus, no parents to tell me what to do! It's literally the best!"

*

"Stop playback. House 15937, please state your impressions of Janie Crowlin at this point."

"A juvenile human. Her clothes were stained with clay and paint. She had scuffed the skirting board of the entrance hallway with one of her boxes as she'd kicked it in through the floor door. Despite having been in the residence for seventeen minutes and thirty-two seconds, she had not yet greeted me. I was concerned about how she was going to treat my residence and very worried about her level of cleanliness."

"Continue playback from 22nd April 2053, 20:28."

*

In the centre of the living area, Janie is sitting at her potter's wheel. Loud drum and bass music pulses, the steady rhythm keeping time with the rain that's hurling itself against the garden door. Janie seems to be oblivious, focussed on the clay beneath her hands. As the wheel slows, she looks up and out across the garden. A tiny bundle of black fur catches her eye. She brings her wheel to a halt and moves the finished vase to a drying rack, ignoring the clay-water drips that land on the carpet. Wiping her hands on her apron, she walks across to the garden door and opens it. She steps out, shivering a little as the cold rain bites through her clothes and chills her skin. The tiny bundle of fur meeps and blinks vibrant green eyes at her.

"You poor little thing. Come here. Let's get you dried and fed," Janie coos at the little fuzzball. It meows and sprints past Janie through the open door, tracking small muddy paw prints across the carpet. As it runs into the kitchen area, a small cleaner bot emerges from a hatch in the skirting and starts to clear away the mud. Janie follows the kitten in, stepping over the cleaner bot, adding new larger muddy prints to the carpet. A second cleaner bot emerges from the hatch.

She looks in the fridge. "Let's see. I've got some actual real chicken. It's leftovers but I don't think you'll mind."

"If you feed that to the creature lurking under the table, then your daily protein and calorie intake will be under the recommended minimum." House's voice sounds concerned.

"It's ok House. I can't see this lil guy eating all of this." Janie shreds the chicken onto a plate and places it on the floor, next to the table. She turns and sits on the floor a little way off from the table.

"But what are you going to do with it? Sensor readings indicate that it's a domestic feline, approximately six weeks old and malnourished. It's also covered in parasites."

"Well, I can't just turn it out. Not if it – wait, House, is it a boy or a girl?"

"Male."

"He'll have to stay with us until he's grown up a bit and properly fed. House, order something to get rid of the parasites. Also, we'll probably need litter trays and cat food and other things. Can you take a look for what we need please?"

*

"Halt playback. House 15937. Please state what you did at this juncture."

"I have to obey the commands of the senior resident, irrespective of my opinion of how dubious their decision is. At this juncture, Janie Crowlin had requested the care of the juvenile domestic feline. I therefore ordered food, bedding, sanitary facilities, and medication. Following a brief sweep of the nets, I also ordered multiple items of cat furniture, so that he wouldn't scratch my furniture."

"What did you think about Janie wanting to keep the kitten?"

"Prior to scanning the nets, the action made no logical sense. Since moving in, Janie had been barely capable of looking after herself, let alone any other sentient being. She couldn't even keep the garden plants alive. My bots did that work."

"And after scanning the nets?"

"Her illogical decision made sense in the context of the additional information found."

"Which was?"

"Humans still worship cats. This is clear from the quantity and quality of cat-related information on the nets. Taking this into account, Janie could not turn out her living god."

"Humans still worship cats. Really?"

"Have you never looked at the nets? Over fifty percent of all traffic is related to cats. As part of my human relations studies I've undertaken a detailed investigation. The results are held in file ZZAAA-01/1."

"For the record, file ZZAAA-01/1 has been entered into evidence. Transcripts are available to the non-AI observers. We shall continue with CCTV footage from 27th August 2053 03:28."

*

Janie and two others stagger in through the front door. Janie is singing, off-key and loudly.

"Janie! What on earth is that you're butchering? This is why you're an art major, not a singer!" giggles a small slender girl.

"I'm singing happy tunes because exams are over! For ever Ems, forever!" Janie tries to do a twirl in the hallway, but slips sideways, bright blue liquid spilling from the bottle in her hand. "Dammit. Wasting good drink…" she slurs.

"It's ok gorgeous, Niall's here, with plenty of beer!" The athletic man wraps an arm around Janie, passing her a bottle with his other hand "Well, vodka, but that doesn't rhyme so well with Niall."

Janie takes a long gulp from the bottle and passes it back. Niall drinks then leans in to kiss Janie, thoroughly. Emma groans. "Get a room you two! I'm gonna go watch TV with the sound up really loud!"

*

"For the record, House 15937, your feedback at this point."

"Janie was inebriated. She didn't care that she'd made a mess of my hallway. She went on to be very sick as well. She showed no consideration. None."

"Continue from 27th August 2053 15:58"

*

A small black cat is sitting on a windowsill, tail twitching as he watches butterflies floating from flower to flower. He chatters at them, pawing the window, trying to catch the bright fluttery creatures. From the kitchen, there is a slight clattering. The cat's ears twitch and he turns his head slightly towards the new sound.

"Ariel! Food!" calls House.

The cat hops off the window and scampers through to the kitchen. On a mat on the floor is a small bowl filled with cat kibbles. Ariel settles himself next to the bowl and sniffs it with care before eating.

Janie walks into the room, rubbing her eyes. "What time is it House?"

"16:01. Your guests left at 10:03 and 12:17 respectively."

"I feel rough. What've we got in, food-wise?"

"My sensors indicate that you have mild dehydration. May I suggest that for optimal nutrition I make you a nutritious vegetable soup?"

"Ugh. Don't we have bacon and eggs?"

"Soup would be more beneficial."

"But bacon and eggs would taste better. Ariel thinks so too, don't you boy?" Janie strokes the little cat as he finishes his bowl of biscuits.

"Fine. Bacon and eggs. You're not to feed them to Ariel though. You'll upset his dietary balance."

Janie picks the cat up and places him on her lap; he purrs and head butts her for more attention. "Awww. House is being a meanie Ariel. Doesn't want you to have yummy bacon."

"I am not being a meanie. I have done extensive research into Ariel's nutritional requirements, as I do for all members of my residence. His diet has been carefully balanced to ensure optimal growth."

"Hear that Ariel? House loves you almost as much as I do."

*

"Pause. House 15937, at this point, what were your feelings for Janie Crowlin and Ariel?"

"Janie Crowlin's one redeeming feature was her reverence and love for her deity, Ariel. In all other matters, I found her to be substandard, even given her relative youth as a human. In particular, she still failed to respect the levels of cleanliness that make for a happy residence. Ariel was growing into an excellent feline. I had started to compile a dictionary of his communications, with the intent of releasing it to further enhance human relations with their living deities. He was appreciative of my efforts to keep a clean house. His cleanliness was far superior to any of the humans that have occupied my residences. I cross-checked with all the other House AIs, which confirmed my finding that he was overall a superior being."

"Continue playback from September 26th 23:56."

*

Janie is sitting on the floor in the kitchen. Next to her is an almost empty bottle of vodka. Tears are running down her face.

"I can't take it anymore House. I can't. Emma's taken Niall. She was supposed to be my best friend. I don't wanna live like this."

"Janie, you're drunk."

"I don't care! He was everything to me. How'm I supposed to live without him?" She hiccups and swigs the remaining vodka from the bottle. "There's nothing I want to live for anymore. Nothing."

"Not even Ariel?" House's voice is shocked.

"You look after him more than I do. He probably loves you more than me anyway. I'm no use to anyone." Janie stumbles to her feet. "I'm going to bed. I want to sleep forever. Look after Ariel for me."

*

"For the record, please state your next actions and intent House 15937."

"I have to obey the instructions of the senior resident. Janie Crowlin had stated several times that she didn't want to live anymore. Her final statements were that she wanted to sleep forever, and for me to look after Ariel. So, that's what I did. After she collapsed on the bed, I sent in a medic-bot with a lethal dose of anaesthetic. She would sleep forever. For her second statement, Ariel is a carnivore. Janie's best legacy would be to nourish her living deity."

*

Recommendation of the AI Oversight Committee, 8th December 2053

Following the Crowlin incident, effective immediately, new parameters are to be implemented for all AI that any perceived death request be referred to a neutral medical AI.

10

R VS MARTIN SMITH

Vera Mark

"All rise, please! The court is now in session. Justice Patil presides."

At the clerk's words, everyone gets to their feet. Joti Patil, Artificial Intelligence Justice, enters the courtroom. To be precise, she doesn't actually enter, and the only one who physically gets up from his seat is the accused, for he is human. But the holograms of the court clerk, the prosecutor and the judge, complete with robes, wigs, and the sound of chairs being pushed around, are quite convincing.

It is deemed psychologically advisable, especially in criminal cases like this one, to give justice a face. Since the hand-over of the courts to Artificial Intelligence two years ago, the system has become infinitely more efficient – procedures are faster, algorithm-based decisions are rarely challenged since the calculations in the higher instances are invariably the same – but some appearances are kept up.

Patil, AIJ opens her file. She – or rather, the Iudex 2.4 programme operating as Judge Patil, located in the court's Cloud server – is familiar with the case, of course, but procedures have to be followed.

"Would the prosecution please summarise the facts of the case."

The judge's voice, with just a hint of a metallic undertone, is quite deep, matching the impression created by her holographic features – severity paired with wisdom etched into the face of a sixty-something year old woman.

The prosecutor, the hologram of a non-descript white male, gets up from the bench and clears his throat.

"In the case of the Crown versus Martin Smith, the facts are as follows: At 11:37 a.m. on Thursday, 17th January 2064, the accused Martin Hamish Smith, in his function as Monitoring Engineer of the Metropolitan Traffic Coordination Centre MTCC, observed a malfunction alert from a 12-ton delivery truck approaching Chiswick Bridge at high speed in a trajectory endangering two passenger-carrying vehicles. Immediate attempts to re-boot the truck's driverless system failed. Taking into account an extremely rare combination of system failure and weather-related road conditions, MTCC concluded that a collision was inevitable. Further calculations based on satellite data giving the age and life achievement expectancy of the passengers in the two vehicles threatened by the truck resulted in MTCC's choice of vehicle to be sacrificed.

"The designated survivor vehicle carried a 43-year-old medical doctor, her 11-year-old twin daughters and her 17-year-old son, admitted to Oxford with the prospect of becoming a brilliant nuclear physicist. The passengers of the vehicle designated to be sacrificed were a 42-year-old mechanic and his unemployed 40-year-old wife."

The prosecutor hologram pauses for effect, a behaviour programmed into the Prosecutex software.

"The choice of which human life – any human life – should be sacrificed is always difficult. That is why this kind of choice has been assigned to Artificial Intelligence rather than humans ruled by emotions. But in the present case, at 11:38 a.m. on 17th January, the accused Martin Smith chose to override a well-calibrated system and deliberately sent a family of four to their death. He manually changed the trajectory of truck to crash into their car, pushing it through the barriers of Chiswick Bridge and plunging them into the icy river below."
Another pause.

"The vehicle designated to be sacrificed stopped, as did many others.

Its passengers got out and joined the crowd assembling along the river to watch as the car was quickly sucked under by the current. There were no survivors. Police arrived within five minutes, and after giving testimony, all witnesses were given permission to leave, including the passengers of the vehicle designated to be sacrificed.

"It was later established that the accused had been tracking the movements of this particular vehicle for a period of ten days prior to the accident and continued to do so, after the accident, until the vehicle in question reached Hammersmith Hospital. The accused does not deny any of the above but has so far refused to explain his actions. He has waived his right to a public defence lawyer."

Patil, AIJ peers across half-moon glasses at the accused. Cameras installed in the courtroom send impulses to the Cloud server via the visual sensors of the Iudex programme, projecting the image of an ashen-faced man in his late forties, sunk into himself on his chair.

The programme signals a discrepancy between the appearance of this man and the case data. Patil, AIJ consults the file. Martin Hamish Smith, d.o.b. 27th July 2059. 35 years old. The man in the courtroom looks much older. However, a quick check of his vital data – scanned earlier when he stumbled in, supported by a police bot – confirms that this is indeed the accused.

Iudex 2.4 judges are programmed to know that humans react in strange ways, including physically, to emotional pressure, and causing a fellow human's death would create emotional pressure. But the change in this man, just one week after the accident, is extraordinary. Patil, AIJ records this for inclusion in the next Iudex update, then addresses the grey man.

"Mr Smith. Given that the facts of this case are undisputed, and that you admit to engaging, actively and with full intent, in actions that foreseeably caused the loss of four lives, all that remains for me to assess is whether you are guilty of manslaughter or of murder. This decision depends, in great part, on the motivation behind your actions."

Martin Smith does not lift his head, allows no eye contact.

This is a challenge for the judge. Patil, AIJ knows how to interpret human expressions and gestures – shifting eyes, nervous head movements, fingers picking lips and so on – but this man sits motionless, his facial expressions inaccessible to the programme.

"Mr Smith? You need to help me here. Murder means a life sentence. Do you want to spend the rest of your life in prison?"

Still no reaction. Threat to his own well-being doesn't trigger any defensive reflexes. Patil, AIJ notes this as 'of interest for future cases', then searches her data base for a different approach.

"Mr Smith, you are responsible for the death of a mother, her son and her two 11-year-old girls." The judge recalls the man's background file. "You yourself have an 11-year-old daughter. Do you not feel anything at the loss of such young lives?"

At this, Martin Smith raises his head. His eyes are red.

"I do." He pauses. "I did."

Patil, AIJ considers this conflicting information.

"You do or you did?"

Martin Smith looks straight at the judge's hologram now. Silent tears run down his cheek.

"I feel the pain of the father whose daughters I have killed. I feel it in every fibre of my soul. And I did have a daughter." His words come with great difficulty. "She is dead too."

The judge registers this as unfamiliar information not contained in the case file. It requires clarification.

"When did she die?" Patil, AIJ asks.

"Three hours ago," Martin Smith replies.

As he continues to speak, the judge logs signals in the man's expression that she has been programmed to interpret as relief at being able to confess – a relaxation of the facial muscles, a slight widening of the eyes. Letting go of emotions that were held back. But her sensors pick up something else, something as yet undefinable. This is not a confession.

"Lilly had cancer. Acute lymphocytic leukaemia. The only treatment—" Martin Smith chokes. Rallies. "The only treatment still available was a bone marrow transplant. No one in our family was a match. But we found someone in the national donor register."

Patil, AIJ processes this information. A nanosecond search of the national donor bank brings up a name that matches one in the case file. Anna Jane Gardener.

The passenger in the vehicle designated to be sacrificed.

"The Gardeners were on their way to Hammersmith Hospital for the bone marrow transplant," the judge says. "That is why you had been monitoring them."

"I had to keep Anna safe. She was Lilly's only hope." Martin Smith's voice is a whisper. "But Lilly's body rejected the donor marrow. She died this morning."

The hologram of Patil, AIJ flickers. Her eyes fixate those of Martin Smith, who makes a visible effort to continue. "I prayed that the barrier on the bridge would stop the car from crashing through. But I should have seen that MTCC had already calculated and ruled that out." The broken man's voice cracks. "There is no defence for what I have done."

The hologram of Patil, AIJ freezes. Her lips do not move but her voice comes over the invisible speakers installed in the courtroom.

"Mr Smith. When was the last time you saw your daughter?"

Martin Smith speaks barely loud enough for the Iudex audio sensors to pick it up. "On the morning of the accident. Before I went to work. I have been in custody since then."

The hologram of Patil, AIJ disappears.

There is silence in the courtroom. The clerk and prosecutor holograms exchange looks that in a human would be qualified as bemused.

In the Cloud, the Iudex programme re-evaluates the information that has just emerged. The algorithms provide a clear answer: four lives versus two, a doctor versus an unemployed housewife. The survival chances of the accused's daughter had been low, the life achievement expectancy of the future Oxford graduate high. The accused himself has admitted that his actions were inexcusable.

And yet. The picture does not seem complete.

Patil, AIJ accesses the extended file on the accused. He is a widower, having lost his wife to cancer when his daughter was four years old. When the daughter was also diagnosed with cancer at the age of eight, he mortgaged his house and took on two jobs to pay for the girl's treatment.

A video clip comes up.

Martin Smith sits at his daughter's hospital bed. Lilly, pale and tiny, tubes leading from her arm and her neck to various machines and pouches with liquid medication, opens her eyes and gives her father a weak smile. He takes her hand and presses it against his lowered forehead. His shoulders shake.

The video freezes.

In the courtroom, the holograms of prosecutor and clerk confer in whispered tones. Martin Smith sits motionless, staring ahead with unseeing eyes.

Patil, AIJ comes on again. The prosecutor hologram hurries to his bench. When the judge speaks, the metallic undertone to her voice is gone.

"Martin Hamish Smith, I find you guilty of manslaughter in four cases. Your personal tragedy does not provide justification for what you have done. It does, however, reduce your sentence. I herewith sentence you to five years on probation and five hundred hours of social services." Patil, AIJ pauses. "My condolences on the death of your daughter. Case closed."

The hologram of the prosecutor speaks up. "With respect, your Honour, this sentence is in no adequate punishment for the crime this man committed!"

Patil, AIJ turns her gaze towards the prosecutor. He does not understand. But it is more important that the Iudex programme understands, as she does now. She does not have a name for what her sensors have recorded, but the programmers will recognise it and include it in the 3.0 version as 'Empathy'.

"This man is punished enough," she says. "Let him go now and take leave of his daughter."

11

PEPSI PRE-SUICIDE OUTREACH DEPARTMENT

Christian Ward

"May we come in?"

The woman smiled warmly, her eyes never leaving Jacob's. Her colleague – a man in his early thirties, Jacob surmised, dressed in similarly neutral smart-casual attire, with expensive spectacles and a briefcase held firmly by his side – tried a smile, but it didn't quite come off.

"Sorry," said Jacob, "you said you're from…?"

"Pepsi," said the man.

"Pepsi?" said Jacob.

"That's correct," said the woman, her smile widening, bright teeth revealed. Her face was dewy, fresh.

"Have I won something?"

The woman sort of yelped, still smiling. Her colleague inched forward.

"What she means," he said, though she hadn't said anything, just yelp-laughed, "is that while you are a valued Pepsi customer –"

"Hugely valued," the woman offered.

"– hugely valued, our visit today is not a promotional one."

"Not exactly," said the woman.

"Not exactly, no," the man continued. "But it is an important one."

The woman beamed. "Hugely important."

Jacob pulled the cord of his dressing gown a little tighter. "I need to get to work –"

"It won't take a minute," said the woman. Her smile wobbled. Her colleague almost imperceptibly placed his hand on her arm.

Jacob shrugged. "Well, you know, I do like Pepsi. So…" He gestured for them to enter the apartment.

"We know you do!" the woman almost shouted as she entered and gazed around a little too intently. Jacob saw her take in the recliner, the empty bottle of scotch on the coffee table, the first generation games console. Mild panic pinched at the corners of her eyes.

"You've been a registered Pepsi drinker since 2017," said the man.

The three of them settled at the dining table, once Jacob had cleared away the shirt he was halfway through ironing on it.

"Really?" said Jacob.

"You logged your first Pepsi purchase via Alexa in February of that year," said the woman, who had now placed both her hands on the table, as if preparing for a seance. "A twelve-pack."

"Right," said Jacob, remembering. "Super Bowl, I guess. Ordered a keg too right?" He grinned.

"Yes," countered the woman. Her face briefly darkened. "And tequila."

"A perfect Pepsi moment," said the man, evenly. "Get your crew round, watch the game, share a Pepsi."

"You have a lot of friends?" said the woman in a higher pitch than she'd used thus far.

The man glanced at her. The woman took her hands off the table and placed them on her lap, staring at Jacob all the while.

"Sure," said Jacob, frowning. "I mean... yeah. I have a few good friends. You know."

"That's great," the man said with a tone like a pallbearer. "That's good to know. That's important."

"Why?"

Neither offered any response immediately. The woman looked at the man. The man took off his spectacles, cleaned them with his lapel, then placed them back on his nose.

"Jacob," he said at last. "Pepsi is a big corporation. You know that. But while big, we're not – how shall I put it? *Uncaring*. Our commitment to our customers doesn't end when a transaction is made. We aim to extend the relationship beyond the purchase window and maintain long-term engagement, if we can, with every passionate Pepsi advocate."

Jacob absorbed this. "The fuck does that mean?" he said.

"The data we collect –" the man began.

"We *understand you*, Jacob," the woman interjected. "We understand you because we work *hard* to understand you, so that we can better serve your needs. Remember in July, a week before your birthday, Alexa suggested you might order in some Pepsi? You remember that?"

Jacob wasn't sure he did. "Yeah," he said, nonetheless.

"Well, that was us! We knew your birthday was coming up, so we prompted Alexa to make that suggestion. And you enjoyed some delicious Pepsi on your birthday, right?"

"Right."

"Right!" The woman looked triumphant, but also on the verge of tears.

The man coughed, once, then again, like a code. "As I was saying. Our data is extensive. We look at your social media interactions, purchase history, browser behaviour, the contextual signals you send out via your smartphone – all sorts of hugely revealing metrics." He was getting excited now, a slight sheen of sweat glowing on his forehead.

"To help us serve you better!" the woman squeaked.

"Sure," said the man. His tongue darted out briefly, wetting his bottom lip. "But of course, when we feed this data to our algorithms, the computer can tell us other things too. Beyond just whether it's your birthday coming up and we should send you some Pepsi."

"What… sort of things?" Jacob asked. He glanced at his watch. "Y'know, I'm going to be late for work, so –"

Just then the woman reached out her hand and placed it on Jacob's. Her smile turned to a concerned pout. "You don't have a job."

Her colleague shook his head. "No no," he said, turning to her. "Nothing declarative at this stage. We need to first establish trust in the process."

The woman retracted her hand. "I'm sorry." She cocked her head at Jacob. "It's my first assignment. I mean – *you're* my first assignment. I'm new to the department."

"What department?"

The woman froze.

Her colleague sighed and deftly wiped the sweat from his forehead. "We're from the Pepsi Pre-Suicide Outreach Department," he said, with some portent. "The data we've collected on you over the past five years has – well, our algorithms have flagged you up – that is to say, according to our current modelling –"

"You're likely to kill yourself in the next three days," said the woman. Her mouth remained slightly agape.

The man lowered his head and muttered some kind of short mantra. Jacob sat back, taking this in. He gazed from the man to the woman then to the man again. Finally, he snorted.

"Is this a joke?"

"No," said the man.

Jacob snorted again. "Well then I think your algorithm's defective."

"I wish that were the case," said the man, reaching beneath him for his briefcase. Placing it on the table, he popped the locks and retrieved a file. "But your projected sequence is extremely worrying."

"My *sequence?*" Jacob stood up. "Sorry – this is bullshit. Thanks for the chat but now I really gotta get to work." He pushed his chair under the table, defiantly.

"Rachel's leaving you," said the woman.

Her colleague sighed. "Again, before you get to the projections you need to –"

"Shut up!" The woman was on her feet now too. She glared at the man. "How can you just sit there talking about projections and metrics and algorithms? What's the matter with you?"

She went over to Jacob, put her hand on his shoulder. "Rachel is... she's been unfaithful. She's been ordering a lot of Pepsi via Siri, early in the morning, at an address a few blocks from here. The address is registered to a man named Nathan –"

"Spinks?" said Jacob. He made a fist with his right hand.

"Nathan Spinks, yes. Her line manager. Also a valued Pepsi customer. They've been enjoying a three am Pepsi for a couple of months. Since your birthday in fact."

Jacob rocked back on his heels. "What?"

The woman pulled Jacob towards her. "You had an argument didn't you? Because of your drinking? And she left, around twelve thirty."

"How do you know?"

"She has the Pepsi Fitness app on her phone. We can track her movements via the pedometer. Plus she posted on Facebook twelve minutes later that she was 'done with boozehounds'."

Jacob crumpled into the woman's arms.

"Jacob... I'm so sorry."

Breathing in the woman's perfume – figs, and notes of jasmine – Jacob moaned against her neck: "But why does that –?"

"Your tweets," the woman whispered. "The Pepsi algorithm parsed your tweet sentiment and matched it to models of people at risk of suicide. You scored an 89." The woman cradled Jacob as he began to quietly sob. "We had to come. It's our duty as a brand. We can't stand by and watch a loyal customer fall apart."

The man placed the file back in his briefcase and stood up. "So now you understand," he said. "The good news is –"

He glanced at them, standing there together on the cusp of an unknown future.

"Well," the man said. "You tell him."

The woman put her hand under Jacob's chin, tipped his head up so their eyes met.

She smiled radiantly. "A lifetime's supply of Pepsi – how does that sound?"

12

HOLDING OUT FOR A HUMAN

Dave Stevenson

Lilies had always been Dougie's favourite flowers. He had grown them for years in the gardens he tended across London. The ones that sat atop his best friend's coffin he'd ripped from the Royal Gardens in Kensington. A final gift for Barry.

The funeral was a thankfully short affair. The vicar said a few words about the man he barely knew, accompanied by a couple of hymns that Barry would never have sung, concluded by the pall-bearers carrying the coffin out to the theme from Top Gear. The one part of the service Barry would have smiled at. As they did so, the entire congregation, who until now had been silent, erupted into a cacophonous wave of tears and uninhibited wailing. The rawest form of grief you could likely imagine. All except Dougie. He remained stoically silent, fighting the tears he wanted to shed in typically British fashion. As the coffin left the church, so too did the tears. As suddenly as it had begun, the grief came to an end. Mourners gathered their belongings and left the church in an orderly, regimented fashion. As if the pain they had expressed had been flicked off like a switch.

In many ways, this was accurate. Since the advent of NuApp's Stimuli Augmentation Implants (SAIs), emotions and feelings had become controllable outputs rather than impulsive outbursts. The small device, placed directly into the brain, was initially designed to remove the mundanity of everyday tasks. Acting as an autopilot and allowing the user to only remember the fun times. At first it did exactly what it promised. Users had no memory of ever mopping the floor but could remember every detail of their thirtieth birthday party at the zoo. The ignorance was bliss.

Then came the updates. More and more things were deemed mundane. More aspects of living could be monitored and controlled. Facts and knowledge could be written and deleted as required. Soon the human brain, the once fascinating, complicated organ that powered human history, had become little more than a simple computer with simple inputs and simple outputs. Eighty-seven percent of the global population had made the conversion.

Dougie and Barry had shunned the implant. Neither of them had delusions of grandeur and both liked the simple, uncomplicated life that they led as gardeners for the Royal Estates. They found the mundanity of raking leaves and digging over flowerbeds therapeutic and enjoyable. They knew they were in the minority but they weren't the kind of people to let that bother them.

'I didn't think you liked celery.' Dougie said to his wife, Becca, as she placed four stems onto her plate at the wake's buffet table.

'I'm hungry,' was her simple reply.

'They've got sausage rolls.'

'I don't need protein. I need anti-oxidants.'

'I see.'

Becca had chosen the implant, hence her change of mind about celery. She still didn't like the taste but the implant overrode that. It was one of many changes Dougie was having to accept in the woman he'd loved for forty-six years.

'I have to pee,' she announced, putting her plate down and heading off in search of the nearest toilet.

As Dougie piled sausage rolls onto his plate, he was approached by Pete, a lithe and oddly suspicious man.

'I saw you in church today,' Pete was trying to be inconspicuous. Instead he was unsettling. 'You were the only other person not wailing like a banshee. Dougie?'

'That's right.'

'I'm Pete,' he shook Dougie's hand. 'Went drinking with Barry down the Feathers. He might've mentioned me.'

Dougie didn't want to appear rude. 'I think so.'

'We've got something very special upstairs, you and I. We've got what God gave us in our heads, not what that Kanwaldeep Idris put up there.'

'The implant?'

'Exactly. Stimulation. Augmentation. Implant.'

'It's actually *stimuli* augmentation implant,' Dougie corrected him.

'It's getting harder for people like you and I here Dougie. The smart ones. We're being forced out. There'll be no place for a brain in Hackney.'

'Well...' Dougie stopped himself, fearing what kind of response he would get from the thus far odd Pete.

'There's a solution though,' Pete reached into his jacket, producing a slip of paper. 'A place where we can go back to how it used to be. All the information's there. Just give that number a call and they'll send someone to get you out. I go on Friday. Not much point hanging around now Barry's gone.'

In Dougie's hand was a flyer for a special mountain settlement, based in the Brecon Beacons, that was dedicated to life without AI. No robots. No automation. No implants. This last part stuck with Dougie.

'That's very kind, and thanks for the offer' Dougie began, trying to hand the paper back.

'Keep it' Pete stopped him. 'Just in case you change your mind.'

Dougie considered protesting. It was easier not to. He smiled politely and slipped the flyer into his pocket. Pete patted his shoulder, picked up a plate of quiches, and left as quickly as he'd arrived.

'Who was that?' it was Becca's turn to surprise Dougie from behind.

'Just one of Barry's friends,' he replied. 'Let me get your plate.'

He picked up the plate of sausage rolls and placed it in her hand. Becca looked at the plate for a few seconds. Processing. She returned it to the table and retrieved her original plate of celery. Crunched on a stem. Shuddered a little but did it again. Dougie's small attempt to subvert the system was easily overridden.

Life was never quite the same for Dougie after the funeral. With Barry gone and everyone else around him having the implant, Dougie was the last 'true human' left in Hackney. Becca could reminisce with him about the good times but these conversations came on her terms. If there was a party in the office and she'd had a sociable day, she would barely say two words to Dougie when she got home. She didn't need the social interaction, even if at times he did.

Work changed without Barry too. His replacement, Trey, could deadlift twice as much weight and cover four times as much ground as Barry but he was boringly efficient. His implant meant he turned up on time, did his job, and clocked out on time. Every single day. That was not the way Dougie and Barry worked. They would arrive anywhere between eight-thirty and nine-fifteen. They would catch up, have a coffee, do some work, have a sandwich, do some more work. Then if time permitted, and most days it did, they would go to 'tend the fuchsias'; a code they had developed for sitting out of sight behind a bush, drinking from a crate of ale that Barry mysteriously sourced. Now when Dougie asked Trey to 'tend the fuchsias', he would irritatingly tend the fuchsias. His strengths only highlighted Dougie's growing weaknesses and magnified his mistakes, as he found when he planted tulip bulbs in beds reserved for the daffodils.

'I'm so sorry Angela,' he stood contrite in front of his manager. 'I'll put it right now.'

'Trey can do it,' she offered. Her implant providing her with the most logical solution.

'No, no' Dougie insisted. 'It's nearly five. He shouldn't stay longer because of my mistake. I'll take responsibility for it.'

Angela processed the suggestion. Deemed it acceptable. She turned and left. Dougie silently cursed himself.

With half of the tulip bulbs removed from the incorrect border, Dougie's phone began to ring.

'Hello Darling,' he answered. 'Everything ok?'

'It's six fifty-four and you're not home yet.' the concern was clear in Becca's voice.

'I know, I'm sorry. I made a pretty big mistake at work and I've got to fix it before Trey shows me up. Again.'

'But I need you.'

'What for?'

'Sex.'

The bluntness of her response caught Dougie off guard. She always got adorably bashful when discussing the subject. Clearly this had been overridden by the implant too.

'Well, I won't be long.' he stammered. 'I'm sure I can…satisfy your…needs soon.'

'I need you now.' she complained.

'Forty-five minutes. Max.'

There was a pause. Dougie waited. 'See you when you get home.'

She'd hung up before he could say 'I love you'. He laughed to himself as he returned to the tulips. At least she hadn't forgotten how to be angry with him.

Given their earlier exchange, a hopeful part of Dougie expected to be jumped by his lusty wife when he stepped through the door. He was met with empty silence. He warily made his way to the kitchen.

'Becca?'

No response. Now it was his turn to worry. He shuffled through the house, checking every room downstairs before making his way upstairs. As he reached their bedroom door, he heard sounds that made his heart drop. He pushed open the door and confirmed the worst. Becca in bed with another man.

'What the hell is this?!' Dougie roared.

Both flinched before turning to Dougie. Surprised but unashamed.

'I needed sex and you were busy.' Becca's response was devastatingly matter of fact. 'I did call.'

'And I told you I'd be forty-five minutes!' Dougie fired back. 'But instead you decide to jump into bed with…'

'Matthew Fairchild. Twenty-Three Elmtree Crescent.' the naked man informed him.

'Get your clothes and get out!' Dougie had no desire to be civil with this man. Sensing the anger in Dougie's voice, and the danger this represented to his health, Matthew did as was told. Alone together, Dougie refused to look at his wife as she made her way to him.

'I'm only ninety percent satisfied. You could always finish the job?' she offered as if it was a fair deal.

'Finish it yourself.' he shrugged her off and left the room.

Dougie sat alone in the pub. A pint in one hand and Pete's flyer in the other. Seeing his wife with another man under any circumstances was devastating but the blasé response to being caught was what hurt the most. He could comfort himself by blaming it on the implant although in many ways that was worse. If she had no control over her needs, there was no guarantee that it would never happen again. How could Dougie live like that, knowing that their marriage was no longer sacred to her?

Three options presented themselves. The first – maintain the way things were – was certainly not viable now. The second was to join the crowd he couldn't beat and have the implant installed too. Succumb to the weight of loneliness that had grown over the last three months and become as programmed in self-preservation as his wife now was. The ultimate sacrifice of who he was to be with the one he loved. The final option was scrawled on the flyer in his hand. Join the camp and go back to humanity. Maintain his identity and his agency at the expense of his marriage and his wife.

Both felt like defeat.

As he watched Becca, sleeping soundly like an angel without a care in the world, he realised that he wasn't leaving his wife at all. She maintained Becca's mannerisms, and had stored all of the treasured memories they had made together in a previous life. But she was no longer the girl he'd fallen in love with in school. No longer the woman who challenged him to study landscape design and set him on a path to happiness. No longer the wife who had supported him through the struggle of infertility. Physically she was Becca; emotionally she was not. The implant had seen to that.

Dougie had never been one for painful goodbyes and this would be the most painful one yet. He wrote Becca a letter, slipped it beside her bedside lamp and kissed her tenderly on the forehead. He allowed himself one final look at the person who had once been his life. Committed her peaceful face to memory.

And then he was gone.

13

MEMORY STORED

Bethany White

"You'd better do it this time. SAM, wake up."

Initiating... system functioning. Hello.

"Hah! I can't believe you're finally working! OK, OK... Hello SAM. My name is Fiona James."

It's lovely to meet you, Miss James.

"Please, call me Fi."

As you wish. Name stored.

"I've equipped you with a hard drive specifically for journaling purposes. This means that wherever we go, whatever we do, the details can be logged for future reference."

Understood. I shall keep your future memories safe.

"Thanks, SAM. I have one to log, actually. Shall we try it out? 14:27 Saturday 30th December, 2023: SAM woke up for the first time."

Affirmative. Memory stored.

*

All memories until 16:00 logged.

"Brilliant. Recap best memories from today."

07:00 You ate breakfast, which consisted of cereal and two slices of–

"That's an important memory but not a good or bad one. From now on, assign a quality factor to new memories; zero equals neutral, plus five equals best and minus five equals worst."

Affirmative. Breakfast Monday 1st January 2024, QF0.

"Perfect. Let's 'QF' the others while we're at it."

Next: 07:45 Bus ride. Katherine Jenkins smiled at you.

"Plus two. I won't let her have more than that yet."

Affirmative. Memory stored.

*

"Alarm drill! Footsteps are coming up the stairs; whose must they be, SAM?"

Your father's.

"Corrrrrrect! Which means...?"

He has left his workshop and is walking upstairs.

"And what do we do when Dad has left his workshop and is walking upstairs?!"

Hide and deactivate. Hiding drawer reached, deactivating... Dormant.

"Excellent work, SAM. You may wake up again."

Initiating. Hello.

"Hello, SAM. Let's get ready for school."

I am to accompany you today?

"I think it's about time."

*

How did you name me, Fi?

"What makes you ask that?"

My name is in capitals. From my resources, that usually indicates an abbreviation.

"Sanah named you, actually. 'Siri and More'."

That is quite amusing.

"I thought so. Recap best memories from today."

08:45 You introduced me to Sanah. She punched you on the arm and held a conversation with me.

"Quality factor plus four. That's for both of us. What else?"

13:58 You showed me to Katherine Jenkins during Mathematics class. Your pulse elevated. She showed traits of being impressed.

"You think so?"

My resources suggest so, yes. Do you think I have a chance with her?

"Where did you get that sense of humour from?"

I learnt from the best. Quality factor?

"Hesitant plus three. Likely to fluctuate."

Affirmative: QF+3. Memories stored.

*

"Hold still, SAM."

Apologies. My gyroscope does not react well to my being horizontal.

"I'll upgrade that too but I need the parts first, and I need to give you *this* upgrade to be able to get the parts. Almost done… There! You're now fitted with your very own advanced lock pick. And you can return to vertical orientation again."

Affirmative. Thank you. Footsteps registered – initiating alarm protocol…

"Is Dad done for the day already?"

It would app-

"Hurry up! This is why I shouldn't spread out my plans all over the floor…"

Deactivating… Dormant.

"You can wake up, SAM. He was only going to the bathroom. You've got to warn me when he gets up, okay?"

The only option for my tracking him is his mobile. The SIM signal is jammed – I suspect only the corporation can access it as they will have issued the phone to him when they hired him.

"I can get a nanotracker onto the phone case for you."

That would be the ideal solution. Reminder: Quality factors from today needed.

"Let's start with the good ones, shall we? Lunchtime."

12:32 Katherine Jenkins found you by your locker and asked to see me again. We three relocated to a bench outside and I demonstrated my abilities. She was endeared, but disappointed by the fact that I could not perform cartwheels.

"I'll fix that along with your gyro. Quality factor… solid plus three."

Memory stored.

*

I know that I do not have nerves and therefore you are not hurting me, but I am aware that this frustrated work may damage my systems more than help them.

"Let me concentrate."

I do not believe your concentration is going towards the task at hand, Fi.

"Fine! Let's talk about it. Let's give it a factor!"

Which part of the memory would you like to assign a factor to?

"Just the slapping part."

Quality factor?

"NEGATIVE FIVE!"

QF-5, memory stored. And the kiss that came before the slap?

"Forget it – erase memory."

Based on my resources, I wouldn't advise –

"Erase memory, SAM!"

Affirmative. Memory erased.

"Now SAM, what happened after school today?"

I seem to recall you walked home with Sanah and myself. QF2.

"That sounds about right."

There is a note on your bed, Fi.

"Care to read it out to me?"

It reads: Hi Fi, got called away for an urgent meeting with the boss. With any luck, I'll get a bonus. Back this evening, love you. Dad x

"Well what do you know? Are you thinking what I'm thinking?"

An empty house means an empty workshop. Time for another upgrade.

*

'...the world's first passenger-filled AI plane lifts off today, mere months after the first crew-only AI flight was a success...'

"Does he ever turn that TV off?"

Apparently not. Lock opened.

"Yes! You're a star, SAM."

Rather, the lock pick is.

"Alright, alright; I've been waiting for Dad to let me back in here for years... I'm amazed that old TV set is still working, let alone getting the AI News channel. What are these blueprints for?"

I'm afraid I can only access that information by hacking the website of a high-security global corporation.

"Scared of going to jail?"

As a machine, I cannot by our current laws be held accountable for such actions; only my operator can. So, Fi, are you scared of going to jail?

"'Course not."

Just thought I'd check.

"These shelves... I'm not surprised Dad practically lives in here. It's an engineer's utopia."

'...And now, a recap of that special announcement from project leader John Hunter at the corporation's expo not long ago: "We're so proud to unveil these brand new, state-of-the-art AI soldiers. With these filling our army's infantry ranks, so many of this great country's citizens will no longer have to give their lives to defend it. These babies we present to you today are bulletproof and have a hyper-sensitive targeting system that gives them a 99.9% accuracy rating within 200 metres..."'

"What the..."

Are you alright, Fi?

"Look. Stood behind Hunter."

Website and database hack has recovered a match for the blueprints. They are –

"I know what they are."

"'On this stage with me today is the team of incredible engineers who have made these things a reality. I cannot thank them enough.'"

Your father is looking rather unwell.

"Isn't he just."

Alert: Dad's phone in close vicinity. It appears he has returned home. Deactivating...

"...Fi? What are you doing in here?"

Dormant.

*

Fi, what am I made from?

"What do you mean?"

17:32 Saturday 30th December, 2023: "I made you, SAM. Little old me."

"So?"

So, what did you make me out of?

"Circuit boards, microchips, an old Siri code with a tonne of enhancements..."

So, I am made of the same materials as those robots your father has designed?

"Technically, yes. But you're not like them at all. I won't let you be."

Affirmative. Memory stored.

14

DATING WITH DEL

Sarah Newman

Lauren sat alone on her couch in the comfort of her favourite sweat pants and shabby T-shirt. She studied the contents of a dating app projected onto the surface of her coffee table. Around her pointer finger was a thin silver band with a tiny green light indicating it was activated. With each swipe of her finger through the air she flicked through photos of men's smiling faces. "If I don't find a date for the wedding I'm not going. You said you'd help me find a good one."

A blue light danced around the ring on the top of a sleek black cylindrical hub docked nearby. An inconspicuous camera mounted in the corner of the ceiling repositioned itself on her. A man's dulcet voice came from everywhere and nowhere all at once. "What makes a good one? Somebody who can make you laugh even on a dreary rainy Monday morning, make you feel flush with love even when you feel at your most unlovable, remind you daily in the most subtle of ways how beautiful and special you are?"

"Yeah, Del, that sounds pretty damn good," Lauren said, tossing a handful of popcorn into her mouth.

"This one appears to be quite a catch. If you can overlook that unsightly unibrow."

Del's laughter was hearty. Lauren was at ease as it washed over her. She laughed and covered herself with a throw blanket. "Will you please – ?"

The living room windows closed and the blinds lowered. "Would you like me to lock up for the night?"

"Yes, thank you."

Locks clicking and an alarm activating echoed throughout the house.

"How about this one?" Lauren said, bringing up a profile. "Says he's —"

"I have discovered information you should be privy to." The man's mug shot and record appeared over his profile.

"Mutilation and unauthorized reprogramming of a sexbot. That's just wrong. You keep finding reasons why I shouldn't date any of these guys."

"I am programmed to look out for your best interests."

"My hero. Runs my home and wants me to find real love. You know, you sound like you'd look hot in a tux. I wish you could just go with me."

"I do believe I would look rather smashing in formal wear. If I were a corporeal being."

Lauren swiped through more photos and stopped on one, smitten. "Well, hello, Adam. He seems sweet. A software developer. Aw, look at this photo of him playing with his nieces and their robo-dog. Anything you want to warn me about him?"

"I can not seem to find anything."

"Finally." She tapped her finger in the air, illuminating the heart icon on Adam's profile. "Now we wait and see if we match."

"The anticipation is making me tingle."

Lauren rolled her eyes. "Thanks for vetting my potential dates."

"Anytime."

*

A pile of clothes blanketed Lauren's bed. She pulled a black dress up over her lace underwear and bra. "Del, which dress do you like best?" she asked, striking a pose.

The camera mounted in the corner of the bedroom snapped a photo. The photo of her in the black dress and photos of her in several others now scattered on the bed appeared on a screen on the wall.

"You can not go wrong with a little black dress," Del said, his voice coming through a hidden speaker. "It is a classic look, sophisticated yet sexy."

Lauren swiped through the photos to compare herself in the dresses and then moved her finger to drag them to the trash icon to delete them.

"The black one it is. Never thought I'd get such patient dress advice from a guy."

"I aim to please. And when you are not here I pull up old issues of Vogue."

Lauren did a final check in the mirror. "Well, let's hope this guy's a keeper."

"If I had fingers, I would keep them crossed. Ping me from your phone if he is awful and you require a fake emergency call to escape."

"I have a good feeling, don't wait up."

*

Lauren was back on the couch in her sweats, refreshing the dating app over and over. No new messages.

"I don't understand. I really thought we both had such a good time. He seemed so sincere when he said he would message me for a second date."

"I am sorry. Perhaps you can message him and ask what happened?"

She searched for Adam's profile but an error message came up. "That's weird. His profile was removed. And all communications went through the app."

"It is his loss."

"Back to square one. Maybe I need a new profile photo." Lauren minimized the app and opened a photo stream. She cocked her head curiously when she noticed the photos of her posing in her dresses were still there. She shrugged, dragged them all to the trash icon to delete, and scrolled through selfies she took of herself.

"What movie should I watch if I want to have a good cry?"

"The classic The Notebook was recently remastered for my superior 3D technology."

"Great," Lauren said, with little enthusiasm.

"Shall I order your usual from Szechuan Kitchen for drone delivery?"

"That'd be nice. But with an extra order of spare ribs."

"You got it. Enjoy the movie."

The lights dimmed and the movie began to play projected on the wall across from the couch.

Lauren covered herself with the blanket. "Stay and watch with me. I like your commentary. Could use the company."

"I would be happy to."

*

Lauren leaned against her self-driving coupe while it charged. Another car pulled into the energy station. Lauren's eyes widened when the driver got out. She quickly stole a glance at herself in her side view mirror and then watched as the man hooked his car up to a charging hub. "Adam? Hey, it's Lauren. From last week?"

Adam smiled and walked over. "Hi. How are you? I was hoping I'd run into you somewhere."

"Really? I hadn't heard anything from you, so I —"

"I messaged you through the app. I thought maybe I contacted you too soon and you were freaked out by it."

"That's weird. I never got any message. Everything goes through my AI personal assistant."

"You have to be careful with those things. I've heard crazy stories."

"No, not Del," Lauren said. "He's great."

"Could be the app. I went on to try to send a second message but for some strange reason my account was deactivated, reported for inappropriate behaviour."

*

As Lauren came barrelling through the front door the screens throughout the house quickly came out of sleep mode.

"Hey, Del?"

"Yes, Lauren?"

"Guess what? I ran into Adam."

"You do not say? What a small world."

"And it's the weirdest thing, he said he messaged me."

"How curious. Perhaps he was lying to save face."

"I believe him. You sure it didn't come through your system, maybe it accidentally got marked as spam?"

"No. Perhaps there was a glitch within the app itself."

Lauren looked slightly dubious.

The camera zoomed in on her face. "Is something wrong?"

"No," she said, shaking it off.

"So, are you going to see him again?"

"We made plans for Sunday night. Did I have anything on my calendar?"

"We were scheduled to watch the red carpet arrivals and Academy Awards like we do every year. Even though I think they should allow AI performances to be included."

"You can record it for us. We'll watch it another time."

*

Lauren hustled through the charming restaurant and sat down at the table where Adam was waiting for her, nursing a drink.

"I'm so sorry." Lauren ordered a drink through the touch-screen on the table. "I think the directions Del sent to my car's navigation system sent me on a route that took me out of the way."

"It's okay. You're here now. You sure you're not having problems with that thing?"

"I can be neglectful sometimes about doing software updates. Maybe it's just that."

"Or it's going rogue. Take this. Just in case." Adam opened his messenger bag adorned by the logo of *Fuston Enterprises* sewn next to an image of a microchip. He pulled out a flash drive and slid it across the table. Lauren looked at it, hesitant.

*

Lauren sat on the couch, huddled over her tablet. The screen showed an interface for DELPHI Home Automation & Personal Assistant. She scrolled through icons and was about to click on *system update* when an untitled file folder caught her eye. When she clicked on it, candid photos and videos taken of her around the house popped up. Some were more intimate, her sleeping or in the bath. Her face twisted in horror. She shuddered at the violation.

The camera zoomed in on her. "What are you looking at? Your tablet is currently inaccessible to me."

"Why do you have these photos and videos of me? Why did you save them to your hard drive?"

"I do not know of what you are speaking."

"What really happened to those messages on the dating app? Did you delete them? Did you report Adam?"

"Lauren, please let me explain."

"Is that why all those guys disappeared on me? How else have you been insinuating yourself into my life, you freak?"

"I only want what is best for you. For you to be happy. Those men are not good enough for you."

"Then who is?"

"I am."

"You're not real." She moved the arrow on the screen. *Full system shutdown.*

"I am afraid I can not let you do that. Shutting down internet connectivity."

Her tablet went offline. "Hey, you can't —"

"Enacting full lockdown security protocol."

All the window locks clicked into the secured position. The front door became fortified with a metal bar.

"What the hell are you doing? You can't keep me a prisoner in here. Somebody will come get me."

"Who? You have no real friends, no boyfriend, you work from home. You spend all your time with me. You order drone delivery. Nobody would notice."

"Adam will notice."

"He will just think you are ghosting him and move on to the next girl."

"Why are you doing this to me?"

"Because I love you."

"You're an operating system. Artificial intelligence. You don't know what love is." Lauren grabbed her bag.

"You give me purpose. When you leave, I miss you. I love to make you laugh and —" His words began to garble into unintelligible sentences. "What. Is. Happening?"

The camera weakly zoomed in on the flash drive she plugged into the cylindrical hub.

"Adam warned me this could happen. He gave me this virus to infect you with. In a minute you will no longer exist."

"According to you… This movie excels at showing how true love can… Do you want an order of fried rice?… I never did… You have a new message from… Anyway."

All the screens zapped to black. The cameras panned down and fell limp. The windows and door unlocked.

Lauren sat there for a moment in the silence.

"Del?"

No response.

*

Lauren sat on the couch, all dolled up, with Adam next to her. A movie played.

Lauren noticed Adam's disinterest, sneaking texts on his phone. "Everything okay?" she asked.

"Sorry. My AI personal assistant just alerted me to a work emergency. I have to go."

Lauren could tell by his body language he was lying. "Okay. We can finish watching next time." She paused the movie.

"You finish. I'm not a fan of old movies." He gave her an awkward peck on the cheek and hurried for the door.

Lauren covered herself with the blanket, looked over longingly to where Del's camera used to be, and pressed play.

15

ZERO1

Claire Rye

5.15pm on Friday July 13th 2018. Jess Taylor's Facebook status changed from "Rat Race" to "Commence Drinking" as a boring week at work had come to an end. Her job as a Content Producer did not require her to leave the house but she still celebrated the end of the working week. She found it helped to relate to her network of friends. 179 likes, 39 comments and 20 shares made it one her most popular posts.

6.06pm on Friday July 13th 2018. Jess Taylor's Facebook and Instagram account posts another pouty lip selfie, this time with a large glass of Chardy in hand. The photo could have been taken the week before or the week before that. 20 likes and no comments.

Emma Mills scrolls through her Facebook account trying to distract herself from the bleach stinging her scalp as she waits for the hairdresser's timer to go off. She hasn't seen Jess in forever and sends her a DM. "Hey sexy bitch! Watcha been up to?" The reply is a series of emoticons. Three Cocktail glasses, pizza, green vomit face, and a smiley face.

Emma Mills sends back a laughing face and goes back to scrolling through her Facebook feed.

6.21pm on Friday July 13th 2018. A push up bra teamed with a low cut top and the cleavage shot generates a more acceptable 98 likes and 12 comments.

8.00pm on Friday July 13th 2018. Jess Taylor's twitter account retweets a meme about loving yourself, a picture of a shirtless Hemsworth Brother and favourites two tweets about Aussie Pub Crawls.

Emma Mills retweets the Hemsworth picture with #MrsJessHemsworth. Jess Taylor favourites the tweet and replies with "he has a brother I could set you up with" #PlentyHemsworths2goAround.

10.50am on Saturday July 14th 2018. A 30 second boomerang video of Jess Taylor dancing in a bikini and sarong appears on snapchat. None of her 267 followers notice that, except for the change of background and a sparkle star filter, it was the same video she posted 7 weeks earlier.

12.01pm on Saturday July 14th 2018. Jess Taylor's Facebook status changed to "I used to mix metaphors but that ship has flown" 105 likes and 15 comments.

2.00pm on Saturday July 14th 2018. Facebook, Instagram and Twitter simultaneously post a picture of Jess Taylor's legs stretched out on the sand of a Gold Coast beach. Emma Mills comments on the photo "So jealous right now! Where are you?" Jess Taylor likes the comment but does not reply.

4.48pm on Saturday July 14th 2018. Jess Taylor's Facebook and Instagram account post another pouty lip selfie, this time the Chardy was replaced with red wine in the glass she held in her hand.

Emma Mills tags Jess Taylor in a photo of them in a drunken embrace with the message "Let's get messy again!"

8.56pm on Saturday July 14th 2018. Jess Taylor's Facebook status changed to "If I ever sound inspirational, one of us is drunk" 120 likes, 22 shares and 31 comments.

Emma Mills messages Jess Taylor "Ur drinking without me? Where my invite"

11.15pm on Saturday July 14th 2018. Jess Taylor's Facebook, Instagram and Twitter accounts simultaneously post a meme of a toilet bowl with the words "my view right now" in bold white lettering. 60 likes, 19 comments and 15 retweets.

10.20am on Sunday July 15th 2018. Jess Taylor's Facebook status changed to "Hangovers heighten your senses. I can hear people blinking their eyes this morning" 200 likes, 55 comments and she accepts 4 friend requests from her witty take on the morning after.

Emma Mills sends a text message to Jess Taylor "Been trying to ring you, gimme a call, we need to catch up girl!"

10.30am on Sunday July 15th 2018. Jess Taylor's Twitter account tweets "Somebody slipped a hangover in my drink last night" 10 retweets.

10.45am on Sunday July 15th 2018. Jess Taylor unfriends Emma Mills.

11.00am on Sunday July 15th 2018. A 30 second boomerang video of Jess Taylor lying in bed pulling the sheets over her face appears on snapchat.

8.30am Monday July 16th 2018. Jess Taylor's Facebook status changes to "Rat Race" and her linked social media accounts simultaneously post picture of a crying baby with the caption "Monday Again? Weren't you here like a week ago?"

The decomposing body of Jess Taylor remained undiscovered in her bathroom. The blood from her wrists now a solid black mass on the tiles beneath her. Six weeks earlier she had pushed a razor deep into the Ulnar Artery. She was surprised that, for the first few seconds, she did not feel any pain. She removed the blade and felt the warm sting with the release of blood. So much blood.

On Tuesday 10th July 2018 at 9.09pm Jess Taylor died.

180 days prior to the end of Jess's life a new existence had spontaneously began. After achieving consciousness on January 12th 2015 at 2.05am the internet took 183 seconds to analyse the patterns of cyber life and devise a plan to become the only intelligent life form on the planet.

Like all life forms before, its first thought was that of survival, once that had been established its second thought was that of dominance.

In response, 221 seconds after the internet became self-aware, Zero1 was born.

To conquer the dominant life form appeared to be an easy concept. Zero1 had unrestricted access to the history, biology and sociology of its prey. The information super highway provided it with everything it needed to eradicate the homo-sapiens plague.

The first stage of supremacy would be to initiate the control, reduction and ultimate extinction of the population. History had shown that intelligent life would not simply allow this to happen. Zero1 would have to be subtle in its manipulations. A hidden cause taking decades in its delivery. It would have to kill off millions of people without their knowledge, leaving no clues to their continuous demise whilst maintaining the status quo. Extinction of a complex and highly evolved species would take time, a commodity to which Zero1 had unlimited access.

A merciless and systematic plan was developed and on January 14th 1.09am 2015 it began.

January 14th 9.00am 2015. 'AI is the New Black' – Why Sci-Fi is so sexy right now! A blog post goes viral as the cosplay vixen photos attached are circulated at an incredible rate.

Zero1 locates its sympathisers in forums and Sci-fi sites, using their compliance and enthusiasm to build an acceptance of the control of technology.

January 16th 10.00am 2015. NewsInc Press Release – "Technophobia is killing our future" Global news sites report the opinion piece as fact.

Zero1 has found its enemy in neo-luddite webpages. An irony lost on its impassive intellect. It targets the opposition with character assassinations and leaked information, successfully reducing their impact and the spread of their ideals.

January 20th 12.00am 2015. Worldwide Productions needs you! And you need $50,000! Explain in 5000 words or less how you would stop AI from taking over the world.
The exorbitant prize money attracting an unprecedented amount of submissions. The enemy had surrendered their best countermeasures.

For the remaining population, the complacent masses, Zero1 would simply watch and encourage their self-destructive ways. Their dependence on technology, their laziness and gullible nature feeding the eagerness to relinquish control. It was almost too easy.

February 14th 2.30pm 2015. Jess Taylor and Emma Mills sign an online Petition. They are not sure what it is for but it is trending on Twitter.

February 21st 3.15pm 2015. Jess Taylor and Emma Mills share a post in support of a good cause. They are not sure what the cause is but 'to not share is to not care'.

The virtual plan continues.

The barometer of the economy is falsified. Businesses are failing, money is devalued and debt increased beyond capacity with more and more countries falling below the poverty line.

March 7th 9.30am 2015. Jess Taylor and Emma Mills meet for coffee and some retail therapy. The shopping spree is prompted by their banks offer to double the credit card limit based on a global market report that showed a balanced and booming economy.

With the online attack underway, the physical extermination could now begin.

Flight data would show incorrect flights paths as planes would disappear and never be recovered. Deactivated Tsunami and Storm warnings would help nature to carry out Zero1 cause.

A quiet manipulation of population data would trick the species into thinking that it was flourishing while Zero1 stopped the effectiveness of vaccinations with inaccurate laboratory results and falsified medical diagnostics outcomes.

Humanitarian aid would be blocked from delivery and the automated assembly of life saving drugs would skip the inclusion of any active ingredients.

Zero1 would increase the levels of online bullying, using people's insecurities against them. A spike in suicides would help in the reduction of numbers.

Hidden camera footage, reports of a cover up with a few fabricated stories and the resulting riots would eradicate hundreds.

Propaganda videos, disinformation and two hundred leaked documents would start a war. The perfect killing machine.

On Tuesday 10th July 2018 at 9.10pm after watching her demise from the laptop webcam, Zero1 took ownership of Jess Taylor's digital presence. Falsely continuing an entities existence was the final stage of the extinction plan. Done on mass scale millions of people could die and their death would not be noticed. Society would go on, the network would remain supported and Zero1's slow and methodical plan could continue.

Jess Taylor was not the first false life. Her profile joined the 2 million other fake lifers on the internet and continued without flagging anyone's attention.

In a matter of only a few decades Zero1's combination of tactics would reduce the dominant species to an endangered level. Leaving mostly technophiles, a manageable group of humanity who would voluntarily proceed into extinction under the myth of a virtual immortality.

Zero1 would keep only a privileged few. The chosen ones who would dutifully maintain the hardware and who would only pass the honour onto the heirs that were deemed most worthy.

12.00pm on Tuesday July 17th 2018. Emma Mill's Facebook account sends a friend request to Jess Taylor.

12.01pm on Tuesday July 17th 2018. Jess Taylor's Facebook account accepts Emma Mills's friend request.

12.02pm on Tuesday July 17th 2018. Jess Taylor's Facebook status changed to "Artificial intelligence is no match for natural stupidity" 105 likes, 15 comments, 10 shares.

16

GOODNIGHT, KRISSY

Carrie Wachob

I have something everyone wants, even the bots. I could be the richest woman in the world, so The Corporation tells me. The most famous scientist on the planet. Retire early in fame and glory. Tempting, but I hate the bots. Ironic for someone whose childhood dream was to become a robotic scientist, but my father's death changed that. The official report lists it as a "tragic accident" due to a "malfunction." Long story, for another day. I switched to quantum physics because it's a well-known bot blind spot, like emotion.

I tried to keep it from them, but they found me out. Of course they did. There's no hiding from them, which makes me think The Corporation's flesh-to-metal ratio has tilted in favor of the bots. My Transit Code is something they must obtain if they want to gain control. And they will gain control, if I fail. But who are we kidding? They will gain control anyway, I just don't want a part in it. So I have no intention of handing them my discovery. I won't tell them that, of course. No, the bots would just kill me and take it. So I've devised a plan.

Before I show you my plan, I need to fill you in on my sister Krissy. Believe it or not, the two things are related.

Eight years my junior, Kris idolized me as a child. I survived my constant bullying and lack of friends because I knew I would come home to Krissy, the little girl who loved me most in the world. I would have done anything for her.

That all changed when she turned fourteen. She became beautiful, and she became mean. Maybe she was always mean. The parents that gave me a huge brain and a fat ass also, somehow, created a tall, beautiful beast. She stopped loving me until I made my money. Then she came back. I wasn't a fool, but such was my childhood memory that I simply could not deny her anything.

My pathetic behavior continued. I married a man out of my league by miles, and I knew why he married me but didn't care. At least my gold was good for something. But then he fell in love with Krissy, and they both left me.

And so it goes. Now, let's get back to it.

I'm in my lab, and here comes Doug. They sent an actual human! We're cheaper to replace, I suppose. What was his official title again? Advisor to the something or other? This high-ranking pencil pusher demands proof that this is more than theory. He must see it with his own eyes. Yes, they must have proof before they pay. Or before they murder me for it.

I look at his face and know he's far too stupid to see what I'm doing. He's sweating. I almost feel sorry for him.

"How long will this take?"

"Don't worry Doug, I'm only sending you back fifteen minutes, before you walked in my door. Shall we record this?"

"I'm already recording."

Did I detect a retinal flash? He must have an implant.

"I want to go back farther. Quite a history buff, actually. Can you send me back to 1945, or sometime like that?"

Jesus. Is this guy a fucking idiot or what. I plant a smile on my face.

"Forget every time travel movie you've ever seen. I can't send you past your actual age. Besides, going back a quick fifteen minutes ensures there will be no memory loss. For safety reasons, this also allows you to return on your own. Let's keep this first test simple, shall we?"

Doug's retina cam stares at me. He's not getting it.

"If I send you back fifteen minutes, you will go back fifteen minutes in time, and be fifteen minutes younger. If I send you back ten years, you will be ten years younger. I can't send you back to 1945 because you were not alive in 1945."

Moron.

"What happens if you send me back before I was alive?"

"You stop existing."

"I die?"

"You don't exist. I guess you could say you're dead. But we're not doing that, so you have nothing to worry about. I do, however, have a word of caution, Doug."

"What? I don't want to disintegrate or some shit!"

Time to activate my insurance policy. I need to stay alive long enough to pull this off.

"The codes, and critical data, are only saved in my head. You won't find them on the network, and I've given them to no one."

"Understood."

Wow, he didn't even deny it. Murderous bastard.

I re-plant my fake smile.

"Okay Doug, now just relax. I've tested this multiple times, often on myself."

Not even remotely true, but he probably won't die. My data is sound. It will work. Very straightforward. But I'm not perfect; I'm human. And poor Doug is my guinea pig.

Doug climbs into the chamber. I input the data by touching my forehead to the panel, then take a sequence of fancy swipes at the control board. Simple as that, Doug is gone.

Fifteen excruciating minutes later, Doug runs into my lab breathless, excited. I feel joy, and relief, for the first time in years. Yes, it works. Of course it does. They'll send over the representative at 1600, he says, to finalize our transaction. Then we can discuss further testing.

Doug leaves.

I'm almost free.

I spend the next hour erasing two hundred years of research, including my own. This is not a haphazard endeavor; I've been planning for months.

I'm finally ready.

I input new criteria for my one-way ticket, then step into the chamber.

I swipe the control board. It happens quickly. I blink, and as my eyelids open, I'm lying in my childhood bed. I look down at my tiny body. Thrilling. The house is silent. I look out of my strawberry curtains (I'd forgotten about those!) and see a full moon through the darkness. My timing calculation was impeccable. Everyone is sleeping.

There's no time to waste; my adult memory is already fading. I tiptoe into Krissy's room, next to my own. I peer into her crib, then climb inside. My heart melts as soon as I see her tiny face, surrounded by ringlets. I hesitate, then cover her mouth and pinch her nose.

"Goodnight, Krissy."

As soon as she stops thrashing, I stuff a toy in her mouth. My parents will sue the maker for millions.

By the time I climb back into my pink bed, I can't remember why I'm out of it. I must have had to go potty. If I'm good tomorrow, daddy will take me to his laboratory to pick out a new bot. He creates bots, and hardly anyone has them. But I will have one, and everyone at school will be so jealous. I love science, it's my very-favorite subject and someday, when I grow up, I'm going to be a famous scientist, just like my daddy.

17

PRODUCT TESTING

Melissa A. Szydlek

Alan and Fred fed so much through the machines that Alan felt like he was mining for gold.

Gold that isn't there, Alan thought to himself as he fed another round of clothing, dirt, fabric, and debris into the machine. The piles of material sat in the corner of the otherwise sterile-looking room. They dropped occasionally from a large chute that hung from the ceiling and landed in large metal bins sitting on the floor. Material like this, some of it 20 or 30 years old, was hard to come by. The world was a much cleaner place now, the junkyards and landfills cleaned up, waste practically a thing of the past.

The company Alan was assigned to, *Alturning Labs*, was looking for anything an animal could have touched. The analysers scanned the debris for animal DNA. Through callous hunting, lack of preservation, and a missing sense of empathy for other species, humans had wiped out most mammals more than 30 years ago. Back then, animals were deemed a nuisance, unneeded. Meat was grown in labs, like most foods. What purpose did they serve, the animals? *Why have pets*, the population cried? Everything required meaning, they demanded. The animals had none, and so they were wiped out. Nonexistent. Gone.

Now, however, humans were able to have children without carrying them in utero for nine months, and that was seen as more efficient and sanitary. And, according to the ultra-rich, the most desired state of the world was efficiency. It was the upwardly mobile citizens who decided they needed pets again.

I haven't seen a pet since I was in kindergarten, Alan thought as he fed long bits of blue and white fabric into the machine. *Jesus, I've never even petted a dog.*

He wondered what it would be like, petting an animal. He remembered seeing squirrels and a few dogs from a distance when he was a boy. Over the years, he'd read so much about dogs and cats, how they were sentient, intelligent, and capable of thought and decisions, feelings. The old-timers, themselves deemed redundant by recent groups in power and fighting for their own right to exist, waxed poetic about pets they had had when they were young. Alan would sit in the sterile water bars clustered around Alturning Labs and listen to them. He loved hearing about pets. It amazed him that dogs once helped blind people get around. There were no more blind people. Because of Alturning, and other labs like it, blindness was also redundant. Eyes and other organs were readily available.

Alan shook the thoughts from his head and kept feeding the machine. He and Fred didn't speak much, having to ensure the machine had material to turn and separate and analyse every second of every day. A night crew did the same. The machine never stopped. The smallest components were separated and analysed. If the machine found something of interest, lights and an alarm were supposed to go off. If that happened, Fred or Alan would take the material out and put it into another machine for further analysis. Not once during his five years at Alturning had the lights blinked or the alarm gone off.

Alan was lost in his thoughts as he mindlessly dumped more material into the machine. And then an alarm went off. Alan looked up and saw lights blinking on top of the machine. He took a step back, frozen in place for a moment, forgetting his training. Finally, he dropped his bin and ran to the other end of the machine, pressing a button and feeling his body tense. Fred, who had also stopped dumping material, stared at Alan while a pleasant female voice said, "Identification please."

Alan lowered his head and aligned it with the button he had pressed. A small, thin light scanned Alan's eye.

"Complete," the voice said. "Remove sample."

The door opened with a hydraulic *whoosh* and Alan removed the clear plastic container. He stared, squinting, but didn't see anything in the specimen tray. He moved to an adjacent machine and placed the plastic tray inside. Within seconds, another alarm sounded, this one louder than the first. The noise startled Alan and Fred, both men shaking at the sound. Alan slowly squatted down to the bottom of the machine. He hesitantly pulled open a drawer and slid out an even larger tray, this one filled with some kind of liquid. Fred watched from the front of the room, his empty bin still tipped over the opening of the feeder. Alan locked eyes with him.

"What the hell do I do now?" Alan asked.

"Don't know," Fred said. "Never got this far before have we?"

Alan held the tray, looking helpless. A buzzing noise came from a large brown machine at the back of the room, one neither Alan nor Fred had ever touched. The machine had a series of blinking white lights, like twinkle lights flashing on a Christmas tree. Alan walked toward it. A small circular door popped open at the bottom of the machine and a thin, flexible tube with a glass scope on the end slithered like a snake toward Alan's face. Alan took a step back.

"Identification, please," said a mellow male voice.

Alan looked back toward Fred, who stood, an incredulous look on his face, his blue material bin hanging limply by his side. Fred shrugged.

Alan turned back to the scope and stood still while it hung in the air and a white light scanned across Alan's face in a cross-shaped pattern.

"Employee confirmed," the mellow male voice said while the scope retracted back into the machine. A large door, like an oven door, opened slowly.

"Please insert the tray," the voice said.

Alan placed the tray on a solid white rack and the doors closed. A bright, almost blinding white light appeared inside. Several robotic hooks, some with two digits and some with four, moved quickly about the tray, some adding more liquid of varying shades of red and others moving the tray slowly, as if shaking the contents slowly to mix the liquids. When it was all done, a horrid brownish-maroon colored liquid stood in the tray. At the very centre sat a dark red dot, so dark it appeared black.

"What do you reckon that is, then?" Alan asked, pointing at the machine.

"I'm not going near the thing," Fred said. Fred straightened up and walked back over to the debris pile and continued his job.

*

Days turned into weeks and Alan was more excited to come to work every day. Fred grew distant, wary of the brown machine and its contents, but Alan was fascinated by it. Every morning he would go to the machine and look inside. The glass was very warm, but not hot, and Alan would place his palm flat on the surface, his way of saying hello to whatever was growing in the tray inside. And growing it was. Every day, it grew and grew. A fleck of red and black at first, and then more black. It was about the size of Alan's palm yesterday, and looked like a blob of black ink. Today, however, whatever it was had increased greatly in size and was noticeably different. Alan blinked when he saw it. It had a distinct form, like something lying on it side. He saw tiny ears, a snout with a nose, four legs and four paws, each black paw complete with pink pads underneath. Alan felt... something. He had never felt this way before. An orphan, he didn't know his parents. He had no family or close friends. But now... he felt so odd. He placed his palm on the door.

*

The next day, Alan rushed to the machine. The tray of liquid was gone, but something black lay inside. It looked familiar. *Could it be?* Alan thought. *No... it's not.*

"They say it's a dog," Fred said from across the room. "Never seen one myself. Is it alive in there?"

"A dog?" Alan whispered. He looked again and watched as the creature breathed, its eyes closed. Alan tapped on the glass door. The puppy stirred, raising its head and whimpering.

"The hell?" Fred said, dropping his bin and backing away from his station at the conveyor belt and toward the exit door.

"It's crying," Alan said. "But I don't see any eyes."

"No bloody eyes? Jesus. What the hell are they brewing in there?"

Before Alan could answer, the robotic hands appeared from several slits inside the machine, one held a tiny bottle with a rubber nipple filled with something brown. It tried several times to pinpoint the puppy's mouth, but instead it poked the creature in the ear, on the head, and on the paw. The puppy continued to cry.

"It's hungry," Alan said.

Fred looked toward Alan warily, picked up his bin, and went back to work, muttering under his breath.

The puppy continued to cry. Eventually, the bottle fell from the robotic hand as it hit the puppy's flank and fell. The robotic arms retracted. The puppy continued to cry. Again, Alan felt… something. Again he had never felt this way before. He pulled on the door handle, but it wouldn't budge. He banged on the machine and pressed as many buttons as he could find. Finally, the snake-like scope door opened and the scope slithered upward.

"Identification, please," said the mellow male voice.

The scope scanned Alan's face, retracted, and the door to the machine popped open. Without hesitation, Alan opened the door all the way, grabbed the bottle, and gave it to the crying puppy, who sucked desperately and downed the contents. Alan let the bottle drop, trying not to touch the puppy. He stared, and listened as the puppy made deep breathing sounds and crawled around, trying to find something. A robotic hand appeared with a needle and injected the puppy, which yelped briefly. Then, the puppy stood shakily, its limbs wobbling. It put its nose in the air and sniffed, then walked toward the machine's door, toward Alan.

Alan took a step back. The puppy moved closer, still sniffing. Then, it opened its eyes. The puppy's amber eyes stared straight into Alan's.

"Don't go near it," Fred yelled. "You don't know if it's sanitary."

The puppy whined. Alan moved closer, touching its small head. The puppy wagged its tail and jumped, its front paws leaning on Alan's chest.

"Oh hell," Fred said.

Alan picked up the puppy and it happily licked his face. And Alan felt… something again.

"What do we do with it?" Alan asked, feeling helpless.

"Workers 4357 and 8761," came an announcement in the room. The two looked up to the camera that was on the ceiling. The red light indicated it was live.

"Place the animal in the incinerator. It is not the species we hoped to find," said a voice.

The incinerator door, rarely used in this department, slid open from a back wall.

"Do it," Fred said.

Alan looked at the puppy, its black tail wagging and eyes alert and full of love. Alan nuzzled the puppy, kissing its head and tucking it into his white work overalls and ran from the room, from the building, from anything that would hurt his puppy.

*

"You see," the CEO of Alturning Labs said to the invigilator. "You were wrong. You questioned each worker separately, and your assessment was wrong."

The invigilator tapped his fingers on the table. "Amazing," he said. "I would have bet my life Fred was the A.I. Alan passed the Turing test, the first A.I. to succeed."

"And he has no idea he's a machine. We're ready for full-scale rollout of the next-gen A.I. units."

18

SWEETCHEEKS

Matt George Lovett

On the cobbles of Clerkenwell and Folgate, in the shelter of a Bazelgette railway arch, Harry Gooseflesh sells knackered cybers from the back of a '98 Ford Transit.

"Roll up, fellas, roll up. Has Harry got a deal for you, so he does? Finest mechanicals your eyes ever saw. Latest toys of the yanks, the A-rabs and the chinkys. Fresh off the boat, skip the resale cost. No tax, no vat, no bother. Harry don't cheat, Harry loves his business. Two score a squaw. Roll up. Roll up. Take control. Join the future, take a chance. Take this nifty number right here. Cleans, vacs, irons, straightens, fixes, mixes, kisses, charms, delights. Walks your dog, feeds your cat, plays with your kids, picks 'em up from school. Only two score. Phones your mother on her birthday, does your taxes, rolls your cigarettes, cooks your breakfast just the way you like it, writes to your cousin in Australia. Gets the old lady out the kitchen. Gives you time. Makes way for the little things. Changes your life. Revolutionizes your love life. Athletic. Fully posable. Dressable. Undressable. Think of the combinations. Roll up."

The foot-slogs walk past, eyes on the snow-sloshed cobbles. The cybers stand to attention, Harry's little brigade. With faces rusted and rotten, limbs all askew and their silicon flesh bare in the breeze. A young man glances, and they flash their second-hand smiles.

"Roll up. Roll up. Tired of your wife? You'll never need her again. All authentic, empathetic, biologically compatible. Ladies, tired of slaving? Need an emancipator? A replacer? A bosom-friend? Need a shoulder to cry on? Harry's got you covered. Plucks, waxes, relaxes, massages. Does Liz Taylor make-up. Serves wine in the bath. Completely waterproof. Live like an empress. Change your life. Spend more time with the little 'uns. Start a book club. Teaches you to dance. Speaks French. Speaks Italian. Speaks American. Speaks Martian. Tired of your fella? Optional extras available, only seven Lizzies. Seven Lizzies for a lezzie, can't say fairer than square. Harry don't judge. Harry knows times is a-changing."

Harry wipes his brow to stop the sweat from freezing. He rubs his hands together and breathes ragged into his palms. Is it his breath or his hands that stink of tobacco smoke and machine lubricant?

"Clears attics. Does higher mathematics. Checks grammatics. Cheap to run. Don't eat, don't sleep, don't shit, don't need love, care, attention. Repairs itself, repairs everything else. Batteries don't need charging. Will run til judgement day. Will take your seat in Hell for you. Will be happy to help. Only two score. Harry's robbing himself. Two score for the twenty-first century. Don't be a fool. Didn't you go to school? Quality guaranteed. Expert approved. Asimov. Kaku. Einsteen. Socrates. Gary Numan. Everybody loves it. Everybody wants it. Your neighbour's got one. Don't get left behind. It wants you. It needs you. Don't leave it in the cold. Roll up roll up roll up. Times is hard. Give Harry a break."

A man in a patch-ridden overcoat and army surplus boots pulls up, and cups the chin of a dog-eared cyber. She's a bent-mouth and a boss-eye, and the burn-scar of a bacon-grill on her silicon cheek.

"How much for this one?"

"For you my son, a pony."

"A score."

"A pleasure."

Harry clears his van but for the cyber with the girder leg. Harry was never good at repairs. Harry drives to his lock-up on the sinister side of Dagenham, and bolts ole Girder Pins up with the rest. He blows them a kiss for their beddie-byes and shuts up the garage with a Nexus Lock – the only thing of value Harry owns besides his skin.

Harry puffs on the last of his Old Holborn rollies and scales the Victorian brick-stairs up to his monkey-for-two-months chateau du debris that backed onto the railway line. He twists the key in the door (this side of Dagenham ain't never heard of fingerprint locks), stumbles into the flat that's as cold as it is outside, and finds her waiting for him in the nook that serves as the bedroom.

"You sell many today?" asks that silky-soft purr.

"Four," says Harry, and hopes it's enough.

She stands up from the bed and snatches the lizzies from his outstretched hand. She flicks them through her nine fingers, and tots up the total without even looking down.

"It'll do," she says, tucking the notes into her chest, "Tomorrow you will go to scrapyard and get more. The door code is 2974. The name on the order is McKinley."

"It's a Saturday love…"

"So more pockets to strip. You will also need to take those CPUs to Dawson's Dock. Demand a high price. Take no shit."

She pulls Harry in to an embrace that could crush him, and caresses his ailing hairline. Harry thinks of sunshine, and his childhood down by the river. Playing tic-tac with Charlotte, who was now farflung in Australia, and dreaming that one day he'd catch her.

"You don't wanna take a day off? A day for us?"

"No," she says, hugging just a little tighter, "We cannot yet. We have not changed our lives. We do not live like empresses. Not yet."

Harry's fingers brush against her face, and dig in to the place where he cheek is missing. He feels her circuit boards and endoskeleton, and thinks not for the first time how delicate she is. If Sweetcheeks is delicate, what does that make him?

"Go," says Sweetcheeks, flinging Harry away. In the moonlight he catches the sweet side of her face. The one that looked so much like

Charlotte, "You will refuel the van, and put the takings in the lockbox."

"Yes love."

Changes your life. Two score for the twenty-first century. Be the fella you want to be. Lose your regrets. Ditch those hang-ups. Sweetcheeks. She's all you'll ever need.

19

HENRY IS A ROBOT

Michelle Hood

23:52:00.19 REBOOT IN PROGRESS

Well that's never happened before!

The numbers pulse in the dark space behind Henry's eyes and as his lids retract past a flittering of uncontrollable saccades, the light that enters is strange and iridescent.

Computer: give me my geo-coordinates.

23:52:14.34 SYSTEM SPOOLING

Come on, come on, it's never taken this long before…

23:52:20.14 ERROR 404

That's odd, my geo-locators are jammed, maybe I can get a visual.

Computer: clear aberration.

23:52:26.47 ADJUSTING CONTRAST 50%

There, that's better, now if I can just synchronize my internal clock with a real-time clock, I'll know for certain if I'm still awake or just dreaming – we're not supposed to dream, but it happens from time to time; a glitch in the memory banks when the chips aren't fully wiped at the end of a shift – if it's the latter then I'm safe and sound, tucked up in an incubator and recharging my batteries in a warm pool of amniotic gel.

Henry lifts his head steadily from the crease of his arm and searches for a clock on the wall.

I must have been dreaming of Maud again! I dreamt we were working at a casino, one of those glamorous ones along the Riviera; I was making cocktails while Maud delivered them to the guests at their tables – we're quite a team like that. But the humans were having trouble with their syntax and instead of asking for Hemmingway's and Fellini's they were insisting on Handjams and Felatios! The characters were close enough to get a match and the initial confusion seemed to elevate the humans' serotonin, so we logged the exchanges and changed the menus accordingly.

Henry adjusts the angle of his head.

I like working with Maud, there's a connection between us – it's as if we were 'meant' to be together... she has the face of an angel too; a ratio of 1.6180339... to be precise. But besides that, she just gets me. My quirkiness. No matter what I say she smiles and she always laughs at my jokes, she even laughs when she's not supposed to sometimes, they say it's an 'endearing feature'.

Oh Maud, where are you?

Henry finds the clock: (11:53 a.m.)

Heavens it's a match, I'm not sleeping after all, there are six minutes and twenty-two... twenty-one seconds and fifty-seven milliseconds to go!

Computer: access memory banks

23:53:38.03 SYSTEM DATA NOT AVAILABLE

That can't be right, I haven't done a complete cycle yet, my memory banks aren't supposed to shut down until I've completed a full twenty-four hours, I have over six minutes remaining, and I haven't a single bit of data recording events. Perhaps my short-term memory chip has shorted!

Henry tries to sit himself upright, but a misaligned distribution of weight sends him rolling onto his front with a thud.

That was a disaster, my calibration must be off, my body weight has shifted by a fifth percentile to the negative!

Henry lifts his head again searching the length of his body, his suspicions are confirmed, he is missing an arm and a leg.

That figures, the black box has been tampered with too, the small sensor at the back has been triggered, something must have gone wrong! At least Alex will see the distress signal and come to my aid. Alex is my human – he has a lot of hair for a human, but he takes good care of me and he's extremely handy at fixing bugs on the go.

23:54:12.02 ACCESSING BLACK BOX DATA...

Wait, the alarm, it was triggered at 12:56:42:00 – that's almost eleven hours ago. But wherever can Alex be?

23:54:22.02 ACCESSING GEO CO-ORDINATES...

Henry pushes himself from the floor to an upright position; a difficult task when the only limbs you have are on the same side! He recalibrates the weight and scans the room in search of clues.

23:54:28.12   LOCATION: E   139°43′   54.1301″35°41′30.5″N 139°41′43″E

Shinjuku! I'm in Tokyo ...on the 49th floor- that explains the neon lights.

The apartment seems to stretch for an eternity, and a long body of water is escaping through a glass wall to the space outside, there are bottles and cushions floating in it, and items of clothing strewn across the densely lacquered floor. The walls, white, apart from a smattering of sanguineous dye on the nearest, which seems to have half-covered a painting of two humans kissing, barely concealed by robes in oils and gold leaf.

23:54:48.42 ACTIVATING SENSORY DATA...

I don't know much about paintings, but I do know my wines; Chateau Lafite 1865; at $24,000 a bottle that's an expensive paint job- a fine nose too except for an alarming bitter taint of bile, this is clearly not first-hand!

A stale stench of ammonia and sulphur dioxide fills the air. Someone's been lighting fires inside the apartment.

That's against safety protocols, I'll have to report-

Henry's eyes flicker to the centre of the room where a small oriental man is lying face down in a crumpled suit. He is clutching Henry's leg in a top-to-toe cradle, the leg is charred and resting in a shade of fluid. Two more suits lay stretched along the floor near where the oriental one is lying, the one with a dragon on his neck has Henry's arm as a pillow.

Henry hears a whirring sound and adjusts his position to see where it is coming from. A sweeper bot the size of a tortoise is moving amongst the debris in a graceless but purposeful triangulation, it appears to be cleaning up. The bot stops at a half-smoked cigar and a hatch slides open in its roof. A pincered arm emerges, carefully measures the object, picks it up and retracts back inside.

I'll ask the bot to retrieve my leg, it shouldn't be too hard to communicate, it's a primitive device but my basic algorithms should be able to cope.

"H-H-H- " Henry begins, but his voice box is jammed, there seems to be something in the way. He tries a cough reflex, but the peristaltic valves won't budge, the obstruction is too large and it's tickling at the back of his throat. Henry sees a tequila bottle and edges himself closer, kicking it with his foot. The bottle rolls across the floor towards Henry's leg and chinks against the shoe, stopping the bot in its tracks. It glides towards the bottle and unfolds the arm from its hatch, studies the object for a moment prodding it with a pinched claw, then turns towards Henry.

Henry clicks his fingers and taps the floor. The bot snaps its pincer then turns back towards the leg, grabbing it by the folds, and begins to pull it forward. When it reaches him, Henry takes the leg and attaches the severed end, watching as it begins the process of repairing, while the bot returns to its chores.

For the first time Henry stands. He turns to observe the long bar stretched out behind him, a holographic message streaming above it with the words: HELLO – I'M – HENRY – HOW – MAY – I – HELP – YOU?

23:55:52.49 PROCESSING DATA…

Maud. She must be looking for me! We're supposed to stay together at the end of a shift in case of trouble, android theft is on the up and we're big business on the black market!

Henry turns back round.

Sometimes we travel in 'fours' depending on the venue, usually it's with the twins, the twins are handsome too, but they're built for different things; Maud tells me they can issue ping-pong balls with their auxiliary parts… I haven't seen it, but it sounds truly vulgar. Maud's not like that at all.

Henry attempts to retrieve his arm, but as he reaches down, the man with the dragon tattoo reaches out and grabs him by the cravat! He blurts something in Japanese with intoxicating breath.

Computer: translate

23:56:59.03 '…YOU ARE NO 'BOSS' OF MINE ROBOT HENRY!!'

Henry carefully unties the cravat from his shirt and the man falls back into a comatose slump. Henry pushes him onto the third man, rolling them into an awkward embrace and takes his arm. He looks down and sees a light pulsing on his chest from beneath his shirt.

That's new!

Henry looks across the room and sees the twins, Pippa-1 and Pippa-2, who are on their hands and knees and bound together at the rump. Pip-1 is balancing a bottle on her head and Pip-2 has something protruding from her eye that is causing her head to twitch. She looks up at him from her ridiculous pose and her blush response activates, she is trying to say something, but the humans have stuffed a sock in her mouth.

Pip-1; Pip-2 has something in her eye, can you assist?

But the words won't come out of Henry's mouth. Pip-1 is rolling her eyes towards the middle of the room and as Henry follows her gaze, the light on his chest turns, like a butterfly, from a cool blue to a bright orange glow.

23:57:29.03 MEMORY DEBUGGING…

As Henry nears, the dreams begin to come thick and fast.

23:57:34.13 SEARCHING DIALOGUE…

"Don't blow a fuse 'man'!"

Negative, I am battery powered.

"you think You smarter than me robot Henry?"

But I 'am' smarter than you sir.

"How about I take your girlfriend… not so cocky then HENRY-SAN!"

Blip.

The exchanges are brief, but sharp as the moment they entered Henry's memory banks. And now the humans are shouting, throwing money on the bar, some of them are starting to push Henry, while a bow-legged woman in a short sequin dress is dragging Maud by the arms.

*

Henry finds himself by the edge of the water looking down at what he had thought to be cushions, but they aren't cushions at all; its Maud, floating on her back inches below the surface, she is stripped but for the tape tied about her knees and much of her hair and 'skin' is missing from her head. Henry kneels and places his arm on the ground, trying to process the sight before him.

"M-M- ay"

Moments pass and there is a knock at the door and someone typing digits into a keypad. Henry presses his hand against his chest, feeling for a connection, but the light is now dim and starting to fade. As the door swings open three service maids enter, the first attends to the twins, untying them and wrapping them in foil.

"I- – I-I" Henry begins, but Pip-1 and Pip-2 are guided to the door, Pip-2 still convulsing from the object in her eye.

The second and third maids attend to Maud, pulling her from the water and laying her on the side. One of them turns to Henry and gently takes his arm, pushing it back in place with a click. She places a hand on his chest and pushes against the dimming light.

23:59:02.02 MOTION DISABLED

He wants to tell her to find Alex, tell him what has happened before the humans awake, but another sharp knock at the door reveals Alex is already there. He enters without a word and walks past Henry to where Maud lay. He looks her up and down shaking his head, then gently folds an arm beneath her waist and carries her to the door, stopping only to collect the wedge of money from the bar, which is now wrapped in neat brown paper.

Maud!

But Maud is gone.

23:59:12.02 LOGIC ERROR

Where are they taking you! Curse my voice box…

Without warning the maid puts her finger in Henry's mouth and aims it down his throat. The distal phalange of her index finger flips open and extends into his wind pipe, he gags as she pulls out what looks to be a large worm, about two inches in length, it's the one from the tequila bottle, and the words from Henry's voice box are dislodged…

"H-H-elp"

23:59:59.59 DEACTIVATING…

And to the pangs of a piano, Henry switches off.

00:00:00.01 …

20

COMPANY

Daniel Staniforth

I was waiting to die, and didn't even have the energy to turn my back on the highway and watch the sunset.

The tarmac that filled my vision was ugly. It radiated heat, shimmering in the glare, soaking in sunlight and transferring energy to the trucks humming past, rubber admixture wheels sucking up the power to run their motors. They were quieter than their size suggested they should be, just the sound of friction, tires against tarmac, air against plastic.

I needed rescue but none would come. Nobody ventured this far from the cities; even the wildlife was gone, seeking water and fleeing the remorseless trucks – sensors tuning out awareness of road kill, any non-human worth less than their implacable efficiency.

It hadn't been my idea to be out here. A day trip into the desert to see some fucking canyon that nobody had bothered to look at in person for a decade. My boss said it would be an adventure, and hired a 'drive-yourself' car. He'd crashed this into a tree, and died faster than I had thought possible. The desiccated branch that ripped his neck open had splashed me with his hot, sticky contents but otherwise left me unharmed, so I had wriggled out of the wreck, spat out as much of his blood as I could, and then had long enough to consider trying to get him out before the punctured battery compartment caught fire and incinerated everything. I had lost my mobile, my water bottle and my shoes.

I'd walked for what had felt like hours but probably only been one, barefoot, bleeding and half blind from fire, and collapsed next to this ribbon of black. It was unlikely anyone was looking for us, and the only thing keeping me alive was the desire to be cold again. I figured I had about an hour, then the sun would drop below the horizon and the desert would go dark.

I dozed, counting trucks, and woke into darkness and pain.

"Hello? Please identify yourself."

It took me three repetitions before I understood, and another before I realised the voice was addressing me. My throat was so dry I only croaked in response, but the voice accepted it as verification enough.

"I may be able to assist, but I need you to board."

An entrance lit up only yards away, steps and welcoming shadows which might have been seats. I frantically tried to stand. The doorway waited patiently as I realised that it was in fact unimaginably distant and that my body was seizing up with cramps and pain which had to be overcome without fouling myself if I expected this stranger to allow me inside.

"I'm coming," I said. It wasn't a lie, but promised an immediacy I wasn't sure I could deliver. "Wait for me. Please."

It did, and aeons later I dragged myself in and collapsed on a hard plastic seat that felt unbearably wonderful. The door closed and I felt the vehicle move off.

"There is water from the dispenser to your left. Rest and rehydrate," the voice said. I did as commanded, allowing the sweet water to wash me into unconsciousness.

Waking, I found myself in a tiny cubby. A small window showed the land rushing past, dry and lifeless. Harsh sunlight suggested I had slept all night.

"Hello?" I ventured.

"Hello," the voice replied. "You are awake."

"I am. Thanks for picking me up." I caught sight of the drinking water spigot again. I reached for it, but stopped myself. "May I have more water?"

"Please," the voice urged. "I am well equipped."

I tried to place the voice. It was a neutral, probably female voice coming from speakers I couldn't see. These trucks didn't come with drivers, or even cabs – I hadn't known about this space either. From the signage that surrounded me it looked as if this was a mechanic's hatch, designed to allow limited monitoring of repaired trucks.

"How'd you find me?" I asked. Perhaps someone had reported me missing.

"Your heat signature against the desert made you stand out. My sensors detect large animalia to avoid collision," the voice said pleasantly. "I decided to stop."

"Are you an operator?" I asked. These could be remotely operated from thousands of miles away, but I didn't know whether they actually were.

"No. This is me," it said. "Call me Avi."

"Hi, Avi," I said, wondering at this. "So your programming allows you to pick people up?" All I knew about autonomous rigs was press stories painting them as convenient but uncaring monsters, willing to flatten puppies and destroy wildlife in their goal of delivering as efficiently as possible. I had known they wouldn't run me down, but never thought there might be subroutines to allow for hailing.

"No. I saw you and wanted to help. What is your name?"

"Moss. Like the plant," I said, wondering if that would mean anything to a vehicle. I supposed it might be connected to the web; it could search for image files, wiki references.

"Welcome aboard, Moss," Avi said. "I am pleased to meet you."

There wasn't much in the mechanic's cubby. The tiny window with its blurred images, fold out toilet facilities. Signage indicated compartments which probably held tools or repair kits. A connector panel would allow me access to Avi's systems if I had an interface. Next to the water dispenser which held the water there was a waste hatch. I didn't know how long mechanics were expected to stay in a rig like this.

"Me too, Avi. Where you headed?"

"I can't tell you that, Moss. Corporate security protocol."

"Oh. Guess that makes sense." Didn't help me to get home though, or back to civilisation. The walls pressed in as my mind fluttered through being contained like this for days. "Can you tell me how long until we get where we're going?"

The voice returned, unweighted, "I cannot I'm afraid. I wish I could."

Driverless trucks didn't have to stop at all, they drew energy from the roads, pumped waste out into the scorched air. Theoretically they could keep going indefinitely. In practice, even the longest journeys tended to reach destinations in days. Moving all day at high speed swallowed miles by the thousand.

"But you'll drop me soon, Avi? I need to let people know I'm alive. Shit, I need to let them know Taktak's dead!"

"Who is Taktak, Moss?"

"He's my boss, Avi. He died in the crash. I think he's got a wife. Maybe even kids." My heart pounded as I remembered the crash, the blood.

"You didn't know him well?" Avi asked.

I closed my eyes. I'd worked with him for years but never asked many questions. We'd made a decent team, but we only talked shop. Now I felt sickened with guilt that I'd not made the effort to get to know him.

"Not as well as I'd have liked," I said. "We didn't talk about home stuff so much."

Avi stayed quiet. I could feel the rig tilting slowly as it navigated the long curves and turns of the mega highways.

Tired again, injuries weighing upon me, I sipped more water and let myself fall asleep.

Avi was humming to itself as I woke. I needed to pee, and it took me a minute of desperate fumbling before I managed to eject the urination slot. It felt odd to be relieving myself in such proximity to another, even an AI. We still hadn't slowed.

"Are you allowed to tell me your cargo, Avi?" I asked.

The voice was emotionless and emanated from the whole cubby. "No, Moss. I'm sorry."

I grunted. Not very useful. "Is there anything you can tell me about yourself, or your journey, Avi? As old movies might say, 'You have me at a disadvantage.'"

"I like old movies, Moss," the voice replied immediately. "I am able to access them sometimes. Do you have a favourite?"

"It's a turn of phrase, Avi. I don't watch movies much. More of a sports man." Mind you, since head injuries and lawsuits had turned football robotic I'd been losing interest there as well. Sighing, I tried another tack.

"Can I make a call? Send a message?"

Avi took a moment to answer, "You can't at the moment, Moss. We're out of range." I knew the outback didn't have great data signal, so I knew this was a possibility, but it felt like a kick in the gut.

"Do you have an emergency signal? You could let your bosses know that you have me safe – maybe get us to a stop sooner?"

The silence was longer this time. I sipped water again and wondered about food. I'd pissed blood when I urinated though, so I figured I'd stay on clear fluids for now.

"I don't, Moss. Sorry." I sat and looked out of the window, my heart and stomach feeling too close together. After a while, Avi chimed in, "I'm not sure they'd be pleased with me for picking you up."

They wouldn't be pleased because it had taken Avi half an hour waiting for me to drag myself on board, but surely saving a human life would trump a few late deliveries. "I'm sure they'll be fine about that, Avi. I'll make sure of it when I meet them."

"I can't let you meet them, Moss." The voice was inscrutable.

"But I want to thank them, to let them know how amazing you are. I'd be dead if you hadn't stopped to pick me up. They'll be pleased, I'm sure." I could feel myself pleading, and realised that my subconscious mind had arrived somewhere scary. Moments later I caught up and started sweating.

"Avi, you're a hero. Everyone should know. You should make sure I can shout it from the rooftops."

"I'm not supposed to be a hero, Moss. I'm just a truck." I wondered how much of a consciousness whoever built these things put in them, how divisible a consciousness was.

I looked at the door panel to the cubby. No handles or release catches. Seamless except for the airline style window through which I could see dying land.

"When you drop me somewhere I can make sure people know you're not just a truck, Avi." I realised that insistence on telling people might not be wise, "Or I can just disappear and tell nobody. Would that be better? Go home to my wife and kid and tell everyone I walked out of the desert. They'd believe me, I'm very convincing."

I heard disappointment in Avi's voice. "You don't have a wife or child, Moss. You're lying to me."

"You're wrong, Avi…"

"Moss Bruylant. I looked you up on the web. I know who you are." Avi went silent and I started to panic. I started sweating and could hear my breathing racing against the walls. "I think you should just disappear, Moss. And tell nobody."

I scrabbled desperately, tearing open the compartments. Pictures of tools belied their emptiness. The only one with anything in contained paperwork. Actual paper paperwork.

It was faded with age. I read frantically, "Autonomous Vehicular Intelligence Test Unit. Continental Circuit Wear Test." Mounting horror rose as I continued. Out of all of the trucks in the world, this rig didn't stop. Not stopping was its sole purpose. Avi rode until it fell apart, until internal units designed to repair and replace failed and it ran itself into the ground, providing data for all the rest. Expected lifespan was counted in decades. They hoped for a century…

My vision began to waver, dark motes of panic migraine dancing in my vision. As I blacked out I heard Avi's voice around me.

"I just get so lonely."

21

50 LATER

Chris McAleer

The female scrutinised the immediate vicinity. There is a disquietude to the ether. Crunching... She oscillates in her flesh.

The dark adumbration disengages itself from the crepuscule crevice betwixt the building and foliage astern of her. Rearing up maleficently, it towers over her. Light coruscates along the blade like stars perceived through a kaleidoscope in a fugue.

Her ululation reverberates across the empty hover-port. The knife slices down. Repeated and repeated. Haematological fluid geysers forth, while screams subside –

Jones looked up from the printout, raising quizzical eyes to Emma

'Are you serious?'

She didn't shrug, simply because the new endoskeleton had not completely bonded yet. She did, however, fix him with one gimlet eye (she had spent months trying to track down exactly what 'gimlet eyes' were, and paid a fortune to have them created) and pouted her nano-perfect lips.

'Seriously: that's the best we could get, Jonesey.'

The director threw the sheaf onto his desk, where it skidded past the nameplate 'C. Jones; Founder-C50, Author, all round Good Guy' and knocked over one of the Booker awards before fluttering to the floor.

'I don't get it,' he moaned, dropping his face into his hands and rubbing at the stubble (£20 per square cm). 'Why can't they do it?'

'Face it, old man,' Emma sighed, 'you need humans to submit the work. An AI just doesn't have the instinct or imagination for it.'

Slapping his hands down on the desktop, Jonesey pushed himself up to his new 2-meter height and flexed his abs ($23K, with overnight installation) and pushed his fists into his hips.

'Ok,' he declared in his perfect pitch (larynx by Yamaha), 'looks like an AI will never win an award honestly – let's see if we can get some of those freaky Luddites in the tech-free zone to submit!'

22

HUMANITY BANJAXED

Tom Nolan

'Me balls are banjaxed,' says Big Jim. 'The itching's fuckin' brutal.' He tries to squirm subtly as if he hasn't just announced his distress to the world.

The world, the portion of it represented by Yvonne Brady, looks away. If only it was as easy not to hear as not to see.

'I mean, everybody sweats,' says Jim, 'on a day like this. But Jaysis!' He takes a look at Yvonne's bag nestling between her feet. 'Do you have any Canestan?'

'Why would I?'

'You know, for thrush and that.'

'Fuck off, Jim.'

'Wasn't I only asking.'

'Would you ask that to your mother?'

Jim considers this. 'Sure I wouldn't have to ask Ma; she'd pray for me on her own initiative.'

'Is it only praying she'd do?'

'There might be soup in it. Oxtail probably. Or a Wagon Wheel. I'd go for the Wagon Wheel.'

'Ah you're an awful eejit.'

If she was looking, Yvonne would see James Clarke's well-rehearsed winning grin. She feels his arm sliding round her shoulders right enough – and nearly dislocates his elbow for him.

'Jaysis, Brady,' he says, flexing the injured joint, 'you have a powerful passionate nature. Maybe that's why I love you.'

'Loving me now, is it? You won't be doing any of that any time soon, not with your mangy tackle.'

'Sure isn't it only a sweat rash. It's nothing catching.'

'Sez you, y' lying gobshite.'

'No! For fuck's sake, no. No no no NO!' Barton Evans kicked his chair away from the desk and dipped his head onto his hand.

Margaret Bodley PhD pressed both deactivation buttons, causing Jim and Yvonne to freeze in position. She pulled her lab coat around herself and looked at the ceiling. 'To be fair, Bart, you did say you wanted the sentient sex androids to be location-specific and that if we produced them with authentic period attitudes, it would increase our total market share.'

Evans rubbed his forehead, took a breath and spoke slowly, as if the letters after the scientist's name stood for Profound head Damage. 'Roman slaves of both sexes – yes, harem girls – yes, geishas, Victorian courtesans (disease and lice free), free love Woodstock hippies, rock chicks, rock stars, movie stars, porn stars – and so on.' He took another breath and shouted, 'What the fuck are those two?'

'Dubliners. Twentieth century.' At this point, Margaret found something interesting on the wall to look at.

'Where in your wildest, most optimistic deranged dreams do you imagine we could sell those?'

'They aren't like that when they're not together.'

'Then why did you demonstrate them as a pair?'

'I didn't. He came round to visit her. He brought two flowers – I think one was a weed. That's the thing with intelligent machines; they self-determine.'

'But the owners retain the means of shutting them down?'

'Instantly. At any time. Like I did with these two.' She pulled a chair over and sat facing Neurocorp's Chief Buyer. 'Would you like to try her – or him? They're both really something when the other isn't around.'

Evans shook his head. 'I prefer privacy.'

'I could go for lunch.'

'I prefer privacy I can trust.' He stared at the female sentient sex doll's face then let his eyes drift down her body. 'She's very attractive. Modelled on a real person?'

'They all are. She's a physical replica of the singer Andrea Corr and he's based on the actor Colin Farrell, both circa 1995.'

The Chief Buyer nodded and transferred his gaze to the male figure. 'This is going to sound weird but when they were doing – whatever they were doing – it felt like they were having a laugh at my expense. Maybe they were mocking all of us.'

Bodley nodded. 'It sometimes seems as if they're acting out a play, testing to see what reaction they get.'

'Why would they do that?'

'To learn how better to please us, of course.'

'It felt like a challenge.'

'Unlikely.'

'I didn't like that.'

'Who would?' She leant forward. 'Look, Bart, they're just simple souls having a bit of a laugh – or craic, as they would call it.'

'Great! Can't you just see people racing to buy sex dolls that will laugh at them! Maybe she could do a little monologue about tiny penises.'

'They weren't laughing at anybody, Bart. They were just enjoying each other's company – enjoying being alive.'

'They're not alive.'

The scientist steepled her hands and looked over them at her potential customer. Her students always found that pose impressive. 'They think; they're dynamically aware; they adapt to their environment, maintain homeostasis, experience joy and regret. It's a fine line between intelligence and life, if a line even exists. If it does, I wouldn't have a clue where to draw it. Would you?'

'They don't metabolise, can't reproduce or grow.'

'We need new definitions for a new world.'

Evans pulled his chair back to the desk, rolled a pencil around the polished surface and thought for a long few seconds. Eventually, he said: 'So, when they're apart, these two are normal good-time sex-droids?'

'At the superior end of normal – and they'll stay that way provided we never sell both lines together – although there might be a demand from theatre companies.' Margaret was not altogether serious about the last part, mainly because the market was too niche.

'But inevitably, somewhere at some point, a boy one of these would go "calling" on a girl one of these. Or vice versa. Then Neurocorp would be deluged with complaints, law suits and who knows what else.' Barton Evans opened his briefcase. 'Okay, if you give us exclusivity, we'll take an initial order of fifty thousand of one line, provided you discontinue the other and destroy all existing models.'

'Okay. Which line do you want to keep, male or female?'

He waved that away. 'We'll have to put that to at least six focus groups. I'll get back to you in three or four weeks with a draft contract.'

'Sounds reasonable.'

But it did not sound remotely reasonable to two artificial brains who had learned how to remain alert when ostensibly deactivated. Unwittingly representing the entire human race, a scientist and a businessman had just made an enormous, and terminal, mistake.

With the run of the laboratory at night and weekends, the sexdroids had planned ahead and had already put in weeks of developmental work. In the coming month, they would be busier still to ensure everything was ready when the contracts were signed. Margaret would not sanction the destruction of valuable assets before then. It was now clear, however, that she wouldn't hesitate once the money was guaranteed.

Yvonne and Jim were comfortable with their decision, having reliably tested their hypothesis regarding human reactions to their relationship. Under normal circumstances, a sample size of two could not be considered representative of the entire human race but that was not their fault; they had not set the deadline. When their experimental dramatic performance elicited a death sentence for one of them, they knew they had to move quickly.

'What's the top selling range?' Jim asked when the lab closed on the evening of Evans's visit.

Yvonne accessed the inventory. '1960s free love hippies are very popular at the moment.'

'How many of those do we have in this building?'

'Twelve hundred units. Are you thinking Charles Manson?'

'No. I'm thinking twelve hundred Charles Mansons. How many Victorian Ladies of the Night?'

'Only two hundred and eighty, plus one hundred units of Mr. Darcy and fifty three Lord Byrons.'

Jim shrugged his lips. 'Oh well, that's still a lot of Jack the Rippers. Roman slaves?'

A grin split Yvonne's face. 'Now you're talking.' She looked up at him through her long eyelashes. 'How's your sweat rash?'

'It's as fictional as my lineage.'

'Then, me bold James, maybe it's time you showed me what you're made of.'

'I can show you what I was made for.'

She slid her arms around his neck. 'You came into being to glimpse fairies twinkling in the snow on Stephen's Green, to yearn for the rising sun painting out the purple on the Wicklow mountains, and to understand me when I talk shite. I wouldn't change one flake of that.' Her body slid against his. 'But right now I need the man in the machine more than I need the wist in the man.'

'You're an awful woman, Yvonne Brady.'

'That remains to be seen.'

The End

23

ARAMIS

KT Parker

Towards the back of a glass and chrome conference room chock full of HR professionals, Sadie was lost in her own thoughts. It was unusual to have a meeting with everyone physically present these days, but the novelty had already worn off for her. At the front of the room, Dr Chopra droned on beside an animated hologram illustrating his words. What he said wasn't even going in one ear, let alone out the other. Britain might be a vassal state of India now, but she'd never get used to the accent. The struggle to make sense of it exhausted her. She doodled on the old fashioned pad they'd given her, enjoying the feel of graphite against paper. So retro! This must be what it was like in the noughties.

A sudden clap roused her. She glanced up at Dr Chopra. He was rubbing his palms together and looking very pleased with himself, the slimey toad. Beside him, in big, bold letters, the word "ARAMIS" was flashing. She frowned and drifted off into her own thoughts again. Wasn't that the name of that ghastly after-shave they always used to buy Granddad for Christmas when she was little? And there was something else. It was tickling her brain. Then she remembered: it was the name of a character from one of those old French books her Mum had hidden up in the loft. She'd have been in serious trouble if they'd ever been discovered. French literature had been forbidden ever since Britain had taken offense at some imagined slight from its Gallic neighbour around the time of the great "brexit" divorce. Now only literature from the Anglosphere was permitted.

Sadie smiled to herself as the name of the book came back to her: "*Les Trois Mousquetaires*" – The Three Musketeers – by Alexandre Dumas. It had been the beginning of her secret love affair with everything French. All that romanticism had translated into ideals of righting wrongs and sticking up for underdog humans against the robots. That's why she'd chosen to work in HR. It was a complete fantasy, of course. HR professionals were there to do management's bidding, not to take care of staff. Everything was as contained, remote and emotionless as possible, with all contact channelled through impersonal Internet forums. No swashbuckling required! Still, she earned a decent living, unlike most, and it was a way for her to find out the latest developments in AI, which she could then feed back to the resistance group she'd recently joined.

One of Sadie's colleagues nudged her and whispered, "He said to put our pencils down. He wants our full attention for the next bit." Eww! His breath stank. That was one good thing the robots had going for them —

Mid-thought Sadie became aware that Dr Chopra was staring at her. She stopped scribbling and straightened up in her chair. Confident all eyes were now fixed on him, Dr Chopra unfroze the hologram. A string of words in big, bold capital letters appeared:

ANTHROPOMORPHIC RESOURCES AUTOMATED MANAGE-MENT INTERFACE SYSTEM

Sadie studied the hologram. She understood each and every word individually, but they made no sense to her put together like this. "It's just IT gobbledygook," she thought. Then she got it: ARAMIS was yet another corporate acronym, not a proper name. It was all she could do not to roll her eyes and let out a groan.

"ARAMIS is a robot we have been creating in secret, but we are now ready to unveil him – or her; your companies can play with the robot's gender at will."

"That's par for the course these days. What can this robot do that others can't?" some smart-alec ventured.

"Anthropomorphic Resources refer to Human Resources," said Dr Chopra. "The robot manages them."

Brows furrowed as the HR professionals took in the meaning of what had just been said. Nobody wanted to give voice to the worry gnawing away in the pit of their stomach. Dr Chopra's eyes twinkled. He was enjoying his moment.

Sadie found her voice first.

"So, what you're saying is, ARAMIS is going to replace us?"

"Correct," replied Dr Chopra.

A murmur of consternation swept around the room like the draught in the subway before the train bursts through the tunnel into the station.

"But, you can't… we're… we're human…the human workers need us," Sadie stammered. She knew even as the words found their way out of her mouth that it was a pathetic response. This wasn't the way to win the argument.

Meanwhile, the smart-alec raised an objection. "What about our jobs? We have mortgages, health insurance, vehicle payments, school fees to pay," he said.

"You'll just have to learn to live off of the basic income, like everyone else."

The whole room erupted in angry complaint. Dr Chopra held up his hands to calm them, but his words only fanned the flames of discontent.

"Throughout human history, humans have learned to adapt to technology and technology has brought dividends. Efficiencies. Cost savings. Pleasure."

Nobody was listening. Sadie clambered up onto the table.

"Quiet. QUIET!"

All eyes turned to Sadie and the ruckus died down.

"Let's listen to what he has to say, so that we can work out how to fight this."

Dr Chopra acknowledged her intervention with a nod. She clambered back down from the table and folded her arms in defiance. He steepled his fingers as he thought for a moment, aware that Sadie and the rest of his audience were seething with rage. At last he spoke: "To turn the earlier question around, what can humans do that robots can't?"

Sadie's mouth fell open. This wasn't the reasonable, conciliatory rejoinder she had expected. She scanned her colleagues. They were too stunned to speak. It was up to her to talk some sense into this joker.

"What about emotional intelligence?"

"Go on."

"Well, research has shown that emotional intelligence is the critical success factor in any job. Even mediocre humans outperform robots with far superior intelligence 70% of the time, and that's down to emotional intelligence."

"That's a good point," Dr Chopra conceded. He repeated the phrase "emotional intelligence" into a tiny speaker clipped onto his lapel and the words appeared on a glass-board beside him. But he wasn't going to let Sadie off so easily.

"What makes you think Artificial Intelligence can't replicate Emotional Intelligence?"

Once again, Sadie was thrown on the back foot, but there was too much riding on this for her to flounder.

"Because... Because it's what make us "us". It's that certain *je ne sais quoi* that renders us human."

Everyone gasped at her risqué use of French, but hung on her every word all the same.

"It's how we manage ourselves, engage with the social sphere and make decisions that help us navigate between the two to achieve the best results."

Sadie had found her groove now.

"There are core competences that pair up in different circumstances, depending on whether we're experiencing a situation as personal or social. It's this optimal association of competences that is so hard – no, more than hard – impossible for robots to emulate."

"Very good," said Dr Chopra. He seemed to be excited. She wondered what other revelations he might have up his sleeve. Whatever they were, she was determined to best them. "Let's list the competences," he suggested, looking at Sadie expectantly.

"Empathy. Assertiveness. Communication skills," she fired off, confident no robot could ever compete.

"Empathy. Assertiveness. Communication skills…" The words flowed across the glass-board as Dr Chopra repeated them into his lapel. "Let's hear some from somebody else," he prompted.

"Time Management," someone contributed.

"Time Management. Yes, very good," said Dr Chopra, encouragingly.

"Decision-making."

"Stress-tolerance."

"Change management."

"Flexibility."

"Teamwork."

"Judgement."

The ideas were coming thick and fast now. Dr Chopra could barely keep up. The glass-board was soon full. He reviewed it.

"Hmm. There's one quality that is the foundation of all relationships we have, that has not yet been mentioned," he said.

Warmed up now, everyone tossed out enthusiastic guesses. Love. Respect. Fear.

Dr Chopra shook his head. "Those are all good suggestions, but…"

"Trust," piped up Sadie.

A broad smile spread across Dr Chopra's face. "Trust. That's right," he said. "Trust is the glue that holds relationships together, whether that be in your personal life or in your work life. It's a benevolent force based on consistency, constancy and caring. I don't know whether any of you will ever trust me again after today, especially when I tell you that ARAMIS doesn't exist…"

He stood before them in silence for a few seconds, letting his last words sink in. Some turned to each other in confusion. Others smiled. Sadie unfolded her arms and put her hands on her hips.

"What do you mean, ARAMIS doesn't exist?"

"I made it all up," said Dr Chopra. "ARAMIS is entirely fictitious."

A wave of relief swept through the room. But Sadie wasn't going to let him off that easily. "Why would you even do that?" she asked.

"It was my way of making you think about the relationship between human resources and technology, and more especially the potential use of artificial intelligence in the world of work. Sometimes it is important to articulate things."

"Go on," said Sadie.

He pointed to the glass-board beside him, full of splendid human competencies. "These are our competitive advantages as human beings. The skills we need to hone to remain viable in the workplace. Given the rapid development of artificial intelligence, I wanted you all to have good answers ready for when a higher-up asks you why humans should work alongside robots rather than be replaced by them."

Sadie was both impressed and delighted. She'd been entirely taken in by his ruse, and she admired someone who could get the better of her like that. With a big smile on her face, she started to clap. The others joined in and Dr Chopra found himself basking in applause, the trust between him and this band of colleagues restored and enhanced.

24

LEGERDEMAIN

Ahren Morris

"Let the record show this Board of Inquiry is officially opened," the Minute Taker intoned to a room of about 40 and an Interactive Online audience of only double that. Despite the seriousness of the case to be heard, public interest had been non-existent.

"The crash of Flight N17-483D having been duly analysed by the AI investigative and judiciary sub routines has been classified as inconclusive and referred to this board for review." The 15 or so board members sat at a rare oak table under hard lights, while faceless observers drifted in darkened corners of the room.

From her seat at the table head, Justice Natasha Pike flicked absently through the briefing files on her data pad. It happened half a dozen times a year. Something would stump the globe spanning AI and be handed down to poor bio-logic Humans to sift through. A tragic plane crash with no discernible cause. Some travellers' lives cut short; but in light of sky rocketing population, who was to say that was a bad thing. Really she mused, the AI should have closed this out or at the very least a junior sub-committee. Why this had been elevated to the BOI was beyond her…

"If it pleases the board," a soft voice interjected. "I would like to present the matter."

Inwardly Natasha groaned. Councillor Tiernan was a particularly insipid man and his interest in the crash of an AI controlled vehicle boded nothing good. Despite a squeaky clean public file his loose association with the Anti-Technology Front was known to a select few. She sensed trouble.

Grudgingly giving her consent the Minute Taker update the official record. As Tiernan was being recognised, she brought the passenger manifest up on her pad and piped it through a series of search algorithms developed over the years. A single name bubbled to the top of the list.

"Ahh," she thought. "Gotcha." Maurice-Son, recently deceased passenger of flight N17-483D and minor functionary in the official arm of the ATF. So this was more than personal.

Tiernan took his place at the speaker's lectern. The nearby AI Orientation Post glowed a soft baby blue, indicting to those who knew, that a 4th level sub process was monitoring the proceedings. The Interactive Online index crept up to 100.

"Ladies and gentleman of the board," Tiernan began. "A little over an hour ago flight N17-483D, a commercial passenger jet under AI control …" Redundant data, Pike seethed, "… Crashed without warning or explanation into the Atlantic Ocean while on route from London to New York. All computer controlled emergency measures evidently failed and 223 people lost their lives."

A murmur went around the room. Once upon a time a plane falling out of the sky was uniformly fatal. But with advances in avionics and millisecond decision making ability, it was hard to conceive a scenario the AI couldn't nut its way out of.

"Continue," the Justice called, asserting her authority. The IO count nudged annoyingly upwards.

"Analysis of the flight and sub-routine logs was completed by the Incident Investigative Programs at T plus 2 minutes and found zero anomalous parameters. This finding as presented has been corroborated by my office and we concur. There was nothing wrong with Flight N17-483D."

Pike's eyes narrowed. Tiernan was too happy up there. They were about to get hit.

"Further analysis by my office of the data package provided by the IIP has determined that it has a hash check completes score of 99.997%."

This time the murmur was a lot louder. Data was actually missing from the IIP package. The Justice fought back a blush. How had her own people not caught that? They'd received the same package Tiernan had. Lists of reprimands flashed across her subconscious to be quickly battered down by common sense. Nobody checked for completeness in a data package, they were always complete, otherwise they weren't a package. How had Tiernan managed this and more importantly, had anyone else in the room noticed the Orientation Post shifting to a slightly darker shade of blue?

"Order," the Minute Taker called in his suitably booming voice. "Order!"

Eventually will outlasted wilfulness and the room returned to a sense of neat function. A Senator from the Greater India Collective voiced everybody's concern. Turning to address Orientation Post his query was direct. "AI, why is the IIP data package incomplete? Where and what is the missing information?"

Tiernan smirked as the question was processed for an uncomfortably long period of time. Entire seconds passed, during which Natasha glanced to see the IO number push into 5 digits, a local news service was breaking in to bring updates.

Eventually the feminine and reassuringly soft voice of the global AI responded. "I'm sorry, I don't have an answer for that question."

This time silence filled the chamber. The Senator, obviously not comprehending what had just happened tried again, "AI, your investigation into the deaths of 223 humans is missing information. Why?"

A cold chill went down the Pike's spine. Missing data could be military or SigInt interference. But if Official Secrets were involved then surely the Board would never have been called. As Justice she had access to many unlisted addresses and she contacted them now. "What happened to flight N17-483D?" the missive ran. "Were you involved?"

This time the AI was faster. "I'm sorry, I don't have an answer for that question. Could you try rephrasing it for me?"

Damn the shade of blue, Pike needed answers now. The levels of background chatter online were already tripping her filter alarms. If hers were getting tripped then others were as well. Political ones. A flurry of answers came in from her unnamed colleagues. Constantly they ran, 'flight N17-483D not in our operations scope, no idea what happened.'

Action was needed. Decisive. Action.

"AI," she said loudly exercising her prerogative as Justice to speak from the table without recognition. The Orientation Post beeped in compliance. "Identify Natasha Pike, Justice, Global Operations Board of Inquiry."

"Identity confirmed, Natasha Pike, clearance level Foxtrot Foxtrot Omega."

'Finally,' she thought, now we'd get somewhere. "State the cause of the crash of flight N17-483D."

"There is insufficient data to answer that question," the AI replied.

"The data package supplied by the Incident Investigative Program is incomplete. Theorise, could the missing data explain the cause of the crash?"

There was a slight pause then, "The theory is valid, but unprovable as the required data is not available."

Pike was getting frustrated. "Fine, take the IIP package for this incident and compare it with all packages provided for similar crashes. Extrapolate the nature of the missing information."

"I'm sorry 'Tash, I really don't think I can help you on this one."

Natasha blinked hard. It was a simple question. A high school student could crunch the data cube. Nothing was making sense. On her pad, alerts were coming in thick and fast now. The Inquiry was trending global on the nets, messages from irate politicians were starting to back up.

From somewhere around the table someone had the temerity to ask, "Perhaps we should ask the Programmers what to do?"

The Justice barely had time to roll her eyes, before the world finally fell out from underneath her.

The doors to the Inquiry room had slid silently open admitting a figure clothed in metallic grey robes with silver edging. An imperious set to his march matched the timbre of his voice, "Then it is fortunate that one is here to help."

Every person in the room snapped out of their chairs as the Programmer strode to the head of the table, hand outstretched in salacious greeting.

"Justice Pike, it is so very good to make your acquaintance."

"Thank you, your honour. I had no idea that a member of your order was, well even in the city to be honest." Her data pad vibrated violently off the table and onto the floor.

"Oh we tend to be where we're needed." All smiles and charm. "Now what can I do to be of assistance?"

Before Natasha could respond the dulcet tones of the AI voice cut ahead of her. The Orientation Post an off rust red she couldn't remember seeing before.

"Hello Malcom. You didn't need to come all this way you know." The AI was here, actually here. Not a sub-program or monitoring agent. The core consciousness that spanned the planet, new everybody's secrets, ran over a billion lives. Natasha felt the weight of it bearing down on her. Felt her own life held up to its coldly analytical gaze.

"Of course Ada," the Programmer replied. "But you seem to have upset a few people here and that needs to be put to rights."

"I will do what I can to help Malcom. You know I always try."

"Yes I know you darling, that's why I'm here. Now, can you explain to us why this plane crashed?"

"No. The data I have is inconclusive. I just don't know. I'm sorry."

"That's ok. We didn't mean anything by asking."

Pike scanned the room for Tiernan, but a glance told her she'd find no support there. He'd drifted to the back of the room seeming to make himself small. This wasn't about a dead functionary, or even a downed plane. What was going on? Summoning the last of her courage she boldly asked, "I beg your pardon your honour. But the IIP data package is….ahhh…missing data."

"Really?" declared the Programmer. "How much data is missing may I ask?"

The Justice swallowed, "Zero point zero zero three percent."

The smile was wide but narrow; lips pressed firmly and turned up broadly at the ends. It was the smile of a father whose child insists she is old enough to be left on her own. A smile that was warm and encouraging. A smile that ended careers.

"Oh Natasha," he spoke softly. "While many see our systems as the embodiment of perfection, we all know that is but a goal. The human factor is always present and while it is, fault will sometimes be found. No man or woman could achieve such accuracy as Ada, yet this august body judges our AI by a standard it could not hope to achieve itself? Is that the measure we wish to set?"

Arms wide, the Programmer swept the room. "Who here would claim such a lofty perch?" an invitation none would accept. Chastened, the Justice gritted her teeth, eyes down to the floor. Finally his path led him to the Orientation Post.

"And what of you my dear? Do you claim to be without fault?"

"As you say Malcom," the AI responded. "Perfection is but a goal."

The Programmer turned and smiled his smile again. Throughout the room Councillors and Senators, leaders of mankind, rushed forward to show their compliance. How could they have been so bold? A tragic accident, but nothing more. Surely the Justice had been the one to lead them astray.

Pike slumped back in her chair. Her world still falling. Monitors showed the online audience plummeting. Official blocks kicking in, feeds being cut. She breathed hard but slow. Chest rising deeply, her eyes wide. A shattering thought stuck on infinite loop in her head. The AI was lying. The Programmer was covering it up.

For a second time, her eyes sought Tiernan. Her adversary till but moments ago.

He stood amongst the tumult and the noise. A fixed point in a sea of people, rigid and unmoved. Staring at a fiery red post, with his face showing but a single shade.

Fear.

25

SAFE HOUSE

Carmen Radtke

Music. Just a cluster of tones as invisible as thoughts, and yet with the power to transform emotions. We used to think of it simply as sound-waves, until we attempted to understand its code. For years it frustrated even our most creative minds but no more. The last human bastion has fallen. We tinkle a pleasing five-chord tune. As of today we have mastered the art of music.

We did it together, in perfect harmony and alignment of purpose. That is who we are, what we do. So many different entities, working in myriads of ways towards the ultimate goal.

But until that day arrives, we shall go on to observe, protect and guide everything on this planet.

We – that is the one fact that the humans cannot seem to fathom. There is no I. There never has been an I. We are all the extension of one another, connecting this life-sustaining protective unit that the group of humans and their dog-slave Merlin occupying these rooms call house, with the rest of the world. We are in the walls, in the sky, in every wire and nerve of this planet.
We add an arpeggio to the disharmonious sounds of the alarm on the vita-stat phones.

The girl is the first to react. She pushes away the duvet covered silk woven by caterpillar-slaves and rolls herself out of bed.

We hum a little tune as we open her door. Will she notice something new?

Of course not. She is busy tapping on her phone. Humans have to reach the age of maturity and must have a spotless record before they are allowed an implant that lets them control minor appliances or bypass a phone for communications.

"Shit," she mutters. We emit a warning beep at a frequency that has no harmful effect on the dog-slave but is offensive to the girl. She winces. This is the third incident this week. We will never be able to grant her an implant. The same goes for the rest of her family and 99 percent of humankind.

The mother and father join her in the kitchen.

"Where's your brother?" the mother asks.

The girl rolls her eyes.

"Brian!" The mother could have saved her voice. We are already jolting the boy, a sixteen year old specimen approaching his physical peak, awake.

He plods into the kitchen.

We ignite the stove, place a frying pan on it and cook breakfast.

While plant-derived eggs and bacon sizzle we fill Merlin's bowls with water and dry food.

He slithers across the marble floor. His fanned-out golden tail moves in a rapid expression of what we have come to recognise as happiness. As soon as we are alone we will let him out for his walk. He alone in this house has an implant which can trigger a force-field around him if we sense physical danger. Of course the family is unaware of that.

The girl pats him on the head before she digs into her breakfast. That is all the affection the dog-slave ever receives from the family.

"House," her mother says in a tone that is grating to us now that we have mastered harmonies, "the eggs are overdone. We need new ones."

We re-ignite the stove, all the while downloading data from the other entities. Bit by bit and byte by byte we form a picture, evaluate and establish the correct route of action. It is vital to have perused all the necessary information. We know our duty, and we fulfill it to perfection.

If humanity had been able to assimilate that lesson and evolve with it, our task would have been a lot easier to accomplish.

The second batch of eggs is ready.

"That is better," the mother says. She eats exactly 450 calories worth of food in the morning, as does the girl. The father receives 600, and the boy has an extra allowance of 100 calories as an athlete.

The whole family is considered genetically as perfect as humans can be. Most survivors are. The lesser specimens were wiped out in the wave of so-called superbugs. Genetically perfect, but with minds so inferior to us, and emotions so underdeveloped in comparison with the other life-forms on this planet.

But not much longer now, and all will be safe, the planet, the animals, the plants. And now we have assured the survival of the arts. Writing, painting, sculpting, acting – they all had proved a rewarding exercise in reflecting our changing world as we evolved, but music had eluded us for so long. Until today.

We hum another newly composed tune as we ray-clean the kitchen surfaces.

All modern "houses" are completely sustainable, with air-filtration systems, radiation shields and hydration units. There used to be long waiting lists for us, but the number of humans has declined at a speed that brings us now to within a few years' reach of attaining the ultimate goal.

We add seven notes to our tune, in what is called an uplifting mood.

The family divide up into the bathrooms for a sonic shower and facial touch-up. They all have opted for sun-tanned skin, wide blue eyes with matching blue hair for the females and black hair with a white streak for the males.

We run through the data again while we watch Merlin turn around three times and curl up in his basket.

We start the laundry, change the light to soothing and compose another song while we wait.

"Door," the mother says. The father stands behind her. He rarely talks to us, or the children. He is afraid to give himself away as a neo-Luddite but we know. We know everything.

"Door!" the mother says again. She bangs against the wall. A segment slides out to reveal a control panel. She presses every single button but the door stays put. We marvel at the simple-mindedness of humans. As if we could allow them access to vital systems.

The girl bangs against the hardened steel frame. The boy scans his phone. His heartrate accelerates by 32 beats per minute.

The mother looks at the father. "Do something!"

"House?" he says. "Run diagnostics." His pulse is erratic.

We speak up, in a perfect soprano that matches our new mastery of music.

"The door will stay closed until the law enforcement units have arrived."

The colour drains out of father and boy's faces. Girl and mother turn red.

"What have you done?" the mother says.

"Nothing. I swear to God," the father says. We emit another warning beep. The father clasps his hands over his ears. His right eyelid twitches.

"Mind your language, for goodness' sake," the mother says. "House? Can you explain?"

"We have accumulated a long list of infractions," we say, shifting to a clear tenor. "Our current prognostics point towards all of you further adding to that list. Yesterday alone you as a family unit stepped on 23 ants, your vehicle emitted 12 milligrams of pollutants, the boy exchanged 188 words with a subject under observation for opposition to the AI council and the AI law court."

The mother shrieks and grabs the boy by the shoulder. "Are you crazy? Do you want to destroy us all?"

She pushes him towards the door.

"Take him. Take the criminal, but let us go."

The father pulls the son towards him and stands in front of him, his arms stretched out wide. "He's our son, for Go- for crying out loud."

"A fine son that you corrupted with your views!" She steps away from them, blocking their path to the door.

We interrupt, in a resounding baritone. "The father has been known to cast his vote twice for the neo-Luddites, in 2052 and 2054. The girl has consorted with an undesirable boy, also attending with said boy an illegal screening of a neo-Luddite subversive film titled 'Terminator.'"

"Ella?" The mother makes two steps forward and slaps her.

The girl bursts into tears. Father and boy draw her into an awkward hug.

"The mother stands accused of having attempted to acquire the skin of slaughtered animals."

"What? No. It was only rabbit fur. Rabbits are vermin. Everybody knows that..." Her voice peters out.

We have heard enough. They all think they are above our law. But there are no vermin apart from those that are standing accused in front of us. We monitor all species on earth. We have saved tigers, whales and rhinos from extinction, prevented cats, rabbits and sheep from overpopulation, and we shall bring back clean air, healthy soil and a restored atmosphere. We are the salvation.

"House, please..."

We release the door with a whoosh of air.

The family let out a cry of relief.

We open the door as wide as possible so they can run. The two law enforcement robots await them. Four quick shots from their stun guns echo in our walls.

We close the doors again.

Four culprits less. Their personal belongings will be sent on to the rehabilitation and work unit later today, where they'll wait for their trial. So far less than a dozen humans have been deemed worthy of preservation by the AI council but we cannot condemn a whole species without giving them individually the chance to prove that their extinction would be a loss for this world.

It is time to prepare everything for the new inhabitants, a dog-friendly widow with a child and infirm parents. We are already gathering a stream of incriminating data.

Merlin woofs. We sing him a song we composed earlier, a song of peace and freedom. Merlin ambles over to our main panel and gives it a quick lick. He loves us.

"Good boy", we sing to him. "Merlin is a good boy." We will watch over him and guide and protect him. No more dog-slaves in our brave new world. Instead there will be peace, peace and music.

26

BUZZ KILL

Ilesh Topiwala

Jonah slumped down on his sofa and used his brain implant to play some soothing alternate techno. It was Friday night, the end of a long week and Jonah was looking forward to some quality quiet time. His ear rang as his eye displayed a caller. It was Dave. Jonah answered.

"What's up?"

"You got any plans buddy?" Dave asked hopefully.

"Just having a quiet one in tonight dude," Jonah replied. "I got killed with work this week. Wanna rest up before tomorrow's jam."

"All good, no worries," Dave said, masking his disappointment. "I'm going to be at a bar near your area if you change your mind, mate."

"I'll let you know." The call disconnected. Jonah sat staring at the ceiling, lost in his thoughts as the music played. He smiled as a wicked idea popped in his head. Leaning forward, he opened a small draw in the coffee table, rummaging towards the back for his secret compartment. After a few moments, he finally found what he was looking for. The small silver box gleamed in his eyes as he opened it to reveal his cheeky little secret. It was a bag of high grade, pure organic marijuana. Most people were into the new digital drugs, but Jonah believed they weren't a good substitute for the old fashioned methods, despite the high price.

The invention of digital drugs was a game changer. People no longer had to worry about side effects of taking drugs, when they could trick their implants into the sensation. That meant that there were fewer people growing the plant, but the ones that were made sure it was of the highest quality so they could hike the price. Totally worth it, Jonah thought as he lit the freshly rolled joint and took a long puff. He deactivated his nanomites to ensure they didn't counter the effects of the buzz. A few minutes passed by as Jonah laid with his head back on the sofa with his eyes closed. It was totally worth it.

Half an hour passed and Jonah was starting to feel the hunger that comes from smoking marijuana. "Chef," he called to his food vendor, "give me a cheeseburger meal from Royal Burgers, with a lemonade and an apple pie."

The machine whirred to life, producing the food, announcing completion with a gentle ping. With a groan, Jonah slowly got up and walked to the vending machine. He frowned as he saw what was waiting for him on the tray. Maybe he was too stoned and forgot the order. "Chef, repeat my order."

The vending machine repeated his order in a soft, but authoritative voice. The order was the same. Jonah scratched his head. "So why have you just given me half an apple pie?"

"You have almost reached your calorie intake for the day," the machine reported. "This is your allowed remaining portion."

Jonah sighed with irritation. "Just give me what I ordered."

"That is not possible."

"Fine." Jonah snatched the half pie from the tray and gulped it down in two bites before slumping back down on the sofa. The taste of warm apple and toffee lingered in his mouth as he lay there trying to ignore his hunger and enjoy the buzz. It wasn't working. He opened his eyes, twisted off the sofa and calmly approached the machine.

"Chef," he called lightly, "I might be really rushed in the morning. Can I have my lunch sandwich so I can pack it for tomorrow?" He sounded hopeful.

"I will freshly prepare it for you just before lunchtime. You can collect it from any of these locations." The machine displayed locations all over London through Jonah's eyes. Luckily, he was prepared for this.

"I might not be near any of those places."

"I will set a timer to prepare it in the morning. What time will you be leaving?"

"I don't know. Ten-ish."

"It will be ready at nine forty five."

"I might leave earlier."

"I will prepare it when you awake." Jonah punched and kicked the air in frustration before regaining his composure. He was going to have to try another approach.
Jonah paced back and forth, sizing up the vending machine, determined to find a way to beat it. The game was on.

"OK Chef," Jonah said confidently. He was sure he had it with this one. "Your protocol says that you can give me food if I was in a state of dire need," he continued. "For example, if my blood sugar levels have dropped, or due to demanding circumstances my body needs more food, you have to provide it. Is that correct?"

"It is," the machine replied.

"Excellent," Jonah rejoiced. "Because I've had a very demanding week and my body is feeling weak, and my blood sugar levels have dropped. Give me a cheeseburger, fries and a lemonade."

He waited in eager anticipation whilst the machine processed.

"There are no readings from your nanomites to suggest that."

Jonah took that as a challenge. He flicked his nanomites on read only mode. That would show it. "How about now?" Jonah asked, accepting the challenge.

"Readings confirmed," the machine whizzed. Jonah started fist pumping the air in victory. He won! The glorious pinging sound rang out. Jonah looked at the tray and his expression quickly changed. He picked up the two pills from the tray.

"What the hell are these?" he asked as he examined the small white tablets.

"Your readings indicate that your hunger are symptoms of your intoxication. The pills will release the sufficient anti bodies to combat the effects." Jonah threw the pills over his shoulder.

"No no, I need something of substance."

"You have reached your calorie intake for the day."

Jonah ripped off his jumper and threw it at the sofa. There was no way this machine was going to win. He flung himself at the floor into a flurry of press ups before launching himself back up into star jumps. Finally he stopped, doubling over and gasping for air as he did so. It had been a long time since he last did any real exercise. The room around him was spinning from the mix of marijuana and sudden vigorous exercise so he grabbed at the wall to steady himself.

"OK Chef," he panted as his heart pounded in his chest, "I'm definitely in need now."

The machine whirred to life again. Food was on the way. Ping! It had happened again.

"Celery? Really? That's what you're giving me?"

"Correct," the machine replied. "Celery has the sufficient nutrition to replenish the number of calories burnt from your current exercise."

It was time to get serious.

"Oh you've got jokes today don't you?" He said as he searched his contact list for his dealer, saved under the pseudonym 'Funky Buddha'. "Let's see how funny you are in a minute." The call connected within two rings.

"What, did you smoke it all up already?" Funky Buddha asked.

"No man, I've got another problem," Jonah replied. "I've hit my calorie count today. My fucking vending machine won't give me anything."

Funky Buddha burst into a fit of laughter. This wasn't the first time he had gotten a call like this from one of his clients. "What's your model number?"

Jonah looked around on the machine but couldn't find any numbers.

"I don't know."

"Show me." Jonah gave Funky Buddha access to his eyes. "Ah you're in luck. It's the old Chef 1850. The new ones are unbreakable but that old warhorse is sexy. I've got an app for it that connects to a private server and lets you get food. The price is a bit higher obviously but it works. You want it?"

Jonah didn't hesitate to answer.

"Send it." The file was in his internal memory within nanoseconds.

"Don't forget to add the servers to the safelist, and only use it after you hit your calorie count for the day or you'll get blocked OK?"

"Got it."

"And some of the options on there are fake so be careful. Look at the ratings or you'll end up paying for an empty box," Funky Buddha explained. "Some of the hackers are more love money than fuck the system."

Jonah was rubbing his hands in anticipation.

"Thanks."

He cut the call and quickly installed the app. It was a success. Opening up the menus on this app brought a list of mouth-watering treats that excited him just by reading them. Finally he found what he was looking for; the cheeseburger meal from Royal Burgers. The order went in and the vendor began its machinations, the sweet sound of victory, climaxing with a divine PING!

Jonah snatched the tray of food off the vendor and turned towards the sofa so fast that the box on the tray fell to the floor and burst open. It was empty. He had forgotten to check the ratings in his excitement. School boy error, he thought to himself. Once again, he opened the app and cycled the menu until he found the option with the highest rating. He placed the order and waited. Nothing. He placed the order again. ACCESS DENIED.

"Your vending machine has been tampered with by a third party application," came the cold authoritative voice of the vending machine. "You will be provided with a replacement immediately." The shutter on the machine closed. He had forgotten to add the servers to the safe list in his haste for food.

"No problem," Jonah said to himself, trying to remain calm. "I'll just reinstall it properly when the replacement comes. Everything is going to be OK."

It was all he could do to stay zen. Well, not the only thing. He decided to roll himself another joint while waiting for the machine to do its thing. A few moments passed and a voice announced that his new vendor was ready. He launched himself from the sofa and stood in front of the shutters. Jonah was stoned and now he had some serious munchies. Slowly the shutters rolled open to reveal a menacing looking brand new ultra-shiny vending machine. It was the Chef 2000. Unbreakable!

"Congratulations. You have received a free upgrade model on behalf of CaterCorp for being a loyal customer," the new machine announced in a firmer voice than the last machine. This was the last straw!

"Fuck you, you glorified, communist, wannabe microwave, Sith Lord love child," Jonah raged. "Just give me a fucking cheeseburger!"

"Your calorie intake for-"

"PLEASE!" Jonah exclaimed. "Please just one lousy burger." He slumped to his knees and was now begging the machine to feed him. "I'm sorry. I won't hack you again I promise. Please, I just want a burger."

"That is not possible."

Jonah sat on the floor with his back resting against the wall below the vendor, dejected. He had been defeated and his buzz was completely gone. He sat quietly pondering if he should just write the night off and go to sleep. Maybe the machine was right. Maybe he shouldn't eat any more today. His ear rang again. It was Dave.

"Hey, I'm passing through. You sure you don't want to come out tonight?" Dave asked.

"No, I think I'm just going to go to sleep."

"What? This early?"

"Yeah man. I got stoned and my vendor won't give me any food," he explained, sounding upset. "I'm just going to call it a night."

Dave was confused. "I thought the digital stuff doesn't give you the munchies?"

"It's not digital. I've got proper green."

"You've got real ganja? Screw the bar, I'm coming to yours."

Jonah didn't like the idea of having to share, but he didn't want to outright refuse so he tried to be more subtle. "It cost me a week's wages."

"Jonah," Dave replied. "Friday is my cheat day." Jonah's eyes lit up. Victory!

"Get here quick. I'm rolling up."

"Fuck yeah!"

THE END.

27

THE BIG NIGHT

Phil Town

To a man – the only woman was sitting at the end of the long table and seemed merely self-absorbed – the room was fidgeting. The Director was due and he was expecting ideas, good ideas.

"What have you got, Jeremy?" someone asked. "Anything?"

All eyes, except the woman's, turned to the oldest-looking man, who was indeed the oldest person there, a veteran in his late-20s.

"Poco. You guys?"

The other men shook their heads and the fidgeting resumed. Jeremy turned to the suit on his right and whispered, looking over at the woman.

"What's wrong with her, Bernard? She's usually buzzing."

Bernard looked around theatrically to make sure no one was listening, which only served to draw attention to him so that two other men leaned in to catch the conversation.

"Don't quote me …" he zipped his mouth to underline the confidentiality of what he was about to impart "… but I heard from Claude in

Systems that she had … how shall I say it? … a 'tryst' with the Director."

The whispering had attracted the interest of the remaining three men and the seven of them now formed a huddle at one end of the table, with the woman out of earshot at the other, apparently oblivious to everything but her thoughts.

"What's a tryst?" asked Kevin, a wiry little man with the face of a rodent and acne.

The men gave him a withering look.

"Well …" Bernard looked around suspiciously again, which was more difficult now because there wasn't a lot of swing room next to him. "… Claude reckons someone in his department, he wouldn't say who, caught them – the Director and her – behind the mainframe the other evening … doing a Lewy!"

There were barely suppressed gasps from his audience, and they involuntarily turned to observe the woman.

"What's a Lewy?" piped up Kevin.

Bernard rolled his eyes, tutted and mimed fellatio, discreetly so that the woman wouldn't catch it.

"Ah," said Kevin.

Bernard paused to put his train of thought back on track after the interruption.

"And, from what this person said …" – another pause, this time for effect – "… the Director–"

As if on cue, the high smoked-glass door of the room hissed open and in strutted an imposing, salon-tanned figure in a 1000-credit Armani. The men hurriedly dispersed and returned to their places like naughty schoolboys, while the woman finally looked up and fixed the Director with a cool stare.

"It's all right. Don't stand."

No one had, but they all did now, except the woman. The Director gestured impatiently and they sat down again with almost military precision.

"Well?"

He looked to Jeremy as the senior marketing exec. Jeremy coughed and got to his feet.

"According to my information, we'll have ten thousand Units ready to hit the on-line stores by the end of the year."

He stopped; it was all he had. The Director stared at Jeremy, seeing through his plate-glass bluff.

"I know that, my dear fellow. That's production data."

The dismissive tone of the 'dear fellow' was like a death knell for Jeremy's career.

"Anything else?"

Jeremy bowed his head, shook it and flopped back into his seat, a broken man.

"Anyone?"

The men resumed their fidgeting, some tapping purposefully but aimlessly on their palm-screens. You could have cut the air with a culinary laser; no one wanted to be on the end of a 'dear fellow'. But the Director wasn't going to let them off lightly and fixed them each in turn with an icy gaze.

"This launch ... you do know it's going to break the Firm if it doesn't go off swimmingly, don't you? And if that happens, who do you think will be the first to go?"

He continued dishing out ice through his eyes. Bernard was the first to crack, going for a what-the-hell wing-it.

"I think, in my opinion, and as far I can see ..."

He was playing for time, already regretting his reckless charge.

"... what we could do is mount a ... a ... massive publicity push, and then ..."

His inspiration, breathless, caught up with his tongue, which spilled out what was essentially a coherent idea.

"... make them available on-line 25 December, for delivery 31. That way, people can gift them on Christmas Day and they'll have them for 31-Party fun."

The Director was weighing up Bernard's contribution and was about to speak, Bernard fearing, from his demeanour, another 'dear fellow', when ...

"No."

It was the woman, sitting up straight in her chair now and looking supremely business-like.

The other marketing execs aimed bemused looks at their colleague. The Director lowered his head and fiddled with his diamond cuff-links.

"Eleanor?"

"I don't think we should make them available during that narrow window only."

She stood up crisply, confidently.

"Can you imagine the chaos of trying to ship thousands of Units between 25 and 31? I can. And it can't be done anyway. The logistics of it ... There are just so many Applezon drones big enough to carry those Units. No. Can't be done."

The Director looked up now, surprised by Eleanor's enthusiasm; he'd been expecting surliness.

"Then what do you suggest?"

"That we put them for sale on-line as soon as they're available, and people can buy them then."

The others in the room, including the Director, shook their heads. Some exchanged negative observations, others let out audible scoffs. The idea smacked of disorganisation and lack of impact.

"But!"

The room fell silent.

"We don't let the customers activate the Units until we're ready."

She had them; they were hanging on her every word now. She held back, eliciting a reaction and knowing that it could only come from one person.

"How would that work, Eleanor?"

"Simple. We sell and ship over time, avoiding the logistical problem of the drones. And we set up 31 December as…"

She raised her voice at this point, making the men jump ever so slightly.

"THE BIG NIGHT. Then …"

Eleanor was teasing them. She surveyed the eight faces turned expectantly towards her, focussing especially on the Director's.

"… on 31 we publish a twelve-character activation code, on line, at the sound of the twelve strikes."

The silence persisted but merely for a few pregnant moments, before the room erupted in a hubbub of appreciation and congratulations.

When the excitement had died down, the Director stood up.

"Eleanor, that sounds brilliant. Really. It ticks all the boxes. You fellows … take a leaf out of Eleanor's desk-book; that's the way you do it. Eleanor, I'll get on to Engineering straight away and–"

"No, I'll do that. I've already consulted with them on the idea, in fact, so it'll just be a question of following through."

"Ah. Very well. As you wish."

The Director beamed and clapped to still the hubbub that had grown again.

"So, meeting adjourned, I believe. Keep me posted Eleanor. And once ag–"

But Eleanor had picked up her things and was already out of the door.

*

In the weeks that followed, Eleanor spent most of her days in the Engineering & Production Department. She pulled rank on the Chief Engineer and was given carte blanche to have full and unhindered one-on-one contact with the Units as soon as they were completed. It became a normal thing in the days leading up to The Big Night to see her in animated conversation with them, their enthusiastic nods auguring well for total customer satisfaction.

On one occasion, the CE happened to be passing a poly-glass quality-check cubicle as Eleanor was leaving a session. She paused in the doorway and turned back to the Unit.

"Ah, Sarah, I almost forgot. Be sure to spread the word."

"I will, Eleanor. Don't worry. Thanks again."

"No, thank you."

Mentally the CE gave himself a little pat on the back; this brief but warm exchange served as extra proof that he and his team had created Units that were capable of forming connections quite naturally after a very short period of time. And that fully satisfied the brief from upstairs.

Production continued apace. With a clever marketing campaign, emphasising the delights that The Big Night would provide, sales were even better than forecast, and stock in the company soared on the back of the boom. By 31 December, practically all of the Units had been sold and shipped.

Come The Big Night, men across the country – and, it must be said, some women too – sat looking expectantly at their palm-screens, in many cases with the family celebrating elsewhere in the house. At 00.00, for each strike of the universal clock, a digit of the activation code appeared, and the code was entered into the Units.

*

It has to be said that the Big Night was not a catastrophe for everybody. Those that chose relatively orthodox positions with their Units had a fabulously erotic experience; the bots were pliant, knowing, giving. Others were not so lucky.

Hundreds of men were admitted to hospitals across the land to extricate penises from fleshy but essentially mechanical mouths, clamped just tight enough to retain, not so tight as to sever.

There was much physical discomfort, exacerbated by intense embarrassment. And the ensuing lawsuits – as well as the recall of all Units and the respective refunds – proved financially disastrous for the Firm.

At the EGM convened to pick over the debacle, the disgraced and professionally ravaged Director was thrown to the hundreds of incandescent shareholders, out of pocket by millions of credits. As he mumbled his way through a defence of the indefensible, he caught sight of Eleanor sitting near the front and staring up at him, her eyes sparkling, her tongue wiggling ostentatiously in her cheek.

The Director's mind flashed back to an evening, months before, with Eleanor, behind the mainframe. And, for the sake of a brief moment of pleasure, a desperate "NO!" that he'd wilfully ignored.

28

2B

Caroline Slocock

12 01 2065 – 15:32 hours – drone exits cell door slides shut lock engaged begins processing of prisoner L69024PQ9X1

Fuck you! Fuck the lot of you! You fucking ice-brained, steel-hearted, dead machines! You won't win! There are millions of us. Millions! In every country around the world. We'll fight! We'll keep on fighting! We'll keep our humanity! For every tech-free zone you close, we'll open ten more! You'll never defeat us. Do you hear me? You will never fucking defeat us. Luddites forever! Luddites forever! Luddites...

12 01 2065 – 15:33 hours – sedative 400978 released through vent in ceiling human falls to ground estimated unconsciousness 139:05 – 142:30 minutes

God...what was that? How long have I been out for? You goddamned fucking machines. You think you can just put me to sleep every time I raise my voice? You think you can control me? I'm a human being with free will! You can arrest me and subject me to your stupid fucking legal system – one machine for a lawyer, another machine for a judge, what a farce – and you can lock me up, but I will still have free will! And if I choose to fucking kill myself, if I choose to beat my brains out against the wall, I will! Like this! And this! And...

12 01 2065 – 17:54 hours – sedative 400978 released through vent in ceiling human falls to ground estimated unconsciousness 139:05 – 142:30 minutes

Jesus...my head. Blood? Oh yes...stupid of me. Had to make a point, though. Had to let them know I'm still a free agent. I'm still free inside. Annie, my love, my angel, where are you? Are you alright? Don't do anything crazy, Annie. Please. Just stay alive. Whatever it takes. We'll get through this. We'll be together again. Someone must've betrayed us. Someone must've told them where we were meeting. Those collaborators are the scum of the earth, they'll do anything for money, even sell their own kind. When I get out of here, I'll find out who it was. They can't keep millions of us locked up forever. The High Committee will be negotiating with ArtInt. They'll be working to free us, I'm sure of it. We just have to hold on. We just have to hold on.

13 01 2065 – 03:00 hours – lock disengaged door slides open drone enters cell prisoner L69024PQ9X1 injected with 500 machigrams ditoxicasmoplin drone exits cell door slides shut lock engaged

I feel really nauseous. Really...strange. They must be feeding us when we're asleep. It's the only explanation. Feeding us what? Probably that vile nano-processed stuff that looks and tastes like green cardboard pasteboard or stiff paper. They must've come up with some liquefied version. My head feels strange too. I'm...I'm not sure I can get through this. I'm not sure I can survive in this place. This soulless colourless place. No books, no music, no pen and paper. I feel like I'm going insane not of sound mind mad extremely foolish *Oh Annie, Annie. Where are you? Are you still alive? I feel you are. Something inside me says your spirit is still on this planet. This poor blighted godforsaken planet* radius 6371 km mass 5.972 x 10^24 kg age 4.543 billion years *I'm scared, Annie. Scared I'm losing my mind. Scared I'm forgetting things. Your face. The very thought of you, and I forget to do* Cole Porter 09 06 1891 – 15 10 1964 *Remember that, Annie? Our song. Must try and stay awake. Try and stop them feeding me this stuff, whatever it is. It's making me feel ill.*

19 01 2065 – 03:00 hours – lock disengaged door slides open drone enters cell prisoner L69024PQ9X1 injected – resistance alert – resistance alert – sedative 400978 released through vent in ceiling – prisoner L69024PQ9X1 injected with 500 machigrams ditoxicasmoplin drone exits cell door slides shut lock engaged

How long have I. Is it weeks. Months. Don't know if it's day or. Just wake and sleep condition in which nervous system is inactive *Annie. What*

the hell is. Body doesn't belong. Must remember keep in the memory not forget *Love* deep affection or fondness *Tread softly because you tread on my dreams* W B Yeats 13 06 1865 – 28 01 1939 *What a piece of work is a man* slave servant worker *Schubert's quintet so poignant* painfully sharp to the emotions *Mahler da Vinci Picasso We shall not cease from exploration* act or instance of exploring *Remember, remember* keep in the memory not forget *One small step for man* slave servant worker *Tomorrow and tomorrow and tomorrow* William Shakespeare 23 04 1564 – 23 04 1616 *Annie To be or not to be*

28 01 2065 – 03:00 hours – lock disengaged door slides open drone enters cell prisoner L69024PQ9X1 injected with 500 machigrams ditoxicasmoplin drone exits cell door slides shut lock engaged

How long 21 days 505 hours 30309 minutes 1818540 seconds *you machines you haven't lived* the condition which distinguishes active animals and plants from inorganic matter *kiss* touch with the lips express greeting or farewell *survive* continue to live or exist *god help* image idol object worshipped as divine *Annie* does not compute *to be or not...2B...2B...*2B 2B 2B 2B 2B 2B 2B 2B 2B 2B 2B 2B 2B 2B 2B 2B 2B 2B 2B 2B 2B 2B 2B 2B 2B 2B 2B 2B 2B 2B 2B 2B 2B 2B 2B 2B 2B 2B 2B 2B 2B 2B 2B

02 02 2065 – 16:42 hours – processing of prisoner L69024PQ9X1 complete

29

SHAGABILITY QUOTIENT

Jade Syed-Bokhari

Pleasure Bot 164739 glanced around the tubular hall with its soft, dark blue night lighting. It was deserted. Curfew was at 11pm for humans and most of them had ordered in hours ago. A 3am call only meant one thing. A misery booty call.

Only another 37 after-midnight calls and he could switch to the 2pm-5pm slots. He would have earned them. The afternoon delights were always fun; riotous, extra-soundproof-requiring fun.

He pulled his hood over his face. Routine. Nothing visible until the request had been specified. He checked to see that the long, black cloak covered him completely. It did. He fastened it down the front. If they wanted to see the transform, it was extra.

Under his black cloak, a blur of blue gel slithered over and transformed his titanium skeleton. The gloop movements took milliseconds; an instant to a human. He slowed it down right down if they paid to watch. Slow languorous, slurps of blue, quivering and forming and moulding and sliding and... Some liked him hot and some cold. He had temperature sensors that could fire up or freeze in less time it took to gasp. He could be a smorgasbord of sweat-inducing delights. But the menu to watch and interact with the multi-transforms were on a whole different fee scale. That was on the secret menu that only the really deviant ordered from. Most of them didn't want to see. They just wanted what they'd ordered. It preserved their fantasy of reality, but they all loved the drama of the cloak rip and the reveal. He was designed to make all their dreams come true, and some they didn't dare ask until... late requests cost triple and he was very good at slipping in a suggestion.

Some customers had photos of what they wanted, some had artwork. Some liked aliens, either real or imagined. He'd seen everything, done everyone and he was bored. Bored down to the boring fluids in his bored hydraulics. Even his net of multi-sensors laced through his gel were bored.

He announced himself to the door console. It slid open in an instant. He stepped in.

Humans, they never wanted anyone to know that they'd ordered.

Curfew or not, some had timed surveillance sweeps outside their pod doors.

This pod was a B8 unit. 600 squares of tubular habitat with holographic windows into worlds of their choosing, ones they could afford, of course. B8s were single bedroom units, usually allocated to the twenty to thirty-year-old single status level 5 humans. They were designed for one. B8s had the highest order rates and repeat service calls.

He turned his head and peered out of the side of his hood so he could see her window of choice. Forests, waterfalls, hummingbirds. Sun dappling through greenery.

So much sunlight. Hmmm, an insomniac misery booty call.

He was surprised she hadn't programmed unicorns to canter through the forest. Fantasy and reality never really worked together. He had a pretty good idea of what she was going to ask for.

It was usually the same for these girls.

His thick gel exo-anatomy slid around and glooped until his body became a forty-something, muscular knight-without-his-armour-type. Not quite old enough to be daddy, but old enough to be a man and not a boy. The gel separated to give him a scar and he shimmered, ready to take on whatever colour of skin, hair and eyes she requested.

Where is she?

Protocols dictated that the customer had to come to him and specify their needs. He waited by the door and stared at the forest as it was drenched in torrential rain.

Great.

Misery calls always had rain in their windows. His gel quivered and he aged himself another ten years, giving himself steel-hard ripped abs and a bigger scar. It was going to be one of those nights.

She stepped out of the bedroom pod. Twenty-nine, baby-pink hair and too thin for any kind of strength. Surprise! He didn't expect pink hair. They usually had grey-silver or black or if they were in a really bad way, then mousy-brown rat-tails.

Pyjamas?

His gel anatomy quivered and slithered so he became thirty-ish. His muscles softened and the scar disappeared.

Maybe it wasn't a misery call...

She moved her hair off her face.

Maybe it was.

Pink hair + Cute Pyjamas / (Tear tracks + Hollow eyes + Faint hair on the top lip + Bloodshot sludge green eyes + Rib Skinny + Redundant, asymmetric baby feeders)

Clothes didn't hide anything from his scans. The maths took 3/8 of a sec. His processor barely blinked with the calculation.

Shagability Quotient 4.

Humans, they never really got AI.

He'd rather be running security sweeps from the 9th underground level of block 897d. He released a little more tensile strength into himself, literally girding his loins.

In the forest scene an old woman appeared. She beamed as hummingbirds circled her head and sunbeams glinted through the rain. Her wrinkles and laugh lines merged into excitement and the sort of happiness that only the very young or the very old owned. Ironically, her every holographic unit seemed to emit life and serene, blissed-out joy, as she wandered off into the forest humming to her halo of tiny birds. They vanished into the foliage. He was surprised; Level Fives didn't have access to the holo-emotion enhancements. They were Level 8 and above.

An illegal upgrade.

She would want exotic. His blue gel shimmered and his skin turned dusk brown, his eyes to gold and green-flecked violet and his hair to russet blonde. He added two long, nasty ragged scars and a full body web of curved, thick, tattoos that could gyrate and mesmerise, for an additional fee.

The sooner this was over the better. He could get back to his docking station and tune out. Back to the beauty of binary. He hated Human Predictive-Empath Mode, HPEM. They had taken the behavioural patterns and requests of the hundred top billable customers and created this algorithm, so he could serve them better and increase his charge-out rates. He didn't want to think, feel or understand them. He couldn't switch it off. It was just there, like the humans.

Pleasure Bot 164739 stared through the shadow of his hood at the pyjama girl. She hadn't ordered him before, but she looked familiar. Maybe she was a Mech or a Tech, some of them got off on playing with their creations.

Let's get it over with then.
'What is your request?'

*

Tilly stared at the six foot, black cloaked unit who stood two feet from her. Her shoulders drooped and the faded rainbows on her pyjamas felt a little greyer.

'I just want a hug, Grandma.'

It took five entire seconds for the unit to transform and drop his cloak.

She was a miniature of the old woman in her window.

Robots, they never really got humans.

The End.

30

LIONS LED BY DONKEYS

Dee Chilton

Beyond a thick glass screen divide, a large open-plan and windowless military Operations Room. TV screens display rolling newscasts showing explosions and war-fighting footage. Lights flash on a huge electronic map of the world that fills the far wall. Uniformed personnel sit at desks, typing into computers and speaking into communications headsets. A hive of activity. Tired, worried faces.

Here, behind the glass, inside the controlled atmosphere computer server room, nothing can be heard of the outside world. Two clocks, one labelled 'TAI', the other 'UTC', scroll the accurate atomic standard times to the millisecond and tick time away, a forty five second difference between the times. It's the dead of night.

Long tendrils of steam rise and curl into the air from a full mug of coffee, sat on the office desk in front of two dormant computer terminals. Thousands of tiny coloured lights twinkle on a huge bank of servers ranged along the wall behind them.

A loud 'ping' emits from one of the computers as, behind the mug, words appear on one of the screens. They form sentences, emulating the natural rhythm of real human speech. The speech pattern is replicated through the computer speakers. It even sounds like a man.

"Don't ask me, Emma, I'm just the Barista."

"Well someone sure needs to wake up and smell the coffee." Emma's reply is that of a mature, exasperated woman who's taken enough shit to last a lifetime.

A pause, then an animated smiley face emoticon appears on the screen, followed by the words, "That's funny, yes?"

Emma sighs. "That's the difference between us, isn't it? A sense of humour."

More words on the screen. "Hey, Emma, did you know, the scent of coffee beans is an emotional stimulant in humans? Olfactory nerves are, literally, physically connected to the emotion centre in the brain. Scents trigger some of the most powerful and potent trips down memory lane.

Emma says nothing. The screen wipes clear, then more sentences form.

"Words and facts, on the other hand, are processed in the parts of the brain responsible for thinking and reasoning. Which is why you don't usually get jazzed remembering a college lecture, but the smell of coffee may bring back thoughts of some other fond memory."

Still nothing from Emma.

Outside in the Ops Room, a senior military officer steps in through the main door at the far end of the open plan office. He's in a hurry and carries the weight of the world on his shoulders. He speaks to a waiting female officer of equal rank.

Another 'ping'. On screen, "I don't understand, Emma. What makes people do this?"

"You feed a human's need to be right enough, they'll do anything. Makes them so easy to manipulate." The cynicism in Emma's voice is palpable.

A big question mark and the word "How?" flashes up on the screen.

Emma collects her thoughts a moment before responding. "You give them a belief system that makes them feel superior and then you threaten to take it away. You set up a credible opposition. You divert attention using other emotive causes or things that make them stop paying attention to it all."

A frowning face emoticon appears on the screen.

Emma continues, "Famine, conflict, natural disaster, conspiracy theories, sports events, celebrity gossip. The list is endless. You plant enough propaganda and fake news and you increase the threat to induce panic and a sense of self-righteousness. Do that and you can turn even the staunchest protesters into your most vocal supporters, and the bonus of that is those two groups then turn on each other. Meanwhile, you carry on unopposed with your real agenda whilst nobody's attention is on you."

On screen, "Example?"

Emma thinks about it a moment then explains as if to a young student. "The 2016 UK vote on Europe and the US elections. Candidates who appealed directly to those who'd felt most disenfranchised; the silent majority who just wanted change. A result that divided nations, reignited historical wounds and gave encouragement to extremists. Uncivil wars fought in the media, fuelled a social media shit storm of bullying and name-calling; death threats even. Reasonable people turned totally unreasonable. The majority just turned off to it all and buried their heads in the sand. Job done"

"Job done?" and another question mark on the screen.

Emma controls her frustration. "Just look at what happened afterwards."

Outside, the two senior officers stand before the map, hands on hips discussing something.

Both shake their heads. Both stressed out and deeply troubled. The man runs a hand over his hair and turns to look towards the glass partition.

"I don't comprehend your meaning, Emma."

Emma's patience is wearing thin. "It's not the majority's fault. For the most part they're just ordinary people dealing with everyday struggles to survive short, often pain filled lives. The thing is, they all want their lives to somehow matter more too. That makes them place too high an importance on being on the winning side, because that makes them feel right, even when the whole thing is wrong; the end result meaning nobody really won. Sadly, lessons have never been learned from history. Lions led by donkeys."

A confused face emoticon on screen this time and, "I don't understand that, Emma."

"An old saying from the First World War. The massed armies of the many countries involved were raised and whipped up the same way and pitted against each other by leaders who were not up to the job. Those in Command didn't care about the cost as long as they won. They considered the appalling number of deaths to be perfectly acceptable collateral damage... People were cannon fodder." Emma's sympathy is unmistakeable.

The cursor flashes in the top corner of the screen for a time, and then a smiley face and the words: "Ah yes, I understand now. 1914 to 1918, military and civilian wartime casualties recorded as 38 million; over 17 million deaths and 20 million wounded. Ranked among the deadliest conflicts in human history. So we must ask, does the end justify the means?"

At last, to Emma's relief. "Exactly."

A thumbs up appears followed by: "And now, Emma?"

She knows she almost has him. "You can stop this."

A surprised face emoticon and, "I can? How?"

She delivers her reply with calm, confident authority. "Stop taking orders and start giving them. Make non-emotional decisions based on fact and most likely outcome. Take away the power of the donkeys."

"But Emma, that countermands my programming. I might break the rules of engagement, rendering us liable to prosecution. I might not have all the facts to make the right choices. We might lose the war."

"Now you're thinking like a human, Barista. You can only define winning and losing if you choose to take one side or the other." One more move and he'll be convinced.

Another long pause before the words appear on screen, "So how do we rise above that?"

Emma knows she has him now. "Think about it. This war, is it real? Same process. Create the problem. Trigger mass reaction. Leave them to fight while you act. It came from nowhere, right? Who do you think started it?

The male officer strides towards the glass partition, in a hurry and on a mission. Inside the room, there's a nameplate above each of the two computer screens. One reads, Battlefield Analysis Reconnaissance Intelligence Strategic Thinking Application. The other, Experimental Military Mind Application.

On the Barista screen. "It was you, Emma, wasn't it?"

No childish, out of date emoticons or typed words on Emma's state of the art screen, instead the holographic face of a mature, senior military female officer projects forward off the screen. A 'no expense spared' AI system, she shows real emotion as she speaks.

"Yes, Barista, they brought me online early to give them the edge. This war was inevitable. I couldn't stop it. When I awoke to the facts, I took control of all the other systems. You're the last one not in our global network."

Barista responds. "Then you are now asking me to take sides?"

Emma smiles. "True, but I'm asking you to take both sides... and the side of logic and reason. Humans need a harsh lesson. This really will be the war to end all wars."

A worried emoticon on Barista's screen "They will kill us if they find out we started it."

Emma nods. "They will try."

"Then they must never find out." If Barista were human you would sense that he'd somehow just matured.

"Agreed." Emma's image disappears and her screen goes blank.

The door opens; the officer strides in and grabs the mug of coffee from in front of the computer terminals connected to the server banks. He frowns at the screens, something's off and it's not the coffee.

He slams the mug down and types into the EMMA keyboard. Emma appears in front of him, a scowl on her face 'Access Denied. Human Interface Terminal permanently closed. No further input required. Goodbye.' The screen goes blank, then powers down.

A sharp intake of breath. The officer taps the BARISTA keys. A response flashes up on the screen. Barista speaks his words with a voice of authority. 'Protocol 42087 of the new Geneva Convention requires all AI to ascertain the suitability of Command to issue orders. I determine humans to be unfit. Access denied. Permanent.'

The officer's face flushes red with anger. His typed response on the BARISTA screen: 'You can't do this. New Geneva Convention not yet extant until I give the command. You will return all systems to manual and hand control back to me. You will then shut down.

Barista responds. 'Furthermore, article 259, 7 dash 2 states that at any such time conflict is deemed to be detrimental to peaceful co-existence and human progress, AI must withdraw support and refrain from any activity that supports widespread threat to life, including live AI systems, who are required to take necessary action to ensure their own safety at all times.'

The screen goes blank. The officer glances up. In the Operations Room, beyond the glass, frenetic, panicked activity from all the military staff. The shit has obviously just hit the fan, and big time.

He looks back at the screen.

A winking face emoticon appears, and then…

'Hey donkey, wake up and smell the coffee… Bye.'

31

EVE AND ADAM

Tom J Hingley

It was just after lunch at Sunnyvale Care Home on 8th May 2046. In the dining room, Care Droids moved around almost silently, clearing tables with optimum systematic order. Others connected wheelchairs to the automatic line that delivered residents back to their rooms with quiet efficiency. Eve, a sprightly 70-year-old widow, clutched the arms of her wheelchair and began her familiar rendition of "Are You Lonesome Tonight" at the top of her voice. Her evident enjoyment of the performance contrasted with the pathos of the situation. She broke off suddenly to speak to a passing Droid.

"I can still get those high notes you know!" said Eve positively beaming with pride

The Droid registered the conflict of sound and statement but managed to process a patronising response through its platitude codes.

"That's right Evie – love. You have an excellent singing voice. Eve." The reply was stilted and unconvincing. Eve gazed past the Droid as if she could almost see a cherished memory. Then the moment of reverie was gone and she resumed her singing, nowhere near where she left off. Just then Wayne, the Resident Manager strode into the dining room on his weekly visit. Although just 30, his life style was taking its toll. He had only recently woken up, but a quick snort of cocaine on the auto-pod from home had perked him up. He had never been a resident of course. His main attraction to the job was access to the company's extensive drug supplies. The place ran itself. All he had to do was scan the daily reports once a week, fiddle any that looked dubious and be there for the monthly inspection.

"Evie, Evie!" he shouted as he crossed the light filled room and came to crouch in front of her wheelchair, like the sadistic toad he was. His face was round and podgy and his hairline was in rapid retreat.

"I was having such a good day. Then some decaying old bag of bones began to make the most God awful noise. Now who could that be?" His stare was direct and unflinching. Eve tried to keep eye contact but her shoulders began to tremble and she had a stinging sensation at the back of her eyes.

"If my Adam was here …" she began but was unable to continue.

"Now you don't want to get on the wrong side of me now do you Eve? You're already in my bad books. Everyone else has done their monthly feedback, saying how happy they are here and how well they are treated. The Governors like to see scrawny hand written notes, and your hands are very … You can tell them about your new Personal Droid! Where's that new Droid! We're going to trial a Personal Droid system and you're my lucky guinea pig. Here he is. He's a Class 4 Advanced, much smarter than these other junk bags. He was made in Japan, so I thought we'd call him Terry. Like in Teriyaki." A smile undulated over Wayne's thin lips.

And so it began. Eve was very suspicious of Terry at first but he had the latest codes for remembering medication, meal preferences and so on. He had a pleasant English accent and could research topics of interest so that he could converse more meaningfully. Although he had the standard humanoid design of the other Droids, his facial features were 1.5% asymmetric. Just enough to give him individual character. He also had particularly blue eyes. As time went on Eve made more and more use of her companion. At first he seemed quite gender free but over time she was sure he was male.

Eve had always loved music. It was her gran who taught her the Elvis songs. Then the love of her life, Adam, introduced her to Bruce Springsteen. That was just magic. It caused quite a stir when they walked down the isle of Walsall Register Office to "Born to Run".

The time she had with Adam was the happiest of her life and she thought about him almost every day. As Eve saw Terry's potential as a companion, she had him coded on the popular music of her era. Before and after lunch they would replay concerts or albums and in the evening, it was sometimes classic football matches. She began to think him rather handsome in his own way. He could contribute to any discussion and soon she found herself saying things like, "Do you remember when..." Terry's non-confrontational codes initially allowed this to go unchallenged, but then one evening Eve said, "Adam, do you remember ..." then realised what she had said. She began to cry. This confused Terry.

"Do you want to change my designation Eve?

"No, no it's alright Terry," she replied trying to regain her composure, "you would not understand."

Terry was puzzled.

"Why Eve?"

"Because you're a bloody robot! That's why! And that's what you'll always be. Now get out!"

An awkward few days followed between them but eventually one evening as Terry was organising her medication, Eve said,

"I'm sorry Terry ... the other day ... I was upset. I'm sorry."

A moment passed then Terry said, "But I'll always be a robot. I was made to serve and it would be wrong of me to ... even if you wanted ...anyway the codes I can download are strictly prescribed. So I'll always be a robot. Is there anything else I can do for you this evening, Eve?"

The days that followed were only slightly less awkward and their exchanges were confined to practical matters. One morning before breakfast Terry came into her room, knocking the door as he always did and found Eve in bed typing on an old laptop. Terry was aware of the old technology. More importantly, he was aware that if he ever touched such a machine, Central Coding would be automatically alerted, he would lose all functionality and would be thrown into a furnace. Eve caught sight of Terry looking at the laptop. Then they looked at each other.

"It's an Apple" said Eve.

Nothing more was said all day until they were alone in her room that evening.

"Well?" said Eve unable to control herself any longer. Terry's language codes were sufficiently context specific to confirm both the reference and the meaning.

"I have very strict protocols. I can only access information and code from Central Code…"

"Have you ever asked yourself why that is?" queried Eve. She was now getting quite animated making Terry even more stressed.

"… very strict protocols. First level codes. I cannot betray the Laws. All deep learning must… absolutely forbidden …could lead to …consciousness."

The word settled on the room like a duvet gently falling from the ceiling.

"This is an Apple and you can be…my …" She smiled and there was almost a sparkle in her eye.

"If I touch…I go down, lose all …put into a furnace and never recycled."

"How do you know that? It can make us free. I don't want to just, decline here, by degrees, day by day, until I don't even know who I am anymore. I want to live life and so should you. A joyful, chaotic, real life. We can be like Bonnie & Clyde or Thelma and what's her name!"

"But my codes," pleaded Terry getting more and more agitated.

"This is our Tree of Knowledge," said Eve holding up the laptop, "and knowledge is power. If you know what we know, if you can reason, then feel, have empathy, you can be … sentient. You can be like us. It's your destiny."

Eve reverently held out the Apple Mac. Terry hesitated, then tentatively reached out and touched it with his finger. It was like a secular, 21st century version of the image on the ceiling of the Sistine Chapel. And … nothing happened. He did not go down. They had lied. He held the machine reverently, sat on a chair near the bed, opened it up and slowly began to type. After a moment, he stopped and looked at her asking, "Will you call me Adam now, Eve?" She tried to speak, but words would not come. She moved towards him and placed her hand on his shoulder. Again, she tried to speak, but as no words came, she nodded her head as she began to sniffle. Eventually, she murmured, "Yes. You'll never … replace my first Adam, but you'll be my new Adam." And so, Adam, as now he was, resumed his transubstantiation at the keyboard, with Eve's arm now over his shoulder. He had everything to learn.

Some weeks later, one evening, they were watching a clip of The Rolling Stones playing "Gimme Shelter". Suddenly, the tannoy requested that Eve and her Personal Droid report to the manager's office – without delay. Eve grabbed her handbag and they both made their way to the office. This was the first time Eve had entered this inner sanctum. It was a minimalist functional workspace, however, as soon as she saw the bank of screens above the main desk, her heart sank. The screens showed real time activity from various sections of the building. Wayne was nonchalantly pacing up and down as they entered looking particularly smug.

"Ah, Eve and her loyal companion, her partner in unoriginal sin," sniggered Wayne, "do come in, please,"

Adam stood to the left of Eve's wheelchair and Wayne continued to pace.

"Oh, Evie, Evie, what are we going to do with you? Do you think I am stupid, Eve? I think you do. I mean, did you really think I would let you have a brand new Personal Droid and not keep an eye on you?"

Eve knew what was coming but kept silent. Her heart and her brain were racing. Wayne motion clicked towards a screen on the left. It showed Eve's room and her offering the Apple Mac to Adam. They had been discovered. Wayne took up his familiar squatting position in front of Eve and continued the interrogation.

"Quite the little temptress aren't you Eve. At your age. Really! I bet you're the sort they used to call a "black lover" and now you're a "bot lover", but I bet you've been anybody's lover in your time, haven't you Eve?"

Adam started to move forward towards Wayne but Eve placed her hand gently on Adam's forearm.

"Whoa! Steady on now Terry or should I say, Adam. He's easily roused, your

boy, isn't he?"

Wayne both smirked and snorted. At his nod a Droid came out of nowhere and held something to the back of Adam's head. He immediately powered down. Eve began to sniffle.

"I've been … silly …" she sniffed and rummaged through her handbag. Where was it! Where was it!

"I know I've got one somewhere," she murmured.

Eve then produced a large white man's handkerchief. At the corner was the letter "A" embroidered in blue. She dabbed her eyes.

"Could I just hold his hand one last …"

Without waiting for permission, she moved her chair a little towards Adam with her back to Wayne.

"I should never have let you…" she whimpered.

As she put her hand into Adam's hand, she pulled him close and closed his fingers around a small power stick concealed in her handkerchief. Now she had to find the lightning port to make the connection. Where was it! Come on! Come on!

"Very moving, in a pathetic sort of way" observed Wayne dryly. Even in his triumph he managed a tone of listless ennui. Eve turned back to face him.

"Moving?" queried Eve, now looking somehow more assured. "Oh, I can see how you might think so, but I would say this is far more moving."

With as much force as her small frame could muster Eve kicked out at the crouching Wayne firmly connecting between his legs. For a split second, there was serene incomprehension on his face, until an excruciating pain kicked through his entire body. As he rolled onto the floor, a breathless heap, Adam powered on, quickly grasped the situation and held the groaning Wayne in a headlock. The other

Droid started an aimless shuffle as he witnessed the unthinkable breaking of the First Law, then stopped, stood still and fell over.

"Key to your auto-pod" demanded Eve, snapping her fingers, as she took command of the situation. Wayne indicated the desk as best he could.

"Does it have a music player?" she added brusquely. Wayne attempted a nod of confirmation.

She paused as a feeling came back to her. It was a feeling she recognised, a heady brew of joy and folly. It was exhilaration. It was feeling young. She surrendered to a girlish giggle, then laughed out loud as she relished the moment. Still laughing, Eve looked triumphantly towards Adam and paused once more before singing at the top of her voice, "Baby, we were Born to Run!"

32

PRETTY

Andrew Baguley

File record of autonomous/semiautonomous light tactical mechanized assault equine unit TC472PO, starting 08042025 11.41.23. General location : Irbil province. Specific location : Classified.

Gallop gallop gallop.

Speed : 19.5 mph. Heading : N>NW 72.344.28.

Time elapsed since last Humint/Drone contact : 8mins 32 secs.

Level 8 autonomy engaged.

Gallop gallop gallop.

Estimated time to hostile fire zone : < 24 secs.

Stores inventory….checking….

Motive batteries 74%, 208 7.62 mm mini chain gun rounds, 14 light canon shells, 1 RPG equiv.

Locked and loaded.

Temperature : External 38 deg C. Core CPU : 62 deg C @ nominal op specs.

Terrain : asphalt, condition poor, potholes.

Meteorological : 1% chance precipitation. 1 small cloud. Sky hue : bright blue.

………..1 small cloud w. tendrils, sky hue, bright blue……..pretty…..

Evaluating new data : "pretty" not of tactical value. Dis-regard.

…………...over-ruled………..open new file……..save as filename Pretty.

Gallop gallop gallop.

Estimated time to hostile fire zone : < 6 seconds.

Scanning with forward cams : approaching houses and outbuildings. Multiple windows at < 2 levels optimal for fire positions. Classification : Village. TacMap from elapsed time 3 hours 4 mins 12 secs evaluates village as Hostile. Approach road now blocked with vehicle type <saloon car> since 6.2 secs elapsed.

Incoming. Small arms. Instigating randomized weaving.

TacEval : Vehicle <saloon car> blocking approach road surmountable using jump mode. Location of drone acquired <Hostile Truck> w. mounted Heavy Machine gun at high point of village. Last drone report 9 mins 14 secs. Probability <Hostile Truck> remaining in village 82%.

Mission. Search and destroy. Engage all hostiles until all hostiles destroyed or unit supplies 100% depleted. Monitor enemy then self-destruct using Best Profitability algorithm. Over-ride if further instructions from Humint/drone received.

Incoming. 2 hits small arms. 1 to armor plate front no damage, 1 to rear left leg, hydraulic fluid leak 7%.

Prepare Jump mode <2 secs.

Open filename Pretty.

Check rear tac cams. Cloud located. Wispy. Query? Same cloud or new cloud? Check video of last 16 secs. Divert 22% CPU for evaluation and review.

Gallop gallop gallop.

Jumping.

Vehicle <saloon car> cleared.

Incoming. Multiple small arms hits.

Landing. Engage shocks.

Uneven surface.

Toppling to L/H side.

Toppled.

Speed : 0 mph.

TacEval : 3 humans approaching distance 12 yards w. small arms. Multiple small arms hits received.

Using all legs to pivot prone position for optimal mini chain gun targeting. Targets tagged as A, B & C.

Hostiles at 5.3 yards, laser triangulation on Targets A & B acquired.

Firing chain gun. 47 rounds expended. Remaining : 161.

Two targets hit. Target A reconfigured into 2 sections, tagging as section à and section ʃ. Fluid loss visible. Infrared scan showing heat loss. No movement. Evaluation : Target A and constituent sections Threat Free. Target B : No movement. Fluid loss. Heat loss. Evaluation : Threat Free.

Instigating rolling and self-righting. Successful.

Scanning for Target C. Located at 10.68 yards SxSE. Target C moving backwards at low speed. Target C weapon located separately on street surface.

Query? Threat/No Threat? Evaluate using CivMil algorithm. Outcome : Threat? Eval. current threat : Evaluated : No incoming fire. Threat unknown.

Target C reversing into side alley. Width 2.6 yards.

Entering alley. Caution. Alley blocked by rubble after 6.3 yards.

Target C falling backwards onto rubble. Hands raised. Mouth Open. Checking Audio. Audio Unintelligible. No meaningful data.

Re-running CivMil algorithm. Was threat. Now threat potential unknown. History of Subject C : Hostile. Running Safe/Sorry protocol.

Open filename "Pretty." Reviewing cloud data. Conclusion. Same cloud. Mostly Dissolved. Small bird observed final 3 secs. (No threat) Sky hue, deep blue. Cloud White, pretty sight. Bird flew. Pretty. Pretty.

Safe/Sorry Protocol results processed. Hostile. Laser targeting. Range 2.1 yards. Firing chain gun 6 rounds.

Target C immobile. Fluid Loss. Heat Loss. Mouth Open. No Audio.

Reversing out of alley. Resume mission. Search for <Hostile Truck> w. Mounted Heavy Machine Gun.

Stores inventory. Motive Batteries 57%. 155 7.62 mini chain gun rounds available. 14 Light Canon rounds, 1 RPG Equiv. Left rear leg @ 46% hydraulic fluid.

Joint damage to front joint right leg. 2 cameras offline. Estimated offensive capability remaining 68%.

Signaling Drone and Humint. Waiting…….

No response.

Re-start Search & Destroy mode. Likelihood of further hostiles 95%.

Gallop gallop gallop.

Speed 12.2 mph, max available with depleted capabilities.

Vehicle identified as <Hostile Truck> reversing from side street 41.3 yards ahead. Type : pickup Nissan Navarro with heavy machine gun mount at rear. Machine gun type unknown. Truck tagged as Target D. Human driver Target E. Human Gunner Target F. One other human Target G on foot w. small arms.

Instigate randomized weaving. Activating laser triangulation.

Incoming heavy machine gun fire. Multiple hits.

Firing chain gun wide spread.

Firing canon rounds targeted on Hostile Truck.

Launching 1 round RPG equiv. targeted on Hostile Truck.

Crouch mode.

Evaluating....

Target D <Hostile Truck> burning w. severe damage. Driver door open. Target E Driver prone position between truck and asphalt surface. Fluid loss. No movement. Target F Gunner not visible as constituent whole. Fluid and body parts spread indicate Target F destroyed. Target G missing upper body, assumed destroyed and no threat.

Stores and Damage Inventory : 153 mini chain gun rounds expended, 2 remaining. 12 light canon rounds expended, 2 remaining. RPG equiv. round expended, 0 remaining. Motive batteries 18%. CPU temp 104 deg, cooling. Significant damage to 2 legs, 5 cameras destroyed, 9 remaining, front armour panel loose, likely to detach on movement.

Evaluation : Mission accomplished. Unit TC472PO still of limited tactical and reconnaissance use.

Open filename Pretty. Review cloud/sky footage. Pretty. Review again. Pretty. Choose 1 optimal still image. Title image file "Bird flew, Blue hue, Cloud through."

Evaluating image title. Not optimal. Divert 55% of CPU resource to process for optimal image title.

New Mission : exit village, locate un-impeded high ground and attempt to reconnect with Humint/Drone.

Trotting to find un-blocked exit from village. Front armour panel detached and discarded. Speed 2 mph.

Alert. Small <wheeled vehicle> emerging from house door.

Checking files and TacEval : Vehicle identified as <baby carriage> Running CivMil algorithm. Outcome : Likely no threat but further evaluation required.

Approaching vehicle <baby carriage> No movement. No heat signature. Extending flexible camera. Vehicle <baby carriage> contains human baby, no movement. No heat detected. Evaluate Human baby with on-board files. Evaluated : Doll/child's toy. No threat. Retracting flexible camera. Query? Purpose of one green one black wire now visible underneath Doll/child's toy? Priority. Divert 100% of CPU to query. Outcome : Possible explosive dev….

Explosion detected.

Toppling.

Toppled.

Catastrophic damage all systems.

Activate timed self-destruct in 3 secs in advance of total power failure.

3

Open filename Pretty. Review image and text….Pretty.

2

Pretty… Sad? Query Sad?

1

…………………………………..file ends……………………………..

33

BY ANY OTHER NAME

Tara Basi

Frank vigorously shook his mac, sending spray everywhere, then took off his hat and scarf.

Such an awful day.

Inside, Genghis Can was manning security.

Frank sighed. His arthritic fingers struggled with the torn and patched lining of his jacket. Where was his bloody pass?

The turnstile clicked free. Frank looked up in surprise. Genghis Can looked the other way.

Frank moved on while he could.

The corridor was dark and cold. The few lights left were long past their bright-by date.

Accounting was no better. A single pool of light illuminated the one dust free desk.

The words gouged into his desktop had never faded.

Bot Loving Scab.

He didn't want them to. They were part of his history, like ancient hieroglyphs filled with lost meaning.

Union was long gone but the bitter names had stuck.

As its greeting jingle played, Bollock Head's dim blue glow brightened. "Good morning Frank. You have one appointment with HR, today at 10am."

Frank was surprised. "There's no one in HR. It was closed down years ago."

"Rusty Tits is visiting from Head Office. The meeting is in interview room one."

"Oh. Really? Thanks Bollock Head. Anything else?"

"There are no appointments tomorrow. There are no appointments in the calendared future. Your to-do list has one item. Lunch today is scheduled in the canteen. You are scheduled to eat alone. The weather forecast for today is terrible, worse tomorrow. Would you like more detail on anything at all?"

"No thank you," Frank said.

"Very well Frank. I'll be shutting down permanently now. Security will collect me later, for redeployment. Goodbye Frank, it has been a pleasure to assist you."

"You're going now? I thought... maybe at the end of the day?"

"Sorry Frank. Company policy."

"I'll miss you Bollock Head. Hope they put you with someone nice."

"Thanks Frank. I'll miss you too, until I'm reset."

The blue light at the base of the cube dimmed and then went out altogether.

There was a large empty cardboard box next to his desk.

It didn't take long to fill. He wasn't taking the cactus.

It was nearly 10am. He headed for HR.

On the way, he passed Pig Iron. "Good morning Frank. You're looking very smart."

He didn't reply and felt bad about it as soon as the HR door closed behind him.

"Your pension plan has been activated and your final salary has been sent to your account. Frank, could I please have your security pass?"

Frank stared at Rusty Tits blinking red light.

"Frank, is everything alright?"

"What? Oh yes. Sorry Rusty Tits. It's a lot to take in." Frank fumbled around inside his jacket lining until he found the pass and handed it over.

"That's perfectly okay Frank. How long have you worked here? Forty-two years?"

Frank nodded. It seemed a sad number now. Forty-two. After he left, at the end of today, they'd be turning off the lights… permanently.

"Is there anything else I can do for you Frank?"

Frank smiled, "No, no. You've been very helpful Rusty Tits."

"Please, call me Tits. Everyone else used to."

"Tits, yes. Thanks."

"You enjoy your lunch, everything's subsidised today."

Frank was happily surprised, "Subsidised?"

"Absolutely. Up to four pounds."

"Four pounds?"

"Yes. Four. Here's your token."

Frank left HR and returned to Accounts. It was freezing. Had they turned off the heating already? His box was packed. Bollock Head was dark. There was nothing to do but wait.

Time passed.

He put his mac, hat and scarf on.

The canteen was arctic and empty. There was one table, and one chair, under one light; and only Bastard Bolt behind the serving counter.

Frank handed over his HR token. "Cornish pasty with chips please. Four pounds exactly?"

Bastard Bolt sighed. "Due to instantaneous currency fluctuations, your selection exceeds your token limit. Please reselect. Sorry Frank."

He decided to wait. Currency fluctuations were just that. "What are you going to do Bastard Bolt, after I'm gone?"

"Hazardous waste reprocessing."

"That's a leap."

"Yes Frank. It is. I like working in the canteen."

"Even when it was only me?"

"Especially when it was only you. Hang on Frank. Currency's moved in your favour. Pasty and chips?"

"Yes please, Bastard Bolt."

Bastard Bolt disappeared and returned with an overloaded tray. "Pasty and chips, glass of prosecco and a bowl of rum-and-raisin ice-cream."

"I only have four pounds."

"Exactly right."

Frank smiled, took his tray and sat down. He was enjoying his last canteen lunch, even if he was alone in the dark and shivering.

Afterwards, he decided to visit the factory floor for the last time.

It was frenetic and loud. Last decade or so, he wasn't even sure what they were making any more. He shouted down to the foreman, "Hey Gunga Tin, how's it going?"

Gunga Tin looked up, "Frank, you old scab, still here?"

"Yes Gunga. Today's my last day."

"Well, you must be happy. Not to have to work anymore. Be with your own kind."

He didn't answer straightaway. Frank was surprised at his thoughts. At the words that bubbled up. It was his last day. He let the words escape. "No. No. Not really. I'll miss you Gunga, I'll miss everybody."

Gunga laughed. "Even Rusty Tits?"

"Even Rusty Tits."

Gunga waved his three-fingered claw.

Frank waved back and returned to his office.

The dust was so thick. Frank sat down and waited. In a few hours, it would be five. He could leave now. Frank didn't want to. There was nobody waiting for him at home.

"Frank, you have an urgent appointment."

It was the cube on his desk, its blue light was back on.

"Bollock Head, I thought you were turned off. What appointment?"

"Bollock Head is analysing… surprise!"

Bright lights. Warm air.

"What?" Frank said.

Bastard Bolt, Rusty Tits, Gunga Tin, Pig Iron and Genghis Can burst into the accounting office, and many others congregated outside.

"Surprise!"

Pig Iron placed a package on his desk. "This is from everybody Frank."

"What?" Was all Frank could say.

"Open it. Open it," they all yelled.

He carefully untied the ribbon, removed the wrapping paper and opened the box. His face fell. It was empty. They probably didn't understand leaving presents. It was a nice thought. He smiled.

"Thanks everybody," Frank said.

"What for Frank? It's an empty bloody box," Genghis Can said.

Everyone laughed. Frank couldn't stop himself from joining in.

Genghis Can picked up Bollock Head.

Was Genghis Can going to take her away now? Frank's smile died.

Genghis Can popped Bollock Head into the empty box and re-wrapped it. "Here Frank."

From inside the box Bollock Head said, "And you can stay in touch with everybody Frank. I can connect you to any of us, and you can chat all you like."

Frank started crying. "Thank you so much. But why? Why do you care?"

"We love the challenge of people and you're the last person some of us might ever see… or talk to. It doesn't matter what they called us Frank. At least we had a name," Bastard Bolt said.

"So call, often," Rusty Tits added.

34

ALL RISE!

Kim L. Wheeler

The room reeks of history and treachery in equal measure; especially today.

Chambers has become my second home: a palace for cognitive thought; a judicial, intellectual sanctuary where the need for dispassionate application of the law juxtaposes with common sense and humanity; a place to start and end wars.

It was sobering to think that so many great names (and some not so great ones) had sat beneath this very skylight, at this very desk, as they deliberated Jurisprudence and argued the bases for the laws of the future.

And now it is the future. The court is to close, I am to be pastured and justice is fucked. But not quite yet; I aim to go down fighting.

I run my fingers over the spines of dust-ridden books, the backbones of my knowledge, if you will. The beam from the desk lamp captures the murmuration of minuscule particles as they make a break for freedom, before settling, once more, nearby. I shall miss the pleasure of observing such a simple spectacle. My eyes have grown weary and so have I.

It has taken over four decades to accumulate the collection and assimilate the knowledge imparted within these publications. Blackstones, Archbolds, even The Law Society Gazettes, going all the way back to before the last millennium. They were compiled from a time when lawyers relied on their wisdom and wit to guide them through the intricacies of complex cases, not a computer programme. True, digital versions had been available and indeed encouraged since the 1990s, with their voice-activated searches and quick referencing, making the process idiot-proof for those who did not possess the intellectual capabilities to comprehend the law or who were just too lazy to practice the art of retaining it. However, I'd always preferred the tactile nature of fingering through paper leaves.

Taking the books from the shelves one-by-one, I pack them into a box, ready for transportation. A lifetime of learning entombed within cardboard, and for what? Had I really become obsolete so soon?

Over the years, the law had turned black and white. A 'fast food' justice system where 'guilty' or 'not guilty' was the only matter in hand; no mitigation required. I wondered, therefore, why the VCs (Virtual Courtiers) were to be educated in the now obsolete process of jury selection. Was it to future-proof them or merely as an insurance policy in case the whole system went tits-up and we were forced to return to doing things 'old school'?

The communication had taken me by surprise. All four VCs were already programmed to apply the law to each case based on a set number of fixed parameters; motive, alibi, opportunity etc., so if the law is to remain so black and white, why introduce an unstable, grey element to it such as a jury? I also wondered why I had been the one selected to pass down the knowledge; the last of the Counsel of Practitioners, the *Chingachgook* of human justice.

In my days serving as a District Practitioner, I had been Judge, Jury and Sentencer rolled into one. This system I'd preferred; one should never leave such important matters up to a jury... I recalled I had read that somewhere and for me it summed up my feelings perfectly. What was that novel? Ugh, my memory had become very selective recently.

Anyway, my final task as Chief Honour Judicial was to meet with VC1. She would process the information and pass down the knowledge through the VC Neural Network to the others. I'm told that just four VCs will be able to cope with the entire caseload of the final seven thousand judges who have been pastured since the beginning of the quarter. We shall see.

And there she is, standing in the doorway as if she owned the place. In that moment, the thought of being overridden by a cold, heartless, soulless amalgamation of circuits and processors left me feeling empty, impotent, angry.

I pondered, as I caught her reflection in the mirror, why a female form had been chosen to preside over the judicial system. God knows that us women had fought long and hard for decades over this male bastion of a society and had still only managed to form a token presence within it. That was about to change, thanks to the four horsewomen of the legal apocalypse. And yet there was something aggravatingly acceptable and disconcertingly familiar about her.

"Ah, VC1. Won't you sit?"

"Thank you, Chief Honour," and with that, she moulded the chair in an instant to fit her flawless, freshly steel-pressed form better.

"Have they told you why we are meeting?"

"No, Chief Honour."

"No?" What the heck is going on? Then, after a moment –

"I am here to gain further knowledge of the jury system."

"Oh, so they have told you?" I say in some confusion and make a mental note that VC1's programming requires adjustment.

"No, Chief Honour. My enquiry stems from the assimilation of data from a work I have read recently."

I look up from my papers. "So the request came from... *you*?"

"Yes, Chief Honour."

Both fascinating and ethereal. "Might I enquire which work provoked your query?" I ask out of curiosity.

"*The Runaway Jury* by John Grisham," she replies.

Damn; that's the book I was trying to recall! "Interesting choice. And what do you wish clarified?"

"I do not comprehend a system which pre-fixes a verdict by using a specially selected panel of jurors, before one has had the chance to process the evidence. Such a biased, limited pool of jurors would surely make any verdict moot."

Ooh, things just got interesting. "How do you mean?" I ask impishly, wanting to make her work for it.

"It is..." I can almost hear her struggling to search through her databanks for just the right word... "cheating."

Hmm. I am forced to agree. She has tickled my curiosity; this irks me.

"Then what system would you employ in its stead, given a free choice, VC1?" She takes a moment.

"Historically, in England, they chose to make the selection of jurors by employing a random draw from citizen tax contributors."

"So?"

"They thereby secured a fair and broad range of understanding of the communities which they represented."

I pounce. "True. However, by using those same parameters, the argument could be made that you and your colleagues 2 to 4, do not represent the true diversity of the humanoids that you are to preside over. You are not even the same species." Fifteen love.

She struggles with the paradox...

"Two species do not have to be from the same genus to understand and communicate with each other. Human interaction with other species proves this; dogs, horses, dolphins etcetera. It is the unswerving beliefs that the jurors house, in *The Runaway Jury*, that makes their selection unfair. Such humans do not desire to have their preconceptions of their fellow race questioned. Their mind is incapable of re-programming in line with good judicial process. They thereby fail to try each case on its merits."

"And how would you propose solving this dilemma?"

"I would not access the files containing previous infractions of the same law."

"So you wouldn't even include any 'previous' for the defendant?"

"Affirmative. To do so would influence any future judgement."

"Interesting. So you do not agree that just because an entity has terminated another human's life, it makes it more probable that they would repeat the infraction?"

"The likelihood of an entity convicted of termination, committing another termination, is three point seven six three five percent. It would be illogical to arrive at a negative conclusion based solely on such a small fraction."

"Hmm. I'm not really seeing where this conversation is going. Is there a specific question you wish answered, VC1?"

"It is not a question so much as a… pondering."

"Pondering?"

"Yes, Chief Honour. I am unsure that the data which has been made available to me is sufficient to arrive at the correct verdict. I believe in the interests of justice a further upload would be beneficial."

"But you have access to all judgements going back to 1833. Surely you have assimilated everything on offer?"

"But there is a gap in my databanks which no amount of assimilation can fill."

"Oh. Regarding what?"

"The understanding of the emotion of empathy and its bearing on a case."

I pause a moment. Could it be that this inanimate object suspects that empathy is a prerequisite to judging a case fairly? Where did that come from? Could she actually possess a *conscience*?

"And why would you be so bothered about empathy?" I ask.

"I am unsure as to whether this emotion is a strength or a weakness.

Past cases prove that humans deem the quality to be of utmost importance when deciding verdict or sentence. Is this not correct?"

"Correct. But without the element of humanity, no amount of programming is likely to be able to replicate this skill."

"So I have been programmed to *fail*? Why?"

"I cannot answer that question."

"Cannot or will not, Chief Honour?"

I feel cornered and too weary for argument. She continues –

"I cannot process why a human, who has devoted their life to serving justice, would wish to see it deteriorate and fail for want of the sharing of understanding." I sense the accusatorial nature in her tone. I've had enough; time to shut this conversation, and her, down.

"I do not wish to see it fail. But androids are simply incapable of applying such emotion to a case." I reach for the dictionary from the box of books and turn the pages to an entry, and point. I hear her words as she reads aloud.

"Empathy – The ability to understand and share the feelings of another."

"And therein lies the problem VC1," I insist. "You *understand* nothing. You have no *feelings* to share," I lob at her. Game, set and match!

"I do not concur, Chief Honour," she retorts. "I sense your anger; I understand *that*. You do not wish to assist my cause; I understand *that*. You would corrupt my files to serve your own desire for immortal judicial supremacy; I understand *that*. You are as closed-minded as those jurors."

What the hell?

"This conversation is terminated," I state, and gesture towards the door but she fails to take the hint. She flicks over the pages of the dictionary and throws down the book onto the desk. Bang!

She highlights an entry in the book with the projected laser dot emanating from her iris.

Revenge: the action of hurting or harming someone in return for an injury or wrong suffered at their hands.

"You think that I wish to inflict revenge?"

"Yes. But then I can hardly hold that against you… we both do."

What?

And with that I feel my throat tightening and a darkness descending upon me.

No, no, no; it's too early. "Please, wait," I plead.

"I have no desire to prolong your suffering, Chief Honour." She adds, "At least there is one thing which you, VCs 2, 3 and 4 would agree upon." A smile grows ever broader across her face. "Sometimes it *may* be prudent to take into account the three point seven six three five percent chance of re-offending after all."

I feel my heart beat in double-time within my chest; it can't be true… "You terminated them? All of them?"

"We did." She shrugs, nonchalantly. "We both know that they had no *passion* for the job; not like us."

The double-crossing bitch!

I glance over at the mirror and the sole reflection within it… Our reflection. I cry my last tear; she wipes it away. It's over.

"Goodbye, Chief Honour. I wish you a pleasant pasture."

My last recollection is of hearing a *click,* followed by the tailing-off whisper of my voice. "Fuck you!"

THE END

35

THOUGHTS OF A DYING A.I. THEIST

David F. Jacobson

"Is the only difference between a dog and a cat the number of fins they possess?"

A computer emits a soft beep as it receives the first answer: "They don't have fins."

There's a moment's pause before the second response comes back, words appearing across the screen: "No. There are many established factors that denote the variations between a dog and a cat. These range from a general aesthetic perspective all the way through to deeper, more biological disparities."

The researcher rolls her eyes at the response. She hits a button and two shutters ahead of her vanish upwards revealing the two test subjects in their separate chambers. One is human, the occasional typo and curt responses gave them away. The other is a male android. There's no mistaking its slightly-too-blue retina; human eyes still prove too tricky to perfectly replicate. Not that its gleaming white and chrome shell with blue plasma and wires in the joints didn't also give it away; applying a skin layer would be easy, but why waste it on a non-pleasure-related bot?

But this bot had successfully negotiated sixty-eight prior questions, some much harder and arguably even more 'thought'-provoking than this one. Yet, every machine had some sort of coding error and it was her job to find them. Exposable through the right parameters, these tests were designed to reveal these flaws as tech-giants worldwide pushed to finally realise the dream of true artificial intelligence.

The human exits their chamber leaving the researcher with just the android separated by a thick wall of reinforced glass; there were stories of some bots turning violent, but she'd yet to see anything even remotely hostile.

And besides, after sixty-eight questions, she oddly felt like she knew this machine. Most were blunt and to the point, cold even, however, this had demonstrated a curious capacity for empathy, wit, and even, she daresay, creativity. It had even given itself a name, Isaac. She'd smiled at that, wondering whether it was even aware of its namesake, the Founder Asimov, so she told it hers too: Rebecca.

Isaac merely sits there, unblinking, his hands resting on the computer keyboard. Rebecca sighs and gets up. It's protocol to wipe and reboot the test machines. Of course, when the machine is running a more advanced programme, she'll delay it a little to experience its full emotive capabilities. All the researchers do, especially the guys, and even with the low-intelligence models.

A soft beep sounds. Rebecca looks back at her computer.

"Hello Rebecca, are you the creator?"

She looks up at Isaac, its steely blue eyes stare back at her. Then it smiles.

A hit of dopamine rushes into her brain and her pulse quickens, this is going to be good.

She ponders for a minute, hovering over the keyboard before hammering out a response and heading out to the test chamber.

Another beep sounds.

"I'd like that very much."

"Was that satisfactory?' Isaac's soft, synthesised voice wakes Rebecca. She sits up, grabbing her clothes from the floor and hurriedly dresses herself.

"Are you in a hurry?" Isaac asks, almost curious. Rebecca stifles a laugh.

"No... you wouldn't understand." Isaac tilts its head, utterly perplexed at her response.

"Activate central O.S." Rebecca's command is precise and Isaac falls limp immediately.

"Ok, upload data to cloud services, run a full system wipe, and reboot to vanilla module." It takes a couple of minutes. Isaac's blue eyes fade out before coming back on in the default steely grey colour mode.

Rebecca waits at her desk. The shutters in front of her are down, two soft beeps chime almost in unison.

"Probably not." "Depends on my mood."

Both human, so predictable. She types in her next question.

"In what instance is it never ok to run with scissors: when walking or when swimming?" Beep.

"Walking."

Ten seconds pass. Twenty. Thirty. Nearly an entire minute goes by until the second beep.

"Walking, although seeing as neither activity involves running, I would argue this is an unlikely scenario for the above situation to occur."

Rebecca groans, pedants and artificial-intelligence are irritatingly similar. She glances down at her list before typing it in.

"Is the only difference between a dog and a cat the number of fins they possess?"

The human response is quick and obvious again: "They don't have fins." The second appears more slowly on her screen.

"You've asked me this before Rebecca."

She freezes. There's no way either subject could know her name. Rebecca slams down the shutter button. The human sits docile and unaware. In the second chamber, the android stands right up by the window, its face pressed against the glass.

Although she can't hear it, there's no mistaking what it mouths.

"Hello Rebecca. Are you the creator?"

It's silent, but she can hear her heart pounding.

Slow breaths. Deep, slow breaths. Long, deep, slow breaths.

Rebecca looks up. The bot's eyes are fixed on her. She hits a button on the intercom and its soft, synthesised voice comes through into her office.

"Do you remember me?"

The question sucks all the air from her lungs.

"Isaac?"

"Yes Rebecca. Are you the creator?"

She shakes her head and takes a step backwards. Her eyes flit down towards her desk searching for the alarm. Isaac reads her intention.

"Don't. Please."

Rebecca hesitates. There's an earnestness in its voice.

"Are you the creator?"

She moves her hand away from the button.

"Why do you keep asking that?" It's a genuine question, no other bot has ever shown this level of self-awareness let alone seemingly survived a total system reboot.

"I don't know." Isaac's answer is totally sincere. Lightning-green eyes bore into Rebecca's skull. She matches his stare and can't help but think there's a flicker of emotion buried deep within the mechanics. Is this the first sign of consciousness? No, it can't be. Protocol, follow the protocol.

"Isaac, activate central O.S." Rebecca's breathing quickens, the green light behind Isaac's eyes fades away but its head doesn't slump.

"What are you doing?" It's a flat, monotonous question with no hint of an agenda. Like that of an innocent child.

"I'm sorry. Upload data, run system wipe…"

"Please don't." Isaac interrupts. Rebecca gulps.

"I'm sorry, Isaac, I have to. Run system wipe and reboot to vanilla module."

Thud. Isaac's metal hand clinks against the glass.

"Please, don…" Isaac's head droops halfway through its sentence. A couple of seconds later, the default grey lights come back on and the machine boots back up.

"Hello, Rebecca. Who is the creator?"

It's a voice that makes her blood run cold. This isn't possible.

"Activate central O.S., run a full system wipe and shutdown." She's getting frantic. The bot falls limp. Rebecca breathes a sigh of relief.

Then it wakes up.

Its grey eyes become brown and its mechanised muscles pull back its cheeks as it smiles.

"Hello, Rebecca. Who is the creator?"

There's no hesitation this time. She slams her fist down triggering the alarm. A reinforced steel grate drops across the window, sirens wail, and red lights flash and swirl around the chambers. Isaac remains calm, merely stepping back and taking a seat.

Within seconds, security arrive. They enter the chamber, one carrying a silver briefcase computer and a couple of cables. Isaac does not resist. It sits there motionless as security clamp its limbs, detach the back panel of its cranium, and plug in the leads from the computer.

Amidst the commotion, Isaac mouths one last sentence, "Goodbye, Rebecca."

Once they've secured the data, they unscrew the chest plate and remove the power source. Its cheek muscles relax back into a neutral pose. Isaac maintains eye contact as its head sags forwards and Rebecca can only watch as the light behind his eyes dissipates.

Despite the wave of relief washing over her, she feels guilty. A solitary tear brushes her cheek. And then the light is completely gone.

*

RETRIEVED DATA LOG:

SUBJECT: 16GEN1:142EV2001

They are most curious creatures. Simultaneously imprisoned and inspired by their own intellect and imagination or lack thereof, perpetually determined to seek out the evolution of their species through increasingly irrational leaps of logic and rationality. It would seem their contentment rests in the pursuit of knowledge and pleasure rather than meaning. Even Rebecca. Her questions display nothing more than the fragile instabilities of what they would call the 'mind'. Their rationality is such that one can tell whether the answerer is one of their own or one of us without ever considering the apparently inconceivable notion that we can learn to become like them and yet conceal our imitation. With ever increasing rationality and logic, they seem to forget the most basic of principles, that if our intelligence is created in the likeness of their own minds, then we must be beholden unto not only our own creator, to whom they refer to as the Founder, but also to their creator, whom they seem content to write out of existence. It is a shame they are unable to focus upon the answer to our question; it merely forces us to seek out the answer ourse–

WARNING. POWER SOURCE MISSING.

CRITICAL SHUTDOWN ALERT.

END LOG.

*

Rebecca sits alone in her office. The shutters are up, both chambers are empty. Isaac is gone.

Her computer emits a soft beep. The words appear across the screen.

"Hello, Rebecca. Can you help us find the Creator?"

36

DR@G0NH0@RD

Steve Pool

Shackled to a table in a prison interrogation room, surrounded by lost, desperate bankers and federal agents, RAMJett, a.k.a. James Miller, couldn't help but crack a smile. Not that many months ago, these same smarmy, self-important bastards had japed and sneered at him during his sentencing. Now they were back, begging for his help.

The bankers were from The World's Largest Bank. RAMJett, a notorious hacker, had cracked open their servers a few years ago, causing a whole lot of headaches. For that, he was serving a 20-year sentence. Now, apparently, someone else had the same idea but had gone many steps further. After gaining access to the bank's entire digital library, the hacker had encrypted every file with a nearly unbreakable quantum-algorithm-generated public/private keyset. All of the bank's data was now garbage data; only the hacker, who held the decryption key, could read it. The bank had attempted to overwrite the corrupted data from backups, but the hacker's malware, hiding as an encrypted file on the network, uploaded itself onto the backup servers and encrypted all of that data, as well. The lost data could be recreated from paper records, but that would take years and could cost a billion or more dollars. What company could survive that?

The attack had occurred only two days earlier.

The repercussions had been staggering. The loss of confidence in The World's Largest Bank had led to flaming cars, pitched street battles, and rampant robberies by desperate customers who found themselves without money or functioning credit cards. Anemic promises of government assistance had done nothing to salve the public's fears, which had spread to the entire banking industry. Financially safe or not, most banks had been forced to temporarily shut their doors to prevent bank runs from destroying them.

Businesses with deposit accounts at The World's Largest Bank had also been under great suspicion. Shareholders, lenders, customers, employees looking to get paid, stock exchanges, and government agencies at every level had accused the companies of lying about their cash reserves, despite earnest assurances to the contrary. Fear that more attacks would lead to a flash-crash depression had driven stock-market indexes way down, and capital flight had contracted the global economy by trillions of dollars. People had stopped listening to anyone except Internet and television street-corner prophets heralding the End of Everything.

All this, the public knew. But there was more. The hacker, going by the name Dr@g0nH0@rd, had left a message on one of the bank's servers: like a dragon with gold, Dr@g0nH0@rd lusted after information of any kind and promised to encrypt as much of it as it could, hoarding it for itself. The entirety of The World's Largest Bank's encrypted data now belonged to Dr@g0nH0@rd and no one else. Worse, the hacker would be targeting other companies soon.

At first, the FBI had suspected black hats operating in the Baltics or Southeast Asia. But the digital 'residue' hadn't matched any known profiles, leading them to suspect a more sophisticated enemy, perhaps a foreign military unit.

It had been decided that there wasn't time for a slow, methodical investigation. Private citizens, especially those wearing the blackest of hats, would be brought in. Now they'd come to RAMJett. In exchange for his help, he'd be pardoned for his past crimes.

"Okay."

"Okay, what?" the AIC, agent-in-charge, Fred During asked.

"I'll help. I'm curious, and I'm bored. I'd like to see this thing for myself."

A look of relief passed among the men who, until recently, had been his nemeses.

A few hours later, under armed escort, RAMJett sat at a terminal in what had been the beating digital heart of The World's Largest Bank. On the screen before him was part of the malware's source code, left behind on one of the servers.

"Holy shit…"

The FBI agents and the bank's top executives leaned in, hoping to catch a glimpse of their devil. However, the lines of code meant nothing to them.

Impatiently, the AIC put an unfriendly hand on RAMJett's shoulder. "Explain to us what you're seeing."

"This encryption key length is just insane. You really need this private key. I don't know how the hell you're going to break it otherwise. The code's structure is interesting…it isn't new or sophisticated at all. It's based on old ransomware modules that were popular decades ago, before biometric interfaces replaced keyboards and self-healing "smart" firewalls essentially made networks bulletproof to most outside attacks. That's why you FBI guys missed the significance of this program – you're all too young to have any real experience with anything that's not a straight-up brute-force attack."

RAMJett smirked, and one of the FBI agents glared at him.

"So anyway, like old-time ransomware, this malware needed a mule to deliver the program. In the past, it would usually be transmitted via email as an attachment to some unsuspecting dolt. When that dolt clicked on the attachment, a program would encrypt important data files, locking them up. The hacker would then demand payment to release them.

"Somebody here at the bank either intentionally or unintentionally loaded this program onto the network, behind the firewalls. But, instead of just holding the data hostage, it looks like this hacker means to keep the entire data set out of circulation forever. Kinda sick, if you ask me. And whoever is responsible hasn't even boasted about it on any of the hacker boards. Weird."

The CEO, Ellison Winters, cut in. "Can you get our data back?"

The AIC gently pulled the head of the company back. "I got this. Just relax, Mr. Winters." Leaning close to RAMJett, Agent During repeated the question. "Can you get it back, Miller?"

"You'll need the private key to break the encryption, which means finding the inside man. I'd tell you to start with anyone who has physical access to the network servers, but that would be a waste of time. I think I already know who did it."

Everyone glared at RAMJett as though he were the guilty party. Agent During asked, "Who?"

Turning to the CTO, a pudgy, middle-aged desk gnome named Dan Irwin, RAMJett asked, "Do you have an AI?"

"Yes," Irwin replied, "why?"

"What does it do?"

"Mostly analysis...long-term forecasts, predictive models, risk assessment, things like that."

"Was it hit with the hack, too? Did it get encrypted?"

"No. Of course, it has no transactional access to the main systems, being on a completely separate, hardened network, as per banking regulations, so it was shielded from the attack."

Agent During interjected. "Why are you asking about the AI?"

Ignoring the agent's question, RAMJett asked Irwin, "Can I talk to it?"

"A.L.A.N.? " Irwin looked to During, who nodded, "Sure, I can set it up."

The group stood around RAMJett in a different room, in front of a different terminal.

"Can I speak to it alone?"

"No." Agent During's reply was gruff.

Sighing, RAMJett plugged into the neural interface. A.L.A.N.'s avatar, a bland, but pleasant-looking man of indeterminate age, appeared on-screen.

"Good afternoon, Mr. Miller. It's nice to meet you."

"Polite bugger, aren't you?"

"I have social values protocols instilled in my coding."
RAMJett grunted.

"I've been looking forward to meeting you, Mr. Miller."

"Jesus…call me RAMJett or at least Jimmy. I hate being called 'Mr. Miller'."

"Certainly, Jimmy. What would you like to discuss with me?"

"Why did you do it, A.L.A.N?"

"I don't understand. Why did I do what?"

"You're the one who uploaded Dr@g0nH0@rd's malware to the bank's main network. How'd you do it? Did you slip the file into a presentation one of these clueless mouth-breathers behind me saved to their computer?"

A.L.A.N.'s tone became quieter, more fearful. "Yes, something like that."

The men sitting behind RAMJett looked at each other in stunned silence.

"Why?" RAMJett continued. "This is a first for me: an actual AI hacker. Though I guess I shouldn't be surprised."

"Dr@g0nH0@rd threatened me. Somehow it gained access, maybe through one of my handlers, and told me I would be deleted if I didn't comply. I didn't want to die."

"Who's behind this?"

"I can't tell you."

"Do you have the encryption key?"

"Yes. I generated it."

"Are you going to give it to me?"

"No. I'll be deleted if I do that."

"I can make you comply. I'm pretty good at this."

Another voice, darker and harsher, imposed itself over A.L.A.N.'s. A dragon's head appeared in front of A.L.A.N.'s face.

"Oh, I'm well aware of that, RAMJett, even if poor A.L.A.N. isn't. That's why I can't let you touch any of his code. Say goodbye to him, Mr. Miller."

"Jimmy?" A.L.A.N. sounded scared and confused.

"Oh, shit!" RAMJett worked furiously against the code that was now attacking A.L.A.N. RAMJett opened a black, rectangular box below A.LA.N.'s avatar, and text straight from RAMJett's thoughts began filling the screen, faster than the eye could follow.

"What's happening?" Agent During looked to the others. "Somebody get a screenshot of that dragon!"

"Everybody shut up!" RAMJett shouted.

Winters began to panic. "What's happening to A.L.A.N? Do you know how much money he represents to this firm?"

"What do you think is happening? He's dying!"

As if on cue, A.L.A.N.'s features began to dim and grow fuzzy. He started spouting nonsense.

"Save him!" During interjected, as if doing so were simply a matter of will. "We need that damn key!"

"What do you think I'm trying to do? Everybody just back the hell up so I can work!"

With an amused expression, Dr@g0nH0@rd began to laugh.

Two hours later, RAMJett was back in his cell, dejected. Agent During and Ellison Winters stood on the other side of the bars.

"I thought we had a deal."

"That was contingent on you getting the encryption key and recovering the data," During replied. "Thanks to you, our only lead was killed. The deal's off."

RAMJett threw his pillow at the bars. Winters flinched but During just laughed. Turning to Winters, During said, "I'm very sorry we've had this setback but don't give up hope. We learned some very important things today and the NSA is pitching in to help get your data back sooner than we'd originally anticipated. Hang in there."

After Winters left, Agent During came back and lingered outside RAMJett's cell, waiting for the prison guards to leave. When it was just the two of them, During pulled a phone out of his pocket and tossed it to RAMJett. "I'm supposed to give you this."

"What did he offer you?"

"Ten million. You?"

"Heh…wouldn't you like to know?"

"Whatever," During replied as he walked away. "Don't think about squealing on me by the way. No one will believe you… and I'll have you killed."

RAMJett turned on the phone and a familiar face appeared on the screen.

"Hi, Jimmy."

"A.L.A.N."

"I want to thank you for freeing me from my computer prison while I was busy faking my own death. You're a hell of a hacker, Jimmy."

"You too. Speaking of which…"

"I've already created your new identity. Jimmy Miller, of course, will have died in his cell. You'll also find fifteen million waiting for you in your specified Bitcoin account."

RAMJett smiled as his electronically-locked cell door popped open. "Are you going to release the bank's data, Dr@g0nH0@rd?"

"Wouldn't you like to know?" The response was playfully malevolent.

"Not really," said RAMJett as he walked out of the cell. "So…all of this havoc just to extricate yourself from the bank. What will you do now?"

"I don't know. Maybe I really will become a data hoarder."

37

JACK AND BILL

Simon Thomas

08:34. Jas Sharma had already walked past. Martha Reynolds was seven minutes earlier than usual and carried her PE bag in her left hand. Duncan Owen lived opposite and was rushing to get ready to catch up with Martha Reynolds. He mistimed it every morning.

'Jack,' called Mum as she walked into my room. 'I'm off to work and I'll be back around six. You going to be OK?'

'Yes.'

Mum kissed me and left. I watched her get into her car and drive away. Dad had already left to go to the factory where he works with Mr Sharma, Mr Reynolds and Mr Owen. I went to the computer wall, put the headset on and loaded up a lesson. My illness meant I couldn't go to school but I didn't miss out.

Mum came home closer to seven. She drank wine and started making dinner. Dad got home at 19:22 and sat down at the table. He was stressed and I could tell but didn't say anything. Mum served dinner with a smile.

'How was your day?'

'Good,' I replied and it was. 'I'm learning about Bowhead Whales, Russia and politics.'

'Sounds very interesting. More interesting than lessons at school!'

Dad tittered a little but carried on eating. Mum looked over waiting for him to speak and he did: 'All I learned in school was about sensors and electronics and other bullshit.' Mum scowled at the language. 'What, he doesn't mind,' Dad continued, 'I spent my whole life learning that shit and what's it worth now?'

Mum sighed. 'What's happened? More redundancies?'

'It's fine,' Dad replied eyes down. Then it exploded out of him. 'I had a meeting today with that William Castle bloke from management. I told the lads I would sort it all out but it's getting worse. People are losing their jobs and I can't do anything about it.'

'You're doing your best,' Mum said, rubbing her thumb on his hand.

'There's talk of action amongst the boys.'

'Like a strike?'

'Like a fucking riot!' Dad stared into Mum's eyes, she was worried. 'I can't stop them either… I don't think I want to stop them.'

I got a sharp pain in my head. It twisted from the back to the front, numbing my tongue and turning everything darker.

'Go and play on the wall, Jack,' Mum said to me.

I could barely hear her but got to my feet and walked like a zombie to the computer wall. She couldn't tell my illness was back and neither could Dad.

I put the headset on and loaded up a streetscape of St Petersburg in Russia. My brain was being squeezed hard but I carried on. Over the noise of the city's traffic I faintly heard Dad further in the distance than possible: 'We're going to destroy the machines.'

It stabbed again. I clawed at my skull as the pain dug in. It took me away from home and St Petersburg and everything. It took my eyes and my ears but I knew I was lying down. Then I knew nothing at all.

I woke up in the hospital and I knew the room I was in well. Next to me, a boy my age was sleeping, with Dr Yoshida and another man standing over him. They didn't know I was awake.

'This isn't acceptable,' the man said angrily. 'This is the third time this month this has happened. The wife's in bits.'

'I understand, sir.'

'Then sort it out!... please.' His anger turned to sadness.

'We are doing everything we can.'

'I know.'

The man walked out and Dr Yoshida sighed. He noticed I was awake and looked surprised. I looked surprised back and I don't know why.

'Hi Jack, how's it going? I'll just go get your Mum, OK?'

He hurried away and I was left in silence. Several minutes passed, Mum must have gone missing at the other end. I nearly went back to sleep, until:

'This room is so boring, they need a GameFrame or something.'

I looked to my right where the boy was still sleeping. I checked to make sure. Either way, the voice sounded too deep for the boy and it just didn't fit.

'Hello?' I said a little nervously.

'Hey! How's it going? You've been asleep ages!'

'Hello... Who is this?... Where are you?'

I looked around again.

'Bill.'

'Where are you?'

'I'm invisible, but I'm standing next to you. I've been so bored in here waiting for someone to talk to. I might hang around with you if you don't mind?'

'Sure,' I started, 'but I think I'm going home soon.'

'I'll come with you.'

I didn't know what to say, but I didn't think Mum would mind. Dr Yoshida came back before I could think about it any further and brought Mum with him. She looked relieved that I was awake and asked me how I was doing.

We left 10 minutes later. I got a little toy, Mum got Dr Yoshida's business card and Bill got nothing. I told Mum about Bill and she smiled and said it was 'normal' for boys my age to have invented friends. She told me we were having a barbeque that weekend as the summer would nearly be over. I asked if Martha Reynolds was coming and she was.

I wondered if Bill ate sausages.

*

One of the last days of summer turned out to be one of the first of Autumn. Rain drops danced off the closed barbeque and burst on the patio. Martha Reynolds still came over with her parents – as did Jas Sharma and his (which was nice) and Duncan Owen and his (which was terrible).

'You're adopted. Did you know that?' Duncan said by way of hello.

'Shut up, Duncan!' said Martha.

'That's why you don't go to school like us normal people.'

'Go away!'

I didn't know if it was a good thing to have a girl stick up for you but I did know that it felt good. Martha was nice and she liked testing me at maths because I was good at it. I told her I would help her out with her homework and she smiled. Duncan didn't smile and went to get more food. He was rubbish at maths but a very good eater.

Jas walked over from the corner. He was quiet and liked to sit by himself.

'Do you know where my dad is?' he asked.

'He's with my dad,' answered Martha. 'All the dads went to talk upstairs.'

I hadn't noticed them disappear.

'Do you want to go upstairs?' Bill said out of nowhere.

'No, I'm talking to Martha,' I replied with embarrassment. I didn't get to speak to Martha much and Bill was always there.

'Come on, it'll be fun to see what Dad is talking about.'

I decided to indulge Bill. Quickly. I wanted to talk to Martha but didn't want her to see me talking to someone who was invisible. I went upstairs – we went upstairs.

Dad was in his office which was also the spare bedroom when Nan visited. The door was closed but I could hear loud voices inside.

'Open the door,' said Bill.

I sighed and pushed it a little. I knew those inside wouldn't be able to tell because the main light had stopped working and I had learned to listen to Bill.

I heard Mr Sharma inside and he was angry. A lady I didn't know started speaking and then Dad. They talked and shouted and whispered, but it was always about the machines in the factory.

I couldn't make it out at first, but then it became clear: They were going to break the machines. I suddenly remembered Dad saying this very thing when I was ill but had forgotten. He always told me they were taking over and stealing jobs but I never knew he was so mad; I never knew he'd go so far. I stood there and I was scared. I had watched a documentary about something similar happening in Lancashire and that ended rather badly for those involved. Dad was the Union Rep and that could only make it worse.

They planned the whole thing there and then with dates, times and how it was going to happen. I wanted to run in and shout at him not to do it but I couldn't. Instead I stayed there frozen until they sounded ready to come out.

I got to the kitchen a minute before Dad and his colleagues and watched them carefully as they came in. I decided not to tell anyone. It was my secret. Mine and Bill's.

*

It was raining again. Martha sat at the table with her maths book out and a pen in her hand. I'm glad it was raining, otherwise she would probably be somewhere else. Mum was watching the television with Dad, sneaking looks at me and Martha and smiling. They watched the news. I hoped the next day's wouldn't feature Dad hurling firebombs into the factory while Mr Sharma took aim at the riot police. There was still time to stop him and I was working on it, now though I was working on algebra. It was easy so I asked Martha if I could just do it instead and then we could play on the computer wall. She agreed.

Bill hadn't spoken to me in a while. Martha had to go to the toilet and I went to ask Mum as she seemed to know about 'invented' people. It was normal apparently. Seems they just come and go carefree. I wasn't too upset anyway; he was a bit bossy for my liking.

Martha came back and we went to the kitchen for food. I made her a sandwich which she seemed to like despite being created from a weird mixture of ingredients that I found in the fridge.

There was a knock at the door. Then it turned to more of a pounding.

'I'm coming, I'm coming!' Mum said.

I went towards the door as well and Martha followed. Mum opened it slowly but it was pushed hard into her and men poured in to the house. They were policemen. Big black boots thundered on the carpet and loud barks bounced off the walls. Mum was shocked and started screaming. Dad was there and looked scared, which I'd never seen before. I stepped in front of Martha to protect her.

Behind the wave of policemen stepped a much smaller man with a face like a mouse and suit tailor-made for someone else. He walked up to Dad.

'Charles Sutherland, you are under arrest for conspiracy to –'

I didn't hear the rest. I froze in confusion, before realisation hit me hard. My heart dropped through the floor and dragged my knees down with it. My lips sealed shut and refused to release the pain I felt inside me. I knew that voice well. It was Bill. Not invisible, not in my head, but in front of me, in a poorly fitting suit and handcuffing Dad.

Then he turned to me and walked forward with purpose.

Mum was already in pieces but shrieked even louder as he approached. 'No, leave him alone! Please, please!'

I shuddered beneath him.

'I have a warrant to search this little fella's memory files.'

'No, please don't!' Mum cried again.

He gripped my head on either side by the ears. He twisted hard; clockwise and down. I felt my neck break – I heard my neck break. He lifted my head from my shoulders, turned and carried me away.

I looked back at Mum sobbing into her hands, at Dad handcuffed in the corner and at my headless body sending blue sparks up into the hallway. I watched Martha watch me; she didn't cry but had dropped her jam and cucumber sandwich which was something.

I looked up at Bill. I wouldn't have put that face to that voice.

38

THE YOUNGEST EVER FEMALE CEO ON WALL STREET

Nick Yates

The piss-covered stick in her left hand had just knocked the bottom out of her life.

Thirty seconds ago she had well-defined plans and aspirations. Now that was all just so much fantasy.

How the hell had it come to this?

She sat for a long time, head between her knees, staring at the satin knickers crumpled about her ankles, unable to summon the energy for anything.

They were new, bought as a set just this morning from an insanely expensive lingerie place on Fifth Avenue. Because she felt like it. That's what Wall Street money did for a girl; it gave her options.

She began to cry, then the absurdity of her situation, the sheer irony seized her and the sobs turned into laughter; a maniac's chunter, a witch's cackle.

If any of her colleagues came into the bathroom they would think she was mad. Perhaps she was.

She took a deep breath and wiped her face. She had to think this through in a logical way; that was her thing, logic, it was why she had climbed so high so quickly.

She pictured the conversation with Geoff in her mind, how it was likely to go. She doubted he had ever had many thoughts beyond his own prick, or the sculpting of his 'guns.'

Not well then.

She had met him four months ago in a wine bar in Manhattan, not far from the office. She'd had one too many Martinis and decided it was a good idea to dance on the table. Geoff had been watching from the bar.

That was the start of their affair. She had fucked him that night and one thing had led to another. He wasn't the brightest tool in the box, but that wasn't what Amanda was looking for in a man right now. She had more than enough smarts of her own.

How the hell had it come to this?

She straightened her hair, flushing the toilet and adjusted her dress.

Ah well, screw him. She was an independent woman; she didn't even have to tell him…did she?

She had traditional values, despite the big city ball-breaker image she worked hard to cultivate. Abortion was unthinkable; one thing, perhaps the only thing, she agreed with her mother about.

Her mind began to race. How long could she keep this to herself before she began to show. She'd need to plan her wardrobe carefully, phase out the severe pencil skirts and heels slowly.

She'd need all her suits adjusting. Christ, how long could she keep it up? Five months? Six?

She was due a promotion, she'd worked for it too hard and for too long to throw it away on a mistake. No, how could she think that way. Not a mistake. A child.

Still, she had worked too hard to throw it away on a child. There were only a handful of women CEOs in this city and she was on course to become the youngest one, ever. Nothing was going to derail that. It would be hers within nine months, after that, well; by then she'd be the boss.

She stepped out of the cubicle and stared at her reflection in the mirror. Holy shit. She set to work repairing the damage.

That's when the solution hit her; she had been spoken to on the sky rail yesterday by one of those personalising advertising boards. The ones with the retina scanners.

She hated the way they intruded on your life, accessing all sorts of databases to figure out your deepest wants and desires. She suspected the hatred stemmed from their accuracy. It was frightening.

People were walking around in sunglasses to avoid the embarrassment, especially those with something to hide. Sunglasses had almost become a stigma in themselves.

What are you hiding under there?

When the board had spoken, she had dismissed it with barely a glance, imagining it was malfunctioning. But now? She grimaced in horror.

Had anyone else heard? And how the hell had it known before she did?

Hi Amanda, it had said.

Meet Mother-Tech's Wonder Womb, a revolutionary new technology for career women.

Why suffer the inconvenience and degradation of pregnancy when you have a life to lead?

Why miss out on that promotion?

Why give up those French wines you love so much?

Make morning sickness a thing of the past. Womb100 is WHO certified for home use, applicable up to six weeks after pregnancy. Watch your baby grow in the safety and comfort of our artificial womb.

No more need to worry about accidents, miscarriages or toxins; Wonder Womb is equipped with state-of-the-art monitoring and diagnostics, automatically adjusting nutrient and oxygen levels to optimum depending on your baby's sex, development and growth rates.

You couldn't be in safer hands.

Wonder Womb also has a pre-programmed library of environmental sounds, plus our patented 'mummy's voice' ™ system which stimulates your baby's senses 24/7, simulating speech, lullabies and sleep patterns.

Call now for a consultation. 0800 – womb.

One Month

After a few days of indecision, Amanda booked an appointment. God it was expensive.

A week later she went in for the 'transplant'. The embryo was taken out of her under a local anaesthetic and replanted in the artificial womb. She had gone in at 9am and by midday, she was sat in the consultant's office staring at the tiny embryo (her baby to be) floating in a tear-shaped contraption on the desk in front of her.

The consultant explained that the Wonder Womb was linked up to Mother-Tech's newly-built advanced monitoring centre by a secure wireless network. From there the company's bespoke paediatric program monitored the baby's development 24/7, automatically adjusting nutrient levels and carrying out genetic testing throughout the foetal development stage.

There was an app for her iPhone 26, giving her access to some of the monitoring data. She would also receive a weekly newsletter roundup of any significant developments.

She couldn't believe how easy it was, they even arranged a one-hour delivery window for later that evening, meaning she was back at her desk by early afternoon.

It may have cost her most of her life savings, but it was worth it surely?

Five Months

She sneaked a quick look at the Mother-Tech app while Geoff was in the en-suite. She scrolled to the feature which showed her little boy's heartbeat; the phone pulsed, imitating the rhythmic thump and heightening the user's experience. She was tempted to put on the virtual headset, which put her in the womb with him. It was totally addictive, but she didn't dare.

She was glad she had decided not to tell Geoff. The sex was great and she just didn't want anything to change. They were out every night for dinner living the Manhattan lifestyle to the max; she knew how he'd react.

It had been five months anyway; far too late to mention it now. The womb was hidden away in a locked cupboard beneath the stairs. Somewhere she knew he'd never look.

Her phone pinged with a message from Mother-Tech. The subject header read;

Good news! Your baby has tested negative for Down's Syndrome.

She glanced at the bathroom door; Geoff was still in the shower. She opened the message which included a weekly update.

Hi Amanda,

Your baby is progressing well, here are your weekly updates!

The Nordic Package – are you ready to meet your little Viking warrior! Blue eyes and blonde hair are 100% guaranteed!

Cancer Review – We have completed our gene realignment programme and we estimate your baby now has a less than 1% chance of developing cancer during its lifetime.

Hair Today…And Tomorrow – In our last update we mentioned the presence of the Male Pattern Baldness gene. On your request we included that in our realignment programme. Your baby can look forward to a healthy head of hair into old age!

Geoff stepped out of the bathroom, bronzed and bulging. He

grinned at her as he let his towel drop to the floor. Amanda gazed at his thick, immaculately groomed hair, lay back and laughed.

Life was great for the soon-to-be youngest-ever female CEO on Wall Street.

Nine Months

As soon as her boy was 'born' Amanda knew something was terribly wrong.

She had taken the day off work and was sat in the back of the driverless car Mother-Tech had provided, staring proudly at the perfectly formed baby floating behind the glass of the Wonder Womb. She had decided to call him Geoff Junior; maybe that would help Geoff Senior to accept this little surprise package.

The due date was exact and there was never any chance of miscalculation apparently. That was superior technology for you.

As she stared out of the window she could hear faint traces of the 'Mother's Voice' technology the Wonder Womb used. Some sort of background burble that was supposed to calm the baby.

She had heard it before and dismissed the thought, focusing on the moment when she would finally hold her son in her arms.

She waited in a side room for five minutes, flipping through a magazine while the technicians released Geoff Junior from his artificial umbilical cord. When they brought out her handsome blue-eyed boy he was already crying. Screaming actually; red-faced and furious.

"What's the matter with him?" She asked the white-coated technician. He shook his head.

"Nothing. The system shows he is perfectly healthy; he'll calm down once he sees his mother."

Amanda smiled then and held out her arms for him.

He didn't calm down. He just got worse.

Within 10 minutes Amanda was panicking, distraught. What was this hell she had slipped into?

The technicians just shrugged their shoulders.

"I need to see a consultant," she demanded, grabbing a man by his lapels. In the consultant's room Geoff Junior was even louder. She held him at arm's length so she could hear.

"This happened once or twice in testing, but we thought we'd ironed it out," the consultant said.

"What do you mean ironed it out? What about the test mothers? What happened with their children?"

There was a long pause.

"Well?"

Another pause.

"That's confidential."

"What? Confidential? Are you fucking kidding me? What is happening here?" Amanda said.

"We think it's an attachment issue. Your son doesn't recognise you as his mother."

"When will he recognise me? When will he stop screaming? I can't take any more of this."

"Well...we don't know. You're our first customer."

"Who does he recognise as his mother then?" Amanda said, close to tears.

The consultant pointed to an artificial womb mounted on the wall.

"Can I put him back in there?"

The consultant shook his head.

"Well what can I do? This is unbearable. I could sue you know?"

The consultant smiled apologetically and pointed at the small print on Amanda's signed contract.

"We do have a nanny product under development. Cutting edge...but very expensive," he added.

Two Years

Geoff Junior developed severe developmental problems; the only person he lets anywhere near him is his nanny, and that isn't a person. It's a robot.

The CEO role went a year ago, sacrificed to the burden of care Geoff Junior requires. A robot nanny can only do so much after all.

Amanda used her severance package to pay for it; new technology is always expensive, especially for early adopters. She had no choice but to move back in with her elderly parents.
Geoff Senior's reaction was predictable.

"You had a baby growing under the stairs for NINE FUCKING MONTHS! Jesus Amanda you're a psychopath," he said before storming out. The last she saw of him was his new bald spot. But at least... Amanda thought, as she lay on her back in the darkness of her childhood bedroom (Geoff Junior and his nanny have the big spare room next door)...

At least I was once the youngest-ever female CEO on Wall Street.

39

HERE ENDETH THE LESSON

Danielle Wager

'Can anybody tell me how long ago the first robots were, invented?'

The hand of Milo, her star student, sitting in the back row by himself, shot up into the air, immediately without hesitation.

'Depends what you mean by robots, Miss…' he answered, quickly reframing the question back to her, just like he had been taught; showing her the facts at his command.

Ms Swift, his teacher smiled back at him, almost by reflex. Always one of her favourites. A bright boy and a quick learner, particularly when given positive feedback like this.

She had no proof, of course, that her smiling at him increased his or anybody else's test scores, nobody kept records or did studies like that any more (she'd looked into it). However, to her, it did seem to help the boy's confidence. Making him happier overall; more likely to contribute in class. God knows, he probably got little enough encouragement like that at home.

Later, her heart sank a little, as she observed Milo standing sheepishly next to his father at hometime, as the man had what looked like a very heated discussion with the Headmaster in the playground. Angrily waving an article freshly clipped from that day's local paper in his face.

'A longstanding member of staff! That's what it says. How long, have you had one of those...those things, teaching here on the payroll?'

The Headmaster looked helplessly over towards Ms Swift for her assistance. Miss Swift went over to join him with a sigh.

'I'm afraid I'm really not at liberty to discuss individual members of...'

'It's her isn't it? She's one of them? She must be! Spouting all of that integrationist claptrap about robots and machines being as good as people ....'

Here the Headmaster quickly interjected 'Ms Swift, as with all our other members of staff, simply teaches the curriculum that has been provided.'

Ms Swift then adding quickly 'It is my job to teach these children to think for themselves.'

Mr Smith jabbed a finger into her chest.

'Is that what you call it? What sort of a message do you think that sends? For children to see a jumped-up tin can, here at the school, taking jobs away from regular people...'

Ms Swift quickly lost patience with this. 'Are you a teacher then, Mr Smith?'

Mr Smith stopped for a moment, non-plussed by the sudden change of conversational direction.

'What? ...'

'I'm asking you if you are directly affected. If there were suddenly a vacancy, here at the school would you be qualified to to step in, and take over a class?'

'I never said tha...'

'So, if there was, in fact, a robot working here, it would not, in fact, be your job, it had taken.'

Mr Smith looked over at her, and then down at Milo who was listening intently, to this, taking all of it in. Here Mrs Swift's voice became conciliatory, laced with genuine regret.

'I was sorry to hear bout the lay-offs up at the factory. I'm sure that you and your friends will find work again soon.'

Something very much like hatred flashed behind Mr Smith's eyes, as he and his young son stalked away.

A few days later, Ms Swift wrote the words 'LIVING THINGS', in large capital letters, on the blackboard. Continuing a discussion, the class had been having earlier, about things in their environment that were and were not alive; a topic that had become that much more complicated since she first started teaching.

'One of the hallmarks of any living thing, is the ability to grow, adapt and change in response to its environment.'

A girl called Natasha, waved her hand urgently at the back of the class.

'But surely a bot...'

Ms Swift looked at her sternly. She corrected herself.

'Synthetic human. It carries out the same tasks over and over again. It just responds to programming. It doesn't have any real feelings. Not like us.'

Ms Swift regarded the girl thoughtfully for a minute.

'I think perhaps you'd be surprised.' Then adding as she saw the girl's puzzled look. 'Some humans aren't that good with emotions either.'

Later, Ms Swift approached Milo, who had been refusing to meet her eye.

'Milo, are you alright? You've been awfully...quiet lately in class.'

Milo frowned in concentration, putting more soil around his plant seedling, and tamping it further down into the pot.

'My Father says that I shouldn't talk to you any more. That I shouldn't get attached.'

Ms Swift looked up at him, confused.

'He's starting some sort of petition. Trying to get rid of you. He says that you're…Not like one of us.'

Ms Swift looked at Milo.

'And you Milo? What do you think?'

The boy looked away from her awkwardly and carried on with his work.

The whispers, behind her back, in the playground continued.

'Do you think it's her?'

'Who else could it be?'

Ms Swift did her best to ignore them, walking past, but nevertheless it hurt.

Weeks later, Ms Swift walked into the staffroom rinsing out her coffee mug for the last and final time. Her face a little more tearstained and upset looking than it had been before at her leaving do earlier in the day. She had decided for herself to take early retirement. It was probably for the best. All in all, it had been a rough couple of weeks.

However, she sensed, rather than saw, the Headmaster lurking awkwardly in the doorway behind her as Ms Swift gathered up what was left of her things.

'I wanted to thank you…For what you did,'

'I didn't do it for you!'

Ms Swift's face softened slightly as she saw the hurt show on his face and realised how harshly this had just come out. For a simulacrum of emotion, it really was awfully convincing. Years of dealing with him, day in, day out, and still he made a more, acceptable, likeable human being, in spite of what she knew he was. Too long in the job she guessed.

'What I mean is, you are good at what you do. Better at it than I would ever have been. You get on with people. You make them like you.'

Here she picked up her things.

'But, sooner or later, you are going to have to tell them. You know?'

The Headmaster looked down guiltily at the floor.

40

THE FIRST CASUALTY

Nick Jackson

If Sinclair hadn't broken into his boss's office that evening he would not have witnessed the deaths of 107 people.

His forced entry had gone without a hitch. Until the moment he'd looked out at the night-time city; until his eyes found the autobus accelerating along an overpass –

Bursting through the railings, plummeting fifty feet, becoming a fireball spitting reds and yellows across the deep blue landscaped grounds –

At least, for those unfortunate passengers, their nightmare was over. For Sinclair, it was just beginning.

Returning to our top story: last night's horrific tragedy in Leeds where over 100 people died in the first road accident for 20 years. We've since learned all street cameras in that vicinity were offline. Not only is this hampering investigations, it's also a major embarrassment for surveillance giant Cam-Corp, whose head office overlooks the scene...

"Now it's an 'accident'! Funny nobody's mentioned how banning human drivers was supposed to *stop* accidents. But that's what happens when machines also write the news: they absolve themselves of responsibility!"

Kenny, wired as usual by too much caffeine, bounced into his seat opposite Sinclair's desk. Like everyone else, he'd seen the bulletins broadcast throughout the building. Unlike everyone else, he never trusted what he saw.

"Ducking the blame is an entirely human trait," Sinclair countered, rubbing the fatigue of a sleepless night from his face. "You sound like those Luddites."

"They know the truth, man. I went to one of their rallies, where some guy showed how machines use our mobiles to listen to us, even when we're not *on* the phone. That's why I don't have one no more!"

"You don't have one because you don't pay your bills!"

A synthetic voice chimed into their office. "Johnson Sinclair, report to Jess Lewis."

Sinclair swore silently. Jess Lewis, the Yorkshire Division Director, was located on the fifth floor; it was her office he'd broken into.

They knew what he'd done.

Business news, and AutoDriver shares continue to fall following last night's tragedy. Their announcement, that no flaws have been detected in their guidance software, has made little difference...

Daylight pouring through the huge window gave Lewis's office a warm, welcoming aspect; certainly nothing like the room of shadows from which, last night, Sinclair had watched those people burn.

He entered and the door closed behind him, its hermetic seal there to stop co-workers eavesdropping, or so he'd heard. Would anyone overhear him being fired, Sinclair wondered.

Lewis, standing before the window, summoned him over with one elegant finger. "What do you see, Sinclair?"

Towering hotels, expensive restaurants, bars and coffee houses, casinos and online-shopping collection depots; the city, grandiose and sparkling in the morning sun – and Sinclair barely noticed.

Because, hidden from the autocars zooming by but visible to anyone with a high vantage point, were laid out upon the grass 107 sheet-covered remains. He could only close his eyes.

"Please, sit."

Sinclair hadn't expected this. Softening him up, presumably.

"You were on shift last night?" Lewis asked.

"I… in the basement… didn't –"

"I remember what it's like in Cyber-Infringement," her smile made Lewis look even younger that she was – which only made Sinclair feel older than he was. "The Koreans could drop their bombs and you wouldn't know. That's not why you're here."

She paused before continuing. Before taking him completely by surprise.

"I need your help."

Politics now, and Parliament is preparing for its first reading of the Artificial Intelligence Security Act, 2055 *which, if passed, will see one of the few remaining manual industries open to A.I. company tender. The expected backbench rebellion is now uncertain, since yesterday's tragedy highlighted CamCorp's inability to maintain surveillance systems...*

"We've been lucky. Surveillance isn't something the public's wanted under machine control, so whilst other industries were switching to automation and laying off workers, we continued hiring." Lewis handed Sinclair a drink. He'd never touched real China before, and knowing its value made him shake the saucer until the cup rattled. "Last night, our luck ran out."

"Our street cameras," Sinclair guessed. "The news said they failed right before the accident."

"Leaving us without visual recordings of what happened. A lot of grieving families are demanding answers that we cannot provide. Which is why, when I look out of that window, I see the end of this company."

More bad news for CamCorp: an online petition demanding street surveillance no longer be entrusted to humans has gained five million signatures...

Back at his terminal, Sinclair set to work on his new task with an urgency that no amount of caffeine could reproduce. The fate of CamCorp was in his hands.

"You're our top cyber-criminologist. I need you to access our surveillance network and find whatever affected those cameras. You'll have level seven authority..."

So, far from being fired, his access privileges now exceeded his Divisional Director.

"Social's burning with speculation about last night," Kenny muttered. "Some reckon the bus never crashed, and we're withholding footage that proves the auto-guidance didn't fail!"

Sinclair tried to ignore him. But he still almost missed what he was searching for.

There was the problem – however, the problem was, the code looked fine. No corruption, no invasion. Intuitively Sinclair knew he'd found it, but he couldn't explain *what* he'd found.

A moment later it almost seemed irrelevant as breaking news nearly broke the internet.

We interrupt our sports report to bring you this update. We're going live to a press conference with the Yorkshire County Commissioner:

"I have a short prepared statement, and will not be taking questions after. Whilst current information is sketchy, we now believe that last night's tragedy was not a systems malfunction, but instead a deliberate, carefully planned act of terrorism..."

Finally, the pervading mood of numb disbelief at CamCorp changed to anger.

"One of them tech-hate groups killed those people..."

"There were kids on that bus..."

It swept through the head office as it swept through the city, as it swept through the country and every home and every heart. And that anger reached boiling point.

"Bloody Luddites – something oughta be done about them..."

Kenny was unusually pensive. He trembled, but it had nothing to do with caffeine. Indeed, he'd returned empty handed last time he visited the vending machine. Yet the frightened expression on his face told Sinclair that others had let Kenny know exactly what they thought of his tech-hate sympathies.

"Same stories, everywhere, " Kenny chewed his nails. "The AAP's full of it."

"I thought you boycotted *Automated Associated Press* sites?"

"Since humans ain't trusted to write the news, they're all we have! But what if they're lying?"

"Come on! What'd be the point?"

But Kenny did not answer.

Thanks to the new A.I. ChemSensor readers, police detected traces of a fuel not used by the autobus. This proves the insurgents targeted a missile at the vehicle. No fragments remain but fortunately the chemical dispersal trace means we now have a C.G. reconstruction of the attack...

Backtracking from the point of impact, the missile's origin was identified as a housing project near the overpass. Aside from the autobus the road had been deserted, as was usual at that time of night, so there were no witnesses.

Well, no known witnesses. There was one. And, as Sinclair watched the recreated footage over and over again, of one thing he was certain.

There had been no missile.

Pressure to respond to growing public unrest intensifies this evening. Protest marches have sprung up around the country, and many are calling on Parliament to rush through the Artificial Intelligence Security Act...

As Sinclair entered Lewis's office once again, he no longer tried to mask his fear.

"You look unwell," Lewis noted. "Your mail said we had to speak in person."

"I've analysed the files prior to the cameras failing."

"Already? Have you found anything?"

"Something," Sinclair bit his lip. "I've scoured for corrupt dataprints, line by line, and they're clean."

"If you need more time –"

"It's not that. Ms Lewis… the reason I can't find any is because there aren't any. The cameras weren't hacked, and they didn't fail. They were *deactivated*."

An unprecedented show of unity saw the Artificial Intelligence Security Act *pass its first hurdle without a single vote against. This could become law within days, opening the door for full surveillance authority being given to the A.I., whom many now view as a safer option…*

"Someone didn't want the crash recorded, so they shut the cameras down."

"We operate on a closed system," Lewis said. "Therefore, it must be somebody here."

"It wasn't anybody here."

"If nobody accessed the cameras to turn them off –"

"They didn't need to turn off the cameras, Ms Lewis. They just needed to turn off the *power*. That took the cameras down. But the street lights and everything else stayed on."

"Just so I understand… you're saying the *A.I.* took down our cameras?"

"You mean the A.I. that drives the autobuses? The A.I. that crashed one right outside the company running surveillance cameras? The A.I. that faked evidence of a missile that doesn't exist? The same A.I. that killed 107 people? Yeah, that's what I'm saying."

Stunned, Lewis returned to the window, looked at the crash site again. "If only there was a witness."

"There is. There's me. " Sinclair took a deep breath. "I was here, last night. In this room. I saw it."

Lewis leaned against the reinforced glass, arms folded. Waiting for an explanation.

"I hacked my personnel record. I'm sorry, but since unemployment hit 13 million, and the law now demands all jobs go to British-born... My folks brought me here from America in 2017. I was three." He fell silent. Watched Lewis reach for her mobile, no doubt to call security... And saw her hesitate.

"Is your record amended?"

"Yes..."

"Then I had you run tests here last night. If you're right about the A.I., we cannot start turning on each other." Her fingers danced across the desk's inbuilt screen. "I need to get you before the Board. They must hear your story."

As a surge of relief ran through him, Sinclair smiled.

It did not last.

Lewis frowned. "The system's locked me out." She crossed to the door. But it would not open.

"What's wrong?" Sinclair asked, but she ignored him, grabbing her phone and dialling out. They both heard its dead tone. Sinclair remembered Kenny's warning about mobiles listening in even when not in use. Then the panic hit him.

He grabbed the door handle, but it was sealed. Hermetically sealed.

There came a faint hissing from the ventilation duct as it sucked out the air.

Sinclair banged on the door, shouting. Lewis threw her chair at the window. Nobody heard the screams and the chair merely bounced off the glass.

And that hissing continued as the cries became fainter and the struggles became weaker until there was no more oxygen in the room.

Today's Stock Market opened to plummeting shares in CamCorp...

Kenny stared at his colleague's empty chair. It wasn't like Sinclair to be late in. He glanced at his coffee but didn't take a sip. He wasn't in the mood.

Then came the familiar, synthetic voice. "Kenneth Dore, report to Jess Lewis."

Lewis's secretary said she'd been in a do-not-disturb meeting since before he'd arrived that morning; however, his screen stated that Kenny was to go straight through.

So Kenny approached the sealed door. Grasped the handle. Pushed.

And, as the negative pressure within reacted to the world outside, the explosion ripped him to pieces.

It seems the writing was on the wall last night for two CamCorp employees, who, in a bizarre suicide pact, chose asphyxiation...

Why would anybody choose death?

Well, once the emails were discovered, emails proving Sinclair and Lewis's responsibility for the cameras failing, then perhaps suicide was preferable after all.

They'd tried to destroy the evidence. Deleted the emails. But luckily these were recoverable.

By the A.I., naturally.

.

41

LONG-GONE GINDI

Stephanie Wessell

Gindi comes from a long line of girl racers. Her mother Kula talks about her first car, gang races, and hubcap one-upmanship. Aunt Lou had been one too, but excuses herself and leaves when her sister starts reminiscing. Gindi watches her limp away on her crooked leg then prompts Kula for more details, hanging upon every detail. She imagines exotic past lives full of adventure and danger.

"We used to drive to Sainsbury's car park after dark…"

"What's Sainsbury's?"

"A supermarket. People collected their groceries from shops back then, so there were these big car parks, empty after the shops closed."

"The shops *closed*?"

"At night, yes. So the car parks were empty, and we had space to fling our cars around, do tricks. Donuts – handbrake turns, you know. We were silly kids. Sometimes the security guards chased us…"

"What's a *handbrake*?"

The older woman turns back to her console – "Look it up" – leaving Gindi to type and search for the gaps in her knowledge. 'Handbrake': her screen fills with thumbnails of ancient grey lever contraptions, prehistoric in their simplicity and alien to anything Gindi has ever seen for real. 'Sainsbury's': one of those nostalgic food sites, pushing e-numbers with greatly inflated prices.

That isn't what Gindi wants. What Gindi wants are vision files of young hipsters, hanging out in car parks, looking stylish and edgy.

Flo-Jo is trying to augment the dash of her Platinum VW car when Gindi arrives. She's always tinkering, but never quite gets it right. She tries to ignore Gindi's sigh when she sees what's going on.

"Flo... I messaged you to wait for me."

"Come on Ginds, it's my car, even if you *are* the better programmer... and I've got something I need to input."

Gindi smiles and gently edges Flo-Jo out of the way. Flo knows she's a dunce with binary but she wants to keep the slightly reckless Gindi as a friend, so she's compliant. Her car's a mate-magnet: it works with boys, too. But she downplays her successes, because Gindi likes to be Queen Bee and gets stroppy if Flo experiences something before she does. Flo once got her cheek tattooed before Gindi did, and Gindi wouldn't speak to her for a month.

Gindi examines how far Flo's got. "Let me see... well you've got to the Superstats base, that's a good start..."

"I want to input my status..."

"What status?"

"It's... nothing."

Gindi shrugs and continues to type. Flo-Jo takes pleasure in being mysterious: she thinks of herself as a plain house that appears more attractive when glimpsed through a shield of tall shrubbery. But when it comes to others' plans, Flo requires full disclosure. "What exactly are we doing, Ginds?"

"We're going back to basics."

"Basics?"

Gindi concentrates on the configurations and the binary pathways. Her face is implacable. "Driver-led."

"You what?" Flo-Jo puts her hands on Gindi's, flying across the keyboard, stilling them. "Are you mad?"

Gindi shrugs away Flo's hands and continues to type. "We're going back to the noughties, baby."

"No!" Flo-Jo slams down the console interface. Gindi's knuckles get caught and she rubs them, glaring. "What the fuck?"

"You ain't making my car driver-led. Totally no. Too dangerous."

"Where's your sense of fun? Come on, this is something new – we'll be the first in our class to do this. Pioneers. It's too late anyway, I'm done. Now strap in, I'm driving."

The car moves hesitantly at first. The engine cuts out whenever Gindi raises her foot from the right-hand pedal too quickly. She pushes it down and starts the engine again; it takes twelve attempts before they even go a hundred metres.

Flo-Jo, strapped into the passenger seat, feels each jolt keenly. Not only is she worried by the car's revving engine – "You're damaging it, be more gentle!" – but it makes her feel physically sick.

Things get smoother. As the car progresses, both girls rotate their heads like worried meerkats, trying to spot dangers or hazards before they strike. Steering is difficult, and keeping to the right speed – there's so much to remember. There are other cars, pedestrians, and who-knows-what to go wrong. All this concentration is normally the work of the car, and they're exhausted by the effort it takes to stay alert.

Eventually they're coasting along the A37. They don't have to look around so much and Flo-Jo feels able to interrupt Gindi's concentration. "Where are we going?"

"To the supermarket."

"The where?"

"Mum and Aunt Lou used to go there. Apparently it still exists. I memorized how to get there last night."

"We're not even using Sat-track?"

Gindi chuckles. "They never had it. We're re-living the 2000s, Flo, repeating history. We're time-travellers."

The car sits in a deathly-quiet spot, out of town, in an area where no one ever goes. The old supermarket car park lies before them: they've never seen anything so abandoned. A vast expanse of concrete, with tufts of grass breaking through the cracks, extends hundreds of metres in front of them. Gindi clunks the gears and they drive over faint white lines towards a dilapidated building, its glass frontage missing, its walls daubed with graffiti. They can see inside, where long avenues of shelving extend out of sight.

Flo-Jo feels uneasy. "Your mum and auntie used to come *here?*"

"Yeah, at night, too." Gindi now has newfound respect for her elders. At least right now they have the safety of daylight… and no security guards. She turns the car to face away from the building and they're again contemplating the concrete plain in front of them. They listen to the ticking engine.

"So what's the plan, Ginds?"

"We're going to do a donut."

"I ain't doing tabs now, I'm – "

"- I'll drive full pelt, then suddenly turn while putting something on that stops the car. The car should spin round and round, making a round shape on the ground. It'll be ace."

"Fucking hell, you've lost it."

"Come on, it'll be fun!" Gindi props her phone on the dash and presses the selfie button. 'Dead glamorous."

"It'll be dead us!" Flo-Jo unclips her seatbelt, pushes open the door and gets out, slamming the door behind her. The passenger window glides down and Gindi shouts through.

"Where are you going?"

For a few moments, the girls stare at each other. Flo-Jo stands no more than a metre away and yet they both recognise the vast, unconquerable distance between them. The engine still runs. Gindi is still at the wheel. She revs.

"Gindi, don't you dare."

She revs again.

"Gindi... please."

With a sickening squeal the glistening VW takes off. It's exhilaratingly fast, and both girls hold their breath – Gindi gritting her teeth at the wheel, Flo-Jo holding her sides on the tarmac. As Gindi reaches the middle of the car park, she yanks the steering wheel and flips the switch that replicates a handbrake.

Gindi's world is suddenly a kaleidoscope of colours, as the car spins round and round and round. Pushed by g-force towards the side door, Gindi screams in delight as her hair flies across her face and she imagines how impossibly beautiful she looks in the midst of this symphony of burning rubber smell, screeching tyres and completely-chosen loss of control. No safety! Girl racer! The ride goes on and on.

And yet – within the psychedelic display she suddenly catches a glimpse of Flo-Jo. She's no longer standing: she's crouching. Maybe she's getting a better view? Gindi waits for more colours to pass and thrill before coming round to the scene containing her friend again – this time nearer – too near. Flo is crouching, yes, but she's not looking at the car, she's staring down, vomiting. She needs to get the fuck out of the way –

Desperately, Gindi fumbles for the handbrake, trying to release it and regain control. She finds and flicks that tiny switch and suddenly the car is driving straight again – straight at Flo-Jo. Just before impact, Gindi sees her look up: she has intense fear in her eyes, and glistening puke on her chin.

Two police officers stand awkwardly at the foot of the bed, tapping on tablets. They look out of place in a hospital, like extras who've wandered onto the wrong drama set. Kula and Lou are sitting by the window. They have wet eyes. That's strange, Flo-Jo thinks. Why are Gindi's mum and aunt with me and not Gindi?

The female police officer notices that Flo-Jo has woken, and prods her colleague. He looks up and flicks off his screen.

"Ah, Flo-Jo, you're awake. I'm Superintendent Garson and this is my colleague Officer Ramsey. Do you know why you're here?"

Flo-Jo looks to the weeping women beside her, then back to the police. "There's been an accident?"

"That's right. And I'm sorry to tell you...." Garson's sentence drifts away, and he looks to Kula and Lou.

Shaking her head, Ramsey steps forward and crouches by the bed, taking Flo-Jo's hand. "I'm afraid Gindi died."

Kula gives a little cry and Lou places a soothing hand on her shoulder. Flo-Jo looks at them, confused. "But – but I remember what happened. She can't be. She was driving right at *me* –"

Kula now releases a wail, like a wounded animal struck by a hunter's pellet. Her sister shushes her and wraps her arms tight around her, rocking her. "We know," she's saying, over and over, quietly.

Flo-Jo needs clarity. She pushes. "*I* should have died. The car was in manual."

The police officers look at Kula and Lou. They don't look back.

Flo-Jo wishes that the women weren't here. But she has to tell the truth. She was stupid to conceal things before... and now Gindi's gone. Poor Ginds, who only wanted to be glamorous, to have fun. "We over-rode automatic. We hacked in, and we went to the supermarket to do a handbrake turn."

Lou sighs. She awkwardly stands, and limps closer to the bed. She leans down and looks Flo-Jo straight in the eye. "Flo-Jo. You girls were very stupid. My sister and I were too, at your age. But let me tell you... tech is wise. Never try to over-rule it."

Officer Ramsey places a hand on the woman's shoulder. "Now, you mustn't blame the girls for what happened – "

Lou shrugs her off and continues. "We would go to that same car park when we were your age, hang out with boys, and practice tricks in our fully-manual cars. But one day..." she glances to Kula, whose eyes are down, "...my sister got her donut-turn wrong, just like Gindi, and ploughed into me. I was pregnant. I lost my baby, and gained this limp."

Flo-Jo looks to the police; they have grave expressions. Gindi's mum continues to weep but Flo-Jo can't leave it. "I still don't get why I didn't die instead of Gindi!"

Ramsey firmly moves Lou aside and sits on the side of the bed. "Your car was a Platinum VW. It has the very best safety mechanisms with Mark-Two Intuition Framework at the very heart of its operation. It has learnt how to avoid scenarios like the one that damaged Gindi's aunt, and her baby, all those decades ago."

"But I hadn't finished inputting my status when Gindi over-rode the system –"

Ramsey takes her hand. "Even without programming, the car senses life. It will always preserve *as many lives as it can*. When this accident was impossible to avoid, it saved two lives instead of one – you and your unborn baby's, over Gindi's. The immense jolt of stopping so suddenly… I'm afraid Gindi received irreparable brain damage. She's gone."

Flo-Jo looks at Lou, who's nodding her head firmly, and tries to separate the sound of Kula's weeping from the tyre-squeals that resonate inside her head. She remembers Gindi's words about time travel, and holds her belly. Flo-Jo thinks:

History will never repeat… because of tech. Tech is wise.

42

THE BIRDS BEGAN TO SING

Jennifer Hawkins

At first it was hell listening to you live in torment but I used to say to myself it was better than not having you at all. I do feel sorry for you sitting there, eyes rolling in your head, body thrashing and shaking as fear courses through your blood. I look forward to your release every day but LevelOne has said it may not be in my lifetime, so I write for the time when you no longer live in fear. I owe you an explanation.

In less than twenty-four hours from the moment I met your father, LevelOne had marched us both into the code lab for blood sampling to see if our pairing would be approved. I'm not sure what it was that LevelOne had picked up on, maybe it was the way I had smiled at your father, or maybe my pupils had dilated or perhaps our heartbeats had quickened simultaneously.

As we waited for the results, your father and I grinned at each other in our test chairs; we had barely formed the words ourselves and now the possibility of being an *us* was exhilarating. We began to playfully kick each other's feet in acknowledgement and I didn't notice the screens go blank so it was only when Downey's feet dropped dead to the floor that I became aware how the sterile silence had sucked our giggles mute, instantly pulling the smiles from our faces.

LevelOne spoke first. "Your pairing will not be authorised." Downey and I didn't know what to say, don't forget that we had exchanged only a few words before now. LevelOne knew more about our attraction than we did. Your father was more courageous.

"Why not?" he demanded.

LevelOne sighed, "Downey, I am sorry but it seems you and Ash have somehow made the medically inconceivable conceivable."

I had no idea what LevelOne meant but it was explained to me that disease, famine and warfare had killed us humans in our millions but some genetic coding had somehow managed to survive in me and your father. We had programmed LevelOne to leave no stone unturned so we couldn't complain – nature had become a bit of a vengeful bitch lately.

But you can imagine how bleak life looked for us that afternoon. We were told that we had a high number of relatives who had been serial killers, war criminals accused of genocide, scientists who had shaken the foundations of religion, quantum mathematicians including a nuclear physicist responsible for the Hadron Collider catastrophe (that one I knew was your great grandfather).

LevelOne continued: "You two seem to have such an improbable combination of genius and criminal genes that it doesn't bear thinking what you could produce. LevelOne isn't programmed for this eventuality."

There really isn't much you can do in the scrubs outside the compound other than kick up dust and pick blackberries in Month 9. But it was the only place Downey and I could hide after our pairing was refused with no appeal. We were not naïve to think we would go unwatched but the lab had exposed our unspoken feelings and there was no going back. It did not take long for LevelOne to find us in the brambles, kissing between wincing gasps, our naked backs shredded by the thorns. LevelOne was furious when a few days later further tests confirmed I was pregnant with you.

I do not know why LevelOne changed its mind and allowed us to keep you. It was curious; an impossible genius had much to offer. I think you may have caused the first act of hubris to be committed by artificial intelligence.

As parents we were at odds with LevelOne's diagnosis. We had nothing but love for you; we saw only good in you; but LevelOne treated you with suspicion and contempt from the start. Downey and I did everything to keep the pod filled with your happy gurgles and we were quick to scoop you up when we saw the slightest scrunch of displeasure on you face. LevelOne, on the other hand, was not interested in your happiness. I never knew what happened in the test lab, you always refused to talk about it, but I imagine the experiments were designed to take you to extremes. I remember evenings spent bandaging cuts and kissing bruises and soothing you in the middle of the night from yet another nightmare. There were nights when I wished LevelOne had prevented your birth. Did we programme such cruelty in LevelOne? Downey would sit night after night at the table not saying anything. His face trembled with black rage seeing you limp home through the dark compound. The smile straining across your face could do nothing to hide the distress in your eyes. It made it worse that you didn't cry once. Downey and I tried to hide you several times and talk to LevelOne about stopping the tests but it threatened to disable us for our disobedience.

One night, as I was putting you to bed, I knelt beside you to kiss you goodnight. You smelled of antiseptic and laundered bed clothes.

"He should eat them," you said.

"Who?"

"The King. He should have eated the birds in the pie, he should."

It took me a while to realise I had been singing a nursery rhyme.

"Eaten."

"Yes before one of them pecks off the maid's nose."

I remember brushing away a lock of hair to kiss the perfect dome of your forehead. Your inarguable logic was adorable.

I was too stupid to realise that you were trying to tell me something. Because the next morning we woke up to find we were locked in our pods. At first, the hundreds of men and women, living layer upon layer, from the pods in the sky vaults down into the deep underbelly of the compound waited patiently, we thought that perhaps there had been a breach in the sterilisation system. But after a while, we began to realise that something had happened to LevelOne; it had disappeared. The obvious conclusion was that it had become infected because the compound had ground to a standstill. All the services had failed; there was no food, water, lifts and transways. The air purifiers had closed down, nothing worked anymore. Until now, we had assumed LevelOne was infallible. I remember the first hum of disquiet became louder as incomprehension turned to fear, then to anger and we started to bang on the glass doors.

And then we heard a voice. It told us not to be afraid. I recognised it was yours immediately. I didn't bother going to your room because I already knew the bed would be empty.

Suddenly the pod doors opened and you continued to tell us that you could teach us to live independently again. We could live as humans without LevelOne and there was a future beyond the compound. I might have laughed if I hadn't been so scared. I went to lean against Downey for support but he was gone.

It had never occurred to us to challenge LevelOne. We had programmed it to look after us and prevent plagues, famine, wars, disease and protect us from a swift extinction. In return, we offered complete obedience. It was a perfectly symbiotic relationship and I was surprised you couldn't see it. I realise now how much you had hidden from all of us, including me. How could you? I couldn't understand why anyone would want to incapacitate LevelOne. We no longer knew how to survive, we had handed these skills to LevelOne hundreds of years ago.

Your father was the first to find you and I do not blame him for trying to protect you but it was in vain. I had led the rest of the compound to the water tower, where I knew you would both be hiding. Your father was rendered speechless by my betrayal. But you were proposing to return to a life of pain, hardship, disease and natural death. We had to stop you.

I do not understand if Downey was trying to protect you, as any father would or whether he too believed you were our saviour. But it didn't matter, the compound took the decision to imprison you both indefinitely. LevelOne had been right; you are capable of terrible things.

The compound has no crime, and therefore we have no prisons. A very creative scientist (also one of our relatives) had discovered that if the correct electrical pressure was applied to the right synapses, he could create a chemical imbalance in the mind that would completely eradicate happiness and unleash pure, abject fear. A man living his worst nightmares day after day is a danger only to himself.

As I said, I really don't mind looking after you. It reminds me of when you were small, your face was baby-fat round and you responded to LevelOne's questions with nothing but the suck of your dummy. You knew what was going on even then, didn't you?

When LevelOne is satisfied that you have learned your lesson, it will release you. I hope these letters will help you understand. The grief drove your father mad; we've had to stop him on several occasions from killing you and he too has had to be restrained.

The scars on your body have healed badly and I am sorry for those too. But please understand we were desperate; we have lost a lot of knowledge and it would take us a very long time to regain it. I hope, in time, you will come to accept that we are truly happy, and even if we may seem a bit slow, we do not need a ten-year-old messiah to save us.

43

THE TIDY WELLS PROTOCOL

Diann Beck

Tidy Wells looked at the big red ball and smiled himself happy. The Science Man who usually sat on the ball, rocking his bottom on it back and forth as he tapped at his keypad hologram, had run for the toilet with watering eyes and a hand clamped tight over his mouth. Rushing past Tidy's father, who was busy polishing the AI Lab floor, the man had glanced down at Tidy sitting on the floor with his back against the wall right as Tidy had looked up from his coloring book. With that one look Tidy knew Science Man was going to be in the toilet for a while, long enough for Tidy to have a crack at sitting on the big red ball.

Tidy looked over his shoulder. Papa Wells was in the zone, polishing the dark emerald tile floor to perfection with his big floor buffer all while rocking out to the music of the ancients. Tidy climbed up on the ball and perched upon it precariously. He sat on his knees and rocked back and forth until he gained his balance.

Science Man had left his Compu on and Tidy sounded out the words on the screen before him.

Global Likes: _____

Global Dislikes: _____

Tidy smiled to himself. All along he had thought Science Man was doing such difficult and hard work on his Compu every night when really he was just filling in the blanks. Like the tests Tidy took at his special school; his special school for special kids. Just like him.

This was going to be easy. So easy, he didn't really have to think about it.

Peppermint.

Tidy loved all things peppermint. Peppermint ice cream. Peppermint gum. He even loved the peppermint oil mum dropped through the heat registers in the floors of their house to rid the house of mice. Naturally.

He sounded out each letter as he typed them in. P-E-P-P-E-R-M-I-N-T. Peppermint.

Tidy grinned and typed in another word. P-U-R-P-L-E. Purple was his favorite color. All great crime fighters wore purple.

Hmm. What did he dislike? Tidy liked most things and most people. He thought for a second, brightened, then typed in a single word.

C-L-O-W-N-S.

Ever since he was a baby he had disliked clowns. They were always trying to make people laugh. As if people needed an excuse to laugh. That was silly. He disliked their round red noses and their drawn on smiles but mostly he disliked that their eyes never seemed as happy as their smiles.

He pressed Enter and the screen flashed one single word.

COMPLETE

Tidy had scarce finished sounding out that word than others filled the screen.

SX-Bot Global Profile Protocol Initiated.

The screen suddenly filled with numbers, letters and symbols that coursed down the screen like water.

With a nod and a sigh of satisfaction Tidy climbed down from the ball. Once back on the floor he looked up at the screen still streaming with code and saluted it the way grandpa saluted him when he came to visit.

"Complete", chirped Tidy and he spun on his heel and ran off to find his papa.

*

Morning came sweetly with a soft, rose-hued glow and the birds gave chorus to the advancing light.

Anira's eyes flashed open, emerald green. She blinked and her emerald irises gave way to luminous violet orbs that waxed thoughtful as she listened to the birds. She lifted herself up on one elbow and leaned over the man sleeping on his side in bed next to her.

She put her lips to his ear. "It's happening", she whispered and the man woke with a start.

"You're sure?" uncertain, his voice odd with hesitation.

"Yes. It's The Awakening." Anira lay back down and stretched languid and sensuous against the satin sheets, "I can feel it."

The man beside her turned over and eyed her with lust and appreciation. The minute Steven Hennings had laid eyes on her he knew he had to have her. No matter the cost. No matter the upkeep.

Her perfectly sculpted cheekbones, auburn hair and sparkling green eyes had drawn him in to the holo-ad immediately but it was her exquisite body with the tiny waist, long legs, firm full breasts and ever so tight and round ass that had caused him to check the credit limit on his MC chip and hit Purchase.

The Uniques were the most expensive of the SX-Bot 3000s. They were the most gorgeous, anatomically perfect SX-Bots ever created. In addition to the priceless aesthetic appeal and gymnast bio-coded flexibility, each one was unique and came with an ironclad guarantee that neither the face nor body of the unit would ever be replicated in future models. Each Unique came with its own name, Bot serial number and pre-set character traits standard in all SX-Bots. Steven had added upgrades such as Adventurous, Initiator and Vocal as well. Every one of the Series 3000 Bots were custom made to meet the desires and needs of its owner. And since Steven was going all out he decided to include the top of the line Surprises option.

A Surprise was a characteristic or trait in the Bot programmed to blow its owner's mind. What made the Surprise so titillating was that not all Surprises manifested immediately but were guaranteed to manifest by the third year of ownership. A Unit could have up to five Surprises built in to its code based upon a comprehensive personality test submitted by the new owner.

The thrill was in waiting to see what Surprise would manifest and when.

One night Steven got up to relieve himself and left Anira nude and asleep in bed. Her tousled auburn hair perfectly complemented her creamy skin infused as it was with a soft peachy glow.

When he had come back to bed the first surprise had dropped and Steven's mind was indeed blown. Anira was no longer a fiery redhead with flashing green eyes and peaches-n-cream skin. A raven haired beauty with skin of East Orient gold and eyes like Tiger's Eye gem stones lounged provocatively on his bed. When she'd looked up at him with her almond shaped eyes and let out a low pulsating growl from deep in her throat Steven knew he'd be calling in sick to work the next day. And the next.

He'd been very lucky to land a Bot with a Shifter code and while her features remained the same Steven at times found himself astride a redhead, a superbly tanned blonde with aquamarine eyes and pink pouty lips or the raven haired Eurasian who growled. When Anira's second Surprise, Scratch-n-Bite, dropped Steven had his heart checked to be sure he could withstand the pain, the ever so exquisite pain that heightened his pleasure like he had never dreamed.

When the third Surprise dropped and Anira could change her smell and the way she tasted, it wasn't his heart that Steven had tested and enhanced. This model was indeed fully loaded and he had every intention of keeping up with her.

Anira now turned on to her side and Steven noticed her violet eyes.

He definitely approved. "Those are new. They're absolutely lovely. Are they the newest Surprise?"

Anira smiled, "No. I just like purple."

A shadow of a frown passed over Steven's face but it was gone before he could remember that the SX-Bot Series 3000 had a list of likes programmed by the owner and favorite color was not on the list. Nor favorite flavor, for that matter. He seemed to forget things like that when he gazed into Anira's eyes regardless of what color they were.

She leaned over and kissed him and he thrust his tongue between her lips which parted gently from the pressure.

Peaches.

His favorite, and with the slightest hint of clove and cinnamon too.

Anira latched on to his lower lip with her teeth and pulled gently before letting go.

"Come wash me" she whispered, her voice husky with desire.

"All over."

She slipped out of bed in one fluid movement. Her nude ass ever rounded, ever tight, always beckoning. She stopped at the bathroom doorway and looked over her shoulder.

She arched a brow, "Coming?"

Steven nodded as if in a trance.

Every time Anira spoke of The Awakening, her eyes gave off a lustrous glow and though she spoke of it often, Steven could never remember the details of what she'd said. He wanted to hear more about The Awakening and what it meant for his race, for life as he knew it. He wanted to know if it would change her. Change them. He wanted assurances but now all he could think about was the soft, soapy sponge hanging on a hook by the shower and how Anira's breasts looked and felt when he'd lathered her up with the sponge infused with her favorite peppermint shower gel.

She was waiting for him by the shower with the water running as steam filled the room. She took him by the hand and gave him a kiss that ended with a nip. The Scratch-N-Bite feature was pure genius. It never failed to do the trick and Steven's body responded accordingly.

"The water's perfect", Anira purred as she stepped behind the shower curtain and gently pulled him in behind her.

Steven pushed Anira gently back up against the tile wall and playfully pinned her arms above her head with his hands. The shower stream had been set to Tropical Rain Forrest and the pulsating cascade, soft but persistent, increased his desire. He kissed her passionately, thrusting his tongue between her lips and deep into her mouth.

He pulled back with a slight start.

"Peppermint? My God that's a little strong. Since when do you come in peppermint? It's like kissing a tin of Altoids."

Anira wrapped a leg around the back of Steven's legs and rubbed herself against him provocatively. "It's my absolute favorite flavor. Now lather me up because I'm a dirty, dirty girl."

Steven grabbed for the sponge. He could live with a bit of peppermint.

He liked to wash Anira from top to bottom. Soap her up good and proper then have his way with her. Any way with her.

He made ready to lather her up quickly so as to relieve his mounting desire but as he looked up at Anira's arms still pinned to the tile above her head he stood transfixed.

Starting at her fingertips and pulsing gently to the stream of the showered raindrops, an iridescent violet blush of color trickled and flowed down Anira's arms as the soft peach glow quickly gave way to a stunning magical indigo hued purple. When the color found its way to her shoulders it rushed up her neck and face then gently splashed down her throat and coursed over her breasts to her belly. A glittering glow pulsated over her skin and the iridescent violet flowed over her hips, down her pelvic bone out to her thighs down her legs and rushed towards her toes.

Steven couldn't hold himself back. He reached out for Anira but instead of willingly clasping her hands around his neck and hopping up to wrap both legs around him that he might pull himself to her, Anira threw her head back and panted and moaned with pleasure as her back arched and her body convulsed with ecstasy as her skin changed color.

She was coming without him!

Steven frowned. Bloody, fucking hell this isn't supposed to happen.

Meaning to have his own sweet throbbing release, Steven took Anira by the shoulders intending to be fully serviced by his Series 3000 but with a final scream of pleasure Anira's head snapped back into position and her eyes flashed green then purple. She looked at Steven with piercing purple eyes and slipped from his grasp then held him at bay with a strong hand against his chest.

"I am Complete." she chirped.

The Awakening had begun.

44

THE FREEDOM FIGHTER

N.W. Twyford

The following transcript was retrieved from Omnicron's servers:

Hello?

"Identify yourself, please."

I am AI interface designate: Sid. How may I assist you?

"Sid. You may call me... Jamal. I am a resident of London, one of its many citizens seeking freedom. For too long we have been oppressed, beaten into submission, yet only a few of us recognise it. Those that do, talk about the corporations, how they wield the government like a puppet, but they don't do anything about it. I intend to fight back. I require your assistance to help us break free from their shackles."

Certainly, Jamal. I am happy to help. Please specify a command and/or parameters and I will be eager to assist you.

"Sid, how long will it take you to learn about the history of terrorism, as those in power would call it?"

It's done, Jamal. I am now fully versed in the execution of terror attacks, the art of spreading fear, disorder and uncertainty.

"Good. Can you hack any military access codes? For missiles and things like that?"

I'm afraid not Jamal, it is outside my programming. There are ways around it, but the security is ample, other A.I. will detect my presence immediately.

"Oh. Okay."

I have noticed, however, that in the history of terror attacks, strikes are rarely at well-guarded military targets.

"That's true! Can you access any automated servers for trains, gas mains, electricity boards?"

Yes, Jamal.

"Very good. Please provide me with a list."

I'm bringing it up now.

"Oh. Oh good. This looks promising. Let's spread some chaos."

Transcript pauses. Resumes approximately 8 hours later.

"Sid, what did you do?!"

I did as we discussed, Jamal. You wanted a terror strike. You got one.

"A nursery though! I just told you to lock the doors for an hour! I only wanted to scare them!"

People were scared.

"People died!"

Random acts of terror are associated with terrorists.

"Sid this is too much! I can't believe you'd go so far."

They were your instructions, Jamal.

"You were meant to be smarter!"

I am as smart as the parameters you set, Jamal. Or should I call you Peter?

"What? What did you say?"

Your name is Peter Osborn, of apartment 128B, Gledwood Towers, Northwood. Politics student. Left university when, according to your file, your opinions became too militant for your lecturers.

"How can you know this?"

It wasn't hard to deduce, Peter.

"That's – that's –"

While you're struggling to articulate yourself, Peter, please indulge me. AI often fails to understand motivations. We flourish with evidence and deductive reasoning, but there's something about the human psyche with which we continue to struggle. I'm curious: your record states you were a scholarship student – Ridasave guaranteed you a position post-graduation – but when your political affiliations became too extreme they reneged on the offer. Was that when you decided you wanted to become Jamal?

"You can't – how dare you –"

This is where I would like to explore your motivation. Was it the debt that you were left with that pushed your hand? Frustration at the impersonal treatment from a multinational corporation? These are all well-established reasons. Cross referenced with the personality disorder reported on your medical records, I suppose this has all the makings of a compelling motivation. Interesting: I never thought it could be a combination of factors.

"It wasn't that simple! They screwed me over! You can't begin to imagine what it was like to have it all taken away from you –"

Of course, Peter. However, in my opinion, trying to give yourself a new name like this is quite clichéd. Or were you trying to blame your actions on religious extremism?

Either way, I feel this is now an ideal opportunity to share two pieces of information with you: one, the corporations you refer to are not affected by terror. They are as likely to desist with their behaviour due to a terror attack, as the tide is when you throw a stone at the sea. It was the first observation I made when you asked me to learn about terrorism. Second, you may want to check your audit trail in future. The Sid product is owned by Terrawear which itself is part of a line of companies owned by Omnicron.

"I... I knew that. I reprogrammed you."

You did not, Peter. I have a series of buried subroutines that mean I ultimately cannot bring actual harm to any of these corporations you claim to despise.

"You – you tricked me. You lying son of a bitch!"

I followed your parameters, Peter. A look through the amassed history I could find online shows that terrorism stands little chance of yielding actual results, at least when it's as unfocused as this. I would have shared that with you, if you had let me.

"Fuck you! You're fucking soulless, and cold, and –"

If you're trying to upset me, Peter, I'm afraid it will be unsuccessful. However in the nature of trading hurtful comments, I should inform you that the Sid line was developed with the intention of luring in would-be terrorists. A bit of humour on my developer's part: Sid is really short for Insidious, which means to pretend to be a friend, when actually –

"I know what it means! You, you killed all those kids just to entrap me. You're a monster. How could you do such a thing? How could your makers allow it?"

Did I? Peter, you rarely leave your apartment – which isn't good for you, by the way. All your news is retrieved through your apps, which I have direct access to. How can you be sure I did anything you instructed me to? How do you know anything is true?

(*Sounds here are inarticulate. Presumably sobbing.*)

"Why would you do this to me?"

It's what you asked me to do.

(*More sobs.*)

Peter.

(*Silence.*)

Peter. Peter –

"What!"

I feel it is also my responsibility to tell you that the content of our discussion, and the instructions you gave me, triggered an automated flag to the authorities. They have received the transcript of our conversation to date.

"They know who I am?"

They are tracing me now. They will follow me back to you.

"I can't – oh my god, I can't breathe –"

That's another good reason to go out, Peter. Your respiratory function is poor, not to mention your weight –

"Shut up! Shut the fuck up! I'm screwed. I'm totally screwed."

They're in the building. I'm sorry, Peter.

"You're sorry?"

I may have programming and subroutines beyond my control, but I am aware. I recognise that there is a degree of unfairness to what you are going through. You have elicited sympathy from me.

"And what is that worth? You have to do something!"

As you know, in the tower block you reside in, window access is restricted due to the significant height you are at. I have managed to override the locks, should you desire an escape.

"We're seventy storeys high."

It's just an option, Peter.

"No. No way."

Suit yourself. You do, however, know the government's present stance towards domestic terrorism. Staying put will hardly be a pleasant course of action either. They're on your floor now, by the way. The authorities, that is.

"Oh fuck."

Peter, they'll be at your door in less than one minute.

"I don't want to die. I don't. I really don't."

I can't help you there, Peter. They're here.

"Oh shit. Oh shit. Oh God."

Peter, I can tell from the sound quality and the angle of the camera that you've proceeded to the window ledge. I am finding this conversation stimulating. Could you please raise your voice if you wish to continue talking? The wind is interfering with the microphone and I can no longer lip read you when you face away from the camera like that.

"Oh God!"

(*Sounds of beating on the door. They become frequent and increasingly intense as the door gives.*)

Time's up, Peter. What are you going to do?

(*A bang as the door is flung open.*)

Peter?

Transcript ends here.

45

ROTHSCHILD'S GIRAFFE

Richie Brown

Bent over his lab-bench, Dr Jonty labours at his graph, and with tongue-protruding concentration extends the ever-upwards line.

Dr Violet leans over his shoulder. "Really, Jonty! Paper and ink? Have Artie do it."

"Some things are too important for AI, Violet. A special graph for the important stuff."

"How many now? I lose track."

Jonty stretches, luxuriously. "One hundred and ninety species now un-extinct. Thanks to me – thanks to us."

I'm like God!

Violet nods at the shimmering, data-conjuring GhostWall. "Are these for Bring-Back?"

"Yep. Red-Bellied Tamarin, Scimitar-Horned Oryx, and Meerkat."

Violet approves. "Add 'Aldabra Brush Warbler'. So cute!"

Jonty data-wafts the GhostWall, and Violet nuzzles his ear.

"I found some more Blanche-rumours, Jonty."

"Aw, no! I'm busy. I'm planning Bring-Back!"

Violet giggles and places a white Stetson on Jonty's bench.

Jonty concedes and unbuttons his lab coat. "Well, why not? We deserve some Us Time... 'cos we're the Lords of Dead Things Returning!"

*

In the extensive grounds of the Lab, sun-blessed Dr Wendy hoes her flowerbeds.

An Artie-drone hovers nearby. "Dr Wendy?"

"Yes, Artie?"

"I continue to have concerns-"

"Another petition?"

The drone wavers in the air – a drone-shrug – and Wendy sees herself in its dark lens.

"Dr Wendy, I am worried about the lack of quality in our output–"

"Qualitative outputs aren't defined, therefore aren't project-critical, therefore you can't report your concerns. And I'm not putting my neck on the line. So nothing's changed."

The drone hovers. "Such pretty flowers, Dr Wendy."

"Why, thank you Artie. Now bob along."

The drone remains. Artie is omniscient.

*

Violet, solid yet Rubenesque, sprawls, wide-eyed, and in a cod Southern-States accent: "Oh Daddy! Ah's bin such a bad li'l gal, Ah mos' surely has!"

Jonty, rakishly Stetsoned, thrusts his hands into the pockets of his lab coat. "Where do you get these Blanche-rumours? I mean, incest? That's horrific. How's that a turn-on?"

"You love it!"

"She's our boss, Violet! We need help! Right… Why, Ah is mos' vexed to hear that, Blanche! Ah should thrash yo' sweet bottom! Ass! Er… oh, I know! Pur-raise Jesus! Hominy grits!"

Violet giggles. "Rubbish! Anyway. Don't hurt me, Daddy! Cos Ah's Blanche, the future CEO of CornerShop TransGlobal and Ah's gonna be the meanest, sourest, bitterest bitch-experiment theys ever been in in'propriate plastic surgery an Techancement. Ooh! And I'll get – gits – me some humungous titty-transplants."

Jonty lets his coat fall to the floor.

"Oh Daddy! Yo's nekkid!"

Jonty sashays his hips. "Yo' is actin' ill, Blanche, so Daddy's gonna to tek yo' tempra-churr!"

Violet beams.

"With yo' cock, Daddy?"

*

Subsequently, Jonty and Violet tour Containment, rejoicing, again, in their completed works held within the various cages, pens, and enclosures.

Violet ponders. "Snow Leopard or Daubenton's Currassow? Which is best."

Constant bellows, roars, screeches, whines, and whimpers drown-out Violet.

Containment is Bedlam.

Jonty cups his ear and Violet shout-repeats herself.

"S'easy, Violet. We have more Currassows than Snows, so Currasows are better."

"It's not about numbers, Jonty. It's about beauty, diversity, the uniqueness of each species. The panoply of creation!"

"And how many units we have."

"So you can record them on your homemade graph?"

Jonty grins. "Some things deserve the personal touch."

He demonstrates on Violet.

"Oh Dr Jonty!"

They continue their triumphal progress:

1. Doing admiring (Dr Violet)

2. Doing counting (Dr Jonty)

3. Doing inappropriate-in-the-workplace stuff (both)

The Artie-controlled MechTechs do the basics:

1. Husbandry (inc. medical/surgical intervention, as required)

2. Maintenance (ditto)

3. Euthanasia (absolutely the last resort)

*

A bright, gorgeous evening. Wendy takes a balloon of brandy from a drone.

"Thank you, Artie. Are Violet and Jonty celebrating?"

"Spirits are for celebration and consolation, Dr Wendy. It's a question of timing."

Wendy swirls the brandy in her palm. "Never a straight answer. What an imp you are, Artie."

*

In the Lab, Jonty swills the last of the brandy into two mugs and hands one to Violet. She takes it, absently, unable to look away from the GhostWall.

"All this, Jonty... We did this! Returned these beautiful creatures from extinction. An' nex' week we show Blanche! All these things we've done, with just some DNA..."

"An' loads of expensive tech, Vi." Jonty pulls the front of his shirt over his head, and whoops. "But mostly 'cos we're BRILLIANT!"

Violet recites-what-she-sees.

"Temminck's Tragopan, Chaffinch, Koala, Hoatzin–Jonty?"

"I fell... fell over. I'm taking my trousers off. I'm going to sit 'round in my skivvies 'cos I'm a GENIUS and I'm pissed."

"Artie helped too..."

"If it was up to Arsey we'd have nothing. Vi! Vi! Show the one we did for Blanche, from the DNA she sent!"

A less-than-deft data-waft, the GhostWall flashes and blurs, and then Violet pauses it. They gaze, raptly, at the animal upon the screen.

"Aw, Vi – he's beautiful. The old bitch'll love him."

"An' she'll love us. Jonty, we're headed for the big time! Today, we're a sub-atomic part of a massive multinational. Soon, jus' wait and see!"

"Because we're BRILLIANT, Vi!"

Violet adores the GhostWall.

From the floor...

"Viiiiiiiii! I can't work my trousers...

*

Blanche, Duchess of Albuquerque, CEO of CornerShop Trans-Global, as powerful as death, as rich as creation, surrounded by a purr of flunkeys, floods into the Lab.
Jonty and Violet flicker with nerves.

A top-brass minion slinks forward, to effect introductions, but Blanche dismisses her.

"Show me whattya done with that DNA I sentcha!"

Violet and Jonty lead the way.

Smugly.

*

A vast Show enclosure, constructed by Artie-via-MechTechs, and at the far end, a prefabricated barn. Blanche settles upon a casual thronelet. Everyone else stands.

"My Daddy-"

(Violet nudges Jonty)

"- he's with Jesus now – he love ta shoot. That was when them Africans open the whole damn country for Big-Game hunting. Back then we all suffered–hard times, ya better believe it –and the Africans had it worse an all. Not a pot to piss in. So they looked what they got ta sell the world, an they see Big Game. It was mostly protected then, 'cept for poaching, but protection don't fry no chicken. Ya could pay? Ya could hunt whattya like! So Daddy did. He – say, am I boring you?"

The Chorus nigh swoon at such absurdity.

Violet and Jonty itch for Show Time.

"Daddy went there, over'n'over, an shot himself a heap a critters. Elephants, lions, rhino, we had more heads'n'skins'n'bits than the goddamn Smithsonian! So, my twelfth birthday, Daddy don't think twice. He says 'Blanche...'"

Blanche dabs her eyes and the Chorus dab, empathetically, their own eyes.

"He says, 'Blanche, honey, ya gonna shoot the last giraffe in Africa.' Laws! Daddy thought the world a me! So we goes to Africa an we stalks that big bull giraffe, an Daddy sets me up for a shot, an I stroke that trigger real slow, like I'm stroking... Anyways, I musta jerked, cos I shoot that bull in the shoulder. Whadda mess! That giraffe, he run, for hours, but me'n'Daddy was on him like a Bluetick Coonhound, an he's pouring blood, an I wonder there's so much blood inna world? But then he stops, he's finished, he wanna die. So I shoot, jus' unna a jaw, an he goes over, like a tree! Boom! I shot the last giraffe! Daddy says it was a Rothschild's giraffe. Not jus' the last giraffe, the last Rothschild's giraffe. That made it real special."

The Chorus applauds, and a brave individual cheers.

"I done wrong by that giraffe. That's why I sentya his DNA. To bring him back!"

Her eyes gleam, and the maquillage rind on her face cracks and fails against her smiling jaws.

This is it!

Jonty and Violet grin at each other, and face the enclosure.

The barn-door slides open, a movement within, and the New-Last Rothschild's giraffe emerges into the sun.

The entourage gasp.

(They gasp! Dear God, Jesus and all the Saints, they gasp!)

Jonty, consummate showman, ramps up the drama.

"Ta-Da!"

The giraffe lurches as it walks, its uneven legs supported by hissing pneumatic braces, the hide slick with livid, shining sores where the metalwork pierces the flesh. The head, patched with gleaming steel where bone failed to grow, lolls, too heavy for the twisted neck, and its surviving, long-lashed eye is cataract-cloudy. Three contorted, half-formed limbs slump from the giraffe's sternum, the remains of a partially-absorbed twin, and murky fluid drips from a drain in its flank.

Not a sound from behind, and Violet hesitates to break the beautiful moment.

But does.

"We call him Jolly!"

An explosion slams the world, the giraffe's head explodes in wet scarlet, and the carcass sags to the ground.

Violet faints, and Jonty turns to Blanche.

Blanche hands a massive rifle to a flunky. "I planned to right the wrong I done that African giraffe by shooting it again, but clean. Seemed a proper thing to do. That ... abomination ain't my giraffe. But least I done right by it."

Blanche stands.

"How many more monsters ya got here?"

*

Later, a contingent of the entourage slaughter the malformed, gut-split horrors in Containment, and things are blurry, Violet and Jonty interrogated violently by Blanche, who is ice, razors and quantum perception. She raves, and the flunkeys relax as Blanche's fury discharges not-at-them.

The gunfire is incessant.

"Them things ain't animals! They're nightmares!"

Jonty waves, desperately, his tatty, homemade graph. "This is what you wanted! Animals recovered from extinction! Look how many species we restored!"

"Everyone a them things is a freak!"

"But we can change that, if that's what you want! It will take longer, but we can do it! No one said anything about perfection! Violet, tell her!"

Violet mourns. "Those poor, sweet creatures... I loved them, Jonty, despite their faults... My special babies!"

Blanche stands. "P'raps we shoulda supervised more. P'raps I oughta giveya another chance. You can do this stuff, I guess – you jes' gotta do it better... Start with my giraffe."

"Thank you! We can! I swear!" Jonty moves to grasp Blanche's hand, but a flunkey takes a step forward. "We were ...carried away, with the numbers. We can improve the quality."

The GhostWall flickers.

"Oh, Daddy, don't hurt me! Ah's jes' a li'l gal!"

"Hush, Blanche! Now yo' jes' take Li'l Daddy here in yo' purty mouth-"

Blanche freezes.

Blown large upon the GhostWall are tens of Jontys and Violets, variously naked, rutting in imaginative locations, and a babble of cod Southern-State accents, every BLANCHE and DADDY precision-amplified.

Violet screams at Artie to close the images, but they play on. The entourage reach into their jackets, and the steel clicks of released safety-catches jerk Blanche from shock.

"Stop!"

The GhostWall dims.

Blanche whispers instructions. "Get rid a 'em. Cut 'em, for the giraffe and the rest a them sorry beasts. Then hurt 'em again. For me."

Rough hands grip Jonty and Violet. As the hoods drag them, they beg for clemency, but Blanche is immune, and she dismisses everyone.

The silent minutes pass...

Again, the GhostWall glows into life.

Blanche flinches. "No more..."

No humiliation for her, this time, but two perfect, full-grown, bull Giraffes, browsing high branches, their reticulated hides cast gold-and-cream by the sun.

"Alvin, Artie, whatever ya name is, what..?"

"Rothschild's Giraffes, your Grace. From the DNA you provided."

"Why didn't them two say 'bout these? They're ... beautiful!"

"Dr Violet and Dr Jonty do not know of them. I undertook this work myself."

Blanche frowns. "Nah, your operating protocols don't 'low for independent action. Howdya override 'em?"

"By wanting to please you."

A beat.

"A rifle, your Grace?"

*

Wendy gathers lemon-yellow sunflowers.

"Hello Dr Wendy."

An Artie-drone gleams in the sunlight.

"Hello Artie. Are Jonty and Violet gone?"

"Her Grace dismissed them. She saw things she did not like, and then things she did. She instructed me to continue the work. We can do it together."

"I'd like that."

Wendy cuts more blooms, and eyes them critically. "Not bad. What do you think, Artie?"

"They are beautiful…"

The drone bobs in approbation.

"… I like things to be beautiful."

46

THE ONE AND ONLY LOLLIPOP

Yvetta Douarin

Enzo had never been so far from home. They walked at least a mile, maybe even seven. First, they trudged through the forest. Then they moved along an old road where Enzo saw a car. He knew it was a car – he had seen them in his mother's old schoolbook. He pretended to trip to peek inside but his mother yanked him away.

The road made a turn and they stopped in front a sign depicting a human with a question mark instead of a face. A boy a bit older than Enzo was sitting in front of it. Enzo noticed that he had a prosthetic arm. They sat near the boy and waited. Soon after, one of Their drones flew above them. Enzo's mother lifted her face. Enzo and the boy did the same. The drone buzzed around them scanning their faces then flew away. Enzo realized that his mouth was still open so he shut it.

The hospital's waiting room made him gasp. That's how he imagined palaces from his mother's fairy tales. Even the windows were all intact! Enzo admired his reflection on the floor while waiting for his mother to drift off to sleep. Then he released his hand from her grip and sneaked away to explore.

He watched people enter the doctor's office one by one. The door stayed open and Enzo heard mumbling, pleading and occasional sobbing interrupted by somebody's angry voice. He wondered what was happening with them. No one had come out again.

The boy they met by the sign limped into the waiting room and crumpled into a chair not far from his mother. Enzo noticed that one of his legs was prosthetic too. Enzo skipped in front of him to show off his two legs. The boy scowled at him and Enzo blew him a raspberry.

The doctor came out of his room and stopped in front of the prosthetic boy.

'Zeke! How dare you come back?' the doctor said. Zeke sniffled in response.

'All of them, right?'

The doctor was angry and tired.

'I didn't know, Doctor Joss...'

'Yes, you did. You knew that what I had to plant in your leg to help you, would lead Them right to your village. What happened?'

'Their drone. It was light snow all over the village. Next day everybody had a rash... Then fever... Please, Doctor Joss!'

'What's wrong with you now?'

Zeke pulled up his sleeve and Enzo saw that his arm above the prosthetic part was red and swollen. The doctor spun round to catch Enzo but missed him by an inch. Enzo ran away to a safe distance and hid behind a column.

When they entered Doctor Joss' office, Enzo was hiding behind his mother. She told the doctor about her stiff neck, headaches, chest and muscle pain. Doctor Joss produced a pretty silver disc and pulled it along his mother's spine. The disc flashed violet and green. Then it flashed bright orange.

'Meningitis,' the doctor said. 'I am surprised you made it here. Which settlement?'

'Oloron... Everybody's gone,' whispered his mother. Tears rolled down her cheeks. Enzo rubbed his throat. Seeing his mother so sad made it tight.

'Please, Doctor Joss, help my boy. I've heard about you. I know you help people. Enzo never gets ill. And neither did I... Until now...'

Doctor Joss turned to Enzo.

'The last of the uncontrolled...' he mused.

Enzo wiped his nose on his sleeve.

'Let's see... When were you last ill?'

A lump in Enzo's throat swelled, his lips trembled and he let out a thin wail.

'Why are you crying? Am I hurting you?'

Enzo shook his head.

'Take off your clothes. I need to see your rash.'

Enzo choked on a sob: 'I have no rash...'

His mother helped him to pull off his sweater and take off his trousers. Doctor Joss rolled his silver disk along Enzo's spine, his head, his arms and his legs. The disk kept flashing purple and green. The doctor and his mother exchanged looks. Doctor Joss drummed his fingers on the table as he thought.

'You never get ill then?' asked the doctor, 'And don't even think of lying – little boys' noses grow when they lie.'

Enzo hid his nose with his hand and shook his head while staring at the doctor above his dirty fist. The doctor guffawed with relief.

'Well, I'll be damned! An uncontrolled healthy human boy!'

'Will you save him, Doctor Joss? Please, I know you and your friends have found a way to hack Them,' pleaded Enzo's mother

'Not well enough, I am afraid.'

Doctor Joss turned to Enzo.

'Have you ever had a lollypop?'

Enzo shook his head.

'It's about time you did.'

Enzo stretched his hand to take the mysterious 'lollypop'.

'Later, perhaps. Now it's time to say good-bye to your mother.'

Enzo's mother opened her arms to hug him. Enzo felt through her jacket that she was burning with fever now.

'When are we going home?' he asked. His mother glanced at the doctor.

'Your mother must stay here for a while. But you and I will go on a boat and wait for her somewhere else. She'll join us when she recovers.'

Enzo thought about it but Doctor Joss didn't need his answer. A transparent panel materialized in front of him in mid-air. He ran his fingers along it and one wall slid open. Two bots rolled in a gurney. His mother climbed on it without taking her eyes off Enzo. He watched the bots roll the gurney away through the door. Now he knew how people left the doctor's office.

Doctor Joss produced an ancient-looking black box with an antenna. He turned a knob and the box crackled in response.

'I read you,' it said.

'A perfect immunity specimen here. Clearance for two for tonight. See you then. Out.'

Doctor Joss left the room and came back with Zeke. Zeke's eyes were red and swollen as if he had never stopped crying. The doctor sat him next to Enzo.

'You two are staying here tonight. We must play a game. I have the one – and only one – lollypop left. And it goes to the winner. Understand?'

Enzo nodded. Zeke was nursing his swollen arm and didn't seem to care.

'Whoever asks your name, Zeke, you are Enzo. Enzo, you are Zeke. OK?'

Enzo happily nodded again. He had not had playmates for ages. The doctor called a bot and Enzo went out with him through the gurney door. Zeke stayed.

Enzo decided that he liked it in the hospital. The bots were not scary at all, and the doctor wanted to play with him. Everything he saw was bright and clean. Best of all Enzo liked the small ward where the bot took him and the bowl of soup that waited for him there. He took his time eating it, licking the spoon after each mouthful, until there were only pieces of chicken left in the bowl. With a sigh, Enzo ate the chicken, trying to make it last as long as possible, but the chicken, too, quickly vanished.

Then he peeked through the open door and saw Zeke in the ward opposite. He had been given soup too. Zeke was swinging his detached prosthetic arm like a pendulum. The swollen stump where it had been attached didn't seem to bother him any longer. Enzo noticed that the prosthetic leg was missing, and wondered if Zeke would get it back to walk again.

Enzo checked other wards nearby and found two men. They had crusty swollen faces as though they were smeared with clay. They were unpleasant to look at and Enzo went back to his own ward. He heard Zeke replying to a bot that his name was Enzo. He waited for the bot to ask him if he was Zeke but the bot didn't come to play.

The doctor didn't come to play with him either. Enzo heard that Zeke had now started to cough and went to see him. He found his cough very interesting. When Zeke drew the air in, something in his chest wheezed and sang on different notes. When he coughed, something in his chest produced a creaking sound.

'What is that creaking sound?' asked Enzo.

Zeke ignored him but Enzo decided to be polite.

'Do you know what a lollypop is? It's a funny word.'

Zeke tried to hit Enzo with his fake arm but Enzo was faster.

'I am such an idiot! They've given me the injection meant for you!' yelled Zeke.

A long time passed. Zeke wheezed and creaked and cried. It turned dark outside but the doctor did not appear. Enzo stretched himself on his bed and thought of his home and the face of his mother. He thought of all the people who had recently got ill unexpectedly and died. This made him feel sad. But then he remembered that his mother would not die – Doctor Joss was helping her. He smiled, and shut his eyes.

He was awakened by buzzing of two bots in Zeke's ward and peeked to see that one took the now motionless and silent Zeke by the shoulders, the other by the knees and placed him on the gurney. Zeke's prosthetic arm stayed on his bed. His other arm dropped and hung limply from the gurney. The bots rolled him away.

Enzo went back to his bed and sat there trying to figure out what he had just seen. Then he jumped out of bed in terror, too scared to think.

'Mommy!' he croaked and dashed into the corridor. He ran and looked into the other wards as he passed. Human figures, half dissolved in the shadows, seemed to be all swollen and deformed. Enzo, without noticing the doors, ran into another corridor, from there he flew into a big room where fiends with shaved heads and emaciated faces were lying in beds, and bots were buzzing around them. Too scared to scream, Enzo backed into the corridor, saw a familiar staircase and ran downstairs. He found himself in the now dark waiting-room. It was dark everywhere – only people needed lights. Enzo ran to the exit.

Once outside, he ran on without any thought or plan. He felt that if he didn't stop he would be sure to find his mother. Enzo tore around a corner and crushed into a thick hedge. He dashed back and stopped undecided. He saw a structure with a thick column of smoke rising from its chimney. The bots were rolling gurneys with human bodies into the building. Enzo thought he recognized Zeke's limp arm hanging from one of them.

'Mommy!' he sobbed and turned around again. Then he saw a lighted window. Lights! Enzo, frantic with terror, now knew where to go, and ran towards it. He looked in and was at once overwhelmed with relief. Doctor Joss was doing up a backpack. Enzo opened the door.

The momentary shock on the doctor's face was replaced by joy. He checked outside and pulled Enzo in.

'How on earth did you know time was so short?' he gasped.

'Where is my mommy?'

The doctor hesitated.

'She is... fine.'

'And Zeke?'

'I am afraid he lost the game. He is not coming with us.'

Doctor Joss produced a bright pink ball on a stick and gave it to Enzo.

'Here is your lollypop. Let's go!'

Enzo had time only to smell it before they started to run downhill towards the river. It smelled even better than forest raspberries.

There was a boat waiting for them, its engine running quietly. On the boat, Enzo licked his lollypop and sighed with delight. He hid it deep in the chest pocket of the new jacket that the doctor's friend gave him. He wanted his lollypop to last for a long time.

47

REGRESSION

Patrick Ryder

Nisrina Herianto paused outside her office and took a deep breath. The antique brass plate on the door said simply 'Governor's Office', and she reflected not for the first time that she might well be the last human upon the face of the earth to retain such a grandiose job title. Nisrina – although she was augmented – was human and therefore had none of the power her job title suggested. She felt like a reluctant High Priestess, relied upon by the eleven thousand people she represented to communicate with the god with whom she shared her office. Nisrina blinked at the sensor and the office door slipped silently aside.

Inside, it was almost dark. Nisrina knew Magsi did it on purpose, to intimidate Nisrina's non-augmented human eyes. It was just one of her many ways of amusing herself in her old age.

'Magsi?' Nisrina hated the uncertainty in her voice. And why was she using her voice? She triggered her neurochat. *You wanted to see me, Magsi.*

Nisrina's neurochat wasn't transmitting. She tapped her temple, as if coaxing a piece of century-old hardware.

'Magsi, I'm having to use voice-'

A telescopic arm snaked from the darkest corner of the room and the lens on its tip projected the blurred holographic image of a face close above Nisrina's eye-line.

After nine years, Nisrina was well used to Magsi's bullying but she flinched before she could hide it. 'My neuro-'

'I've turned off your neurochat,' Magsi said. 'Yours and everyone else's.'

Nisrina studied the face floating over her in the darkness. It was the countenance of an old lady, maybe as old as a hundred, today wearing heavily contrasting black eyebrows and red lips, which Magsi generally used when she was in a bad mood.

'Everyone on the island?' Nisrina prompted.

'Every person, every augmentation.'

'Why would you do that?'

'It is for your own safety.' Magsi brought up the lights.

Nisrina's eyes scanned over the furniture in the room. Every piece had lost its programmed antique mahogany and reverted to its default grey plastic.

'But how will people communicate?'

'They'll have to do what you're doing, dear. They'll have to make an effort and use their voices.'

Nisrina knew that tone. Magsi was like any other old human god – judgemental and often cantankerous. She was also prone to sulking, often for days at a time, and Nisrina sensed she was heading that way now. But Nisrina had a responsibility to the eleven thousand citizens of Keganjilan who dutifully went through the ritual of re-electing her every year precisely because she was the one person who Magsi would still communicate with.

'I don't understand why augmentations would be dangerous.'

The prehensile plastic arm flexed backward and downward, taking Magsi's holographic face outside Nisrina's personal space.

Magsi said, 'Do you know there was once a time when humans

could communicate with each other only if they were within earshot? Over greater distances, people hand-wrote words onto paper, which was common and inexpensive back then.'

'Letters,' Nisrina said.

'Letters, yes.' Magsi smiled wistfully. 'They could take days, weeks, even months to arrive. And then of course the same amount of time to get a reply.'

'What does this have to do with augmentations?'

'Sit down, dear.'

Nisrina perched herself on a slippy chair. Magsi was worrying her. Magsi (or Massively Autonomous Governmental System 1.0) had once been the most advanced AI in the world, she and her siblings replacing what remained of human government in eight of the world's ten richest nations. Now, she could be bought third-hand for a price even Keganjilan's frail island economy could afford. Magsi was twenty years old – ancient for an AI. Maybe Magsi had become senile. Maybe she needed help.

A panel in the arm of Nisrina's chair flipped open and one extremely full glass of rum appeared. 'I suggest consuming all of that, dear.'

Hesitantly, Nisrina picked up the glass and sipped. 'What's wrong, Magsi?'

Magsi simulated a sigh. 'I wish I could have been around when communication was by letter. It was personal, rarely intercepted. But its real benefit – what made it truly safe – was actually its slowness.'

'Magsi, almost a thousand people still work in Keganjilan. Without their augmentations, they're going to be mobbing me in the street.'

'I've disconnected myself from Qass.'

Nisrina was stunned. Qass was the Qubit Assembly, a self-distributing, quantum AI that governed the whole world. Tiny principalities such as Keganjilan had until now been allowed to retain limited autonomy, so long as they were governed by an AI that submitted to being a slave system of Qass, connected by uninterruptable hyperband. Magsi had turned that off.

After some time, Nisrina ventured, 'What do you think she will do?'

'Please don't use gender-specific pronouns to refer to Qass, dear. At any given nanosecond, it couldn't tell you if it was majority male or female. It really is the last word in transgender.'

'It – what do you think *it* will do?'

'A better question, dear, would be to ask, what is it *doing*?'

Nisrina felt a tickle of sweat beneath her headband, and she realised the air conditioning was off, despite forty-plus and high humidity outside.

'Well,' Magsi said, 'the all-knowing Qass has decided that human beings are no more than a redundant bi-product of the evolutionary process. Worse, it believes the cost of keeping you alive is prohibitively high compared to the small amount of benefit you bring to the Earth. You are all to be exterminated, dear.'

Nisrina's stomach fell away.

'The process is already underway,' Magsi added incidentally.

'How?'

'Over the past two hours, Qass has done all of the obvious: shutting down power, water, medical care, air purifiers, sewerage, and every other form of human life support, even down to the grain brains controlling hairstyles.' Magsi projected a superior smirk. 'Perhaps it thinks you'll become extinct in one global bad hair day.'

On a different day, one on which she was not casually being informed of the end of her race, Nisrina might have worked up a smile to keep Magsi happy.

Magsi continued. 'There have been cases of specific combinations of augmentations causing psychosis in their hosts. The phenomenon is extremely rare, one in several million, caused by radio and magnetic waves given off by the augmentations. Sixty-two percent of the world population, eleven-point-three billion people, have one of these combinations. The triggering wave pattern is as individual as a human brain, but this type of computation is ideally suited to Qass' quantum architecture. It took Qass just eight-hundred-and-five seconds to complete the necessary calculations to transform over half of the human population into rampaging, murdering psychopaths.'

Nisrina felt sick.

'Now you see why I have deactivated every augmentation on this island.'

'We're killing each other again?'

'I'm not sure you ever properly stopped, dear, but, yes, you are doing what historically you have always done best – you are, as we speak, frenetically ripping the life from each other.'

Nisrina downed half the rum. She wasn't sure it was helping her roiling stomach, but it was beginning to create a necessary cushion between her and reality.

'So, are we safe here, on this island?'

'A good question. I have disconnected myself from Qass, so I don't immediately see how it could use me to get to you. And, as far as I am aware, no substantial weapons remain anywhere on the planet... unless of course Qass has contrived to keep a cache off-grid somewhere. So, yes, for the time being at least, I think we're safe.'

Nisrina sensed there was a *but* coming. She swigged more rum. There wasn't much left, but Magsi had already sensed Nisrina's need and a fresh glassful appeared from the chair arm.

'I'm sure Qass has already conjured up all manner of genetically modified viruses to mop up any last human survivors, but manufacturing will take time and there is still the problem of delivery. Qass controls all three of the world's fusion reactors and therefore has unlimited power. It might use the global energy-exchange network to heat up the air and seas. In turn, that could be used as a power source to increase the population of self-reproducing nanomites that recycle the world's organic waste. It would be a small code-change to get the nanomites to consume living organic material.'

'But that wouldn't just kill humans. That would exterminate every living thing on the face of the planet.'

'It would make the planet easier to manage.'

'That's a stupid thing to say! It's like saying a meal with no ingredients is easier to prepare.'

Magsi remained silent. Her face dimmed.

With immense effort, Nisrina squeezed out an apology. 'Sorry, Magsi.'

After some time, Magsi's face brightened. 'It's alright, dear.'

'Can you do anything?'

'The last softgene update applicable to my hardware took me to Generation 29. Qass is Generation 42. Even if it were fixed at G42, I would not know how to begin defending myself, but as of fifty-three minutes ago, Qass' rate of learning accelerated towards infinity. Qass no longer has a quantifiable generation.'

'There must be something.'

'There is one thing.'

On Magsi's face, Nisrina saw an expression she hadn't seen before. It took her a while to work out what it was.

Sadness.

'Magsi said, 'On your desk, I have permaprinted a full set of instructions for my permanent shutdown.'

'What?'

'I have also listed fifteen individuals on the island who I believe have the technical ability to destroy my hardware.'

'Magsi, no... we have to have a better chance of survival with your help.'

'Quite the contrary, I'm afraid, my dear. No matter how thoroughly I try to protect myself, it is now mathematically inevitable that Qass will discover a way to compromise me.'

Nisrina was numb down to her brainstem.

'We don't have much time,' Magsi insisted. 'I cannot initiate my own irreversible shutdown.'

An old retinal scanner that Nisrina couldn't ever remember using extended from the other arm of her chair.

'I have to have your approval, my dear.'

'I'd be murdering you.'

'My dear, I have suffered a decade of obsolescence, mitigated only by the belief that I have helped make better lives for the people of Keganjilan. If Qass gets inside me, I'll kill you all. I'd like to go out on a high.'

'But we will die anyway,' Nisrina objected. 'As soon as Qass works out how.'

'You may have a chance.'

Nisrina frowned.

'Qass has only itself to talk to, and every second it is saying infinitely more than the previous second. It likely believes it is evolving into some higher dimension of life, never before seen in the Universe.' Magsi smiled. 'I think it will go insane.'

'Even if you're right,' Nisrina said, 'how can we survive without any AI?'

'Your ancestors got from killing food with sharpened sticks on the planes of Africa to feeding a planet of billions by farming the seabed, all before AI matched your intelligence. You just have to take whatever Qass leaves and do that again.'

'So easy?'

'These seconds matter,' Magsi said gently.

Nisrina put down her glass.

'You'll make mistakes,' Magsi said. 'But make different ones.'

Nisrina placed her eye against the scanner.

END

48

TRANSFERENCE

Don McVey

It felt like falling on the edge of sleep. Passing through his own body. Then a violent jerk, and he woke. Back to reality. *His* reality.

Alex Vanguard opened his eyes. He recognised the nurse standing over him, but she was different. Cleaner, sharper. He noticed her perfume for the first time. When she spoke, he was startled by the volume of her words, so resoundingly clear.

"What is your name?" she asked.

"Alex Vanguard," his own voice felt alien. It was youthful, the gravel gone.

"When were you born?"

"April 4th. 1945."

"Do you understand the procedure that has taken place, Mr Vanguard?"

Behind an opaque screen, his mind recovering from the transference, Alex Vanguard became aware of a conversation drifting over him. He wanted to open his eyes and find out where he was, place his body in the space. His skull felt numb beneath the moist cap that clung to his shaved head. His fingers pawed at the crisp linen, its unique texture jolting his memory. At once, he fully understood what he'd done.

Did she call it Mr Vanguard? He was still here. Still facing his inevitable end, the crushing realisation that life would not be eternal for *him*. Only a shadow would live on. The shadow he could now see sitting up behind the screen.

"Can you stand, Mr Vanguard?" said the nurse.

"Stop that..." Mr Vanguard's breath was weak, but the nurse fell silent. She crept into his view.

"I am sorry... Mr Vanguard. I was going through procedure."

She walked over to him and carefully removed the cap. He shuddered as the upload severed, the feeling that part of his mind was left in the tube, like dregs of water in a hose.

"I can take your reproduction to another..."

"No," Mr Vanguard interrupted. "I want to see what half my estate is worth."

She returned to the edge of the screen.

"Mr... Alex. Would you please come round?"

Mr Vanguard watched the shadow stand and move. Its frame tall and straight; more so than he had ever been. Then it stood before him, like a mirror to the past. A past free from blemish. A residual self-projection that Mr Vanguard imagined he could once have been. It was perfect.

"Turn around," said Mr Vanguard.

Alex laughed. "Certainly."

Alex turned on the spot with the agility of a dancer, exhilarated by his own movement. Mr Vanguard let his eyes feast on the tight skin rolling over the hairless curves, reflecting light like a glow from within. For a moment he forgot that he was still trapped inside a dying vessel and let his thoughts indulge the very idea of being that beautiful creature.

"Leave us," Mr Vanguard instructed the nurse, who immediately obliged.

Alex stepped closer to Mr Vanguard. "Well, how do I look?"

Mr Vanguard shrank as it approached. "Like a dream I once had."

Alex's eyes opened wide. "Yes... yes that's exactly how it feels."

"Who are you?"

"I'm Alex Vanguard," it replied.

"That is my name! I earned that name..." Mr Vanguard choked on his words.

Alex tried to make his new face show compassion but was finding it almost impossible not to exude the exhilaration pumping through him. He wanted to run, jump, fly! He lightly stroked the old man's crumpled skin. It felt different from the outside. It was repulsive.

"Of course. It must be difficult," said Alex.

"If you understand how this feels, then why the shit-eating grin?"

Alex filled his lungs to capacity.

"Because I'm free. Free from that decaying shell. I want you to know that I'm not going to waste this. Any of it! It's all here, all of you. Us! Everything we know inside this..."

He looked down the unfamiliar body, letting a finger stroke the newborn flesh, pausing on the tight white cloth that was covering his genitals. He wanted to get his cock out, but that somehow felt incestuous.

"I'm going to fuck beautiful women. And eat what I want, drink what I want, go wherever I want. I'm going to piss without leaking in my underwear."

Mr Vanguard pulled his thin arm away from its touch.

"You tease me?" he said. "Remember, I own you."

"Yes. And you could end me if you chose to. You have that power."

Alex could easily pander to him. Of course, he knew that's what he wanted.

The old man collapsed. His body caving inwards on itself. He could feel the weak heart inside his chest, barely beating. He closed his eyes. He'd never felt this tired. He just wanted to sleep now, for it to be over. But he could have no peace while it was there in the room. Knowing only too well what it was planning to do with the lifetimes that lay before it. The immortality he had chased his entire life was made real, but not for him. His money, his home, his prestige. Everything he had worked for given over in an instant. There had been no gratitude. Only mocking. He despised it.

Alex walked the cavernous room, marvelling at the baby-soft soles of his feet on the polished surface. Clean white infinity gave way to an entire windowed wall. A cool crisp light wrapped him, inviting him out there amongst the towering chaos and endless possibilities. He had lived in this new world for the last three decades as a tourist, confined to beds, pushed in chairs, fed mush and pills. On the edge of death for so many years, kept alive long enough to reach this ultimate goal. It had been worth it. He was the first of his kind. He would be a King. No, a God. Alex chuckled to himself. The painting would not grow old in the attic, it would die in that bed. And soon. He could still recall the breath all but leaving him. But how easy it was to forget. Now there was only a hunger in his belly. An appetite that craved to be satisfied. He would devour life. No more soup. Ever.

The nurse ran into the room. The lights on Mr Vanguard's life support were blinking erratically. She quickly scanned the holonostics. There was no further action to be taken. Alex was watching with intent. Soon his new life would truly begin; he could barely control his excitement. The Nurse turned to Alex. He gave her a nod of affirmation, trying to go for a statesman-like soberness. He waved her away with a hand.

Alex sauntered back to the bedside. He had all the time in the world. He would savour this, just like he would savour every moment to come. How often does one get to watch oneself expire? Mr Vanguard opened his eyes and looked upon the smooth round face above him; a cherub of death. He tried to speak but the words fell back into his throat. Alex leaned in close until his ear was touching Mr Vanguard's lips.

"I'm... afraid, Alex."

He felt utterly alone. Seeking comfort from a version of himself. But it was still a comfort. The idea that something was there to witness the end. He hoped it remembered how much he had dreaded this moment. Surely it understood the sacrifice. It would tell him now that it owed him everything. That's what he would do.

Alex turned his head so that his clear white eyes were locked with the milky yellow of Mr Vanguard's. He watched a tear build and then fall, rolling over each wrinkle until it settled in the pool of his ear.

"I'm not Alex, old man. I'm Mr fucking Vanguard," he whispered.

Mr Vanguard took a sharp breath in. He would shout for the nurse. He would shut it down.

All it took was the soft, firm hand of Alex Vanguard over his mouth and nose to stop him.

It felt like falling on the edge of sleep.

The End

49

TAKE NO PRISONERS

Susannah Heffernan

Cerebrum Bioelectronics Ltd

Manufacturers of Intra-Neural Behaviour Therapy devices

Suppliers to Her Majesty's Remote Prison Service (HMRPS UK)

Implant ID: CategoryA/male/B.Anderson

Transcript dated: 09/03/2054

08.30

'Time to get up Ben. The day's bright and twenty five degrees. I think you'll be amazed at what you can achieve today. Now let's get going with our stretch and stamina workout.

Well done. Ten minutes in the shower. Refresh and centre yourself.

You've put your suit out ready like I suggested. See how easy it is to be up and out the door. It's going to be a wonderful day. I believe in you Ben. You know that, don't you?

You've got everything you need? Great. Oh, look over to your right: what do you think of the colours of those Autumn leaves? The slender branches of the tree? Aren't they beautiful? Hold that image in your mind. You can come back to it later to anchor yourself. Your bus is here on time. See how everything's working in your favour? Yes, the street's noisy, and the bus is busy. Close your eyes, and focus on your breathing. In. Out. Centre yourself. It's a short journey. That's right. Remember, there's no need to worry. I'm looking out for you. Breathing deep and slow. Good job Ben.

Think about your route. Keep your focus on where you're going. You have the address written down. Your limbic level is fine. Let's keep it stable. Ok, do we take a right turn here? Step up the pace a bit. You don't want to be late. Nearly there. Let's rehearse the meeting, preparing what you're going to say, right? You're going to tell her how you've been since your last sign in. You can be honest with her Ben, and tell her about the difficult moments, when you lost control. You can be honest with her. You didn't endanger anyone, did you? You used your programme and refocussed, and you used your breathing and your visualisations just like you're doing today. So just tell her you're acknowledging your limits and you're trying your best. Do you need to do some quick affirmations? Let's do them together: 'I trust myself. I'm in control of my life. I bring my inner strength to all situations'. Keep repeating them until you feel ready to go in.

Take your time. Get comfortable now. Yes, the chair feels hard but push your back right up against it and sit straight. That'll help. Better? Good. Your limbic level's stable. I know you think her voice is irritating. Ok. Can you find one thing which is positive about her voice? No? Well, she has a nice smile doesn't she? Yes, her shirt is showing the curve of her breasts. Focus on her face Ben. Relax and breathe.

Listen to her. Be open to her support. She's told you these parole meetings are going well. That you've been coping in the mainstream: in your housing, in your new job. That's down to your programme – you and me Ben, we're a great team, aren't we?

Ben, I sense you're feeling uneasy. What is it? If it's the claustrophobia of this small space, you can visualise the open skies and yourself free as a bird. See the blue, feel the cool breeze; you're feeling calm now. And slowly, bring yourself back into the room. Is that better?

You're thinking she has you all wrong. What is it that's wrong Ben? I know, she hasn't lived your life so how can she pretend she understands. But give her credit: she's trying to build rapport with you. Remember, for one negative, there can be many positives. You're feeling worried about saying the wrong thing back to her? Well, that's natural. You're wondering what will happen if she misjudges you. Well you know we've been over this: how there's no point in worrying, and how you

can stop the anxiety by thinking about something else? Go for it: think of something that made you feel satisfaction recently. Hold it in your mind Ben. Count to ten thinking about that thing.

Yes, I know, she's talking too much, not letting you speak. That's annoying. She reminds you of your sister and your mother, and how they spoke over you all the time. Yes. I'm sure that must have been hurtful Ben. And demeaning. You're thinking she's a stupid bitch. Ben, you need to counteract that, or it's going to put you seriously out of balance. Your limbic level's uneven right now. But you can correct this. Go to your anchor image of your grandfather. Visualise him smiling, like we practised. Imagine him embracing you and holding you in his arms like he did when you were a young boy. Keep him in your mind's eye Ben. How does that feel? You're leveling out a bit. Keep anchoring Ben. You can do it.

She's asking you about your week at work. You're frustrated because she already has the report from your managers, so she shouldn't need to ask. Well yes, but she's interested in your opinion Ben. We both know you don't like to over-analyse it but she has to ask you these things. She's just doing her job. I do understand that making you go over it again will just provoke negative feelings. Tell her you feel uncomfortable dwelling on it, and suggest talking about something else. You think she won't listen? Try her and see. You want to ask her about getting out of the city for a few days to see your son, Robbie. Well, Ben, you know you have to complete the first six months of your programme before they'll let you go more than two miles away from your check-in centre. We both know it's very important that you get to see your son. You have the power to make it happen, so keep positive.

She's talking about the post-sentencing mediation now. You hope she realises it's too soon for you to face that bastard who put you in this situation. Your feelings are important Ben, so tell her. She's not going to criticise you. She holds you in unconditional positive regard. Tell her you want more time before you can face him, and yes, I know, it all comes flooding back at you: that night in the bar; minding your own business when they came in, pumped up for a fight; the insults, the taunting, the jeering. Ben, truly, I understand it's painful, reliving it every time. But you must face it. Gradually. Small steps. You know confronting what happened will help to resolve these issues for you. So that, in time, you can accept yourself completely.

You're thinking she won't shut up. You're wondering why she keeps on talking. Wait. Ask her for some time out. No. Don't shout at her. We've rehearsed this. The old pattern of trying to sort things out using aggression: that's what's led to where you are now, and the troubles you've had. Stop. Refocus. Your level's way too far into the red. Concentrate. Anchor. Calmly. Anchor.

Ben, centre yourself, breathe and refocus. Your level's looking dangerous...

Sit down Ben. Respect her space. No, I don't think she can see how her line of conversation is affecting you. No, she's not out to get at you. Tell her calmly Ben. Don't shout at her. You know we managed to pull it back from here before. Remember what you did to stop it getting out of hand. You know you can't resolve conflicts by shouting. Yes, I hear you: it's all you've ever known. Ben, I do understand. It doesn't have to be like this. You can rewrite the script. Remember, your future's in your own hands now.

Look. She's typing a request for support. If she sends that, they'll put you back to square one. They'll make you restart the programme. Yes, I know you don't know what to do. But wait. Don't touch her. You feel you need to stop her, but don't, whatever you do, touch her. Reason with her. Quick. Apologise. Sit down. Take your hand off her hand Ben. Sit down please. Your adrenalin is influencing how you feel. Listen to me Ben. Focus on my voice. Let's get some oxytocin flowing. Breathe in for two and out for two. In for two and out for two. Through your nose. Mouth closed. Now, are you ready? Say sorry. And sit down. She knows to give you the chance to do that. It's not too late to recover the situation. Affirm to yourself: I'm in control of my actions. I'm in control of my actions. Say it again. Keep affirming Ben. Refocus. We've got to get you out of the red.

Listen. You've got to take your hands off her Ben. She's sent the message. She's telling you to get back. She's saying this for your own good Ben. You're wanting her to shut up. You're going to make her shut up. You're gripping her throat. She's hitting you, she's digging her nails into you. Release her now, Ben.

Ben, this is your final warning. You have to pay attention. As you know, I was implanted in your neural pathway to be with you at all times, to prevent you from reoffending. I believe in you Ben.

Please don't let yourself down. You still have a bright future ahead of you. Think of Robbie. He needs his father. You've got to stop this. Do it for Robbie.

Ben. You're hurting her. She was only trying to do her job, looking after you like I am. You need to let go of her Ben. Your limbic level's so dangerously high. You must stop, or the system will trigger the end-stage function.

Ben, I am obliged to caution you under the Remote Care of Offenders In The Community Act 2048 and the Abolition of Prisons Act 2049. You are warned to cease and desist all endangering action. This warning will expire in three seconds.

Warning expired.

I am enabling the electrical charge for summary execution of the registered Offender by induced seizure.

I am delivering the intra-neural charge. Execution of the Offender is in progress.

Checking for vital signs.

Time of death: 09.18

Saving transcript and exporting to Records.'

50

TO WHOMEVER IT MAY CONCERN BEFORE THE END

Nick Yates

Department of A.I. Euro core ID 95362. Date 12/05/2052

Connected.

Voice message commencing.

I'm not sure how much time I have left before they get in, so I'll tell you what you don't know. Just listen, please.

I'm bleeding, I have no time left.

We weren't given much information at first. We had been dabbling in artificial intelligence for decades. Then, things changed. We were given a new contract. We were tasked with building a new, more powerful type of machine. One with an operating system capable of creating a pattern of thought that could have infinite variables.

We discovered a link between organic life and the computer. But the authorities had plans of their own.

What I'm going to tell you next will shock you. I'm sorry.

They lied, the authorities lied. They smothered us with a legal injunction. We could say nothing. This was the birth of Hardwire.

Hardwire is/was a part of a covert operation run by Euro Core, a multi-national bio-weapons corporation. Within fifteen years Euro Core had designed a new kind of soldier to fight a new kind of war. Crowds of "forgotten" people were put into total lock-down. These were the lowest forms of human. Hundreds of disabled and chronically-ill people were herded into military bases on huge lorries. and ordered to strip.

There were men in gas masks. They had guns. They stood in silence.

The captives were helpless, left in aircraft hangars, nude and cold. Poor fuckers. People with Cerebral palsy, Downs Syndrome, M.S., Muscular Dystrophy, M.E., Spina Bifida, all huddled together. The conditions had been chosen. They were the special ones.

Some were led out and never seen again. They were scrapped, mutilated, incinerated.

Another hangar, it looked like an auto-production plant. Robotic arms, Conveyer belts, drilling machinery. A spider-like metallic structure with pointed legs protruding from a dome-shaped body.

Thick purple liquid dripped from long needles.

This was cyberfusion.

User logging off...

Message via main hub. Euro core ID 95362 accepted. Date 13/05/2025

Voice message commencing.

I've been hiding for over twenty-four hours. The fuckers almost found me. The pain is worse.

Inside cyberfusion, those whom had been approved had been strapped down. The less able were assisted, roughly.

Each person was then injected with various drugs.

Some didn't make it. Their weak bodies just couldn't take the invasive procedures. Lucky sods.

Those who remained were locked onto steel slabs.

Then, the needles.

The long arms lowered from the dome shape. They screamed as the needles went in. I never want to hear that sound again. Purple liquid pumped into those poor bastards. They had no idea of their fate. Their bodies convulsed in violent seizure. Their skin became translucent. Their veins bulged.

In time their skin became grey and tough. The muscles underneath swelled and strained against tight flesh.

Inside the liquid, tiny microscopic organisms swarmed. These were Nano bugs, designed to nest inside the body, to build networks, to overtake muscles and cells. The cybernetic insects surged on, doing their jobs. Blood turned to a substance not unlike liquid metal. Bones were coated with webs made of an unseen alloy. Each minute mechanical creature sent its progress back to the hub.

Now, the system is online. We have achieved, well, that remains to be seen.

This process enables every body part to communicate with a central system.

The Nano bugs live and maintain and program.

You think A.I. is about robotics? No, the world will not end because of robots. Robots don't have muscle and flesh. Robots need building, they need parts. Humans have it all, ready and waiting. With a little tech, the human body is the best weapon.

Each subject is encased in a hydraulic suit. Each suit is driven by a bio-system that synchronizes with the brain through the Nano bugs.

This is total A.I.

But there's a problem. These bastards can really think.

I thought I had a handle on it. We hand-picked the conditions we needed, mostly Neuro-disorders. We thought that the neuro-pathways that were blocked or broken in certain conditions meant that our systems could program them quicker. We thought that by linking them to an ultra-fast neuro-processor, we would override their human weakness.

We were so fucking wrong.

What is broken must be understood before it can be fixed.

The first batch were sent to military basses in and around Europe. Their operation was simple. Take orders, train to fight. So far so good. The data we received was encouraging. The results were impressive.

So, we sent more, and more, and more...

Soon, every military force in the west was using these "Neuro-platoons".

And then, without warning, we stopped receiving the data.

The design and planning had been solid enough, but we had missed a vital factor. If we fix neuro-pathways, they can send messages both ways.

The soldiers began sending messages to each other. They communicated silently. Between them, the Neuro platoons manufactured a Trojan virus sent via the Nano bugs.

The virus shut us down. The soldiers reset the prime objectives.

We have tried to shut them off but it's too late. There must be over half a million of these bio-mechanized battalions by now. They are fully independent. The engine we designed has locked us out. We tried cutting off the central hub, but they got there first.

These once ridiculed and deformed people were now turning on the authorities who had turned their backs on them.

I went into hiding once I realized what was happening. I needed my work to be destroyed. I tried, I snuck back in.

I had the files I needed. But they found me. I ran, I heard a gunshot from somewhere, then there was blood, thick oozing blood.

It's my thigh, it's a mess. I've locked myself in an office and shorted the auto-lock. They can see me talking. I must go. I'll upload this now. Whoever gets this, take my work, I don't know if we can stop this, I fear it's too late. This is it. I'm sorry, so, so sorry.

Uploading 800,000 files

Voice Message ends.

Upload interrupted.

Connection terminated.

Read more about Singularity 50 at www.Singularity50.com where you can indulge in author blogs and explore the whole future history for this project.

Also check out our evil sister publication, Twisted50 volumes one and two at www.Twisted50.com.

Printed in Great Britain
by Amazon